THE INQUISITOR

THE INQVISITOR

URBANA FREE LIBRARY

Catherine Jinks

St. Martin's Minotaur
New York

www.minotaurbooks.com

ISBN 0-312-30815-9

First published in Australia by Pan Macmillan Australia Pty Limited

First St. Martin's Minotaur Edition: October 2002

10 9 8 7 6 5 4 3 2 1

To John O. Ward (again)

Salutatio

𝕿o the most blessed Father Bernard of Landorra, Master General of the Order of Preachers.

Bernard Peyre of Prouille, friar of the same order in the city of Lazet, a servant of little use and unworthy, sends greetings in the spirit of supplication.

When the Lord appeared before King Solomon and said unto him: 'Ask what I shall give thee', King Solomon replied: 'Give therefore thy servant an understanding heart to judge thy people, that I may discern between good and bad.' Such was the prayer of Solomon, and such was my prayer too for many years, as I strove to make inquisition of all heretics and their believers, fautors, receivers and defenders in this, the province of Narbonne. I do not claim the wisdom of Solomon, Reverend Father, but I do know this: that the search for truth is long and painstaking, like the search for a man in a foreign country. The country must be explored, with many roads followed and questions asked, before the man can be found. Thus one might say that the quest for understanding resembles that form of rhetorical discourse which we call a syllogism – for just as a syllogism moves from universals to particulars, presenting a certain unchangeable truth if it is made up of true propositions, so the full understanding of one fateful act will follow from an understanding of all the people, places and events which surrounded or preceded it.

Reverend Father, I need your understanding. I need your protection and your good regard. Stretch forth thine hand against the wrath of mine enemies, for they have sharpened their tongues like a serpent; adders' poison is under their lips. Perhaps you know of my plight, and would turn away, but I swear that I am falsely accused. Many people have been falsely accused. And many people have looked without seeing, preferring to sleep in contentment with the darkness of their ignorance, rather than gaze upon the light of truth. Reverend Father, I implore you – regard this missive as a light. Read it, and you will see far, and understand much, and forgive much. *Blessed is he whose transgression is forgiven*, but my transgressions have been few, and small. It is through guilt and malice that I have been so cruelly punished.

Therefore, to illuminate your path, in the name of Almighty God and the Most Blessed Virgin Mary, mother of Christ, and of the blessed Dominic our father, and of all the heavenly court, I hereby record those events which took place in and around the city of Lazet, in the province of Narbonne, relating to the assassination of our venerable and respected Brother Augustin Duese on the Feast of the Nativity of the Blessed Virgin, in the year of the Incarnate Word, 1318.

Narratio

The shadow of death

hen I first met Father Augustin Duese, I thought: 'That man is living in the shadow of death.' I thought this, firstly, because of his appearance, which was bloodless and attenuated, like one of the dry bones from Ezekiel's vision. He was tall and very thin, his shoulders were bowed, his skin was grey, his cheeks were hollow, his eyes were almost lost in their deep, shadowy sockets, his hair was scanty, his teeth were decayed, his step was faltering. He looked like an ambulant corpse, and this was not simply because he was so full of days. I came to feel that death was hovering near him, attacking him ceaselessly with the weapons of illness: inflammation of the joints – particularly in the hands and knees – poor digestion, failing eyesight, constipated bowels, a problem with the passing of water. Only his ears were unaffected, for his hearing was very acute. (I believe that his skill as an inquisitor stemmed from his ability to detect the note of falsehood in a person's voice.) I am also convinced that the penitential quality of his meals may have contributed to the degradation of his stomach, which was forced to digest food that St Dominic himself would have spurned, food that I would hesitate to call food, and which was consumed in very small quantities. I would even go so far as to say that, if he *had* been dead, he might perhaps have eaten a little more, although to eat large portions of the victuals he favoured – bone-hard bread, boiled vegetable peelings, cheese rind – would have been more difficult than swallowing a thorn hedge. Doubtless he offered up his suffering as a sacrifice to the Lord. Myself, I believe that such a diet should be observed with a little less zeal. The Angelic Doctor told us that austerity is taken up by religious life as being necessary to mortify the flesh but, if practised without discretion, it carries with it the risk of faltering. Not that Father Augustin paraded his mortifications: his abstinence was not a vain and faithless gesture, of the kind against which Christ warns us when He condemns the hypo-crites who fast with a sad countenance, and disfigure their faces that they may appear unto men to fast. Father Augustin was not like that. If he mortified the flesh, it was because he felt unworthy. But he made no friends among the priory's swine-herds with his demands for mouldy turnips and bruised fruit. Scraps of that kind have always been regarded as their property – in so far as a Dominican lay brother may own even a cabbage stump. I once remarked to Father Augustin that, while he starved himself, he starved our pigs also, and a fasting pig was of no use to anyone.

He said nothing, of course. Most inquisitors know how to use silence with the most expert precision.

In any event, Father Augustin not only looked and, I am quite sure, felt like a dying man, but behaved like one as well. By this I mean that he seemed to be in a very great hurry, as if he numbered his days. And to give you an example of this strange urgency, I shall describe what happened shortly after his appearance in Lazet, not three months before his demise, in response to my request for help in the praiseworthy task of 'catching the little foxes who seek to destroy the vineyard of the Lord' – that is to say, apprehending certain enemies by which the Church is hedged about, like a lily among thorns. Doubtless you will be familiar with these enemies. Perhaps you have even encountered these purveyors of heretical doctrine, these sowers of discord, fabricators of schism, dividers of unity, who question that holy truth proclaimed by the Roman See and soil the purity of the Faith with their diversely erroneous teachings. Even the early fathers, after all, were plagued by such emissaries of Satan. (Was it not St Paul himself who assured us: 'There must be heresies, that they who are approved may be made manifest among you'?) Here in the south, we battle against many perverse dogmas, many pestiferous sects whose names and practices differ but whose poison corrupts with equally harmful effect. Here in the south, the ancient seeds of that Manichaean heresy denounced by St Augustin have become deeply rooted, and flourish still, despite the pious efforts of St Dominic's holy order.

Here, the lives of many friars are devoted to the defence of Christ's cross. When I was first appointed vicar to Jacques Vaquier, Lazet's inquisitor of heretical depravity (how long ago it seems!) the intention was not that I should spend the better part of each day pursuing those workers of iniquity, but that I should ease Father Jacques's burden whenever he found its weight overwhelming. As it happened, however, Father Jacques was easily overwhelmed. I spent a good deal more time on Holy Office matters than was my original intention. Nevertheless, Jacques Vaquier did make inquisition of many souls which, like sheep, had gone sadly astray, and when he died last winter, the volume of work that he left behind was too great for one man. That is why I appealed to Paris for a new superior. And that is why Father Augustin arrived at the priory late one summer afternoon, six days before the Feast of the Visitation (when he was actually due), unheralded, unexpected, unaccompanied save for his young scribe and assistant, Sicard, who served as his master's eyes.

Both were too weary to attend supper, or Compline. As far as I know, they went straight to bed. But at Matins the next morning I saw Father Augustin in the choir-stall opposite, and after Tierce I joined him in his cell. (For this, of course, we were given special permission.) I should explain that in the priory of

9

Lazet, brethren appointed to serve the Holy Office are given the same privilege as that enjoyed by our lector and librarian – namely, their own cells, and permission to shut the doors of their cells. Father Augustin, however, did not shut his door.

'I prefer not to speak of unholy matters in a place dedicated to God,' he explained. 'As far as possible, we shall speak of the limbs of the Antichrist only where we attack them, rather than poisoning the air of the priory with wicked thoughts and deeds. Therefore I see no need for secrecy or closed doors – not here.'

I agreed with him. Then he asked me, in formal tones, to join him in a prayer, that God might bless our efforts to cleanse the land of heretical morbidity. It was already apparent that he and Jacques Vaquier had been cast from different moulds. Father Augustin was wont to employ certain learned phrases when denoting heretics – 'the foxes in the vineyard', 'the cockle in the harvest', 'deviants from the right way', and so forth. He was also very precise in his use of those terms defined by the Council of Tarragona, last century, concerning the different degrees of culpability in heretical association: for example, he never called someone a 'concealer' of heretics who was really a 'hider' (the distinction, as you know, is a fine one), or a 'defender' who was really a 'receiver'. He always called the house or inn where heretics might congregate a 'receptacle', as the Council decreed.

Father Jacques called heretics 'pond-scum', and their houses 'pest-holes'. He was not, as St Augustin might have put it, one of those men who joined their hearts to the angels.

'I am aware that the Inquisitor General wrote to you with a full account of my history and education,' Father Augustin went on. His voice was surprisingly firm and resonant. 'Are there any questions you wish to ask me concerning my experience as an inquisitor ... my life in the order ...?'

The Inquisitor General's description had indeed been thorough, with exact dates given for all of Father Augustin's teaching posts, priorships and Papal commissions, from Cahors to Bologna. But there is more to a man than his appointments. I could have asked a great many questions about Father Augustin's health, or his parents, or his favourite authors; I could have asked him for his views on the role of the inquisitor, or on the poverty of Christ.

Instead, I asked him the question which you were doubtless wondering yourself, and which he must have answered a thousand times. 'Father,' I said, 'are you related to the Holy Father, Pope John?'

He smiled a weary smile. 'The Holy Father would not recognise me,' he rejoined obscurely, and would say nothing else on the subject, then or at any other time. I never discovered the truth. It is my opinion that, as a Duese from Cahors, he *was* related, but that somehow the two branches of the family had become disunited, and that as a result he did not benefit from Pope John's renowned generosity to men of his own blood. Otherwise, he would have been a cardinal by now – or at least a bishop.

Having avoided my question, Father Augustin proceeded to ask me questions in return. I had been identified as a Peyre of Prouille; had I indeed been raised in sight of St Dominic's first foundation? Had its proximity inspired me to join the Dominican order? He spoke reverently, and I was sorry to inform him that the Peyres of Prouille had been ruined long before St Dominic arrived there. Even in St Dominic's time the fort had been dismantled, and the Peyres' seigneurial rights relinquished to a family of rich peasants. I know this from reading an account of the monastery's early days, which, quite unexpectedly, reassured me on a point that had always been of some concern – for I had been most uneasy as to the exact circumstances of my family's decline. In this part of the world, fallen glory is very often the result of heretical beliefs: I was relieved to discover that my ancestral property had not been confiscated by the Holy Office, nor, indeed, by the armies of Simon de Montfort, but had simply been lost through weakness or stupidity.

I told Father Augustin that I had been raised in Carcassonne, and that my father had been a public notary and consul there. If I had any relations in Prouille, I knew nothing of them. Indeed, I had never even visited the place.

Father Augustin seemed disappointed. In a chillier tone he asked me about my progress in the order, and I quickly reviewed it for him: solemn profession at the age of nineteen, three years of philosophy at Carcassonne, teaching philosophy at Carcassonne and Lazet, five years of theology at Montpellier Studium Generale, appointment as Preacher General, definitor at various provincial chapters, Master of Students at Beziers, at Lazet, at Toulouse . . .

'And back to Lazet,' Father Augustin finished. 'For how long now?'

'Nine years.'

'You are comfortable, here?'

'Comfortable. Yes.' He meant, of course, that my pace had slowed, that I appeared to be at a standstill. But as one grows old, one begins to lose the passions of youth. Besides which, there are certain men in the order who do not laugh as I do. 'The wine here is good. The weather is good. There are sufficient heretics. What more could you want?'

Father Augustin looked at me for a little while. Then he began to question me about Father Jacques, about his history and habits, his tastes, his talents, his life and death. I realised very quickly that he was driving me in a particular direction, the way dogs will drive a hart towards a hunting party. The way I will drive a heretic towards the truth.

'Father, there is no need to prevaricate,' I told him, interrupting a careful inquiry about Father Jacques's friendship with some of the city's leading merchants. 'You want to know if the rumours are based on fact – if your predecessor did, indeed, secretly accept money from accused heretics.'

Father Augustin exhibited no manifestations of surprise or annoyance. He was too experienced an inquisitor for that. He simply watched me, and waited.

12

'I too have heard these tales,' I continued, 'but have been unable to confirm their truth or falsity. Father Jacques brought to the order many rich and beautiful books, which he professed to have received as gifts. He also had many well-endowed relatives in this region, but I cannot tell you whether their wealth came *from* him, or went *to* him. If he did accept illicit gifts, it cannot have occurred very often.'

Still Father Augustin remained silent, his gaze fixed on the floor. Over the years, I have learned that no one, not even an experienced inquisitor, can read the hearts and minds of men as he would read a book. For man looketh on the outward appearance, but the Lord looketh on the heart – and Father Augustin's outward appearance was as blank as a stone wall. Nevertheless, with a vaulting and no doubt undeserved confidence, I believed that I could follow the direction of his thoughts. I believed that he was naturally suspicious of how far *I* was implicated, so hastened to reassure him.

'I, on the other hand, have no rich relatives. And my wages as your vicar are transferred directly to the priory – when they are paid at all.' Seeing my superior's puzzled frown, I explained that Father Jacques, despite repeated requests made to the Royal Steward of Confiscations, had been owed three years' wages when he died. 'Confiscations are not as profitable as they used to be,' I added. 'The heretics we see now are mostly poor peasants from the mountains. Any rich heretical lords were captured and skinned long ago.'

Father Augustin grunted. 'The King is responsible for the expenses of the Holy Office,' he said. 'This is not Lombardy or Tuscany. The Inquisition of France does not depend on confiscations for its survival.'

'Perhaps not in theory,' I replied. 'But the King still owes Father Jacques four hundred and fifty livres tournois.'

'And yourself? What does the King owe you?'

'Half that.'

Father Augustin frowned again. Then the bell rang for Prime, and we rose together.

13

'After Mass,' he said, 'I wish to visit the gaol, and the premises where you conduct your interrogations.'

'I shall take you there.'

'I also wish to meet this Royal Steward of Confiscations – and of course the Royal Seneschal.'

'That can be arranged.'

'Naturally, I shall inquire into the matter of wages,' he went on, and moved towards the door. It appeared that our dialogue had reached its conclusion. But as he crossed the threshold, he turned and looked at me.

'Did you say that the lost sheep in our prison are mostly poor peasants?' he inquired.

'I did, yes.'

'Then perhaps we should ask ourselves why. Are the rich all faithful Catholics? Or do they have the means of buying themselves their freedom?'

I could find within me no answer to this. So after waiting, briefly, for a response, Father Augustin once more set off for the church, leaning heavily on his staff and stopping, sometimes, to catch his breath.

Following him, I had to walk more slowly than was my custom. But I was compelled to admit that, although his body might be infirm, Father Augustin's mind was very vigorous indeed.

It occurs to me that you will not be familiar with Lazet, except in the most simple terms: you may know that it is a large city, only slightly smaller than Carcassonne; that it lies near the foothills of the Pyrenees, overlooking a fertile valley bisected by the River Agly; that it trades mostly in wine and wool, some grains, a little olive oil, and wood from the mountains. You may even know that it has been a royal possession since the death of Alphonse de Poitiers. But you will know nothing of its appearance, its important features, its prominent citizens. So I shall set down a faithful description of the city before I proceed to my account of the events which took place there, and may God lend my hand an eloquence which my tongue lacks.

Lazet is built on the crown of a low hill, and is well fortified. When you enter the northern gate, which is called the St Polycarpe gate, you soon reach the cathedral of St Polycarpe. It is an old church, rather small, and simple in its construction; the canons' cloisters beside it are more elaborately decorated, having been completed more recently. The Bishop's palace used to be the canons' guest-house, before Pope Boniface XIII created the bishoprics of Pamiers and Lazet in 1295. Since then this building has been quite transformed (or so I am told), and boasts many more rooms than even an Archbishop could possibly require. It is undoubtedly the most handsome building in Lazet.

There is an open space in front of the cathedral where five roads intersect, and here you will find the market. Many people frequent it to buy wine, cloth, sheep, wood, fish, pottery, blankets and other goods. At the centre of the market stands a stone cross, raised above a kind of sheltered, shallow pit, like a grotto, which is the property of the canons of St Polycarpe. I have heard tell that long ago, before the city was built, a pious hermit lived for fifty years in this grotto, never once emerging (or even standing up, to judge from the dimensions of the space), and that he prophesied the building of Lazet. His name was Galamus. Although he was never sanctified, his grotto has always been regarded as a holy place; for countless years people have been leaving gifts there, anonymously, for the canons – sometimes money, more often bread or vegetables, a roll of cloth, a pair of shoes. These offerings are collected every day at sundown.

The fact that there has been very little to collect, these past few years, has been blamed on the Holy Office – which tends to be blamed for most of the bad things in this part of the world.

From the market, if you walk down the Street of Galamus,

you will pass the Chateau Comtal on your right. Once the home of the counts of Lazet (a line now extinct, thanks to its heretical tendencies), this fortress is now the headquarters of the Royal Seneschal, Roger Descalquencs. When King Philippe visited our region some fourteen years ago, he slept in the room where Roger now sleeps – as Roger himself will take care to remind you. The monthly assizes, over which he generally presides as a magistrate, are also held in the chateau, and the royal prison is accommodated in two of its towers. Much of the city's garrison is stationed in the barracks and gatehouse.

The priory of the Friars Preachers lies to the east of the chateau. As one of the oldest Dominican foundations, it was visited many times by St Dominic, who graced it with a small collection of crusts and garments which are carefully preserved in the chapter house. Twenty-eight friars live here, as well as seventeen lay brothers and twelve students. There are one hundred and seventy-two books in the library, fourteen of them acquired (through some means) by Father Jacques Vaquier. According to that well-respected work by Humbert of Romans, concerning the lives of our early fathers, Lazet was the place where a certain Brother Benedict, plagued beyond endurance by Seven Winged Devils (who beat him unmercifully, afflicted his entire body with pustules, and filled his nostrils with an evil smell), went entirely mad, and had to be chained to a wall for the protection of his fellow friars. When St Dominic exorcised these devils, their master appeared in person – having assumed the shape of a black lizard – and argued theology with the saint until defeated by a very powerful collective enthymeme.

Fortunately, such things do not happen here any more.

From the priory, it is only a short walk to the premises of the Holy Office. Nevertheless, when I conducted Father Augustin along this route, I was greeted four times by passing acquaintances – a glove-maker, a sergeant-at-arms, a tavern keeper, a pious matron – and was conscious of my superior's quizzical, sidelong glance. 'Did you not tell me,' he said, 'that the Holy Office is regarded with hostility among the people here?'

'I fear so.'

'And yet they seem to regard you as a friend.'

I laughed. 'Father,' I replied, 'if I were in their position, I too would make a friend of the local inquisitor.'

This seemed to satisfy him, though it was not an entirely truthful explanation. The fact is, I have taken great care to keep on good terms with many of Lazet's citizens, for to construct a detailed mental image of the city's most notable family trees, business partnerships and blood feuds, it is necessary to pass time with the people involved. I guarantee that you will learn more about a woman's amatory secrets by exchanging a few words with her maid or her neighbour, than by interrogating her on a rack (which is something that I have never done, by God's grace). *Behold, I send you forth as sheep in the midst of wolves: be ye therefore wise as serpents, and harmless as doves.* These are words to live by, not only for the preacher, but for the inquisitor also.

I have always said that a good inquisitor does not need to ask his witness many questions. A good inquisitor already knows the answers. And he will not find all the answers in books, or in the contemplation of Christ's Ineffable Majesty.

'Here, as you see, is the prison,' I announced, when we had reached the city wall. For in Lazet, as in Carcassonne, prisoners of the Holy Office are held in one of the fortified towers that adorn the city's encircling wall much as jewels adorn a necklace. 'We are fortunate, here, in that our headquarters were specially constructed to abut the prison, allowing us to move freely and easily between the two buildings.'

'A good plan,' Father Augustin agreed, in grave tones.

'You will not find the appointments as lavish as those in Toulouse,' I added, because I knew that he had spent some time working with Bernard Gui, who conducts his business in that house near the Chateau Narbonnaise donated to St

17

Dominic by Peter Cella. 'We cannot boast a refectory or a great hall, as they do in Carcassonne. We have stables, but no horses. Our employees are few.'

'Better is little with the fear of the Lord,' Father Augustin murmured. Then I showed him how the stables were built, hewn out of a gentle slope so that the big wooden doors, barred from the inside, opened onto a street somewhat lower than the road on which the main entrance was to be found. In effect, although the building was three storeys high – with the stables forming the lowest level – from the north, there appeared to be only two storeys, huddled against the prison tower like a lamb seeking refuge against the flank of its mother.

But perhaps it is inappropriate to compare the headquarters of the Holy Office to something weak and tender like a lamb. The repository of many grave secrets, it was as well fortified as the prison beside it, with thick stone walls pierced by three small loopholes. The main door was barely wide or high enough to admit a man of normal proportions and, like the stable door, it too could be barred from the inside. On that morning, however, we met Raymond Donatus coming out as we were going in, so there was no need to knock.

'Ah! Raymond Donatus,' I said. 'May I introduce Father Augustin Duese. Father, this is our notary, who devotes most of his time to our special requirements. He has been a faithful servant of the Holy Office for eight years.'

Raymond Donatus looked shocked. I surmised that he had been stepping outside to empty his bladder (for his hands were fumbling with his garments), and had not been expecting to find our new inquisitor on the doorstep. Nevertheless he recovered himself quickly, and bowed low.

'You grace us with your presence, Reverend Father. My heart rejoices.'

Father Augustin blinked, and muttered a blessing. He seemed slightly taken aback by Raymond's exaggerated – one might even say, histrionic – courtesy. But that was a characteristic of Raymond: he was ever extreme in his use of words, which were either as sweet as the bread of angels, or like the hammer that breaketh the rock in pieces. He was a moody fellow, swinging from gloom to exultation many times each day, quick-tempered, loud in his opinions, hilarious in his good humour, gluttonous, intemperate, and as lascivious as a goat (whose blood is so hot that it will melt diamonds). A man of humble birth, he prided himself on his education. He also dressed in fine clothes, and talked a great deal about his vineyards.

These little faults, however, were as nothing beside his mastery of legal language, and the awe-inspiring deftness of his hand. I have never, in all my travels, met a notary who could transcribe the spoken word so quickly. One's first sentence would barely have left one's mouth before his contraction was on the page.

To conclude with a description of his appearance (what Cicero would call an *effictio*), I will say that he was about forty years old, of medium stature, plump but not obese, ruddy-faced, with abundant hair as black as the third horse of the Apocalypse. He had good teeth, and was always proud to display them, beaming at Father Augustin so fiercely that my superior appeared to be somewhat disconcerted.

To fill the awkward silence, I explained that Raymond Donatus was in charge of the inquisitorial records, which were kept upstairs.

'Ah!' said Father Augustin, suddenly animated, and crossed the threshold at a surprisingly rapid pace. 'Yes. The registers. I wish to speak to you about the registers.'

'They are quite secure,' I said, following him. As our eyes adjusted to the shadows, I pointed to my desk, which occupied one end of the room we had entered. The only other furniture to be seen were three benches, arranged along the walls to our left and right. 'That is where I do a good deal of my work. Father Jacques used to leave much of the correspondence to me.'

Father Augustin peered like a blind man. Then he shuffled

over and touched the wooden lectern – again like a blind man. I had to lead him into his own room, which was larger than the anteroom, blessed with a loophole that admitted some light. Having explained that it was Father Jacques's custom to interrogate witnesses in this room, I showed his successor the inquisitor's desk, the inquisitor's chair (an impressive piece of furniture, elaborately carved) and the chest where Father Jacques had kept certain works of reference: Guillaume Durant's *Speculum judiciale*, the *Summa* of Rainerius Sacconi, Peter Lombard's *Sentences*, Raymond of Penafort's gloss to the *Liber Extra* of Gregory IX. These books, I said, were now in the care of the priory's librarian, but if Father Augustin should need to consult them, he had only to ask.

'And the registers?' he inquired, as if I had not spoken. There was a cold intentness in his manner which puzzled me. I took him back into the anteroom, and up the circular stone staircase which had been built into a narrow corner turret, connecting all three floors. When we reached the top floor, we found Raymond Donatus waiting for us there, together with the scrivener, Brother Lucius Pourcel.

'This is where we keep the registers,' I explained. 'And this is Brother Lucius, our scrivener. Brother Lucius is a canon of St Polycarpe. He is a quick and very accurate scribe.'

Father Augustin and Brother Lucius exchanged a fraternal greeting, Brother Lucius with his usual humility, Father Augustin as if his mind were on matters more important. I realised that nothing would distract him from his purpose, which was to locate and examine the inquisitorial registers. So I conducted him to the two great chests in which they were contained, and bestowed on him the keys of his predecessor.

'Who else has been given keys?' he asked. 'Yourself?'

'Of course.'

'And these men?'

'Yes. These men also.' I looked over to where Raymond Donatus and Brother Lucius stood, an ill-matched pair, the one so well padded and richly dressed, so robustly coarse in his

20

appearance and appetites, the other so pale and slight and subdued. Often I had heard Raymond talking to Lucius, his plangent voice clearly audible from downstairs, as he tabulated the attractions of a female acquaintance or discoursed upon matters pertaining to Catholic dogma. He had many opinions, and liked to air them. I cannot recall hearing Brother Lucius express his thoughts on anything, except perhaps the weather, or his smarting eyes. Once, out of pity, I asked him if he would prefer to see less of Raymond Donatus, but he assured me that he was not dissatisfied. Raymond, he said, was a learned man.

He was also a man who burned incense to vanity, and was not at all flattered by Father Augustin's apparent inability to remember his name. (That, at least, was how I interpreted his peevish expression.) Father Augustin, however, was consumed by one overriding concern. Until he satisfied himself on that score, nothing else could hold his interest.

'I cannot unlock these chests,' he declared, presenting his swollen and tremulous hand for my inspection. 'Kindly open them for me.'

'Are you looking for a particular book, Father?'

'I want all the registers containing all the inquisitions conducted by Father Jacques during his time here.'

'Then Raymond will be of more assistance than I.' Gesturing to Raymond Donatus, I heaved open the lid of the first chest. 'Raymond keeps these books in order.'

'With great zeal and diligence,' added Raymond, who was never shy of proclaiming his own virtues. He bustled forward, eager to lay claim to the stewardship of our inquisitorial registers. 'Is there a particular case you wish to review, Reverend Father? Because in the front of each book there are tabulations – '

'I wish to review all the cases,' Father Augustin interrupted. Squinting down at the piles of leather-bound volumes, he frowned and asked how many there were.

'There are fifty-six registers,' Raymond said proudly. 'Also several rolls and cahiers.'

'This being, as you know, one of the oldest headquarters,' I pointed out. It had occurred to me that Father Augustin was almost certainly incapable of lifting even a single register, because each codex was quite large, and weighed a good deal. 'It has also been one of the busiest. At present, for example, there are one hundred and seventy-eight adult prisoners.'

'I want all of Father Jacques's registers put in the chest downstairs,' my superior commanded, once again ignoring my remarks. 'Sicard will help me to review them. Can we enter the prison from this floor?'

'No, Father. Only from the floor below.'

'Then we shall retrace our steps. Thank you.' Father Augustin nodded at Brother Lucius and Raymond Donatus. 'I shall speak to you again later. You may return to your duties now.'

'Father, I cannot,' Raymond objected. 'Not without Father Bernard. We were planning to conduct an interrogation.'

'That can wait,' I said. 'Have you written up the protocol for Bertrand Gasco?'

'Not entirely.'

'Then finish it. I shall call you when I need you.'

Father Augustin descended to the anteroom slowly, for the stairs were narrow, and the light dim. But he held his tongue until we were safely behind my desk, near the door of the prison. Then he said: 'I wish to ask you frankly, Brother – are those men reliable?'

'Raymond?' I said. 'Reliable?'

'Are they trustworthy? Who appointed them?'

'Father Jacques. Of course.' As St Augustin says, there are some things which we do not believe unless we understand them, and some things which we do not understand unless we believe them. But here was something which I understood and *still* did not believe. 'Father,' I queried, 'have you come here to make inquisition of the Inquisition? Because, if so, you should tell me as much.'

'I have come here to prevent ravening wolves from depraving the Faith,' Father Augustin replied. 'To do so, I must ensure that the records of the Holy Office are secure. The records are our greatest resource, Brother, and the enemies of Christ understand that. They will go to great lengths to obtain them.'

'Yes, I know. Avignonet.' Every soul who works for the Holy Office has engraven on his heart the names of those inquisitors killed at Avignonet last century. Not so many know that their registers were stolen, and sold later for the sum of forty sous. 'Caunes, too. And Narbonne. Every attack against us seems to end with the stealing and burning of registers. But this building is well guarded, and copies of every register have been made. You will find them in the Bishop's library.'

'Brother, the greatest defeats of all are those contrived by traitors,' Father Augustin rejoined. Leaning heavily on his stick, he added: 'Thirty years ago, the Inquisitor of Carcassonne uncovered a plot to destroy certain registers. I have seen the depositions – copies are lodged at Toulouse. Two of the men implicated were employed by the Holy Office, one as a courier, the other as a scribe. We must be vigilant, Brother – always. *Take ye heed every one of his neighbour, and trust ye not in any brother.*'

Once again, I was confounded. I could find nothing to say except: 'Why were you consulting thirty-year-old depositions?'

Father Augustin smiled. 'Old records will tell you as much as new records,' he said. 'That is why I wish to review the registers of Father Jacques. By extracting the name of every person defamed for heresy in his depositions, then matching the names against those listed as charged and condemned, I shall see whether anyone has escaped punishment.'

'They may have escaped punishment because they are dead,' I pointed out.

'Then, as prescribed, we shall exhume their remains, burn their bones and destroy their houses.'

Through the wrath of the Lord of Hosts is the land darkened, and the people shall be as the fuel of the fire. Doubtless I am faint of heart, but the pursuit of departed souls has always seemed excessive, to my way of thinking. Are not the dead in God's domain – or the devil's?

'The people of this city will not look upon you kindly, Father, if you dig up their dead,' I observed, thinking again of those episodes to which I had already referred – to those attacks made on the Holy Office in Caunes, and Narbonne, and Carcassonne. To that incident described in Brother Guillaume Pelhisson's *Chronicle*, where Brother Arnaud Catalan, Inquisitor of Albi, was beaten bloody by a hostile populace for burning hereticated bones.

But Father Augustin's reply was: 'We are not here to make friends, Brother.'

And he regarded me with a faintly accusatory air.

Among the many remarkable works housed in the priory of Lazet is Pierre of Vaux-de-Cernay's *Historia albigensis*. This chronicle contains an account of those deeds which, but for God's gift of letters, would almost certainly have been forgotten, since few wish to remember such bloody times, or the roots of bitterness that caused them. Perhaps (who knows?) they are best forgotten; certainly the shameful history of this province's fascination with perverse doctrines is not one which I would care to see widely published. Suffice it to say, however, that if you consult the *Historia albigensis*, you will gain a very full understanding of those dark infidelities which drew down the wrath of Christendom upon us, here in the south. I cannot hope even to attempt a synopsis of the events described by the said Pierre, who, in the train of Simon de Montfort himself, bore witness to so many battles and sieges, as the crusading armies laid our mountains and our heritage waste for the dragons of the wilderness. In any event, it was a war that has little bearing on my own humble narrative. I draw your attention to Father Pierre's work only because it gives such a faithful account of the extent to which that 'abominable pestilence of heretical depravity', the sect of the Manichaean or Albigensian heretics (also known as the Cathars), had infected my countrymen before the crusade was launched against them. From the highest to the lowest, they wandered hither and yon through the pathless wastes of error; in Pierre's own words, even the nobles of this land 'had nearly all become defenders and receivers of heretics'. And where nobles proceed, as you must be aware, base folk will always follow.

Why do they follow? Why do they turn their faces from the light? Some say that the Holy and Apostolic Church itself is at fault, for its greed and ignorance, for the vanity of its priests and the simony of its pontiffs. But I look around me and I see pride – I see ignorance – at the root of all dissent. I see base men who aspire, not just to the priesthood, but to the mantle of prophecy. I see women who presume to teach, and peasants who call themselves bishops. (Not at present, thank the Lord, but in times past the Cathars had their bishops, and their councils, too.)

Such was our plight some hundred years ago, or thereabouts. Today, thanks to the diligence of the Holy Office, heresy has been driven into hiding: the disease is no longer widespread and exposed, like a leper's sores, but festering in dark concealment, in woods and mountains, behind false piety, beneath sheep's clothing. As far as I can ascertain, after consultation with Jean de Beaune at Carcassonne, and Bernard Gui at Toulouse (and also with the new Bishop of Pamiers, Jacques Fournier, who has recently instigated his own attack on unorthodox beliefs in his diocese), the latest outbreak of this infection was occasioned by the labours of Pierre Authie, one-time notary of Foix, who was burned for his misdeeds in 1310. Pierre and his brother Guillaume were converted to error in Lombardy; they returned to their homeland late last century as Perfects – or priests – to convert in their turn. Bernard Gui estimates that they must have ministered to at least a thousand believers. In effect, they sowed a seed which has sprouted, flowered, and seeded again, so that the slopes and passes of the Pyrenees are now thick with this noxious weed.

25

Hence the number of mountain peasants confined in our prison – ignorant souls for whom one might feel pity, if they were not so stupidly stubborn. How tenaciously they cling to their foolish errors, insisting, for example, that where there is no bread in the stomach, there is no soul. Or that the souls of bad men do not go to hell or paradise after the Last Judgement, but are thrown from cliffs by demons. Or even that those who move their hands or arms from their sides, when they walk, do great evil, since movements of this kind throw down many souls of the dead to earth! I doubt that the Manichaean Perfects themselves teach such nonsense (for they have a code of beliefs which, though mistaken, is not without logic in its perversity). No, the strange convictions of these illiterates are of their own devising. Taught to doubt and question by the Perfects, they create their own doctrines to suit themselves. And what does this lead to? It leads to men like Bertrand Gasco.

Bertrand came from Seyrac, a mountain village full of heresy and sheep breeders. Because the Perfects teach that copulation, even between man and wife, is sinful (and if you consult the first part of the *Historia Albigensis*, you will see that the author tabulates this particular error in the following way: 'that holy matrimony is nothing else than harlotry, nor can anyone fathering sons and daughters in that state achieve salvation'), because, as I say, this is one of the Manichaean tenets, Bertrand Gasco used it to his own ends. A squat, unhealthy, grim-visaged weaver, of few possessions and no education, he none-theless was able to seduce any number of women – I have not yet calculated the total – including several who were married, one who was his sister, and one who was his half-sister. To justify such monstrous sin, he told his ignorant victims that to be known carnally by one's husband was more sinful than to be known carnally by any other man, even a brother. Why? Because the wife did not believe that she was sinning, when she was known by her husband! He also said that God had never ordered that man *not* accept his blood sister as his wife, since at the beginning of the world brothers used to know their sisters carnally. In this declaration, I instantly detected the influence of someone more literate than Bertrand, and was able to extract from him a name – the name of a Perfect, Ademar de Roaxio. As it happened, this same Ademar had also been apprehended. He was already immured in the prison with Bertrand.

I do not believe that Ademar taught Bertrand such perverse dogma with the intention of encouraging him to pursue his female relatives. Doubtless these errors were presented simply to support the proposition that carnal knowledge is a sin, whether in or out of wedlock, whether between strangers or siblings. Ademar, being a man of ascetic temperament, would not have approved of Bertrand's activities. I would speculate that the Perfect lived as he professed to live – as heretical doctrine decreed that he should live: chastely, poorly, on a diet precluding meat, eggs or cheese (these having been begotten by coition), eschewing oaths, begging and preaching. Some authorities maintain that heretics claim falsely, when they claim to be chaste, or poor, or pure in any way, and it is true that many heretics are liars, fornicators and gluttons. But a few are not. A few, like Ademar, are true believers. And they are all the more frightening because of it.

From the deposition of a witness named Raymonda Vitalis, I learned that on one occasion Ademar was asked to bless a dying child with that blessing known as the *consolamentum*, comprising many prayers and prostrations. This, the heretics believe, will ensure that a dying soul shall gain eternal life – but only if he or she takes no food or water afterwards. 'Do not give your daughter anything to eat or drink, even if she asks for it,' Ademar instructed. When the child's mother replied that she would never deny her daughter food or drink, Ademar told her that she was imperilling the child's soul. Whereupon the father removed his wife, forcibly, from the presence of the child – who died crying out for milk and bread.

They call this terrible fast the *endura*, and believe that it is a holy form of suicide. Doubtless the philosophy behind it is somehow derived from their disgust with the material world, which they call the creation and domain of the malign god, Satan, to whom they ascribe a power equal to that of the Lord. But I digress. My intention here is not to explore the intricacies of heretical doctrine. My intention is to narrate a story, as quickly and clearly as possible.

Suffice it to say, therefore, that Ademar himself was fasting thus when Father Augustin first inspected the prison.

'This man is an unrepentant Perfect,' I informed my superior (and I must confess that I spoke with some pride, for Perfects are a rare breed, these days). 'He is dying.'

'Dying?'

'He refuses to eat.'

I opened the hatch in Ademar's cell door, but it was too dark to see anything. So I unbarred the door itself, knowing that, faint with hunger and chained to the wall, Ademar would offer us no threat. He was alone, because Perfects have to be placed in solitary confinement, no matter how crowded a prison might be. If they are not, they will poison the minds of other prisoners, persuading them to recant their confessions and die for their principles.

'Greetings, Ademar,' I said cheerfully. 'You look very ill, my friend. Will you not reconsider?'

The prisoner stirred a little, so that his fetters clinked. But he said nothing.

'I see that Pons has left you some bread. Why not eat, before it goes stale?'

Still Ademar remained silent. It occurred to me that he was too weak to talk – perhaps too weak to pick up the bread. In the dim light, his appearance was deathly, his long, bony face as white as the seven angels.

'Would you like me to feed you?' I asked him, with real concern. When I broke off a piece of bread and placed it on his lips, however, he turned his head away.

Sighing, I straightened, and addressed my superior.

'Ademar has made a full and honest confession, but refuses

28

to renounce his errors. Father Jacques's instructions were that all uncooperative witnesses and obdurate sinners should be made to fast, on bread and water, so that bodily rigours might open their hearts to the light of truth.' I paused, overcome for a moment by the close, fetid air of the place. 'Ademar's fast is a little more stringent than I would wish,' I concluded.

Father Augustin inclined his head. Then he advanced until he was close to the prisoner, raised his hand, and intoned the words: 'Repent, and ye shall be saved.'

Ademar looked up. He opened his mouth. The voice that emerged from it was faint and unearthly, like the creaking of a tree in the wind.

'Repent, and ye shall be saved,' he rejoined.

I had to conceal a laugh behind a cough. Ademar was incorrigible.

'Renounce your errors, and be with God,' Father Augustin demanded, even more grimly. Whereupon Ademar replied: 'Renounce your errors, and be with God.'

Looking from one man to the other, I was disturbed to recognise a certain similarity between them. Both were as immovable, as implacable, as the brass mountains of Zechariah.

'Your life is not your own, to end as you wish,' Father Augustin informed the Perfect. 'If need be, I can hold an *auto de fé* tomorrow. Do not assume that you can escape the flames in this cowardly fashion.'

'I am not a coward,' Ademar croaked, rattling his chains. 'If you were truly a servant of God, instead of a walking cash-box, you would know that hunger bites more keenly than any fire.'

This time I simply had to laugh.

'That remonstrance might well apply to me, Ademar, but not to Father Augustin. Father Augustin's reputation precedes him: he is renowned for living on nettles and knuckle-bones. He knows what hunger is.'

'Then he should know that it is slow, very slow. The flames

29

are quick. If I were a coward, I would throw myself onto the pyre, but I am not.'

'You are,' I said. 'You are a coward because you condemned a child to death, and walked away. You left her parents to endure her cries alone. That is the act of a coward.'

'I did *not* walk away! I stayed to the end! I watched her die!'

'And I wager you enjoyed it. I know what you think of children. You told a pregnant woman that her womb was cursed with the fruits of the devil.'

'You walk in darkness, benighted monk. You have no understanding of these mysteries.'

'True. I cannot understand why you would give your life for an erroneous faith which must disappear one day, since no pious believer may have children. Foolish fellow. Why court death in this way, if, as you believe, your soul may very well end up in a chicken, or a pig? Or even a *bishop*, God prevent it!'

Ademar turned his face to the wall. He closed his eyes, and refused to speak. So I addressed my next remark to Father Augustin.

'With your permission, Father, I could send Pons in here with some nice stuffed mushrooms ... perhaps a little wine, a few honey cakes ... something to tempt the appetite.'

Father Augustin was frowning. He shook his head impatiently, as if my words had displeased him. Then he limped towards the door.

'Ademar,' I said, before following my superior, 'if you die in this cell, it will accomplish nothing. But if you die in the sight of others, perhaps they will be moved by your courage and steadfastness. So it is of little concern to me, if you die here. You are not defying me with this fast – you are helping me. The last thing I need is a Manichaean martyr like you.'

Father Augustin was waiting in the corridor when I emerged from Ademar's cell. It was a very noisy corridor, because

30

prisons are noisy places (no matter how much straw you put down, every voice echoes like a bucket hitting the bottom of a stone well), and the cells were well stocked with angry, unhappy people. Nevertheless, he lowered his voice to speak to me.

'Your remarks are ill-considered, Brother,' he said – in Latin.

'My remarks . . .?'

'To call that firstborn of Satan a martyr to promise him influence over a sympathetic crowd.'

'Father, all he needs is an excuse,' I replied. 'One excuse to eat, and he will do it. I gave him that excuse. And since I assume that you were, shall we say, *exaggerating* when you told him that you could arrange an *auto de fé* for tomorrow – '

'That was not true,' he admitted.

'Exactly. If he does not eat, he may be dead by tomorrow. Certainly by the end of the week. And deaths in custody are not . . . they are not desirable.'

'No,' said Father Augustin. 'An example must be made of this sprout of infidelity.'

'Ye-e-es . . .' I must confess that I was concerned, not to offer a lesson to the populace, but to ensure that questions were not asked among people in elevated positions. Only twelve years before, Pope Clement's investigation into the Holy Office prison of Carcassonne had resulted in an official reprimand.

Besides, death is outside the bounds of inquisitorial authority. It is the secular arm which bears the responsibility for taking life.

'As you can see,' I remarked, moving on to less disturbing subjects, 'on this floor are prisoners condemned to the regime of *murus strictus*, and those who are obdurate in refusing to confess. The floor above us houses the *murus largus* prisoners, who may exercise in the corridors, and converse there. Do you wish to see the lower dunjon, Father? It can be reached through that trapdoor.'

'No,' said Father Augustin, abruptly. Then he said: 'Has it often been used?'

'Only when I need space to question people.' A good inquisitor has no need of torture. 'Father Jacques employed it for other purposes, on occasion, but not recently. Shall we proceed up the stairs, now? Pons lives with his wife on the top floor, so we may finish there, as you requested.'

My superior had, in fact, wished to inspect the gaol before meeting its gaoler. He gave no reason for this preference, but I surmised that if Pons' stewardship was deficient in any way, Father Augustin would surely make note of the fact, and demand an explanation at the close of the tour. As I conducted him past the rows of *murus largus* cells, some of them with two or more occupants, owing to an insufficiency of space, he questioned me closely about the procedures employed to ensure that prisoners received those goods bestowed on them by friends and family. Did such goods, he asked, ever pass through the gaoler's hands?

'Rest easy, Father,' was my response. 'As far as a gaoler can be honest, Pons is that.'

'How can you be sure?'

'Because I know many of the prisoners' friends and relatives. I ask them what they give, and I ask the prisoners what they receive. There is never a discrepancy.'

Father Augustin grunted. I sensed that he was perhaps unconvinced, but I decided – as ever – that it would be foolish to challenge him on an uncorroborated assumption. *In quietness and in confidence shall be your strength.* He said nothing; I said nothing. We proceeded. On our way up to the top floor, I introduced him to several guards, and to our familiar Isarn, who often delivered summonses. Isarn was himself a reformed heretic. He was also a sickly, earnest young fellow, the child of heretical parents (long deceased), and regarded the gaoler and his wife as foster parents, eating with them, giving them most of his meagre wage, and sleeping on their table.

I had always found him to be harmless enough, indeed barely worthy of remark, so was surprised at Father Augustin's response when I mentioned his unfortunate history.

'That youth was a follower of falsehood?' he exclaimed, on receiving this information.

'As I said. But no longer. He renounced his errors years ago, when he was a child.'

'How can you be sure of that?'

I looked at him in astonishment. We were climbing the stairs to Pons' chambers, at the time, so I was forced to stop and turn in order to do this.

'I have never approved of using such people,' he declared. 'It is not safe. It is not wise. The plot at Carcassonne was facilitated by a man of similar tendencies – '

'Father,' I interrupted, 'are you telling me that there is *no such thing* as a "former" heretic?'

'I am telling you that we cannot employ that youth,' Father Augustin replied. 'Get rid of him.'

'But he has never given us any cause – '

'At once, if you please.'

'But – '

'Brother Bernard.' Father Augustin spoke with great severity. ' "Can the Ethiopian change his skin, or the leopard his spots?" '

'Father Augustin,' I rejoined, 'your namesake was himself a reformed heretic.'

'He was a saint, and a great man.'

'And he once wrote: "None save great men have been the authors of heresies".'

'I do not wish to engage in a rhetorical dispute, Brother. Surely you do not incline to sympathy with the wood cut from the vine?'

'No,' I said, and I spoke the truth. An ancient father of the Church once wrote: There is no heretic except from contention. St Paul himself criticised dissension and division, from which nothing springs but ruin, misery, despair. The concord of unity is the bedrock of the Christian world. Only the vain-glorious, moved by pride and passion, would seek to split this rock and watch our civilisation tumble into the well of eternal darkness.

By their fruits ye shall know them. Families rent apart, priests assassinated, sisters seduced by their brothers, dying children deprived of food. It has come to pass that good heretics would be more reluctant to kill a chicken than a monk. And they make this choice. As you probably know, 'choice' is what 'haeresis' actually means.

They choose the deviant way, and must suffer the price for so choosing.

'No, Father,' I said. 'I do not incline to sympathy with any heretic.'

'Then you must be vigilant. Is it in the power of man to discover what is in the heart of another man?'

'No, Father.'

'No. Not unless he is enlightened by the spirit of God, or instructed by the care of the angels. Are you so blessed?'

'No, Father.'

'Nor am I. Therefore we must be on our guard. We cannot allow the Enemy of Mankind to become our friend.'

For the third time that day, he defeated me. Truly he was forceful in the power of his will. I bowed to him, signifying consent, then took him to display his royal letters of appointment to the Seneschal, the Bishop, the Royal Treasurer, and the Royal Steward of Confiscations. Back at the priory, he also attended Compline, after speaking privately to the Abbot.

And that night, as I lay on my pallet, I fell asleep to the sound of poor Sicard's low drone as he read through the registers of Father Jacques in the adjoining cell. He was still reading when the bell rang for Matins, in the early hours.

Was it illogical that I began to regard my new superior as a man living in the shadow of death?

A lion in secret places

The Holy Office would be troubled on every side, were it not for the assistance of certain low functionaries – scriveners, guards, couriers, even spies – who are generally known as 'familiars', and who are regarded with disdain by many respectable citizens, often unjustly. Isarn may have laboured under the burden of an heretical past, but he was a good and humble servant, without vanity or guile. Father Augustin was also without vanity or guile, a soul fruitful of virtues, enriched with the manifold grace of God's holy spirit – but in casting off poor Isarn, he did wrong. Manifestly, he did wrong. In matters such as these, one should not be too quick to condemn, for mercy and truth are virtues which often walk hand in hand. Blessed are the merciful, with blessings that are very rich – as I myself can testify.

Some three years ago, I acquired a familiar whose services were almost beyond praise, a man of such exceptional wit, so masterful in his craft, that my pen falters as I attempt to deal justly with his excellence. Yet he was a Perfect (or so it appeared), and unworthy of trust. How easily I might have disregarded his strange proposals! How staunchly I might have clung to my suspicions, and lost the chance which he offered!

Yet I was reckless. I listened; I pondered; I agreed. And the fruits of this decision were bounteous.

I saw him first in his prison cell, to which he had been lately delivered. I knew little about him, save that he had been caught – with a fellow Perfect – at the fair in Padern. I also knew his name, but I shall not transcribe it here. His identity being a closely guarded secret, I shall merely call him 'S'. In appearance (and once again, I cannot give you a full and detailed *effictio*), he was tall and pale with small, very clear, very measuring eyes.

'So! My friend,' I said to him. 'You have requested an audience with me.'

'I have.' His voice was soft, and as smooth as butter. 'I wish to confess.'

'Then you should wait until tomorrow,' I advised. 'The tribunal will be in session, and a notary will be present to record all that you have to say.'

'No,' he said. 'I wish to speak to you alone.'

'If you want to make a confession, it must be recorded.'

'I wish to make a suggestion. Give me a little of your time, my lord, and you will not regret it.'

I was intrigued. I am usually 'my lord' only to frightened peasants and respectful sergeants-at-arms; never before had a Perfect addressed me in this way. So I told the prisoner to proceed, and he began by saying: 'I am not a Good Man, my lord.'

Knowing that 'Good Man' was another appellation for Perfect, I replied: 'Then this is no confession, because I already have testimony that you are.'

'I dress like a Good Man. I wear a blue robe and sandals. I eat no meat, when I eat with others, and talk of the Great Babylon of the Roman Church. But in my heart I am no heretic, and never have been one.'

At this I laughed out loud, and would have spoken, except that he forestalled me. He said that his parents had been Cathar believers; that his father had been burned as a lapsed heretic, and his mother imprisoned; that his patrimony had been con-fiscated and the house of his birth destroyed. He said that, at six years of age, he had lost everything that once was his. His youth had been spent sleeping in relatives' barns, minding their sheep, eating their scraps. He narrated all this calmly, in his gentle voice, as one might speak of a cloudy day, or a stale loaf.

'The Good Men destroyed my inheritance,' he concluded. 'Yet they still came to me, expecting to share my bed and my food, expecting to be guided from here to there, expecting to be hidden and helped and listened to even while they put the whole village at risk. My relatives always welcomed them, and I used to lie awake at night, dreading that someone would inform the inquisitors.'

'You should have informed us yourself,' I remarked.

'And gone where, my lord? I was only a child. But I swore that one day, I would win back my inheritance by destroying those who had robbed me of it.'

He spoke with a quiet intensity which I found utterly con-vincing. Yet still I was confused.

'They were your enemies, but you joined their ranks. How is that?'

'To betray your enemy, you must know him well,' 'S' replied. 'My lord, the Good Man, Arnaud, was captured with me. I led him to your door. I can tell you all about him, and about other Good Men, and their habits, and their haunts, and the trails they use, and the people who lead them. I can give you the past five years of my life, and the whole of the Cor-bieres district.'

'For the sake of enmity?' I asked, but he did not understand. (He was not, I soon discovered, a highly educated man, though he had a quick mind.) So I was forced to rephrase my question. 'Because you hate the heretics so much?'

'I hate them, yes. And I wish to profit from them. The past five years I give to you freely, as a sign of my goodwill. The next year, you must pay for.'

37

'You are offering to spy for me?'

'For you, and only for you.' He looked at me with his small, clear, honey-coloured eyes, and I knew that he must have been a powerful preacher, for his gaze was compelling. 'No one else must know. I will tell you my story as a reformed heretic. Because I betray so many people, my punishment will be light. You will let me go, and I will return to my ministry in a new district – the Rousillon district. In one year's time, you will arrest me at Tautavel. I will tell you all that I have learned, and you will pay me two hundred livres tournois.'

'Two hundred? My friend, do you know what *my* wages are?'

'Two hundred,' he said firmly. 'With that I will buy a house, some vineyards, an orchard . . .'

'How will you do that if you are imprisoned? I cannot release a relapsed heretic. You will go to the stake.'

'Not if you help me to escape, my lord.' He paused, then added: 'Perhaps, if you like my work, you can hire me for another year.'

And that is how I acquired the most accomplished familiar ever employed by the Holy Office – not for one year, nor even for two, but for as many as he would give me. What a whited sepulchre that man was! As wily as a parandus (which changes colour according to its hiding place) and as dangerous as a lion among the beasts of the forest. Yet I gave him my trust, and he gave me his in return. *Be strong, and of good courage, for the Lord thy God is with thee wherever thou goest.*

I will freely admit, however, that not all familiars are worthy of trust. Some sell their righteous for silver and the poor for a pair of shoes. Grimaud Sobacca was one such; his molten image was falsehood, yet Father Jacques would fling him a few livres, on occasion, for services of a low and dishonourable kind. Sometimes Grimaud would spread false rumours, causing divisions between people who would thereafter denounce each other as heretics. Sometimes he would pretend to be a prisoner, and become the recipient of secrets that were later reported to Father Jacques. Sometimes he would bribe maids, threaten children, steal documents. If Father Jacques ever did accept money, it was almost certainly Grimaud who collected it.

Then, with the death of his patron, Grimaud looked to Father Augustin for succour. He brought rank scraps of gossip to the Holy Office as a stray cat might bring dead mice to a kitchen – except that he was more a rat than a cat, and, like most vermin, always found a way in. One evening, as we were returning to the priory for Compline, my superior asked me about Grimaud. He told me that Grimaud had come to him that very day, with a tale about heretical women living in Casseras. They had moved into the old Cathar castle there, and did not go to church.

'Do you know about these women?' Father Augustin inquired. 'I was not aware of any castle at Casseras.'

'There is none,' I said. 'There is a forcia, a fortified farm, that was confiscated some time in the past when its owner was convicted of heresy. I believe the lands now belong to the crown. When I was last in Casseras, no one lived in the forcia, which had been largely dismantled.'

'Then Grimaud was lying?'

'Grimaud always lies. He walks in the streets of Babylon, and wallows in the mire thereof, as if in a bed of spices and precious ointments.'

'I see.' The strength of my condemnation clearly impressed Father Augustin. 'Nevertheless, I shall write to the priest there. Who is the priest there?'

'Father Paul de Miramonte.'

'I shall write and ask for confirmation.'

'Did you give Grimaud money?'

'I told him that if we arrested any of these women, after due inquiry, then he would receive a small sum.'

'If there are any heretics in Casseras, Father, the priest would have told you. He is a very reliable fellow.'

'You know him?'

'I make it my business to know most of the parish priests hereabouts.'

'And many of their parishioners, too, I gather.'

'Yes.'

'Then perhaps you can tell me about these people.' Whereupon my superior recited a list of six names: Aimery Ribaudin, Bernard de Pibraux, Raymond Maury, Oldric Capiscol, Petrona Capdenier and Bruna d'Aguilar. 'These are people whose names were mentioned in some of Father Jacques's depositions, but who have never been charged or convicted.'

'Aimery Ribaudin!' I exclaimed. '*Aimery Ribaudin?*'

'That name is familiar to you?'

I stopped, took his arm, and pointed down the street to our right. This street was filled with impressive hospita – twostoreyed dwellings with great, vaulted shops and warehouses on their lower floors. 'Do you see that hospitum? That belongs to Aimery Ribaudin. He is an armourer, and a consul, and a wealthy man.'

'Has he ever been defamed, in your hearing?'

'Never. He is a patron of St Polycarpe.'

'What of the others? What of Bernard de Pibraux?'

'Pibraux is a village to the west of Lazet. The seigneurial family has three sons, and Bernard is the youngest. I have never met him.' We had halted in our progress, but seeing the curious looks being cast in our direction, I began to walk again. 'Raymond Maury is a baker – he lives near the priory. A badtempered fellow, but then he has nine children to support. Bruna d'Aguilar is a widow from the Saint-Nicholas parish, well off, the head of the household. I *have* heard tales about her.'

'What tales?'

'Foolish ones. That she spits three times to bless her bread. That her pig can recite the *pater noster*.'

'Hmm.'

'The other two names are strange to me. I know of several Capiscols, but not an Oldric. Perhaps he is dead.'

'Perhaps. He was seen at a gathering which took place forty-three years ago.'

'Then he may be dead. He may have been charged and convicted long before Father Jacques' time. You should check the old registers.'

'I shall.'

And he did. He had Raymond searching through the records for fifty-year-old books, and he had Sicard reading them, every night from Compline to Matins, until poor Sicard was red-eyed and hoarse. Then one day, at our headquarters, as I was penning a letter to Jean de Beaune, the Inquisitor of Carcassonne (who wanted a copy of certain depositions in our keeping), Father Augustin came shuffling down the circular staircase, and stopped in front of my desk.

'Brother Bernard,' he said, 'have you been referring to the records lately?'

'I? No.'

'You do not have any registers in your possession?'

'Not a one. Why? Is there a book missing?'

'It appears so.' Father Augustin seemed somewhat distracted in his manner; his gaze wandered over my pens and fuller's earth and pumice stone as he spoke. 'Raymond cannot find one of the old registers.'

'Could he be looking in the wrong place?'

'He said that you might have sent it to another inquisitor.'

'I never send originals, Father, I always have copies made. Raymond should know that.' I was beginning to share my superior's concern. 'How long has the book been missing?'

'That I cannot establish. Raymond is uncertain – the old records are so rarely consulted.'

'Perhaps both copies have been put in the Bishop's library by mistake.'

'Perhaps. In any event, I have told him to find the Bishop's copy, and bring it here.'

By this time I was concentrating hard. Such a mystery could not go unsolved. 'Has Brother Lucius seen this book?'

'No.'

'Has the Bishop?'

'I intend to ask him.'

'No one else would have access to our records. Unless ...'
I paused, and by some marvellous concordance of reckoning,
Father Augustin finished my sentence for me.

'Unless Father Jacques took it.'

'Unless he misplaced it.'

'Hmmm.'

We gazed at each other, and I wondered: had Father Jacques
been covering his tracks? But I said nothing, for he that refrai-
neth his lips is wise.

'I will look into the matter,' my superior finally announced.
He seemed to push it aside with an abrupt movement of his
hand; all at once he was addressing himself to another topic
entirely. 'I shall need horses, tomorrow,' he said. 'What are
the procedures for securing them?'

'Horses?'

'I wish to visit Casseras.'

'Ah.' Having explained that the Bishop's chief ostler would
require notification, I asked my superior if he had received
fresh information from Father Paul de Miramonte. 'Have
Grimaud's suspicions been confirmed?' I inquired. 'Are there
heretics living in the forcia at Casseras?'

For a long time, Father Augustin remained silent. I was on
the point of repeating my question (unaware that his hearing
was particularly acute), when he suddenly demonstrated that
he had heard me after all.

'As far as I can ascertain,' he replied, 'the women in question
are good Catholics. They do attend church, but not regularly,
because of ill-health. Father Paul says that the forcia is some
distance from the village, and that this may also prevent them
from worshipping in bad weather. They live simply, and
piously, keeping fowl and exchanging eggs for cheese. He sees
nothing questionable in their habits.'

'So ...?' I was confused. 'Why the journey?'

Again, Father Augustin thought for a while before speaking. 'Women living together in such a fashion invite danger and calumny,' he said at last. 'If women want to live chastely, serving God and obeying His laws, they should seek the protection of a priest or monk and enter a convent. Otherwise they run a grave risk, firstly because they are living an isolated life, vulnerable to rape and pillage, secondly because people remember that the female followers of Albigensian error once lived in similar circumstances, founding many heretical 'convents'. People distrust women who appear to favour the life of Mary over that of Martha, yet who reject the disciplined guidance of ordained authority.'

'That is true,' I agreed. 'There is always a question in such cases. As you say, why not enter a convent?'

'Besides which . . .' And here Father Augustin paused before emphatically repeating himself with all the deliberation of that rhetorical form known as the *conduplicatio*. 'Besides which, one of them can read.'

'Ah.' How mixed a blessing is the gift of literacy, among lay folk! 'Not Latin, surely?'

'I would think not. But as you know, the half educated are in far more peril than those with no education at all.'

'Yes, indeed.' I had myself witnessed the stubborn vainglory of men and women only partly acquainted with letters, who might have learned a few passages of the Gospel by heart, yet esteemed themselves superior to the most learned authorities. I have heard ignorant rustics expound scripture falsely and corruptly, as in the Epistle of Jean's 'His own received him not', translating 'His own' as 'pigs', mistaking *sui* for *sues*. And in the psalm 'Rebuke the wild beasts of the reeds', they say 'Rebuke the animals of the swallows', mistaking *harundinis* for *hirundinis*.

They assume the appearance of learning like a mantle, which for other illiterates hides the depths of ignorance beneath.

'If these women are courting error, living in a dangerous fashion, then I shall endeavour to set them on the right path,' said Father Augustin. 'One paternal admonition may be all that is required. A gentle discourse.'

'In the manner of St Dominic,' I concurred, and he seemed pleased with this comparison.

'Yes. Like St Dominic.' Then, in his dry but forceful way, he added: 'After all, *Domini Canes* are not hounds of the Lord simply because we attack the ravening wolves. We are also here to round up those sheep who stray from the flock.'

Having delivered himself of this sentiment, he limped off, puffing like bellows and leaning heavily on his cane. I must confess that a culpable thought crossed my mind, at that moment – the image of a very old, bald and toothless, three-legged dog – and I smiled down at the pen in my hand.

But my smile faded as I asked myself: how do toothless dogs sustain themselves, if not by scavenging for dead creatures?

Father Augustin was clearly determined to pursue defamed heretics to their graves, and beyond. I knew that he would bring trouble down upon us, if he did so. There would be protests and recriminations. There would be a marshalling of influential patrons.

I did not, however, expect the worst. And in this I lacked foresight.

Casseras lies near the larger village of Rasiers. From memory, I would estimate that Rasiers is inhabited by three hundred people or so, among them the Royal Provost. It is this Provost who occupies the castle, formerly a possession of the same family which built the forcia outside Casseras – a family of whom I know little save that its master, one Jordan de Rasiers, surrendered his castle to northern forces a hundred years ago. Having consulted our Holy Office records, I can also tell you that his grandson, Raymond-Arnaud, lost the Casseras forcia, as well as a town house in Lazet, when he was convicted of heresy in 1254.

Both Rasiers and Casseras were infested with heretics long

ago. I have seen the depositions, hundreds of them, from the interrogations of 1253 and 1254, when most of the villagers were summoned to Lazet, in small groups, for questioning. As far as I can recall, about sixty people from Casseras were convicted, all belonging to four families. (I have often observed that heresy infects the blood, like certain inherited illnesses.) These families are no longer represented in the village: their members were imprisoned, or executed, or dispatched on long pilgrimages from which they never returned. Some, mostly children, were sent to live with distant relatives. As Jerome declared in his commentary on Galations, 'Cut off the decayed flesh, expel the mangy sheep from the fold, lest the whole house, the whole paste, the whole body, the whole flock, burn, perish, rot, die'. With the infection of heresy cauterised, Casseras was restored to health (though one must, as Father Augustin used to say, be ever vigilant).

To reach the village from Lazet, you must ride south for half a day until you come to Rasiers on its verdant plateau of pasture, woods and wheat fields – an harmonious arrangement of natural wealth which yields both refreshment to the eye and varied gifts of produce to the zealous labourer. *Oh Lord, how manifold are Thy works! In wisdom hast Thou made them all: the earth is full of Thy riches.* Casseras lies even further south, among foothills, and the land there is not so fruitful. There are no orchards or vineyards, no carts or horses, no mill, no inn, no priory, no smith. Only two houses can boast separate outbuildings for the sheep and mules and oxen. The church is a modest receptacle of God's grace – a dark limestone box containing a stone altar, a wooden crucifix, and a locked chest for the chalice, paten, linen and vestments. There are also paintings on the walls, badly executed, and in bad repair. Of course, better it is to be of an humble spirit with the lowly (and so forth), but there is little there to glorify Christ's majesty.

From Casseras, a stony path leads up through village plots and uncleared woods to the terraced pastures of the old de Rasiers forcia. Here you will often see sheep grazing, and they belong to certain local families, who pay the Provost paturage and forestage for the privilege of using royal land. (There are many complaints about such taxes: everywhere I go, I hear them. Too many taxes, the peasants say. How can we give to the Church, when the King wants so much?) The path of which I speak is as steep as a staircase in some places, and as deep as a trench in others, almost impassable in wet weather, perilous in the snow, more suited to goats than people, and challenging even to the most skilled, experienced riders. Thus it was that Father Augustin and his sergeants-at-arms, having crossed the River Agly, urged their mounts across rugged hillsides beneath a blazing sun, and risked their lives traversing a dense forest renowned for its population of brigands, were faced, at the very close of their journey, with the most difficult climb of all.

They also decided to retrace their steps the same day, and more quickly, too, so as to reach Lazet before the gates closed at sundown. That is to say, Father Augustin made this decision, and a foolish one it was, for it almost destroyed him. As a consequence, he spent the next three days in bed – and why? Because he was reluctant (or so he attested) to miss the celebration of Compline. Now, I understand that it is the duty of every Dominican brother to attend Compline, that Compline is the crown and culmination of our day, that no absence will go unnoted and no excuse will suffice. Nevertheless, as St Augustin points out, God has created man's mind rational and intellectual, and reason dictates that a weak man, made still more infirm by the pains and fatigue of a long ride, will be absent from Compline on many more occasions than a man who wisely breaks his journey with a night spent under the roof of a local priest.

I delivered myself of this opinion when I visited my superior in his cell on the second day of his recovery, and he agreed that he had overestimated his strength.

'Next time, I shall stay the night,' he said.

I was startled.

'You intend to *return*?'

'Yes.'

'But if these women are unorthodox in their faith, you should summon them here.'

'They are not unorthodox,' Father Augustin interrupted. His voice was a faint and laboured croak, but, with my head lowered almost to the level of his mouth, I was able to catch both the words that he uttered and the hint, the merest echo, of the choler with which they were imbued. It puzzled me, this choler, which sprang from some hidden source. I could see no reason for it.

'They need spiritual guidance,' Father Augustin continued, his eyes shut, his breath foul on my cheek. I could trace very clearly the contours of the skull beneath his skin.

'Surely Father Paul could provide them with that?' I said, and he shifted his head irritably, almost feverishly.

'He cannot.'

'But – '

'Father Paul is a simple man with more than a hundred souls in his care. These women are well born, and quite intelligent, in so far as a female may exercise those faculties more highly developed in the male.'

He paused, and I waited, but no further explanation was forthcoming. So I dared to hazard my own.

'That is to say,' I remarked, 'if they are wedded to error, and Father Paul remonstrates with them, they will probably convert *him*. Is that what you mean, Father?'

Again, my superior rolled his head in a fretful fashion, like those who drink the wine of the wrath of God, and have no rest day nor night. His infirm state was beginning to affect his demeanour, normally so calm and cold.

'You are irreverent,' he complained. 'This mocking . . . you torment me . . .'

Instantly contrite, I begged forgiveness. 'Father, I am at fault. I should not speak thus, it is a weakness of mine.'

'These are grave matters.'

'I know.'

'Yet you make a mockery of them. Always. Joking even with the prisoners in their chains. How can I understand you?'

And I thought: Hear ye indeed, but understand not. It was ever so, I fear. Whatever order they might belong to, monks are generally enjoined to speak quietly and without laughter, humbly, gravely and in few words.

'Father Paul would not be *converted*,' my superior continued, his breath rattling in his throat. 'But maybe he would not *convince*.'

'Of course. I understand.'

'The women are in need of pastoral guidance. It is my duty, as a friar of St Dominic, to prevent them from falling into error. I have offered to visit them occasionally and minister to the health of their souls. It is my duty, Brother.'

'Of course,' I said again, but without comprehending. Pastoral care is the duty of the secular clergy, not the Friars Preachers. There may be a few exceptions (Guillaume de Paris, as you know, has been the King's confessor for many years), but St Dominic's Rule, though it dispatches our brethren to the farthest corners of the earth that we may spread God's word with the persuasive powers of sweet-tongued rhetoric – though it invites the common folk into our very midst, to worship with us at Compline – nevertheless does not encourage the kind of intimacy fostered by the bonds of pastoral care. Moreover, it certainly does not encourage free and frequent intercourse with women.

This, I must confess, is what puzzled and concerned me above all else. I need not present you with a demonstrative argument regarding the dangers of friendships between monks and women, whether they be matrons, virgins or harlots. St Augustin was firm in declaring such friendships occasions for sin. *Through an immoderate inclination toward these goods of the lower order, the better and higher are forsaken.* St Bernard of Clairvaux has asked: 'To be always with a woman and not to

48

know her carnally, is not this more than to raise the dead?' Even the most divinely inspired associations, such as that of St Christina of Markgate and the hermit Roger, can be fraught with peril – for did not the devil, that enemy of chastity, take advantage of their close companionship and overcome the man's resistance?

Now, there are many men in holy orders who, because Eve violated the forbidden tree and broke the law of God (and because more bitter than death is woman, whose heart is snares and nets), will forbear to speak, even to look, at any females who cross their paths. In this they lack the spirit of charity, and are excessive in their fear of fleshly contact. Did not Christ himself permit the ministering woman to kiss his feet, and wash them with her tears, and wipe them with the hairs of her head? Did he not speak to her, saying: 'Thy faith has saved thee; go in peace'? I have spoken to many women in the street, outside the priory, on doorsteps, and behind the walls of convents. I have preached to them in churches and listened to them in prisons. Such discourse can be most beneficial in all kinds of ways.

But to eat with a woman, to sleep under her roof, to meet with her often, and to open your heart to her – therein lies great danger. I know this (and here I must make a shameful confession), because I courted such danger when I was a young man, and exposed myself to sin and disgrace. As a youth, before taking orders, I knew women carnally – sinfully – outside the bonds of marriage. How diligently I studied the art of love! How earnestly I perused the works of the troubadours, and employed their honeyed phrases like arrows aimed at the hearts of many a maiden! When I took the vow of chastity, however, I did so with the solemn intention of keeping it. Even as a preacher ordinary, travelling through the countryside with an older, more experienced Preacher General (the revered Father Dominic de Radel), I was ardent in my wish to dash against Christ, as against a rock, those evil and lustful thoughts which rose up in my mind. I was sedulous in turning my gaze from every female form, striving to attain that love of God which is perfect, and casteth out fear.

But we are all sinners, are we not? And I fell, like Adam, when confined to a village in the Ariege for several weeks by an illness which overtook and incapacitated my companion. My preaching in the local church moved a particular young widow to approach me, seeking spiritual guidance. We conversed, not once, but many times, and ... have mercy upon me, O Lord, for I am weak. Not to dwell on a profane and discreditable incident, we were joined together in sensual gratification.

Of course, I did not expect Father Augustin to succumb in a like manner. The state of his health, I suspected, would not allow it. Furthermore, I regarded him as a man who walked firmly in the Lord's statutes. (I would say *limped* in the Lord's statutes, if it were not unnecessarily flippant.) In effect, he was as a green olive tree in the house of God, and I could not imagine that his soul would be knit with the soul of another, any more than the flame of ungodly lust would be ignited in his loins.

Nevertheless, his trips to Casseras became a source of irritation to me. They were not regular, nor overly frequent, but they were frequent enough to retard the progress of the Holy Office. And to understand why, you must understand the extent of the *inquisitio* then underway.

I had received notice from Jean de Beaune, in Carcassonne, that he was interrogating witnesses from Tarascon, or thereabouts. One of these witnesses had implicated a man from a village called Saint-Fiacre, which lies within Lazet's domain. When summoned and questioned, this man had defamed almost every inhabitant of Saint-Fiacre, accusing even the local priest of harbouring and aiding Perfects. Confronted with such a mass of testimony, I was at a loss. Where should I begin? Who should be summoned first?

'Arrest them all,' Father Augustin commanded.

'*All?*'

'It has been done in the past. Ten years ago, the former Inquisitor of Carcassonne arrested the entire population of a village in the mountains. I forget its name.'

'But Father, there are more than one hundred and fifty people in Saint-Fiacre. Where can we hold them?'

'In the prison.'

'But – '

'Or in the royal prison. I will speak to the Seneschal.'

'But why not summon them in small groups? It would be so much easier if – '

'If the rest escaped into Catalonia? Doubtless there *would* be less work for us, if they did.' My superior did not add: 'Will that be your excuse when you are finally resurrected to confront Him from whose face the earth and heaven will flee away?' But his stony expression spoke the words as clearly as any tongue. Doubting that the entire population of Saint-Fiacre would decamp over the mountains, I nevertheless had to admit that at least some, particularly the shepherds, might avail themselves of that route. So in great weariness of spirit, I undertook the task of convincing Roger Descalquencs to lend us his support – for without the Seneschal, we had no means of impelling more than one hundred and fifty people to march as far as Lazet, let alone deliver themselves into the hands of the Holy Office. (Naturally, Roger had taken the oath of obedience required from everyone holding official station, but even so he was a busy man, and sometimes had to be propitiated.)

I also had to placate Pons, our gaoler, who was not pleased by such an enormous influx of prisoners – and I had to secure the services of another notary. Even Raymond Donatus, for all his speed and skill, could not cope with such a large number of interrogations. Father Augustin and I were obliged to gather testimony, not only from the inhabitants of Saint-Fiacre, but from witnesses who might serve to implicate those four suspects identified by my superior as having very possibly bribed Father Jacques: that is to say, the suspects Aimery Ribaudin, Bernard de Pibraux, Raymond Maury and Bruna d'Aguilar. Since Father Augustin was dealing exclusively with these cases, the Saint-Fiacre depositions were left largely to me. As a result two notaries were needed, so we applied to the Royal Steward of Confiscations, and he gave us a few, grudging livres tournois for the employment of Durand Fogasset.

Durand had worked with me before, on occasion. He was a lanky, sallow young man with inky fingers, worn clothing, and a great shock of dark hair falling over his eyes. His skill and experience were commensurate with the modest sum that we paid him. Indeed, it was only through necessity that he worked with us at all, for Lazet was oversupplied with notaries, and there were no rural openings either, at the time. Though his comportment was not out of keeping with his position, he made no effort to conceal his opinions about the Holy Office and its functionaries. For this reason, perhaps, and because he was not as efficient as Raymond, Father Augustin held him in very low esteem. 'That untidy youth' was Father Augustin's epithet for Durand. As a result, the young notary worked only with me.

Reviewing the previous paragraph, I am concerned that it may be misleading. Durand expressed no culpable or heretical views. He never opened his mouth during my interrogations, nor berated me afterwards for anything I might have said. It was simply that sometimes, with a grimace or a sour remark, ('Would you like me to disregard all pleas to the Virgin, in the future, or include them in my transcript?') he managed to convey a certain muted disapproval.

Once, after questioning a sixteen-year-old inhabitant of Saint-Fiacre, I asked Durand frankly what he thought. The aforesaid witness had spoken for some time about her devotion to her aunt, and, as is my habit, I had allowed her to stray from the path along which I had been prodding her, knowing that some subjects have to be aired and exhausted – giving relief to an overburdened heart – before others can be examined. (In such a manner, too, I contrive to demonstrate my own sympathetic stance.) At the close of the session, I told Durand that when he wrote up the protocol in its finished form, he could excise most references to the witness's aunt.

'Her remarks about the Holy Sacrament are relevant, and, of course, the Perfect's visit. The rest we can discard.'

Durand looked at me for a moment. 'You think it *irrelevant?*' he said.

'To our inquiry – yes.'

'But the aunt was like a mother to this girl. She nurtured her so tenderly. With such devotion. How could the girl have betrayed her? It would have been against nature.'

'Perhaps.' But to argue about nature, and what it comprises, is to flounder into a theological swamp. 'Nevertheless, it is irrelevant to our inquiry. We are gathering evidence, Durand. Evidence of heretical association. It is not our place to look for excuses.'

I paused, and regarded Durand, who was frowning and staring at the floor, the pages of protocol clasped to his bosom.

'You think me unjust?' I inquired gently. 'You think I was cruel to that girl?'

'No.' He shook his head, still frowning. 'You were quite ... you have a kind manner, with people like her.' Then he gave me an ironic, sidelong glance. 'It is your way, I have noticed. Your technique.'

'And it works well.'

'Yes. But you coax these confidences out of people, and then you discard them. When they could be important.'

'In what way?'

'In her defence.'

'You mean that she was impelled by love to betray the Holy and Apostolic Church?'

Durand blinked. He hesitated, looking confused.

'Durand,' I said, 'do you recall the words of Christ? "He that loveth father or mother more than Me is not worthy of Me."'

'I know that she was wrong,' he replied, 'but surely her motives were less blameworthy than those of her aunt, say ... or her cousin?'

'Perhaps. And they will be taken into account when she is sentenced.'

'But *will* they? If they are not recorded?'

'I shall be present at the sentencing. I shall see to it that they are.' Observing Durand's furrowed brow, I added: 'Recall the state of the Holy Office finances, my friend. Can we afford to expend hundreds of *ares* of parchment on the intimate ramblings of every witness we interview? If we did, we would be unable to afford your salary, I fear.'

At this Durand twisted his face into the most extraordinary expression, compounded equally of distaste, regret and embarrassment. Then he shrugged, and ducked his head in his usual, sketchy attempt at a parting bow.

'You have me there,' he remarked. 'I shall go and write this up, then. Thank you, Father.'

I watched him as he loped towards the staircase. Before he reached it, however, I was moved to reinforce my argument with one last observation.

'Durand!' I said, and he turned. 'Remember also,' I appended, 'that the girl made a choice. In the end, we all make a choice. That kind of freedom is God's gift to mankind.'

Durand seemed to consider this. At last he said: 'Perhaps she *felt* that she had no choice.'

'Then she was wrong.'

'Doubtless. Well ... thank you, Father. I shall keep that in mind.'

But I digress. This dialogue has no bearing on the main theme of my narrative, which is the flurry of work occasioned by Father Augustin's inquiry into his predecessor's morals, and the arrest of Saint-Fiacre's entire adult population. We were so busy, as I said, that we needed another notary (Durand); so busy that I was once late for Compline, and was chastised for my disobedience during the Chapter of Faults. Yet, in the midst of this great confusion, Father Augustin visited Casseras three times. Knowing the weight of business with which we were burdened, he nevertheless absented himself, and I must confess that my very bowels boiled, God forgive me. I thought, like Job: I will not refrain my mouth; I will speak in the anguish of my spirit; I will complain in the bitterness of my soul.

Therefore I went to my confessor.

To purge one's heart of spite and resentment is difficult in a priory. A friar speaks so rarely, and then mostly in formulae – his infrequent conversations are generally overheard, because he is hardly ever alone. A friar must sequester his feelings, and give the appearance of bearing everything inflicted on him with a quiet mind. But I need not explain this to you; we have all lain awake at night, drinking from the cup of wrath as we silently curse our brother, who is often lying, awake and fuming, in the very next bed!

For us, only confession offers relief. We can, in the act of describing our blameworthy sentiments, catalogue the faults and injustices of our brethren. And that is what I did, closeted with Prior Hugues. I confessed to my bitterness, and went on to give a full account of its source. The Prior listened with closed eyes; he and I shared a long history, having met at the priory school of Carcassonne, and we respected each other's judgement.

'I am at a loss,' I told him. 'Father Augustin is so constant and persevering, so diligent and zealous in his search for truth, yet every so often he wanders off to Casseras – for no good cause, as far as I can ascertain, unless he has strayed from the Rule in some fashion.'

The Prior opened his eyes. 'In what fashion?'

'Oh, there are women involved, Father. Who can help but speculate?'

'About Brother *Augustin*?'

'I know it seems unlikely – '

'It certainly does!'

'But *why*, Father? Why is he doing this?'

'Ask him.'

'I have.' Briefly, I recounted Father Augustin's explanation of his conduct. 'But we are not parish priests, we are monks. I cannot understand.'

'Do you have to understand? "Am I my brother's keeper?"'

I would have said 'Yes' – because in a priory, the Prior is the keeper of all his brothers in Christ. But I knew that such a pleasantry would only puzzle my old friend. Though sage and serene, he was not one to banter witticisms.

So I remained silent.

'Brother Augustin truly feels that he is doing God's work,' the Prior continued, in his placid way, and I realised that, as the vigilant shepherd of our flock, he must have raised the subject with my superior already. 'An inquisitor,' he pointed out, 'is entrusted with the salvation of souls.'

'At the expense of his work in the Holy Office?'

'My son, forgive me, but you are not correct in questioning the actions of your superior.' With his benevolent smile, the Prior was able to chastise me thus without giving offence. 'It is your place only to serve, and to bear your cross with fortitude.'

Again I said nothing, for I knew that he was right.

'Be satisfied that I am watching over our brother,' the Prior concluded, 'and will see that he comes to no harm. Confine yourself to your duties, and cleanse your heart of these angry thoughts. What will they do, but poison your existence?'

So I strove to render my soul as peaceful as a watered garden, while Father Augustin, apparently at ease with his conscience, proceeded as before, visiting Casseras every week or two, stubbornly pursuing an outcome which was hidden from those around him. The journeys always left him seriously enervated; indeed, I warned him several times that they would kill him.

And I was right, because he was visiting Casseras on the day of his death.

♦

Father Augustin died during the Feast of the Nativity of the Blessed Virgin. His absence from the priory on that day was much commented upon, and it certainly struck me as an error of judgement, not to say disrespectful. The fact that he did not return for Compline, however, occasioned no remark; it had become his habit to spend the night with Father Paul, in Casseras, before returning to Lazet.

It was only at noon on the following day, when he and his entourage were still absent, that I became concerned.

At this point in my narrative, I must attempt a *demonstratio* of events which I myself never witnessed. It is a difficult task to paraphrase the words of others, so that I may recreate vividly certain episodes whose aspects are only vague in my own mind. Nevertheless, it must be done, for these episodes are crucial to your understanding of the fate which has befallen me.

The aforementioned path from Casseras to the forcia was, as I have said, a rugged, inhospitable thoroughfare, little employed by any villagers save those grazing their sheep on the King's land. Its final, steepest stretch, lying between rocks and new forest, was almost never used. Only the inhabitants of the forcia – and, more recently, the inquisitor who called on them – were obliged to struggle up and down this goat track. But on the day after the Feast of the Nativity, two young boys decided to visit the forcia, that they might greet and admire both the inquisitor's bodyguards and the marvellous horses on which these magnificent men rode. The boys were, of course, children from Casseras.

Their names were Guido and Guillaume.

Guido and Guillaume had never seen horses before the arrival of Father Augustin. Nor had they ever seen a sword, or mace. Consequently they welcomed with great excitement those evenings which brought the Inquisitor of Lazet to their priest's house, for the inquisitor was always attended by four armed men and their mounts, who slept together in Bruno Pelfort's barn. The two boys were infatuated with the notion of warfare. They were frequently to be found trailing our familiars Bertrand, Maurand, Jordan and Giraud like shadows, and were sometimes rewarded for their assiduity with scraps of food, or a short time in the saddle.

Therefore, when their heroes passed through Casseras on the Feast of the Nativity and did not return that night, they were hugely disappointed. Like the rest of the village, they assumed that Father Augustin had decided to sleep at the forcia. ('We thought yon friar was making merry with his lady, at last,' was how one inhabitant later put it.) So the next morning, they scampered off to visit their idols, anxious not to miss the opportunity.

When I came to converse with Guillaume, who was the elder of the two, he described that morning in vivid detail. According to Guillaume, Guido was slightly afraid of the forcia, because it was popularly supposed, among the children of the village, to be haunted by 'devils'. The full significance of this remark has always escaped me, since the adult villagers seemed quite well disposed towards the women on their doorstep. Perhaps the notion of 'devils' derives from the heretical beliefs of the de Rasiers family. Perhaps certain demonic apparitions had indeed manifested themselves there. In any event, Guillaume was obliged to coax his friend along the path, pointing out that no devils could possibly remain at the forcia, since the Inquisitor of Lazet must have chased them all away.

They were discussing the Inquisitor, and how many devils he might have imprisoned in cages at Lazet, when they noticed a foul smell. (Recall, if you will, that this was the month of September, and the days had been very warm.) As they progressed, the stench grew stronger; Guillaume immediately assumed that somewhere, not far away, a sheep had fallen victim to disease, or dogs, or one of the many sad fates to which sheep, I gather, are particularly prone. He made some remark to this effect, and Guido objected, for no sheep had been reported lost.

Then they heard the sound of flies. At first they feared that a swarm of bees might be approaching, and Guido was anxious to retreat with expedition. Guillaume, however, had applied his powers of reasoning to the matter: by tracing the connection between the smell and the sound, he deduced that a dead animal was attracting insects, and that since there were so many insects, the dead animal must be very large.

So he pressed on somewhat fearfully, a sharpened stick in his hand, and where the path levelled out on a small plateau, hemmed in by thick growth, he found the remains of Father Augustin's party.

You will doubtless have heard that Father Augustin and his bodyguards were hacked to pieces. Perhaps you do not fully understand, however, that when I employ the phrase 'hacked to pieces', I am not making use of an hyerbole, but a literal and precise description of the victims' state. Their bodies had been divided into small portions, and the portions scattered like seed. Not a fragment of clothing remained. The *translatio* one might apply to the condition of the corpses is that of a looted crypt – or perhaps even the Valley of Bones – except that these bones were not clean and dry. They were coated with blood and purulent flesh, and, beneath a mantle of flies, they cried to heaven for vengeance.

Only consider the sight that assaulted Guillaume's vision: a scene of the most terrible slaughter, dust dark with blood, leaves and rocks spattered with it, fragments of blackened flesh adhering to every surface, and, hanging in the air, a stench so powerful that it seemed to have a corporeal presence of its own. (Guillaume confessed to me later that he found it hard to breathe.) At first, the dazed children were unable to identify what they saw. Guillaume thought, for an instant, that a sheep had been dismembered by a pack of wolves. But, when he moved forward, and disturbed one cloak of flies so that it lifted and dispersed like fog, he saw a human foot lying before him, and knew what had happened.

'I ran,' he told me, when I questioned him. 'I ran, because Guido ran. We both ran back to the village.'

'Not to the forcia? The forcia was closer.'

'We never thought of it.' Looking a little ashamed, he added: 'Guido was afraid of the forcia. Guido was afraid. Not I.'

'And then?'

'I saw the priest. I told the priest.'

As you may imagine, Father Paul was horrified, and somewhat at a loss. He went to Bruno Pelfort, who was the richest, most important man in Casseras, and together they sought assistance from other villagers. It was decided that a party should be sent to examine the site of the massacre, and retrieve what was left of the corpses. Various farming implements were collected to serve as weapons in the event of an ambush. On Guillaume's advice, several buckets and sacks were also assembled. Then fourteen men, armed with scythes and spades and mule-goads, marched off towards the forcia.

They returned a long time later, pursued by swarms of flies.

'It was terrible,' Father Paul told me. 'The smell was terrible. Some of the men who had to pick up the pieces . . . they were ill. Vomiting. Some said it was the devil's work and were very frightened. Afterwards, the sacks and buckets were burned. No one wanted them back.'

'And no one thought about the women?'

'Oh yes, we thought about them. We were scared that it might have happened to them, too. But no one wanted to go and see.'

'Someone did, though.'

'Yes. When we reached the village, I sent a message to the Provost, at Rasiers. He has a small garrison there – very small. He came with some soldiers, and the soldiers went to the forcia.'

Meanwhile, there was a great deal of discussion concerning the remains. It had been established that they were male remains, and most villagers shared the opinion that they belonged to Father Augustin and his men. But no one could be sure, because no heads had been found. There were other members missing, too, and certain people were accused of leaving them behind.

Father Paul, however, insisted that all visible body parts had been retrieved. He had been very careful to satisfy himself on this point.

'If anything is missing, then we must look elsewhere,' he said. 'In the woods, perhaps. We should set the dogs to work.'

'But not now,' said Bruno. 'Not until the soldiers come.'

'Yes. After the soldiers come,' Father Paul agreed. Then someone asked him what they should do with the remains already in their possession, and there was more debate. One person advised instant burial, but was shouted down. How could you bury half a man, when his other half was still lying around in the woods somewhere? Besides, these corpses belonged to the Holy Office. The Holy Office would no doubt lay claim to them. Until then, they would have to be kept.

'How can you say that?' Guillaume's mother objected. 'They will *not* keep. They are not sides of salt pork. You can smell them from here.'

'Hold your tongue!' Father Paul snapped. He was very shaken, for of all the villagers only he had been intimately acquainted with Father Augustin. (I subsequently learned that, after fixing his gaze upon the scene of slaughter, he had dropped to his knees, and had been unable to walk for some time.) 'Do not speak so disrespectfully! These men are still men, no matter how barbarously they have been used!'

There was a long, pensive silence. Then one of the villagers said, 'Perhaps we *should* salt them – like pork', and cautious glances were exchanged. The suggestion seemed almost blasphemous, but on the other hand, what else were they to do? Slowly, even Father Paul was brought to admit that the choice lay between salting and smoking. So, reluctantly, he gave his sanction to the use of salt, and there followed a fiery argument as to who would donate their time for this task, and who their brine barrels, for no one was eager to undertake such a dreadful duty.

One matron was even heard to declare that Father Paul should be responsible, since he, like the Inquisitor, was a man of God.

But Father Paul shook his head. 'I must go to Lazet,' he remarked. 'I must tell Father Bernard.' And everyone agreed that this labour was, indeed, best accomplished by a priest. Father Paul was urged to wait until the Provost, Estolt de Coza, arrived, so that he might borrow the Provost's horse; the priest, however, was keen to start out on foot as soon as possible. 'If the Provost wants to send a horse after me, then the horse will catch up,' he said. 'I must make haste, for if I leave immediately, I should reach Lazet before sundown.'

He decided to take Bruno's son, Aimery, with him, and set off soon afterwards with a modest supply of wine, bread and cheese. The two men had not gone far when they were joined by one of the Provost's sergeants-at-arms, riding a horse which he bestowed on Father Paul – so it was apparent that Estolt had arrived in Casseras within a very short time of the priest's departure. Mounted, Father Paul had no great need for company. Therefore, he pressed on alone, while Aimery and the sergeant retraced their steps.

Back in Casseras, the Provost had taken charge. He listened gravely to Bruno Pelfort's account of the morning's work. He viewed the remains of Father Augustin and his familiars. Then, with his band of sergeants, some brave volunteers from the village, and his own lymer hound, he made his way cautiously to the site of the assassination.

'My dog is a good hunting hound, with a very keen nose,' he told me when I visited him. 'Though frightened by all the blood, he soon sniffed out a head and another piece which were hidden deep in the undergrowth. I realised that they must have been flung there.'

Unlike Father Paul, Estolt had the presence of mind to examine the ground for tracks. Unfortunately, the sun-baked earth was as hard and as dry as old bone, but he did find sufficient evidence in the way of broken foliage and blood smears to suggest that horses had plunged into the woods, and very possibly had been led out again. 'I did not know,' he said, 'if the assailants were at the forcia, or if they had made their escape.' It had not occurred to him, at this point, that they might have returned to the village.

With the newly discovered body parts carefully rolled in someone's cloak, Estolt and his party made their way to the forcia. The path they used was defiled by no drops of blood, nor any other suspicious traces. A column of smoke was rising from the ruins, but it was thin and wispy, and came from a cooking fire. Women's voices could be heard, and these voices were not raised in fear; they were joined in a tranquil murmur, like the cooing of doves. As Estolt later said, it was a sound which told him, more clearly than any words, that he would not find the assassins in that particular place.

Instead he found four peaceable women: an elderly woman called Alcaya de Rasiers; a toothless, bedridden crone who (ironically) went by the name of Vitalia; a widow, Johanna de Caussade, and her daughter Babilonia. They were unaware of the butchery that had taken place not far from their home, and seemed appalled when they were told about it.

'They had heard nothing; seen no one,' the Provost informed me. 'They had no explanation to offer. I spoke to Alcaya – she was a descendant of old Raymond-Arnaud de Rasiers, so I suppose she felt that she had some stake in the place. I spoke mostly to her, because she seemed to be in charge. But it was the widow who returned to Casseras with me.'

And there, I discovered, she took it upon herself to salt the remains of the five murdered men. It was an act of almost exalted devotion, which the villagers regarded as highly suspicious. I suppose, in light of what I subsequently learned, their suspicions were not unfounded. Nevertheless, I believe that Johanna de Caussade applied herself to the terrible task out of a sense of moral duty, and should be praised for her resolution.

Though I honoured Father Augustin, and respected him, I could not have done such a thing myself.

Behold, I tell you a mystery

When Father Augustin failed to return as expected, I was naturally somewhat disturbed. After consulting Prior Hugh, I dispatched a pair of armed familiars to Casseras with a letter for Father Paul de Miramonte. They would have passed Father Paul somewhere near Crieux, for he reached Lazet shortly before Vespers. Consequently, I did not attend that office; indeed, I was absent even during Compline, occupied as I was with the unhappy task of informing both the Bishop and the Seneschal that Father Augustin's carcass was now meat for the fowls of heaven.

The dead shall hear the voice of the Son of God: and they that hear it shall live. I believed then, and believe now, that Father Augustin is destined for the Life Everlasting. For him, death is surely the portal to Paradise – and with what joy must his soul have abandoned that frail and sickly mortality! I recall the words of his namesake: 'There praise to God and here praise to God, but here by those full of anxious care, there by those free from care; here by those whose lot is to die, there by those who live forever; here in hope, there in hope realised; here in the way, there in our fatherland.' I know that Father Augustin will find eternal glory in that city which hath no need of the sun, neither of the moon, for the Lamb is the Light thereof.

I know that he must walk in white among those who have not defiled their garments. I know that he died as a witness to the Faith, and is therefore assured of salvation.

Nevertheless, I found no comfort in this knowledge. Instead I was haunted by an image of butchery which gave me no peace, and left me secretly fearful. Like a lion in secret places, this fear advanced on me slowly, step by step, as my shock was dispersed by the activity that followed Father Paul's announcement. It was the Seneschal, Roger Descalquencs, who first gave voice to my dread, during our initial discussion regarding the murder.

'You say there were no clothes?' he asked the priest of Casseras.

'None,' Father Paul replied.

'Not even a trace? No rags? Nothing?'

'Not a single thread.'

Roger thought for a while. We were sitting in the Great Hall of the Chateau Comtal, which has always been a place of confusion, filled with smoke and dogs and sprawling sergeants, sticky trestles, discarded weapons, the odour of ancient meals. Every so often, one of the Seneschal's young children would pound through the door, complete a circuit of the room, and depart again.

Whenever this occurred, we were obliged to raise our voices over the extraordinary squeals emitted by this child – which were not unlike the squeals of a slaughtered pig. In this way, the assassination of Father Augustin was made public, for many of the garrison sergeants heard, and spread the news quickly. Indeed, many even joined our conversation, offering up their opinions without any kind of encouragement.

'Thieves,' said one. 'It must have been thieves.'

'Thieves might take the horses and the clothes,' Roger rejoined, 'but why would they waste their time chopping off legs and arms?'

This was, I think, the key question. We pondered it for a while. Then Roger spoke again.

'The victims were mounted,' he said slowly. 'Four of them were mercenaries – is that right, Father?'

'Yes.'

'Four of them were trained mercenaries. To overcome properly armed professional soldiers … well, in my opinion, no ragged little band of hungry peasants is going to do that.'

'Not even with arrows?' one of the sergeants inquired.

Roger frowned, and shook his head. It occurs to me, as I review this text, that I have not provided an *effictio* of the Seneschal, nor even a brief account of his life, although he is of great importance to my narrative. At the time of which I speak, he had served the King for twelve years, vigorously, judiciously, perhaps a little rapaciously, but only on the King's behalf; his own manner of life is not characterised by an excessive attachment to worldly goods. A man of about my age, with campaigning experience and a stocky, muscular form, he has retained a good deal more hair than I have (in fact, he is one of the most hirsute individuals of my acquaintance), and has been thrice married – his first two wives having perished in childbirth. With their assistance, however, he has succeeded in producing seven children, the eldest of whom is married to the Count of Foix's nephew.

With his brisk and slightly rough-hewn manner, Roger Descalquencs is generally able to disguise the depth and subtlety of his intelligence. He likes to breed dogs and hunt pigs; he is illiterate, often taciturn, untutored in many fundamental points of Catholic doctrine, with no interest in history or philosophy, no desire to extend his geographical knowledge, no devout concern for the salvation of his soul. The appearance he presents, in his stained wool and worn leather, is more like that of an ostler than a King's official. I have read that Aristotle, in a letter to King Alexander, once advised the King to select as an adviser 'one who is instructed in the seven liberal arts, learned in the seven principles, and master of the seven gentlemanly skills. I consider this true nobility'. By these standards, Roger is not of the nobility at all.

Yet he is a man of acute political insight, who possesses a very careful, clear and logical mind. This he demonstrated as he reasoned through the evidence so far presented.

'To attack armed and mounted mercenaries, you would have to be armed, and perhaps even mounted, yourself,' he mused, 'unless there are a lot of you, and I doubt that there were in this case. Most thieves have no money for weapons and horses, unless they happen to be living off some sort of wealthy pilgrimage route. There are brigands like that on the road to Compostella, I hear, but not around Casseras – not as far as I know.'

'So you doubt that this was the work of common thieves?' I asked, and he spread his hands.

'Who can tell?'

'But you wondered why thieves would waste their time dismembering the corpses?'

'Yes. I also wonder how they knew where to place their ambush. If you ask me, this attack was no chance meeting. What armed brigands would be drifting through that kind of fallow ground? It *is* the perfect place for an ambush, but who would they hope to rob there? Someone must have told our murderers about Father Augustin.'

I have already acknowledged, in these pages, the impossibility of divining another man's thoughts. As St Augustin himself once wrote: 'Men may speak, may be seen by the operations of their members, may be heard speaking; but whose thought is penetrated, whose heart is seen into?' Nevertheless, I believe that the progress of my calculations was keeping time with Roger's. For when I spoke, he nodded, as one would nod at a familiar face.

'Father Augustin's visits were not regular, or publicly announced,' I said. 'No one would know about them unless that person saw him on the road.'

'Or lived in Casseras.'

'Or perhaps received word from the Bishop's stables,' I finished. 'The Bishop's stables were always notified the night before he left.'

'No one in Casseras would do this thing,' Father Paul insisted vehemently. 'No one would even *think* of it!' But I regret to say that he was ignored.

'I tell you what seems odd to me,' the Seneschal remarked, tapping his chin with one finger as he stared off into space. 'Hacking someone to pieces is an angry thing to do. You would only do it because you hated the person you were doing it to. So if thieves did this, then they must have had a grudge against the Inquisitor. And if they were *not* thieves, then why take the clothes?'

'They must have undressed the bodies before dismembering them,' I pointed out. 'More time wasted.'

'Exactly.'

'A hired assassin might want to keep the clothes,' I hazarded. 'If his horse and his weapons were provided by somebody else, he would be poor enough to consider retaining even torn and blood-soaked garments, which could be washed and repaired.'

Roger grunted. Then he stretched his limbs, and ran his hands through his heavy thatch of grey hair several times, as if he were carding wool. 'With some men, it would be easy to find one enemy who hated them enough to slice them up,' he observed. 'With an inquisitor, half the world would gladly boil him alive. If I were you, Father Bernard, I would be very careful where I went, from now on. The fact that the guards were chopped, too, might mean that whoever did it hates the whole Inquisition – not just Father Augustin.'

With this reassuring observation ringing in my ears, is it any wonder that I failed to sleep that night? Not that I would have been expected to sleep, for a vigil was naturally held for Father Augustin's soul. But you must know how it is with vigils (and, indeed, with Matins) – no matter how earnest one's intentions might be, one tends to lose consciousness occasionally in the darkest hours. That night, however, I was kept awake in the contemplation of this death, so cruel and unwarranted, and so very close to my own life. I must confess that I was not moved to sorrow so much as fear, and disgust, and even (God forgive my irreverence) self-pity, for my superior's demise had left me with the burden of his various inquisitions to complete. How vain we are, we men, though our days are as a shadow that passeth away. How attached we are to the business of this world, even in the shadow of that mystery which is death. Thus, instead of offering up prayers for the soul of the departed, I found myself reviewing the events of the day, which had been a full one: the Seneschal had gone to Casseras to claim the bodies and examine the site of the assassination; Prior Hugues had written to the Master General, informing him of this most heinous crime; the Bishop had written to the Inquisitor of France, requesting a successor to Father Augustin. And I? Although I was confronted by a mountain of work, I had spent most of the day considering who, of all the people being pursued by my superior, might be in a position to have him assassinated. For it had occurred to me that many of them would not have been capable of killing him themselves. They were still in prison, you see.

Father Augustin had been at Lazet for only three months: in that time he had proceeded against Aimery Ribaudin, Bernard de Pibraux, Raymond Maury, Bruna d'Aguilar, and the entire village of Saint-Fiacre. I believed it likely that one of the townsfolk had been responsible for my superior's death, since few, if any, of the villagers had family outside prison, or the wherewithal to pay and equip hired assassins. This was my first thought. Then I began to wonder if, as the Seneschal had speculated, the attack had not been aimed at Father Augustin personally, but at the Holy Office itself; in that case, the culprit could have been someone pursued on *my* orders – or even on the orders of Father Jacques. It occurred to me suddenly that Father Augustin was the first inquisitor for many years to have set foot outside Lazet. His predecessor had remained behind the city walls for as long as I knew him; I myself had rarely travelled. Therefore one might conclude that Father Augustin had been an obvious target. It was possible that some malevolent sinner had been brooding for years on this bloody act, only carrying it through when the opportunity finally presented itself.

At which point I realised, with despair in my heart, that the aforesaid sinner would never be apprehended if it could only be done by examining inquisitions of the past twenty years. There were so many, and the resources of the Holy Office were so inconsiderable. Even if the Seneschal's investigation revealed new evidence, and that evidence narrowed the field of suspects, we would still *require* a field of suspects, for which the records of the Holy Office must naturally be the source.

This is what occupied me as I knelt in the choir during Father Augustin's vigil. I did not pray for him, as I should have; I did not fix my heart on Christ's suffering and deliver my vanity into the hand of God, humbling myself until I was as lowly as the chaff of the summer threshing floors, and therefore worthy to seek divine forgiveness on my superior's behalf. I did not reflect on his savage wounds, and weep for them as I should have wept for the wounds of our Saviour. Instead, I was given over to the cares of this world (where we shall have tribulation), groping in the darkness when I should have lifted my gaze to the light.

I did not even think: my friend is dead; I shall see him no more. Reading this, you must regard me with disfavour, and condemn me as stony hearted. But I find that I have come to miss Father Augustin more intensely with the passing of time, and I realise now that this is a consequence of our friendship's rare quality. True friendship, so the authorities tell us, is a path unto virtue – and many walk this path hand in hand. Ailred of Rievaulx, in his *Spiritualis Amicitia*, puts it thus: 'The friend, adhering to his friend in the spirit of Christ, is made one heart and one soul with him and so rising up through the stages of love to the friendship of Christ, he is, in one kiss, made one spirit with him.' Now this is a lofty ideal, but it has little bearing on my own congress with Father Augustin. Father Augustin and I kept our hearts and our souls firmly separated, I fear, mostly on account of my own culpable self-esteem.

Nevertheless, I knew that he walked in the Lord's statutes, and recall the words of Cicero in *De Amicitia*: 'For I loved the man's virtue, which is not extinguished.' Father Augustin and I shared no pleasant jests or tender secrets. We did not find joy in each other's company, or seek each other out to unburden our hearts when the weight of the world's cares made them heavy. But on the road to virtue he walked before me, a lamp unto my feet and a light unto my path. He was a model and an ideal, the perfect inquisitor, zealous yet even-tempered, strong in his faith, unflinching in his courage. I drew from his presence a new strength which I did not really notice until its source had departed. In Father Augustin I had identified a sense of mission absent in his predecessor, and blindly I had let it guide my own steps, knowing that Father Augustin would not lead me astray.

Without him, I had no one to follow. Once again, I was forced to make my own way, straying down paths which led me into swamps and nettles − for I was ever one to let my perverse humours and my curiosity, my sloth and my pride, govern those virtues which seem to have such shallow roots in my character. If Father Augustin had lived, perhaps ... but if Father Augustin had lived, none of this would have happened.

I know that he would have died bravely. Though feeble in body, he was strong in spirit, and would have faced the final stroke as calmly as any man could, his thoughts and emotions fixed on eternal rewards. I also believe that he was better prepared for death than most of us, having lived for so long in its shadow. But now, when I recall his trembling hands, his fragile form (as defenceless as a nestling's) and how slowly, with how much effort, he would accomplish even the simplest task ... when I recall these things, my very bowels ache, and my eyes fill with tears, for I know that when the first blow fell, he would not have had the time or the strength even to raise his arm, or duck his head, in a futile attempt to shield himself. Indeed, his sight was so poor that he might not have seen the blade as it fell.

To kill him would have been like killing a tethered lamb.

It is strange that I can weep for him now, but did not do so then. I suppose I feel that I know him better now, for reasons which will become clear to you presently – and I am also very different, in many ways. Events have conspired to stretch the boundaries of my affections.

For all that, however, I should have been moved to grief when I first laid eyes on his mangled remains. Instead I was left feeling queasy and somewhat ill at ease. Perhaps, confronted by such terrible proof of life's transience, one naturally flees from the notion that these bloody rags of flesh, these shattered bones, could possibly be human in their essence. Or perhaps it was simply that they bore no resemblance to Father Augustin – since his head, that most distinctive member, was still missing.

But I should not speak of the remains just yet. They arrived somewhat later, with the passing of another two days. I should learn not to jump ahead in my narrative, when there is ground in-between to cover.

The Seneschal, as I said, did not return with the victims' bodies for another two days. In the intervening period, I was kept very busy. One of the dead familiars (and only one, by God's grace) was a married man, with children; I was bound to attend them, and offer what comfort I could – little enough, I fear, though with the Prior's and the Bishop's consent, I was able to promise the bereft widow a small pension. It was also my duty to inform the inquisitors of Carcassonne and Toulouse that Father Augustin had perished, and to warn them that they themselves might be in danger. I was reluctant to dispatch messengers with this correspondence, lest, as servants of the Holy Office, they be slaughtered on the way. But by using three men from the Bishop's household, I was able to assuage any fears I had on this account.

In addition, all the work hitherto performed by Father

Augustin naturally fell to me. With what remorse I now reflected on the time, so lately past, when I had nursed a resentment against him for his trips to Casseras. How burdened I had thought myself then! Now, consulting his schedule of interrogations, I realised that he had been trying to atone for his absences by shouldering far more than could legitimately be expected of anyone – let alone a man of feeble health. I was ashamed, and I was also appalled. How could I even hope to replace him? The answer was that I could not. Many people would have to languish in prison for many more months, waiting to be interviewed, because the Holy Office did not have the resources to address their cases immediately.

Needless to say, it had occurred to me that the agent of Father Augustin's death might very well be found among those with whom he was most recently involved. Therefore I was eager to sort through his effects, and review the documents which dealt with his latest inquisitions. I found nothing of interest in his cell, for here were kept only such humble impedimenta as the Rule required: his three winter tunics and pelisse, his spare leggings and socks and underclothes, the three books issued to most of us who proceed to the higher levels of learning – Pierre Comester's *Historia Scholastica*, the *Sentences* of Pierre Lombard, and the Scriptures. His scapular and tunic, his black mantle and leather belt, his knife and purse and handkerchief ... these, of course, were missing. I found and disposed of certain salves and cordials prepared for him by our Brother Infirmarian, as well as a scented candle that was reputed to have a salutary effect on aching heads and smarting eyes. The herbal pillow I gave to poor Sicard. I have neglected Sicard in this narrative, but his role is a very minor one. He entered the order as an oblate, and possessed many of those qualities characteristic of people fresh from a cloistered childhood: a muted voice, a ravenous appetite, a very slight stoop and a somewhat acquisitive reverence for books. (Brother Lucius, our scrivener, was similarly endowed.) Though Sicard had never impressed me as a youth of great intelligence or accomplishment, he had served Father Augustin loyally and efficiently as a scribe, and was shaken to the very soul by my superior's death. I therefore kept him near me for several days after it had occurred, as one would shelter an orphaned kitten, allowing him to retain that pillow belonging to Father Augustin in the knowledge that it would comfort him a little. This I did with the approval of the Prior, who soon took him off my hands. By the month's end, he was assisting the Brother Librarian, and sleeping a good deal more than he had in Father Augustin's care.

He will never be a preacher, that one. He has not the capacity.

But I was speaking of Father Augustin's effects. Having cleared his cell, I went on to examine his desk and document-chest at headquarters. Here I found four registers from Father Jacques's time, each marked and glossed wherever the names Aimery Ribaudin, Bernard de Pibraux, Raymond Maury, Oldric Capiscol, Petrona Capdenier and Bruna d'Aguilar appeared. I also found an old register, marked in several places, wherein I discovered the entire, sorry tale of Oldric Capiscol.

Forty-three years ago, as a youth of thirteen, Oldric had once adored a Perfect at his father's request. Three years later, someone present during the adoration had defamed Oldric, who was imprisoned for two years; when released, he was obliged to endure *poena confusibilis* – the name we give to that humiliating punishment whereby the penitent is required to wear saffron crosses on his breast and back. Oldric displayed the shameful insignia for a year but, upon finding that they prevented him from earning a livelihood, finally discarded them and obtained employment as a boatman. Needless to say, he could not escape punishment so easily. *Be sure your sin will find you out*. Having been discovered and cited to appear in 1283, he was afraid to do so, fleeing from the wrath of the Holy Office – which subsequently had him excommunicated. After remaining under censure for a year, he was declared a heretic in 1284. In 1288 he was captured, at last, but escaped on the road, only to be recaptured near Carcassonne. He was sentenced to life imprisonment on bread and water.

I found this surprising, for I knew that Father Jacques, had he presided at the *auto de fé*, would have condemned him to death. In a marginal gloss, Father Augustin had noted that no Oldric Capiscol was currently residing in prison, concluding that, since no mention had been made of another escape, the prisoner must therefore have died in captivity some time between 1289 and the present day.

So Oldric could not be blamed for Father Augustin's demise — although I wondered uneasily if he might have descendants who bore a grudge against the Holy Office. None of the Capiscols *I* knew seemed to be of a rancorous temper; they were poulterers, and all the poulterers of my acquaintance (so frequently occupied, as they are, with the beheading of fowl) display a peculiarly serene disposition, perhaps because they are able to vent their evil humours on their livestock. Nevertheless, I realised that there might be a branch of the family unknown to me, and sitting there at my superior's desk, leafing slowly through the dusty record of old names and misdemeanours, I became quite apprehensive. Could there be anyone in Lazet whose life had not been touched, in some fashion, by our relentless pursuit of errant souls? How was it possible to search out and identify the assassins, when so many people had reason to hate — or fear — the dead man? At Avignonet, Guillaume Arnaud and Stephen of Saint-Thibery had been killed by heretical knights, many of them unknown to their victims, who had come all the way from Montsegur simply in order to murder these two champions of the Faith. Had a similar fate befallen Father Augustin? Were his assassins simply heretics, without any direct link to the man they had so brutally cut down?

But then I reminded myself that the culprits had known both where and when to strike. Preparing an ambush would have been impossible without a base near Casseras — or an informant among the Bishop's household. If the Seneschal's investigation was thorough, some name or description must surely surface. Meanwhile, it was incumbent upon me to provide my own list of names, which might be matched against anything uncovered by the Seneschal.

This is what I endeavoured to do, in the two days before he returned. And I began with the bribery suspects.

Of all these suspects only one, Bernard de Pibraux, had been arrested and incarcerated by Father Augustin. Raymond Maury, on the other hand, had been summoned to appear before the tribunal five days hence. Father Augustin's reasoning was clear to me, in this – for a baker with nine children was very much less likely to disappear than a vigorous, unmarried young noble with (as far as I could deduce from various depositions) no prospect of inheriting the family wealth. Indeed, neither of the accused men appeared to be endowed with many worldly goods, and I wondered, at first, how they might have found the means of persuading Father Jacques to overlook them. But Bernard de Pibraux did possess a doting father, and I recalled that Raymond's wife's relatives were fairly well placed, being a family of successful furriers. Most families would be willing to pay a good deal in order that they might not be branded with the infamy of a heretical connection. It is, of course, an hereditary stain.

Upon examining Father Jacques's registers, I made myself familiar with the original accusations against Bernard de Pibraux and Raymond Maury. Both names had been mentioned, in passing, by witnesses summoned on unrelated matters. One witness had heard Raymond remark in his shop one day that 'a mule has a soul as good as a man's'. The other witness had seen Bernard de Pibraux bowing to a Perfect, and giving him some food. Neither incident had become the subject of inquiry by Father Jacques, though Father Augustin had since interviewed Bernard, who maintained that he had been ignorant of the Perfect's identity. Having met this purveyor of false doctrine in the house of a friend, he had bowed out of politeness, and given him some bread that he did not want himself. Bernard denied ever having paid money to Father Jacques, for any reason.

In such cases as this, it is very difficult to discern the truth. Father Augustin had interviewed a number of witnesses, none of whom could attribute to Bernard any other acts which might be described as unorthodox. The young man attended church, though not unfailingly: his parish priest condemned him as 'a thoughtless youth, given to excessive drinking, and often neglectful of his soul's good – like so many hereabouts. He is one of a small group of friends who share the same habits. I cannot persuade them to leave the young maidens alone.' In his usual efficient manner, Father Augustin had taken care to garner the names of this 'small group of friends': they were Bernard's cousin, Guibert; Etienne, the son of a neighbouring castellan; and Odo, the son of the local notary. I wondered if they were of a violent temperament, and went to ask Pons whether Bernard de Pibraux had been visited by any friends of about the same age.

'No,' said Pons. 'Just his father and brother.'

'Did the father vouch for the brother?'

'If he did, there was no need.' Pons actually smiled – a rare sight, let me assure you. 'They were cast from the same mould, those three.'

'How did they appear? Did they impress you as very angry? Was there anything furtive in their demeanour?'

'Furtive?'

'Did they look as though they might be up to no good?'

Pons frowned. He scratched his jaw. 'Everyone looks scared when they come in here,' he pointed out. 'They think they might not be allowed to leave.'

This was a valid point. One forgets what an awful effect the prison has on most visitors. 'But what about Bernard?' I asked. 'How is he taking imprisonment?'

'Oh – now *that* I can tell you. Bernard has the devil's own temper. Never shuts up. Three buckets of water I threw over him and it made no difference. Some of the other prisoners have complained.'

'He is violent, then?'

'He would be, if I let him. Once I put him in chains, it calmed him down a little.'

'I see.'

With this information I returned to my desk, and pondered. To me, it appeared that Bernard's guilt or innocence in regard to the 'veneration' of the Perfect would never be established one way or another – unless he confessed to an heretical act. Father Augustin must have felt the same, for he had taken great care to ask Bernard for the names of any enemies who might wish him ill. This procedure, designed to apprehend false witnesses, is a useful one if a person's guilt is difficult to establish. But since Bernard had not named the witness responsible for accusing him, there was no suggestion of a conspiracy.

Faced with this dilemma, I considered what Father Jacques would have done. For him, there would have been two alternatives. He would have starved a confession out of Bernard, before recommending a lenient sentence, or he would have ignored the whole incident. Once or twice, in the past, I had myself witnessed this tendency to overlook certain reported misdeeds 'for lack of evidence', and I am not convinced that my superior was moved by a passion for lucre, rather than an inclination towards mercy. 'If a man chooses not to kill a chicken for his mother-in-law,' he expostulated on one occasion, 'it does *not* follow that he was a heretic at the time. This woman is a scold and a shrew. Who would choose to sacrifice a good, plump hen for such a one? Tell her to go away.'

I had never told Father Augustin about these little lapses, for they had been infrequent, had involved people without the funds to pay a gate toll (let alone a bribe), and had normally occurred when Father Jacques was feeling particularly careworn. Indeed, I would commend him for his clemency, if not for the fact that he was also subject to the most unpalatable bouts of vindictiveness. As far as I was concerned, the fact that

Bernard de Pibraux's lapse had been passed over indicated nothing out of the ordinary, as regards the behaviour of Father Jacques.

In Raymond Maury's case, however, I could see that something was wrong. To say that a mule has a soul as good as a man's is to attest to that belief, held by the Cathari, that the souls of men and beasts have been taken from the Kingdom of Light by the God of Darkness, and infused into corporeal bodies until they can be restored to heaven. Now, it is possible that one might insult an enemy, saying 'he has the soul of a mule, and the morals of a rat', or some such remark, and that this insult might be misheard, or misunderstood. But Father Augustin, upon interviewing certain friends and acquaintances of Raymond Maury, had extracted from them further evidence that the aforesaid baker was a man of deviant opinions. One neighbour, on informing Raymond that he intended to complete a pilgrimage in order to secure an indulgence, heard Raymond say: 'Do you believe that any man can absolve you of your sins? Only God can do that, my friend.' Another acquaintance remembered going to the church of St Marie of Montgauzy, to pray that stolen goods might be recovered; on the way, she met Raymond Maury, who scoffed at her intentions. 'Your prayers will do nothing for you,' he is reported to have said.

As you can see, Father Augustin had collected some damning evidence against Raymond – and in doing so, had also raised serious doubts about Father Jacques. It really did appear that the former inquisitor's honesty must be brought into question, else why had Raymond Maury not been arrested long since? I could not believe that Father Jacques's apparent blindness had stemmed from a merciful impulse, no matter how many children Raymond might have possessed; in such cases, mercy should properly be displayed at the sentencing. No: I became convinced, even as I read through the depositions, that some sort of illicit payment must have changed hands.

It saddened me to think so, but I was not entirely surprised. What *did* surprise me was the document I found concealed in one of the registers. After perusing it carefully, I was able to identify it as a letter, but did not recognise the hand in which it had been written.

Although I cannot reproduce the text of the letter faithfully, to the best of my recollection it ran as follows.

Jacques Fournier, Bishop, by grace of God humble servant of the Church of Pamiers, to his worthy son, Brother Augustin Duese, Inquisitor of heretical depravity, greetings and affection in the Lord.

I received your letter of charity with joy. Now as to that matter about which you sought counsel: would that there might be as much discernment as love in what I say, that I might give my dear son valuable advice. You refer to a young woman, of great beauty and spiritual worth, 'possessed by demons'; you seek invocations by which she might be freed from this curse. In my library, as you speculated, I do indeed possess literature describing such exorcisms, but before you attempt any rituals of this nature, I would urge you to examine diligently the form and symptoms of her malaise. Is it, as you say, a case of possession, or is it an instance of insanity, promoted by some foe learned in the diabolical arts? The Angelic Doctor himself has warned us against those old women who can inflict harm, particularly on children, with the evil eye – and there are others, even more dangerous, skilled in the conjuring of 'infernal kings', about whom I know little. Be sure to gird yourself well with the armour of Faith and courage, before drawing your sword against such an enemy.

As to the formula for banishing demons, I give it here:

Let the subject hold a candle, sitting or kneeling; let the priest begin with 'Our help is in the name of the Lord', and those present chant the responses. Let the priest then sprinkle the subject with holy water, place a stole around his neck, and recite psalm seventy, 'Hasten thee, O God, to deliver me' – and let him continue with the litany of the sick, saying, at the Invocation of the Saints: 'Pray for him and be favourable: deliver him O Lord.'

Then begins the exorcism, to be recited thus.

'I exorcise thee, being weak but reborn in holy baptism by the living God, by the true God, by the God who redeemed thee with His precious blood, that thou mayest be exorcised, that all the illusions and wickedness of the devil's deceit may depart and flee from thee altogether with every unclean spirit abjured by Him who will come to judge both the quick and the dead, and who will purge the earth with fire. Amen ...'

But I shall not recite the formula in its entirety, since it has no bearing on my tale. The letter concluded with a respectful salutation (Let the peace of our Lord Jesus Christ be with you, etc.) and a request for copies of certain depositions which, again, are not relevant to this narrative. The date given was a day not three weeks before.

I say that I was surprised at this letter, but in fact I was more than surprised: I was so astonished that I almost fell off my stool. Who was this 'young woman, of great beauty and spiritual worth'? Certainly no one whom *I* had encountered. Perhaps, I thought, she was one of the women at Casseras – the daughter of the widow, for instance. But why should Father Augustin have concerned himself with her tribulations? Demons, whether invoked or in possession of a benighted soul, were not the domain of the Holy Office. Pope Alexander IV had specifically warned inquisitors not to concern themselves with cases of divination (or suchlike) unless they manifestly savoured of heresy.

As for the formulae given, I could not see how they would have profited my superior at all, since he was not a priest, and should properly have applied to one before turning to the Bishop of Pamiers. It was just one mystery among many. But

I knew that my superior could not have written to the Bishop himself, his vision being too poor – so I went to Sicard, and asked him about the letter.

'Yes,' he said, blinking up at me with his large, pale eyes. (He was inspecting certain volumes of the Angelic Doctor's *Summa*, for bookworm.) 'I remember transcribing that. He sent it to Pamiers with some other documents. But you would have to ask Brother Lucius about the other documents.'

'What did the letter say? Can you recall?'

'It was about a woman. With the devil in her.'

'Do you know who she is? Did he mention her name?'

'No.'

I waited, but soon realised that if I wanted anything more, I would have to extract it, like teeth. Sicard was ever thus – the discipline of the cloister had trained him too well. Or perhaps it was Father Augustin who had insisted that he speak only when spoken to, answer only the questions put to him, and make no observations freely until such a time as he might have reached a high level of maturity and education.

'Sicard,' I said, 'did Father Augustin mention where she lives, or with whom she lives? Did he offer any detailed descriptions of any kind? Think, now.'

Obediently, Sicard thought. He sucked in his bottom lip. His delicate fingers played nervously with a quill as he shook his head.

'He only said that she was young. And of great spiritual worth.'

'And he offered *you* no explanation?'

'No, Father.'

'And you never thought to ask him for one?'

'Oh *no*, Father!' Sicard looked shocked. 'Why should I do that?'

'Because you were curious. Surely you were curious? I would have been curious.'

The poor boy stared at me as if he were not familiar with the word 'curious', and had no desire to become better acquainted with it. I saw then that Father Augustin had chosen his scribe with great wisdom, selecting someone wholly incurious, innately deferential, sadly impercipient – and, for all these reasons, almost incapable of revealing Holy Office secrets. Therefore I left him, with an encouraging word, and went off to Compline still musing on this remarkable letter, which I decided (sagely, as it transpired) to keep concealed, for the present.

I did, however, silently pledge that I would visit the women at Casseras, so as to satisfy myself that all was as it should be there. But I was reluctant to do so until after the Seneschal had returned; I wanted to hear his report before making any further decisions.

As it happened, he returned the next day, so I was unable to present him with a list of possible suspects. I had not even interviewed Bernard de Pibraux at the time. Perhaps I had been too confident of my abilities, but in all frankness, I had not expected the Seneschal back so soon. If the investigation had been under my command, I think I would have moved more slowly and delicately.

We all have our different ways of working, I suppose.

I was writing letters when the corpses arrived. It had occurred to me that I should undoubtedly speak to Bernard de Pibraux's three cronies – Etienne, Odo and Guibert – in order to establish, if I could, their whereabouts on the day of Father Augustin's murder. At least two of these young men had very probably been trained in the art of battle, and since they were young, hot-headed and hard-drinking, there was every reason to believe that they might have urged each other to inflict a terrible revenge on the agent of their friend's downfall. This speculation was strengthened, in my mind, by Bernard de Pibraux's possible innocence. A band of wild and passionate youths, convinced that their friend has been wrongfully imprisoned, would in all likelihood be moved to the kind of reckless fury needed to accomplish such an obscene act of destruction.

So far, at least, they were the most likely suspects.

You may not know that there is a procedure and formula for summoning individuals to appear before the tribunal. One writes to their parish priest, thus: *We, the Inquisitors of Heretical Depravity, send greetings, enjoining and strictly instructing you, by virtue of the authority we wield, to summon in our names so-and-so, to appear on such a day at such a place, to answer for his faith.* In this instance, of course, I named three names, and requested that they appear before me at different times, on different dates – for I desired to question them each on his own.

I had sealed this letter, and was sharpening my pen in preparation for the next (summoning Raymond Maury's father-in-law), when there was a knock on the outer door. Since it was barred from the inside, as is our practice at headquarters, I rose and went to open it. I found Roger Descalqencs on the threshold.

'My lord!' I exclaimed.

'Father.' He was bathed in sweat and grey with dust; in his right hand he held the reins of his palfrey. 'Will you take these barrels?'

'What?'

'The bodies are in these barrels,' he said, gesturing at the horses behind him. Each was laden with two small wooden barrels bound with ropes. Six or seven weary-looking sergeants were in attendance, all bearing the stains of a hard ride. 'They were salted.'

'*Salted?*'

'They were put in brine. To preserve them.'

I crossed myself, and two of the sergeants, seeing this, imitated my actions.

'I thought you might want me to bring them straight here,' the Seneschal continued. His voice was hoarse, his breathing heavy. 'Unless you have a better notion?'

'Oh ... um ...'

'They smell pretty rank, I warn you.'

By this time Raymond Donatus (ever vigilant) had descended from the scriptorium; I could hear him behind me, making shocked noises.

'They will have to be examined ...' I faltered. 'I should ask our Brother Infirmarian ...'

'You want them at the priory?'

'No! No ...' The thought of such grisly remnants defiling and disturbing the peace of the cloister was repugnant to me. I knew how much they would agitate many of my brethren. 'No, take them ... I know.' I had recalled the empty stables under our feet. 'Take them downstairs. This way. Raymond, will you show them? I must fetch our Brother Infirmarian.'

'Jean can do that. I need to talk to you. Jean! You heard.' The Seneschal jerked his chin at one of the sergeants. 'Arnaud, you supervise the unloading. Where can we talk, Father?'

'In here.'

I ushered the Seneschal into the room formerly occupied by my superior, and invited him to sit down. Seeing him collapse into the inquisitor's chair, I was also moved to offer him refreshments. But he waved this suggestion aside.

'When I get home,' he said. 'Now, tell me, has anything happened while I was away? Have you learned anything that might help us?'

'Ah.' It was evident that his news was not good. 'I was going to ask you the same question.'

'Father, I am no lymer hound. I do *not* have a nose for this kind of business.' He sighed, gazing down at his beautiful Spanish boots. 'All I can say is, if the villagers were involved, it was all of them. Every last one.'

'Tell me what you accomplished.'

So he did. He told me that his sergeants had searched Casseras, looking for hidden weapons, horses or clothing. He told me that he had questioned all the villagers, asking them what they had been doing on the afternoon of Father Augustin's death. As far as he could recall, there were no discrepancies between their accounts.

'There was nothing. No one saw any strangers that day. No one seems to bear a grudge against the Holy Office. And no one was away that night – which is probably the most important thing I learned.'

'Why?'

'Because more pieces were found.' It appeared that, during the Seneschal's soujourn in Casseras, two remarkable discoveries had been made some distance from the village. In one instance, a shepherd had found a severed limb high in the mountains, and brought it to Casseras because he wanted to give it to the nearest priest. Similarly, a head had been found near a village on the road to Rasiers – a village where the priest had heard about the Casseras massacre, and had therefore dispatched the head to Estolt de Coza with all haste. Estolt, in turn, had sent it to Roger.

'These pieces were scattered far and wide,' the Seneschal pointed out. 'The arm was a good day's walk from Casseras, so if someone from the village left it there, he would certainly have been away that night – '

'Even if he rode a horse?'

'Even if he did, he would have had to walk back, because there was no horse in Casseras, Father.'

'I see.'

'Do you? I wish I did. It seems as if the murderers split up and went in different directions.'

'Scattering bloody members on their way.'

'Does it make sense to you?'

'Not at all, I fear.'

'At least we can say that there were two – probably more – and that they were not from the village. I feel sure they were not from the village. The skills they would have needed, the distances they covered ... no. If you ask me, they were from somewhere else.'

Having delivered himself of this opinion, Roger fell silent.

For a short time he sat frowning at his boots, apparently lost in thought, as I reviewed his arguments in my own mind. They seemed sound enough.

Suddenly he spoke again.

'Do you know how much it costs, to hire a team of assassins?' he asked abruptly, and I was unable to suppress a smile.

'Oddly enough, my lord, I could not even hazard a guess.'

'Well ... it depends on what you want. You could hire a couple of pedlars for next to nothing, I suppose. But there were two mercenaries tried at my court, not long since, and they were paid fifteen livres. Fifteen! For just two!'

'And where would anyone in Casseras get fifteen livres?'

'Exactly. Where? Say the fee was twenty livres – well, you could buy half a house for that in Casseras. I fancy even Bruno Pelfort would have to sell a good portion of his flock, and he is the richest man in the village. But the priest says his flock is the same size as it ever was, more or less.'

'So unless all the villagers contributed – '

'Or unless they got the money from someone like Estolt de Coza – '

'But you think not?'

'I can see no cause. If Father Paul is to be believed.'

'And I think he is.'

'So do I. Have there been no heretics in Casseras recently?'

I shook my head. 'Not that have come to our attention.'

'What about Rasiers?'

'Nor from Rasiers.'

'What about those women in the forcia? Father Paul says the Inquisitor went there to give them spiritual guidance. Is that true?'

I hesitated, not knowing how to reply. I was uncertain as to whether it *was* true. Seeing me at a loss, the Seneschal twisted his face into a very discomforting grimace.

'This was no affair of the heart, surely?' he expostulated. 'Some of the villagers are saying it was – '

'My lord, is that likely?'

'I want to know what *you* think.'

'I think it unlikely.'

'But not impossible?'

'I think it *very* unlikely.'

Even as I spoke, I knew that the emphasis I placed on these words, and the expression on my face as I uttered them, were culpably irreverent – for they implied that someone of Father Augustin's age and appearance surely must have renounced all claims to the pangs of love a long, long time ago. To my surprise, however, the Seneschal did not respond as I had expected. Instead of answering with some wry acknowledgement – perhaps even a smile – he frowned, and scratched his jaw.

'I would think it unlikely, too,' he said, 'if I had not met the women. Their eyes were red with weeping. They talked and talked about his kindness and his piety and his wisdom. It was very . . .' He paused, and then he did smile, but rather as if he were reluctant to do so. 'You see, Father, if they had been talking about *you*, then I would have understood. You are the kind of monk a woman might weep over.'

'Oh!' Naturally, I laughed out loud, though I must confess that I was flattered, God forgive me. 'Is that a compliment, or an accusation?'

'You know what I mean. You have a way of talking . . . augh!' Apparently uncomfortable with the topic, Roger pushed it aside with a rough movement of his hands. 'You know what I mean. But Father Augustin was a . . . a born monk.'

'A born monk?'

'There was no blood in his veins! He was dry as dust! God help us, Father, you must know what I mean!'

'Yes, yes, I know what you mean.' It was not the time for teasing. 'So you think that these women were genuinely affected?'

'Who can tell? A woman's tears . . . But I *did* think that if Father Augustin was investigating them, then they might have had a reason to kill him.'

'And the means?'

'Perhaps. Perhaps not. They live simply, but they must live off something. Something more than a few fowl and a vegetable garden.'

'Yes. They must,' I said, thinking of the letter from Jacques Fournier. It lay in the very next room, and I could have produced it, then and there, for the Seneschal's scrutiny. Why did I hesitate? Because I had not yet presented it to the Prior? Perhaps because I was eager to safeguard Father Augustin's reputation. If, on my forthcoming visit to Casseras, I should happen to discover that he had formed a shameful association with these women – an association which had no bearing on his ultimate fate – then it would be my duty to conceal his irregular conduct from the world at large. 'Unfortunately, the women were not being investigated,' I declared. 'As far as I know, Father Augustin was trying to convince them to enter a convent. For their own safety.'

'Oh.'

'And if they had wanted to discourage him, they could have done it without chopping him to pieces.'

'Yes.'

At this juncture we both fell silent, as if exhausted, and occupied ourselves with our own thoughts. Mine were concerned with Bernard de Pibraux, and the pile of unfinished work on my desk. Roger's, evidently, were concerned with the Bishop's stables, for after a while he said: 'Have you spoken to the Bishop's ostler, by any chance?'

'No. Have you?'

'Not yet.'

'If we can find out who knew about Father Augustin's visit – outside Casseras – '

'Yes.'

'And then match those names against the names of anyone he might have offended – '

'Of course. And you might see about your dead familiars, too – if they mentioned their trip to anyone.'

'There will be a *great* deal of work to do,' I sighed. 'It may take weeks. Months. And it may be fruitless.'

The Seneschal grunted. 'If I send word to every bailiff and provost and castellan within a three-day ride of Casseras, we might find a witness who saw the assassins fleeing,' he said, delivering himself of a cavernous yawn. 'They must have stopped, those men, to wash off the blood. Perhaps someone will find one of the stolen horses.'

'Perhaps.'

'The murderers might even boast about what they did. It often happens.'

'Pray God it does.'

Once again, a sense of fatigue seemed to settle over us like mist. Manifestly it behoved us to finish our dialogue, rise from our chairs, attack our duties. Instead we simply sat there, as the room slowly filled with the smell of horse sweat. I remember looking down at my hands, which were covered in ink and sealing wax.

'Well,' Roger said at last, speaking almost with a groan, as if the effort involved was too burdensome, 'I suppose I should go and speak to the Bishop's ostler. Get those names you wanted. And a description of the missing horses.'

'The Bishop is very grieved about his missing horses.' My intention in saying this, I fear, was an uncharitable one, but the Seneschal responded only to my words, and not to my tone.

'Five of them gone?' he said. 'I would be pretty grieved myself. It will cost a fortune to replace them. Are you going to take charge of the bodies, Father?'

'Naturally,' I assured him, rising even as he rose. From beyond the closed door I could hear shuffling, muttering, creaking noises which indicated to me that the barrels containing Father Augustin's remains (and those of his familiars) were being transported to the stables. Could I discern the hollow slap of salt water against wood? I realised, then, that I would have to examine the gruesome contents of these receptacles personally – a task which I was most reluctant to undertake.

'My lord?' I said, arresting Roger on the threshold. 'If you have no objection, my lord, I should like to visit Casseras some time soon.' (In making this request, I knew that I would have to tread carefully, or risk offending him with what could have been regarded as a lack of respect for his methods.) 'Since I am more acquainted with those signs indicating the presence of heresy, I might uncover certain clues that you overlooked. Through no fault of your own.'

'*You?*' On the Seneschal's face was written astonishment and alarm. I do think it wonderful, the manner in which a man may speak without words – for just as heavenly vials full of odours are the prayers of the saints, so the shifting of shadows is the language of a man's countenance. '*You* go? But that would be foolish!'

'Not if I was accompanied by some of your men.'

'Father Augustin was accompanied. Look what happened to him.'

'I could double the guard.'

'You could send for the villagers. It would be less dangerous.'

'True.' The thought had occurred to me. 'But that would frighten them. I want them to regard me as a friend. I want their trust. Besides, we have no room in the prison.'

'Father, if I were you, I would think again,' Roger warned. He shut the door (which had just been opened), and put his hand on my arm – where it left a grey stain on the white fabric. 'Where will we be if you get slaughtered?'

I tried to laugh off his concern. 'Since I shall be using your horses, my lord, we will know, at least, that the culprit did not derive his information from the Bishop's stables,' I quipped. And indeed, my demeanour was one of careless courage, though inwardly I was quaking. For although my intellect told me that Father Augustin's assassins had left the scene of his murder far, far behind, my heart was filled with an illogical fear that I was determined to suppress.

Unfortunately, as you may have anticipated, my first glimpse of Father Augustin's remains served only to nourish this fear.

That I may know him

Amiel de Veteravinea is the priory's Infirmarian. He is a small, wiry man of brisk demeanour, with a clipped and hurried way of speaking. Although his pate is perfectly hairless, his eyebrows are luxurious in their growth, thick and dark like the northern forests. I would say that his character is not as sympathetic as one might wish in an Infirmarian; however, he is very accomplished in both the diagnosis of complaints and the preparation of remedies. He also exhibits a profound and learned interest in the art of embalming.

This ancient skill, by which, through the use of certain spices and mysterious techniques, dead flesh is preserved from corruption – this skill, as I say, is one about which I can demonstrate little knowledge. I have never found it an appealing subject. For Brother Amiel, on the other hand, it is a source of intense fascination, such as a theologian might derive from debate over the essence of the Godhead. And Brother Amiel's interest is not purely theoretical, for after consulting various rare and time-honoured texts (some of them written by infidels), he will often sully the stainless integrity of his newly acquired wisdom by applying it to the corpses of small birds and beasts.

It was therefore to Brother Amiel that I turned, when

confronted by the pitiful remnants of five murdered men. No one else of my acquaintance would have had the stomach to examine each body part with the care required for proper identification. He arrived promptly, bearing several large, linen sheets, and I saw at once that my intuition had served me well, for his eyes were bright, and his step positively eager. Upon reaching the stables, he spread his sheets side by side on the floor, then rolled up his sleeves as a man might who faced the prospect of a delicious meal, and did not wish to have any portion of his raiment trailing in the goose grease.

I should tell you, at this point, that the stables were already somewhat repellent in their odour and aspect, having been used to house Pons' swine about two years previously. The animals had not thrived there, however, and the smells had been most objectionable to those of us working on the floor above. So, having butchered his precious pigs (in one of the troughs designed to water our non-existent horses), Pons had abandoned his dream of home-cured bacon, and the stables had become less frequented than ever.

They were, in effect, perfectly suited to the storage of decomposing human remains.

'Ah!' Brother Amiel exclaimed, upon producing a sodden joint from the first barrel. 'Knee, by the look of it. Yes. A knee.'

'I – um – if you will pardon me, Brother ...' With one corner of my mantle pressed against my nose, I cravenly edged towards the stairs. (There were two means of egress from the stables: through a small door up the stairs, or through a pair of large doors that opened onto the street. These were always barred from the inside.) 'I shall return when you have completed your examination.'

'Now *this* is not Father Augustin's hand. I knew his hand, and this is much larger.'

I turned to go, but Brother Amiel prevented me.

'Wait!' he said. 'Where are you off to?'

'I am ... I am very busy, Brother – '

'Did you know these dead sergeants? You must have. They worked here, did they not?'

'I knew them, but we were barely acquainted.'

'Then who knew them well? I need help, Brother Bernard, I cannot put these bodies back together alone.'

'Why not?' I regret to say that his meaning escaped me, at first. 'Is something too heavy, for you?'

'Brother, the pieces must be *identified*.'

'Oh. Yes. Of course,' I said quickly, but as I gazed at the swollen, black-and-purple object in his grasp, my powers of reasoning were suddenly restored to me. 'Brother, surely this advanced degree of putrefaction will prevent us ... I mean ... I doubt that most people would recognise these body parts, no matter how well they might have known the victims.'

'Nonsense.'

'I assure you.'

'The hairs on this hand are black. The ones on the knee are grey.' Brother Amiel spoke condescendingly, and a little sharply, as one might speak to a stupid child – but I was feeling too nauseous to take offence. 'There are always features which putrefaction does not expunge.'

'Yes, but you must take into account our natural revulsion,' I gasped, realising, even as I did so, that Brother Amiel had experienced no natural revulsion whatsoever. 'The sight of these remnants ... they will affect people so strongly ...'

'Then I am to have *no* help?'

'Brother, you must expect none. I am simply warning you – that is all.' And having delivered this warning I retreated in haste, to seek out poor Giraud Gantier's wife, together with such familiars as might be persuaded to scrutinise what was left of Giraud and their other comrades.

When I returned, I brought Pons with me. Of the seven remaining sergeants on our staff, four had agreed to come down one at a time, owing to the constraints of their duty roster, and three were asleep at home, having worked the night shift. I had sent Isarn's replacement, the new messenger, to fetch Matheva Gantier. God knows that I was reluctant to seek her assistance, but there seemed to be little alternative.

'Christ in Heaven!' Pons croaked, upon entering the stables. In my absence, Brother Amiel had emptied the salting barrels, and had spread their contents across his linen sheets. I noticed at once that some of the pieces seemed to be grouped in arrangements that were vaguely reminiscent of human forms, with heads laid at the top of the sheets, and feet laid at the bottom.

I could see only two heads.

'We have a lot of missing members, here,' Brother Amiel announced, without sparing us a glance. 'A great many. It makes things very difficult.'

'Oh, Christ God . . .' Pons muttered. His hand was across his mouth, and he was as white as the second horse of the Apocalypse. I put a sympathetic hand on his arm.

'Perhaps you should ask your wife to bring down some herbs,' I suggested. 'Strong herbs. To mask the stench.'

'Yes. Yes. At once!' The gaoler fled precipitately, so that I was left alone on the threshold. It was some time before I summoned up the courage to advance. Brother Amiel simply ignored me, minutely inspecting each dreadful artefact by the light of his oil lamp, until I joined him where he squatted.

'You see, I have found what is left of Father Augustin,' he pointed out. 'The head is not here, but I know his body well. His hands were so deformed, they are unmistakable. His feet, too – you see? Only one. This, I am sure, is the upper portion of his back. Remember how he stooped . . . the curvature is distinctive. His arms were very thin and feeble.'

I turned away.

'The rest are more difficult. Of course there are two heads, and we can, to some degree, distinguish between certain types by the consistency and colour of their body hair. Father Augustin's hair is grey, so we can put all the grey hair in that group. We also have black and brown, and the black is thick and coarse, whereas the brown seems finer. But there is also some thicker brown, and three arms with black hair – therefore one must take into account the differences between hairs growing on diverse parts of the body – '

'Uh – Brother? Would you speculate that this was done with an axe?'

'I would speculate that it *had* to be done with an axe. Look how the spines are cut through! I doubt it could be done with a sword.'

'Would you have to be very strong, then? To do this?'

Brother Amiel hesitated. 'You would have to be strong enough to chop wood,' he said at last. 'I have seen children chopping wood, and pregnant women. But not invalids.'

'Of course.'

'"I will praise Thee, for I am fearfully and wonderfully made",' Brother Amiel murmured, '"... and in Thy book all my members were written, which in continuance were fashioned ..." If we had the Lord's book, Brother, we should be able to identify every last piece.'

'Undoubtedly.'

'I fear that they will have to be buried in one grave,' the Infirmarian continued, 'and even then, what will happen at the Resurrection? How can Father Augustin rise to face God's judgement when his head is lost in the mountains, some-where?'

'Yes indeed,' I muttered, then lifted my own head as his observation cut through my queasiness like the clear, clean chime of a bell. Could *this* be the reason for dismembering Father Augustin? Was it the intention of his killers that he be denied resurrection?

I found it difficult to believe that anyone would have been so impassioned in their hatred of him.

'If these had been dry-salted, I would be much happier,' Brother Amiel went on to complain. 'Rotten meat cannot be preserved properly in brine. But I daresay that the salt supply in Casseras would have been insufficient – '

'Um ... I can identify the heads, Brother.' I had found

myself looking at them, and it had occurred to me that they were recognisable – if only by their beards. 'This is Giraud, and this Bertrand.'

'Ah? Good. And which was the taller?'

'That I cannot tell you.'

'We are desperately short of members, here. There are only five feet.'

By this time I was growing quite dizzy from the stench, but knew that it behoved me to remain, if only that I might be of comfort to Matheva. She was a small and delicate woman, recently recovered from a feverish illness; as I had feared, she exhibited acute manifestations of profound anguish upon seeing her husband's head, and had to be carried out of the stables. As for the sergeants, they too were of little help: one vomited on the stairs (though he insisted later that he had been poisoned by a bad egg), and the rest were apparently of an unobservant nature, responding to Brother Amiel's queries with blank expressions and gruff pleas for forgiveness.

Even so, the Infirmarian was partially successful in his appointed task. By Compline he had sorted the remains into four groups: one comprising the members of Father Augustin, one comprising those of Giraud Gantier, one comprising 'black-haired portions' – of which there was a most confusing abundance – and one comprising the head of Bertrand Borrel, together with various pieces (mostly hairless) which were impossible to classify. Each of these distinct collections having been wrapped in a separate sheet, they were borne away to the priory, so that only the salting barrels were left.

I gave orders that these were to remain where they stood, until I was able to inquire of their owners whether they should be returned or simply destroyed. I could not imagine anyone wanting to keep them, but knew that the proprieties had to be observed. It would be easy enough to settle the matter when I visited Casseras; the only effort involved would be committing such a minor concern to memory. I doubted very much that the villagers even expected to see their barrels again.

In regard to my visit, I was able to arrange an escort of twelve sergeants-at-arms from the city garrison. The Seneschal even lent me his own battle-mount, a great black stallion called Star, who impressed me as a beast of the most intimidating prowess, surpassing an elephant in size, a bull in strength, and a tiger in speed. But before describing the course and outcome of this journey, I wish to record here two notions which crossed my mind during the three days which elapsed before I set out. The first was an addendum to my theory concerning Father Augustin's dismemberment; the second, an entirely new theory which struck me with the force of a tempest one night, as I was lying in bed. Both are worth considering, since they modified my perceptions thereafter.

I shall begin with the addendum, which occurred to me when I was in conversation with the Bishop. Once again, I have omitted an important *effictio*, in my neglect of the Bishop, whose position alone should have ensured him a personal appearance in this narrative long since. But perhaps you have already met him? If not, let me introduce you to Anselm de Villelongue, a former Cistercian abbot turned prelate, at least two-score years of earnest self-advancement behind him, skilled in the arts of poetry and hunting, confidante of several highly placed lords and ladies (especially ladies), a man whose heart and soul are wed, not to the base obsessions of local politics, but to the far more exalted realms of diplomacy among counts and kings. Bishop Anselm presides over the spiritual concerns of his flock with a polite and abstracted indifference, allowing the duly appointed authorities to act as they see fit. He spends a good deal of his time writing letters – and will probably be elected Pope one day. As to his appearance, he is neither too fat nor too thin, too tall nor too short; he wears fine clothes and eats delicate foods; he has a pleasant, kindly smile, beautiful teeth, and a smooth, round face with an even colour.

His hands are thick and stumpy, but he nevertheless draws attention to them with his enviable array of jewels. One must search very hard, I assure you, to find the episcopal ring to kiss. If you should comment on this display, he will very generously provide you with a history of each article, citing its worth, its former owners, and the means by which it came into his possession – usually as a gift. *The poor is hated even of his own neighbour: but the rich hath many friends.* Bishop Anselm's friends are legion, and growing in number every day; few, however, are of local provenance. Perhaps the citizens of Lazet are weary of trying to capture his attention.

It was necessary, for example, to discuss at great length the various features and foibles of Bishop Anselm's missing horses, before the Seneschal and I could shepherd him towards more gainful topics. We were sitting in his reception room, as I recall – on damask cushions in carved chairs – and even Roger Descalquencs had lost patience with all this chatter about hocks and spavins long before the Bishop had exhausted his own interest in the mysteries of horse breeding. (I have always wondered: is the Bishop insensitive only to the boredom of his inferiors, or do the likes of the Count of Foix and the Archbishop of Narbonne also find horseflesh and jewellery subjects of vital concern?) At any rate, I remember that I was describing to Bishop Anselm the exact condition of the murdered men, while he sat there wearing a pained look – but rather more as if he had bitten into a sour grape than as if the sins of the world were rending the caul of his heart – and I was telling him also that much of Father Augustin's corpse was still missing, though it appeared that another head had been found near a village towards the coast (along with one of the Bishop's missing horses). This head was being transported to Lazet even then; God willing, Brother Amiel would identify it as belonging to Father Augustin.

'Brother Amiel says that there are still insufficient members,' I explained. 'He says that he could not piece together four bodies with what he has, let alone five.'

'God have mercy.'

'Whoever did it must have been full of rage,' the Seneschal

interrupted. 'Father Bernard thinks that it might have something to do with the Resurrection.'

'The Resurrection?' Bishop Anselm echoed. 'How is that?'

I was then obliged to repeat my theory, and did so with some reluctance, for I still regarded it as improbable. The Bishop shook his head.

'O ye sons of men, how long will ye turn My glory into shame?' he intoned. 'What a monstrous act, to deny a soul his final salvation! Undoubtedly this is the work of heretics.'

'Well ... no, my lord,' I said, realising even as I spoke the full implications of what I had proposed. 'In fact, the Cathari do not believe in bodily resurrection.'

'Oh.'

'There are, of course, the *Waldensian* heretics,' I continued, 'but I have never encountered a Waldensian. I have only read about them.'

The Bishop waved his hand dismissively. 'All progeny of the hateful power,' he replied. 'And you said earlier that the man who discovered my horse – or the horse that appears to be mine – you say he is a monk?'

'A Franciscan, my lord, yes.'

'A man beyond reproach?'

'So it seems. He claims to have found it wandering in his priory's own grazing lands. We have sent for him, naturally.'

'And he is bringing the horse with him?'

'I believe he will be riding it, yes.'

'Oh?' The Bishop clicked his tongue. 'How worrisome. So many Franciscans are like bags of meal, in the saddle. It comes of their walking everywhere.'

Apprehensive, no doubt, that the conversation would turn once more to matters equine, the Seneschal quickly interjected. 'My lord, we have been questioning your ostler,' he said. 'It seems that only four people were told of Father Augustin's visit to Casseras: your ostler, two of the stablehands, and yourself, of course. The ostler mentioned it to one of the canons. Did *you* mention it to anyone? Anyone at all?'

The Bishop, however, had not been attending — lost, perhaps, in his concern as to the wellbeing of any horse mounted by a Franciscan. 'Mention what?' he inquired.

'My lord, Father Augustin's visit to Casseras.'

'I had no idea he was going to Casseras.'

'Then no one asked your permission? To borrow the horses?'

'Oh, the *horses*. Yes, of course.'

So we struggled on, as if through a lake of mud, and a somewhat futile endeavour it was. That night, however, I was reviewing the conversation in my mind when my thoughts became centred on a particular remark that I had made: namely, '*He says that he could not piece together four bodies with what he has, let alone five.*' It had been a curiously unpalatable observation, though powerful in its depiction of Brother Amiel's difficulties. Its full — indeed, its literal — meaning did not become apparent to me until that moment. I remember I opened my eyes suddenly, and stared into the darkness with my heart pounding.

Brother Amiel could not make up five bodies. One might speculate, therefore, that only four bodies were present.

My thoughts seemed to snag on this supposition for a long, long time; then, with a jolt or stagger, they leapt forward and began to race along the paths of reason with the speed of a lightning bolt. Perhaps the best *translatio* I could use would be to compare this phenomenon to a mouse surprised in a barn: first, in shock, it will stay motionless; then, in fright, it will flee. My thoughts fled hither and thither like a frightened mouse — I asked myself question after question. Were only four men killed? Had the other been kidnapped or, more believably, had this one man been a traitor? Had the bodies been torn apart and widely scattered to conceal his absence? Had the clothes been removed to facilitate such a deception?

I realised that my new theory accounted for several features of the massacre which had remained mysterious in our eyes. It accounted for the odd combination of savagery and thoroughness inherent in the labour of chopping someone to pieces. It accounted for the missing clothes. And it accounted for the source of information regarding Father Augustin's visit to Casseras. After all, who would know his movements better than one of his bodyguards?

The familiars had always been instructed as to their duties the evening before Father Augustin left. A traitor, therefore, would have been given sufficient time to alert his homicidal cronies, who in turn would have commenced their journey at once (and spent the night on the road), or, alternatively, at first light. In the latter case they might even have followed Father Augustin – at a discreet distance – knowing that they would be able to prepare their ambush while he was visiting the forcia.

And then? Then, on his way back to Casseras, Father Augustin would have been led straight to his death by the traitor beside him. Afterwards, this pestiferous hypocrite would have fled, seeking refuge in some distant land. I wondered who might have paid him for his treachery, because he could not have hired his fellow brigands on a familiar's wage; I also wondered where he was now, if he was not dead – for you must understand that this theory was still a theory. I had no proof, none whatsoever, and could not be sure that my suspicions were justified.

But if they were, then the identity of the traitor would be easy enough to establish, providing that the third head, now on its way to Lazet, did not belong to Father Augustin. If it did, then we were faced with a choice of two suspects: Jordan Sicre and Maurand d'Alzen. As I drifted off to sleep, I vowed that I would inquire into the histories of these two men.

I also vowed that I would keep my suspicions to myself, until further evidence arose which might support them. I did not want to be precipitate in announcing that one of Father Augustin's killers had been nurtured in the bosom of the Holy Office. Admissions of this sort are difficult to retract, if they prove to be mistaken – perhaps because so many people would like them to be true.

A most famous proverb is related of a certain Greek, and said to have been found on the tripod of Apollo: 'Know thyself, and see thouself as thou art'. There is nothing clearer in human nature, nothing of greater value, nothing, finally, more excellent. It is through these qualities that man is, by a singular prerogative, preferred to all sensible creatures, and is joined also, by a bond of unity, to those incapable of sensitivity.

I have striven to see myself as I am, and in doing so, have recognised a shameful lack of humility in my arrogant self-will, my flouting of the Lord's commandments, my belief that I could visit Casseras, that abode of danger, without falling into peril. I was advised against it by the Seneschal; I was advised against it by Raymond Donatus and Durand Fogasset; I was advised against it by Prior Hugues. And instead of submitting myself with all obedience to my superior (imitating our Lord, of whom the Apostle saith 'He was made obedient even unto death'), I ignored every plea with a blameworthy insolence, stubbornly adhering to my purpose, and therefore engendering the kind of punishment that I should have anticipated – since we are warned in the Scriptures not to follow our own wills.

I shall omit any description of the journey, which is of no great relevance, except to say that my passage was noted and much commented upon, owing to the number of my retainers. Indeed, I felt rather like a king or bishop with my twelve heavily armed guardians riding all around me. They were, for the most part, men of lowly origins, crude in their manners and rough in their speech. I sensed that some of them were perhaps not entirely pleased to be included in the excursion, more on account of my own presence than because of any risks that they were slated to run: at first I suspected that this dissatisfaction stemmed from an aversion to the Holy Office, but gradually came to realise that they were uncomfortable when obliged to remain in close proximity to anyone with a tonsure. It appeared that they were not much accustomed to prayer or worship. They knew their *pater noster*, and their Creed, and attended church on certain feast days, some even confessed themselves devoted to particular saints (chiefly the warrior saints, such as George and Maurice). For the most part, however, they seemed to regard the Church as a kind of strict and tiresome parent, always chastising them for their sins, as rich as Solomon but stingy, withall – the customary view of people whose life precludes much in the way of spiritual practice or insight. They are not heretics, these people, for they believe what the Church tells them to believe; however, they are the stuff from which heretics are often made. As St Bernard of Clairvaux reminds us, the slave and the mercenary have a law of their own, which is not from the Lord.

I should add that I discovered all this not through close questioning, which would have confirmed their worst fears about the Holy Office, but after complimenting them on the condition and design of their weaponry. There is nothing closer to a soldier's heart than his sword or mace or spear; by admiring these sinister objects I reassured their owners, and by exchanging pleasantries about the Bishop (God forgive me, but there is no one more despised in the whole of Lazet) I endeared myself further. By the time we reached Casseras, our party was in a pleasantly congenial temper, though tired and in need of refreshment. Indeed, one of the guards went so far as to congratulate me on being 'not at all like a monk' – something of which I am frequently accused by my brethren, though in a very different tone.

Casseras is a walled village, having no castle nearby to which the villagers might flee in times of peril. (The forcia is but a fortified farm, and of fairly recent construction.) Fortunately, the disposition of the land is such that it allows the houses to be built in concentric rings around the church; if the village had been positioned on steeper ground, this would not have been possible. Two wells are sheltered behind the walls, as well as several gardens and threshing floors, two dozen fruit trees and a couple of barns. The whole place smells strongly of manure. Naturally my arrival was greeted with astonishment, and perhaps some apprehension, until I was able to inform the inhabitants that my enormous retinue did not pose a threat to them, but had been brought along in case *they* posed a threat to *me*. Many laughed when I said this, but others were affronted. They assured me angrily that they had not been involved in Father Augustin's murder.

Father Paul seemed pleased that I was well protected. Unlike so many priests in similar remote villages – who regard themselves as little lords, beyond the reach of episcopal authority – he is a good and humble servant of Christ, somewhat careworn, perhaps a trifle too submissive to the desires of the wealthy Bruno Pelfort, but on the whole a reliable and earnest parish priest. He professed himself happy to accommodate me that night, apologising, as he did so, for the nature of his hospitality, which he described as 'very simple'. Naturally, I commended him for this, and we talked for a while about the virtues of poverty, though taking care not to adopt an over-emphatic stance – neither of us being Franciscan monks.

Then I told him that I wished to visit the forcia before sundown. He offered to accompany me, so that he might point out the scene of the massacre, and I readily agreed to his proposal. In order that he might keep pace with the rest of us, I insisted that one of my bodyguards surrender his horse to the priest and remain in the village until we returned: I had barely finished speaking before the soldier to my right had leapt from his saddle. (I wondered later if the wealth of pretty girls in Casseras might have contributed to his haste.) There followed a burst of activity which I shall not bother to relate here, and we set off while the sun was still high in the western sky. By some mysterious means, during our brief delay at Casseras, many of my guards had acquired hunks of bread and smoked pork, which they generously shared with those of us whose allure was not as powerful or productive. I could not help but speculate as to what else they might receive during their night in Bruno Pelfort's barn.

I have already described the path to the forcia. To me, the dry ruts and encroaching foliage seemed ominous – threatening – though I understand that my perceptions were coloured, somewhat, by my knowledge of what they had silently witnessed. It was very warm; the sky was hard and pale and cloudless; the birds were largely mute. Insects buzzed, leather creaked. Occasionally, one of the sergeants would spit or belch. No one appeared much inclined to converse; the riding was so difficult that it required concentration.

I did not have to be alerted, when we reached the site of Father Augustin's death, because the blood was still visible. Though some of it was obscured by dust or dry leaves, a good many dark stains could be detected – unmistakable, not on account of their colour, but because of their shape: drops and smears, pools, sprays, trickles. Even my escort was subdued by these traces, and by the faint but inescapable smell of corruption. I dismounted, and said a few prayers; Father Paul followed my lead. The rest of the party remained in the saddle, watching for any sign of a threat. Our fears, however, were groundless – no one attacked us on our way to the forcia. No one even emerged from the woods to stare, or greet us. There seemed to be no one around at all.

We reached the forcia quite suddenly, for the lay of the land is such that one approaches it up a steep slope like a hill, except that the crest of the hill is cut off sharply to form a triangular plateau. It is on this plateau, girded by lofty peaks, that the forcia is constructed; it stands in the middle of poorly cleared grazing land, some distance from that point at which the path gains the plateau. Therefore the traveller has no glimpse of his destination until he completes his climb.

Then he is confronted by a distant stone wall, clearly ruinous and pierced by an undefended gateway. The gateway opens onto a kind of bailey, which encircles, not a fortified tower, but a very large, very dilapidated house. Although much of its shingle roof has collapsed, the fact that part of it was inhabited, at the time of which I speak, could be deduced from the drift of smoke mounting into the sky above it. Other signs of habitation were the fowl strutting across the beaten earth of the bailey, and the garments draped along a low wall, which might once have belonged to a barn, before it was dismantled. The remains of several outbuildings, built at intervals against the enclosing wall, could still be seen. Undoubtedly this farm had once been a wealthy and prosperous possession.

What it now was I could not quite discern, at first glance. Although rather impoverished in appearance, it did not have the disreputable look of a lepers' refuge, or indeed the odd shepherds' cabin of my acquaintance. A single glance was enough to tell me that someone had been sweeping the yard around the house, and assiduously tending the garden planted under the southern wall. The chickens had a sleek, well-nurtured plumpness. There was no litter of old bones and nut shells underfoot, nor any smell of excrement hovering in the air. Indeed, the air was scented with the perfume of various herbs laid out to dry in the sun; it was also redolent of that inexplicable, almost exultant purity which seems to come with the proximity of mountains.

I noticed all this even as a woman emerged from the house – drawn, no doubt, by the noise of our arrival. Not wishing to alarm her, I dismounted some distance away, and approached her on foot, with Father Paul close behind me. I realised at once that she was not the young woman of Father Augustin's letter. She must have been nearly my age, and while very handsome indeed – quite the most ornamental matron that I had encountered for many years – she could not have been described as a woman of 'great beauty'. Her thick, dark hair was streaked with grey; her figure was tall and straight and imposing; she had fine features evenly distributed around a rather long face, and a calm but critical gaze (*in whose sight shall no man living be justified*). Only her skin was truly beautiful, as white as the heavenly robes of the martyrs. With her immaculate grooming, her firm though graceful stance, the very manner in which she had arranged her hair – with all these things, she seemed to transform her surroundings, so that where formerly I had noticed the dirt and the desolation, I now became aware of the imposing mountainous vista, the neatness of the vegetable garden, the delicate and colourful figures woven into the blanket which had been spread on the ground beneath the aforesaid drying herbs. While the place was not one in which she seemed to belong, exactly, her very presence served to elevate or refine it, so that one regarded it differently, as one might regard a piece of rag or a fragment of wood that has been touched by a saint. Not that I would describe this woman as saintly – quite the opposite! I simply wish to convey the impression I gathered, from her appearance, that she had been born and bred among people accustomed to rich and beautiful things.

Yet for all this she was wearing very simple clothes, and her hands were dirty.

'Father Paul!' she exclaimed, then turned to me, bowing. The priest traced a cross in the air above her head, blessing her.

'Johanna,' he said, 'this is Father Bernard Peyre de Prouille, from Lazet.'

'Welcome, Father.'

'He wants to talk to you about Father Augustin.'

'Yes. I understand.' The widow (for so it was) spoke in a soft and musical voice, very pleasant to the ear, and oddly out of keeping with the directness of her gaze. She had the voice of a nun and the eyes of a judge. 'Come this way, please.'

'How is Vitalia?' Father Paul inquired, as we moved towards the house. 'Is she any better?'

'Not at all.'

'Then we must pray, and pray hard.'

'Yes, Father, I have been praying. Will you come in, please?'

Stopping at a doorway in the northern wall of the house, she gathered up the curtain that fell across it, and stood back so that we might enter. I must confess that I hesitated, wondering fleetingly if an assassin lay in wait for me on the other side of the door. Father Paul, however, had no such qualms, perhaps because this territory was familiar to him; he proceeded fearlessly, and could be heard greeting some unseen host – without violent interruption – soon after crossing the threshold.

I therefore followed him, conscious of the widow behind me.

'Vitalia, I have brought Father Augustin's friend to visit you,' Father Paul was saying. In the dim light I could see him standing over a low bed, or pallet, in which lay the tiny, huddled form of an old woman. At the other end of the room, which was quite large, stood a brazier; since there was no hearth, I surmised that the original kitchen was not habitable, and that this had been built as a bedroom or storeroom of some kind.

There was hardly any furniture – just the old woman's bed, a table made from a worm-eaten door placed on cut stones, and some benches constructed on the same principle. But I noticed that the cooking utensils were numerous and (as far as I am qualified to pass judgement) of good quality, as were the bedclothes, the food storage equipment, the brazier itself. I also noticed a book. It was sitting on the table, like a cup or a piece of cheese, and exerted upon me an irresistible fascination. Most Dominicans of my acquaintance are incapable of ignoring a book: do you find it so?

Surreptitiously I picked it up, and examined it. To my surprise, I found it to be a translation, in the vulgar tongue, of Hildegard of Bingen's *Scivias*. Poorly transcribed, incomplete, with no title given, it was recognisable to me because I am familiar with the works of Abbess Hildegard. The words I read were unmistakable: 'The visions I saw neither in sleep, nor madness, nor with my carnal eyes, nor with fleshly ears, nor in hidden places; but awake, alert, and with the eyes of the spirit and the inward ears, I look on them in the open and according to the will of God.' (Execrable translation.)

'Whose book is this?' I inquired.

'It belongs to Alcaya.' The widow answered me, and I saw that she was smiling. 'Alcaya can read.'

'Oh.' For some reason, I had expected that she herself would be the literate one. 'And where is Alcaya?'

'Alcaya is with my daughter, gathering wood.'

This was a disappointment, for I had wanted to meet the daughter – who was, I felt sure, the young woman mentioned by Father Augustin. But her mother, no doubt, would provide me with at least some information.

So I expressed the wish that she would join me in a private place, where we would discuss certain matters relating to Father Augustin and his death.

'We can talk in the bedroom,' she replied. 'Through here.'

'And I shall stay with Vitalia,' Father Paul suggested. 'We shall pray to God in His mercy. Would you like that, Vitalia?'

Whether Vitalia agreed or objected, nodded or shook her head, I shall never know – because I was in the bedroom before the priest had finished speaking. Evidently this room had once boasted a hinged door and shutters, but every trace of them had been removed long since; the openings that remained were now hidden behind lengths of cheap cloth, which were nailed to the wooden lintels. There were three pallets in the room, and a very impressive, carved and painted wedding chest. I examined it curiously.

'That is mine,' the widow remarked. 'I brought it here.'

'It is very handsome.'

'It was made in Agde. Where I was born.'

'You came here from Agde?'

'From Montpellier.'

'Ah? I studied theology in Montpellier.'

'Yes, I know.' As I looked up in surprise, she added: 'Father Augustin told me.'

I considered her for a moment. She stood with her hands folded at her waist, watching me with some interest, and with no fear whatsoever. Her demeanour puzzled me. It was so unlike that of most women, when they are confronted by a representative of the Holy Office – and yet it was not in the least insolent or aggressive.

'My daughter,' I said, 'Father Augustin visited you here many times, so I feel sure that you must have talked of many things. But what was the purpose of his visits? Why did you need him so urgently? Surely for spiritual advice you could have gone to Father Paul?'

The widow seemed to think. At last she said: 'Father Paul is very busy.'

'No busier than Father Augustin was.'

'True,' she agreed. 'But Father Paul has no legal knowledge.'

'*Legal* knowledge?'

'I am involved in a property dispute. Father Augustin was advising me.'

She spoke carefully, and with an obvious lack of candour, but I retained the amiable visage which it is my custom to assume on these occasions.

'What kind of property dispute?' I asked.

'Oh, Father, I would not impose on your time.'

'Yet you were willing enough to impose on Father Augustin's.'

'Only because he was not as pleasing in his ways as you are, Father.'

Her smile, as she said this, unsettled me somewhat, for it contradicted the glint in her eye. On her mouth was a simper; in her glance was a challenge.

I pondered this curious contiguity.

'My ways can be as displeasing as any man's,' I replied, in gentle tones, but with a certain unequivocal emphasis. And to demonstrate that I was not easily deflected from my course, I added: 'Tell me about the property dispute.'

'Oh, a sad affair.'

'In what way?'

'It has disturbed my sleep.'

'For what reason?'

'Because it is so desperate and complicated . . .'

'Perhaps I can help.'

'No one can help.'

'Not even Father Augustin?'

'Father Augustin is dead.'

I began to feel as if I were playing chess (a pastime which occupied me greatly before I took my vows). Sighing, I recommenced my attack using somewhat blunter weapons.

'Kindly explain to me this property dispute,' I said.

'Father, it is much too boring.'

'Let me be the judge of that.'

'But Father, I *cannot* explain.' She spread her hands. 'I cannot explain because I have no understanding. I am a simple woman. An ignorant woman.'

And I, Madame, am a leper king, was my immediate response to this remark (so manifestly disingenuous). But I refrained from uttering the thought aloud. Instead I observed that, if she had indeed sought help from Father Augustin, she must have had some means of communicating her difficulties.

'He read the papers,' she replied. 'There are documents – '

'Let me see them.'

'I cannot. I gave them to Father Augustin.'

Suddenly I became impatient. It does not often happen, I assure you, but my time was not limitless, and she had exhibited an almost insolent subtlety in her rejoinders. It behoved me, I thought, to show her that I was aware of certain important facts.

'Father Augustin wrote to the Bishop of Pamiers about your daughter,' I declared. 'He mentioned that she was possessed by a demon. Could that be why you needed his advice, and not the advice of a poorly educated, rural priest?'

To use information in this way is to use it like a weapon. I have done so often, when interrogating witnesses, and the response is always gratifyingly intense. I have seen people gasp, weep and change colour; I have seen them fall to their knees in supplication and claw at my face in fury. But Johanna de

Caussade continued to regard me without a change of expression. Finally she said: 'Augustin often talked about you'. And it was I who responded with a gasp.

Had she *intentionally* omitted that all-important prefix?

'He said that you were very clever and persistent,' she continued, 'and that you worked hard, but that you did not have the soul of an inquisitor. He said that you treated it all as a sport, like hunting pigs – that you did not feel about it as he did. He disapproved of such levity. But I do not.'

Can you imagine my sensations, at this juncture? Can you imagine being told, by a strange *woman*, that your late, revered superior regarded you as deficient in some fundamental impulse? And that she should have the gall to *say* as much! I assure you, I was speechless.

'I think it shows that you have some human weakness, and sympathy,' the widow remarked. Then, without asking permission, she sat on her wedding chest with a sigh. 'I shall tell you this because if I try to conceal it, I know that you will find out regardless. You will never rest until you do. But I would ask that you keep it to yourself, Father; it is not for other ears.'

At last I found my voice. With great relish, I informed her that I could make no such promise.

'No?' She pondered, a little. 'Have you told anyone else about my daughter?'

'Not yet.'

'Then you know how to keep your own counsel,' she said. What a compliment! I, an inquisitor of heretical depravity and long-time confessor to countless brethren – I, Bernard Peyre of Prouille – had been judged as a man capable of keeping my own counsel!

Suddenly I was angry no longer, but amused. The woman's audacity was so extreme, it almost compelled one's reluctant admiration.

'Yes,' I agreed, folding my arms, 'I know how to keep a secret. But why should I keep yours?'

'Because it is not only mine,' she rejoined. 'You see, my daughter is Augustin's daughter.'

Believe me when I tell you that at first, I did not comprehend the full meaning of this revelation. Then, as her words penetrated the very depths of my soul, I lost command of my body, and had to steady myself against the wall – else I would have collapsed.

'She was born twenty-five years ago,' the widow proceeded to inform me, in a matter-of-fact way, without allowing me time to gather my thoughts. 'I was seventeen, the only daughter of a wealthy importer of fine cloth, and I was very devout. I wanted to become a nun. My father, who desired a grandson, tried to persuade me that I should marry, but I was moved by stories of martyred virgin saints.' Upon making this remark, Johanna smiled a wry little smile. 'I saw myself as the next St Agatha, you understand. My father, in desperation, went to Father Augustin, with whom he was acquainted. At that time, Augustin was forty-two years old, very tall and regal, like a prince. Very learned. Very ...' She paused. 'He had a fire in his belly,' she said at last, 'and it shone out of his eyes. How his eyes stirred me! But I was *very* devout, you must remember. And young. And pretty. And stupid. And when we talked about loving God, I thought about loving Augustin. It seemed the same thing to me, then.'

Suddenly she laughed out loud, and shook her head in wonder. Her disbelief, however, could not match mine. On trying to imagine Father Augustin as an impassioned, vigorous, soul-stirring object of desire, I failed miserably.

'He promised my father that he would look into my heart, to see if I was truly a bride of Christ,' the widow explained. 'We talked several times, sitting in my father's garden, but we talked only of God and Jesus and the saints. The love of the divine. I could have listened to him talk about anything – I could have listened to him reciting the same word, over and over again! It would have made no difference.'

There was another pause. It stretched on until I was obliged to prompt her.

'And then?' I queried.

'And then he decided that I should not be a nun. Of course he must have known that I was in love with him – perhaps he saw me for what I was, an emotional girl with silly ideas. At any rate, he told my father that I would be better off married. He told me the same thing. And he was right, you know, he was quite right.' The widow nodded to herself, her demeanour suddenly serious; she was not looking at me, but at the wall behind me. 'Even so, I was very unhappy – I felt so betrayed. When I met him in the street one day I refused to look at him, or speak to him. I walked straight past. Such a stupid, childish thing to do. But would you believe it, Father ...' (Here she laughed again.) '... would you believe it, I offended him dreadfully! I think I offended his pride. He came to my house, and I was alone, and we had such an argument. It ended as you might expect: I was weeping, and he took me in his arms ... well, you can guess what happened.'

I could, but I tried not to. Harbouring such impure thoughts is hardly better than acting upon them.

'It was only the once, because – well, because he was so ashamed. I know that he never forgave himself; he had broken his vows, you see. And then I found myself with child. I told no one, but a child is something you cannot hide forever. My father saw what had happened, and beat me until I gave him Augustin's name. Poor Augustin was sent away – I never knew where. His Prior was very eager that no scandal should attach itself to Augustin – or to the priory – so the whole matter became a great secret, by God's grace. As for me, with the aid of an enormous dowry my father persuaded Roger de Caussade to marry me and support my child. My only child. My daughter.' At last, the widow looked at me. 'Augustin's daughter.'

This, then, was Johanna's tale. I did not find it incredible; I believed every word, though my imagination failed me (thanks be to God) when I tried to picture Father Augustin passionately embracing a seventeen-year-old girl. I also found it impossible to equate the naive and hot-blooded object of his desire, conjured up before my inner eye like a ghostly apparition, with the woman who sat on the wedding chest, so calm, so self-possessed, so manifestly past her prime. It was as if she spoke of another person altogether.

'And your husband – he is dead, now?' I inquired.

'He is dead, and his brother has taken his house, though my father's property is mine. Roger's family has never liked me. They suspect that my daughter is not his.'

'But what are you doing here?' This was the question uppermost in my mind. 'Did you come here because of Augustin?'

'Oh *no!*' For the first time, she became really animated: she lifted her hands and clasped them under her chin. 'No, no. I had no idea where he was.'

'Then why?'

'Because of my daughter. I had to find a place for my daughter.'

In response to some delicate but persistent questioning, she revealed that her daughter, while a sweet and beautiful girl, had never been 'quite well'. Even as a small child, she had been troubled by nightmares, sudden rages, periods of unnatural lethargy. Fiery sermons had moved her to weep uncontrollably and mutilate her own flesh. At the age of twelve, she had experienced a 'vision of devils', and had begun to scream every time her cousin approached her, saying that he was surrounded by a 'dark halo'. Her troubles had worsened with the passing of the years: she would fall to the ground, spitting and screaming and biting her tongue; sometimes she would sit in corners, rocking back and forth, uttering gibberish; sometimes she would scream repeatedly, for no apparent reason.

'And yet she is a good girl,' Johanna insisted. 'Such a good, sweet, pious girl. She has done no wrong. She is like a little child. I *cannot* understand – '

' "Such knowledge is too wonderful for me; it is high, I

cannot attain unto it." The Lord's ways are mysterious, Johanna.'

'Yes, so I was told,' she replied, rather impatiently. 'I went to many priests and nuns, and they told me that God's punishments could be cruel. Some of them told me she was plagued by a devil. People would throw stones at her in the streets because she was screaming and spitting. My husband grew to fear her so much that he refused to let her in the house. No one would marry her. I had no choice; she was sent to live in a convent. She wanted to go, and I thought it might help her. I paid all her dowry over to the Church. If it had been any smaller, she would have been turned away, I think.'

'Do you?' Although there is a great lack of charity in the world, I could not believe that somewhere, among all the communities devoted to Christ's service, there was not one to which the succour of a haunted soul would fail to recommend itself. God knows, I have met enough maimed and bedeviled monks, in my time. 'But she was admitted, at last.'

'Yes, for her sins. They tried to *beat* the demons out of her! They told me that she was dying, and when I came to see her, she was lying in her own ... her own filth.' The memory still affected Johanna; she flushed slightly as she recounted it, and her voice trembled. 'So I took her away. My husband had died, so I took her away. I went to Montpellier, where no one knew us well enough to stone her in the streets. And I met Alcaya.'

'Ah yes. Alcaya.' Alcaya, it transpired, was the granddaughter of that very Raymond-Arnaud de Rasiers who had built the house in which we were sitting. As a small child, she had been sent from her home to live with relatives in Montpellier, after her parents had died in prison. She had married, but had deserted her husband to live, for a time, with some religious people. (Johanna spoke of these people so vaguely, with such an evident lack of understanding, that I was unable to identify them.) When Johanna met her, Alcaya was living what might best be described as a mendicant life, begging for food, sleeping under the roofs of charitable friends, spending much of her time sitting beside municipal wells talking to the women who were collecting water. Sometimes she would read to them from one of the three books that she carried with her. It seemed to me, from what I heard, that she saw herself as a preacher – and I found this very troubling.

'One day my daughter fell down in the street,' Johanna related, 'and someone threw a bucket at her. Everyone was frightened by her screams, except Alcaya. Alcaya took my daughter in her arms, and prayed. She told me that Babilonia was special, and close to God; she spoke of many female saints (I cannot remember their names, Father) who, when they saw God, wept for days, or danced about like drunkards, or screamed without cease until they awoke from their trance. She said that my daughter was exalted in her love of God.' The widow looked at me in a worried, hesitant fashion. 'Is that true, Father? Do saints behave like that?'

There can be no doubt that many holy women (and men) have been driven to conduct which might appear almost deranged, in their mystical exaltation. They rave of visions; they appear dead; they spin about or speak in tongues. I have read of such holy madness, though I have never witnessed it.

'Some blessed servants of God have been driven to strange acts, in their ecstasy,' I replied, with some caution. 'I have not heard, however, that they are given to biting their tongues. Do *you* think that your daughter is ... um ... entering into the joy of the Lord, when she falls down and bites her tongue?'

'No,' the widow replied, bluntly. 'If God is with her, then why are people afraid? Why was Augustin afraid? He thought it the work of Satan, not God.'

'And you?'

The woman sighed, as if weary of confronting a dilemma that had grown old and stale. 'I know only this,' she said flatly. 'I know that she is better when she eats well, and sleeps well, and is free to roam where she chooses, without being troubled. I know that she is better when she is loved. Alcaya loves her.

Alcaya can soothe her, and make her happy. So I have come here with Alcaya.'

'And why did Alcaya come?' I inquired. 'To claim her inheritance? This place belongs to the King, now.'

'Alcaya wanted to find peace. We all wanted to find peace. Vitalia, too. She has had a hard life.'

'*Peace*?' I exclaimed, and she caught my meaning at once.

'It *was* peaceful here. Before Augustin came.'

'He wanted you to leave.'

'Yes.'

'He was right. You cannot live here in winter.'

'No. In winter, we shall go elsewhere.'

'You should go now. It is unsafe.'

'Perhaps,' she said quietly, her gaze on the floor.

'Perhaps? You saw what happened to Father Augustin!'

'Yes.'

'You think yourself defended from such a fate?'

'Perhaps.'

'Indeed? And why might that be?'

'Because I am not an inquisitor.'

She raised her eyes as she said this, and I saw in them no trace of tears. The look on her face was grim, exhausted, impatient. I said to her, with genuine curiosity: 'Did you welcome Father Augustin back into your life? Or did he trouble you?'

'He had a right to trouble me. Babilonia is his, as well as mine.'

'He was concerned for Babilonia?'

'Of course. He had no interest in me. But when Father Paul told him our names, he wanted to see his daughter. He ran a great risk, you know. I could have shamed him before the world, when he arrived here with his guards. I could have revealed everything – he had no assurance that I would not. Yet he came. He came to meet Babilonia.' The widow shook her head. 'And when he did, he said nothing. He seemed unmoved. A strange man.'

'And when he saw you? How did he react then?'

'Oh, he was angry with me. He was angry with me for bringing Babilonia to this place.' Johanna's puzzled expression became sardonic. 'He *hated* Alcaya.'

'Why?'

'Because she argued with him.'

'I see.' In fact, I saw only too well. Johanna's *notatio* of her friend was not an appealing one. It seemed that Alcaya was perilously unorthodox in her behaviour, if not in her beliefs. 'Would Alcaya have wished him dead, do you think?'

'*Alcaya?*' the widow cried. She gazed at me in astonishment, then burst out laughing. But her laughter was quickly extinguished. 'You cannot believe that Alcaya killed Augustin,' she said. 'How can you think such a thing?'

'Consider, Madame, that I have never met Alcaya. How would I know what she is capable of?'

'They were hacked to pieces! Five grown men!'

'Assassins can be hired.'

She peered at me in such dismay — such manifest perplexity — that I found myself smiling. 'I will admit, however, that she is not high on my list of suspects,' I added.

She seemed to accept this; our conversation turned to other topics, drifting from the weather to Montpellier to Father Augustin's manifold virtues. Culpably, perhaps, I found it a great relief to discuss my superior with someone who had known him intimately, and who was not a fellow monk.

'He *drove* himself,' she remarked at one point. 'He despised his own weakness. I told him: "You are too sick. If you must come, then stay longer". But he refused.'

'He was an ardent soul,' I agreed. 'Awake all night — living on kitchen scraps. He must have felt that his life was drawing to a close.'

'Oh no, it was ever thus. It was his nature. A good man, but almost too good. If you know what I mean.'

'I do, yes. Too good to live with.' I laughed. 'And is your daughter the same?'

'Not at all. She is good like a lamb. Augustin was good like ... like ...'

'An eagle.' I reminded her, gently, that she should be referring to him as 'Father' Augustin. 'I wonder – did he often think of her, over the years? If I had a child, I would pray for her every day.'

'You are not like Aug – like Father Augustin.'

'No need to remind me of *that*, I assure you. My faults are many.'

'So are mine. He was always telling me so.'

'The chastisement of your peace,' I said, but she missed the allusion. 'Believe me, none of us measured up. And did he scold his daughter, too?'

'Oh, no. Never. You cannot scold Babilonia, because none of her sins are her own.' For the first time, I saw the widow's eyes moisten. 'He loved her. I am sure of that. He had a great heart, but he was ashamed of it. Poor man. Poor man, and I never told her – '

'Never told her what?'

'That he was her father,' the widow sobbed. 'She was afraid of him at first, and I was waiting. She was beginning to know him, and he was beginning to smile at her ... it was so cruel. So cruel.'

'It was,' I said. The sight of her tears had convinced me, as tears so rarely do, that Johanna was in no way responsible for my superior's death. They were not easy tears, you see: they were wrenched out of her, a source of profound shame.

Their softening effect on the parched clay of my affections almost moved me to pat her hand. But I restrained myself.

'Forgive me,' she gasped. 'Forgive me, Father, I have not been sleeping.'

'There is nothing to forgive.'

'I only wish that I had loved him more. He made it so hard.'

'I know.'

'He could be so annoying! I wanted to hit him sometimes,

and when it happened – that terrible thing – I felt as if I had caused it – '

'Would you like me to hear your confession?'

'What?' She looked up, and blinked; she seemed startled. 'Oh, no. No, no,' she said, recovering immediately. 'There is no need for that.'

'Are you sure?'

'I am not *hiding* anything, Father.' Her tone was curt. 'Is that why you came? To find out if I killed him?'

'To find out *who* killed him. And to do that, I must know as much as there is to know. You are an intelligent woman, Johanna – you should understand. What would you do, in my place?'

She looked at me, and her rancour subsided. I could see it flow out of her face. Nodding slowly, she opened her mouth to speak, but was interrupted by a babble of raised voices. It appeared to come, not from the next room, but from further afield. It sounded like an argument.

Alarmed, Johanna and I exchanged questioning glances. Then we hastened outside, to see what was amiss.

For Thy light is come

St Augustin once wrote: 'All things are as present to the blind man as to the seeing. A blind man and one who has sight, standing on the same spot, are each surrounded by the same forms of things; but one is present to them, the other absent ... not because the things themselves approach the one and recede from the other, but on account of the difference of their eyes.'

Now, I have found that this same observation also applies when two people are both sighted. One of them may look and see a certain person, a certain thing, or a certain event, while the other may not, at first, see the same person, or the same thing, or the same event, but another entirely. So it was when the widow and I emerged from the house. My own impression was that my guards (all gathered now in the bailey) seemed to be sharing a jest of some sort, for their demeanour was jovial and relaxed. They had dismounted, and were passing a wineskin from hand to hand.

Johanna, in contrast, saw a band of armed soldiers threatening her dear friend, Alcaya. I know this because she clutched my arm, and said: 'What are they doing?' in a voice urgent with dismay.

'Doing?' I said. 'What do you mean?'

'Those men!'

'They are my retainers.'

'They are threatening her!'

'Do you think so?' Looking again, I saw an elderly woman trying to disarm one of the sergeants, who was successfully eluding her grasp. One of his comrades grabbed her from behind, then collapsed in mock torment, amid much laughter, when she slapped him feebly on the wrist. 'It seems to me that she is threatening *them*.'

Nevertheless I stepped forward, and inquired as to the meaning of this confusion.

'Oh, Father, she wants us to leave!' Evidently, such a request was regarded, by men dedicated to the profession of arms, as a huge joke: something unworthy of serious consideration; a demand which must have been made in the same light-hearted spirit as that in which it was received. 'I told her, we take our orders from the Seneschal!'

'That is Alcaya,' murmured Father Paul, who had followed me from the house. 'Alcaya, what troubles you? These men are here with me.'

'Father, you are welcome. They are welcome. But they have frightened Babilonia. She is hiding on the mountain. She will not come until they go.'

'Oh, but it is so late,' Johanna protested. 'She *must* come down.'

'She will not,' the old woman replied. Studying her, I was surprised to note that her manner was neither belligerent nor in any way overbearing; she wore a serene expression, and her voice, while harsh with the harshness of age, seemed to crackle warmly, like a kitchen fire. She had bright blue eyes (a colour one rarely sees in these parts), and they seemed as innocent as a child's as she looked at me. 'You are a tall man, Father,' she said. 'I have never seen a monk so tall.'

'And you are a small woman.' I was surprised into an infantile retort. 'Though not the smallest I have ever seen.'

'This is Father Bernard Peyre of Prouille,' the priest

interjected. 'You must show him respect, Alcaya, for he is an Inquisitor of heretical depravity, and an important man.'

'I can see that, from the size of his escort.' Alcaya spoke, I am convinced, without any ironical intention; her tone was sweet and grave. 'You are very welcome, Father. We are honoured.' And she bowed low.

'Johanna tells me that you can read,' was my response – for I was interested, intensely interested, in what it was that she read. 'I have seen one of your books, by Abbess Hildegard.'

Alcaya's face brightened. 'Ah!' she exclaimed. 'What a blessed book!'

'Indeed.'

'What wisdom! What devotion! What a pattern of female virtue! Father, have you read this book?'

'Several times.'

'I have read it many times. I have read it to my friends.'

'And your other books? I would like to see your other books. Will you show them to me?'

'Of course! With joy! Come, they are in the house.'

'Wait.' It was Johanna who spoke; she had been watching us carefully (upon catching her eye, I had realised, from the dawning comprehension therein displayed, that Father Augustin must have exhibited a similar interest in Alcaya's reading matter), but now her concern was for her child. 'What about Babilonia? She is scared to come down from the mountain. She cannot stay there, Father, it will be dark soon.'

'Never fear. I shall send my guards away.'

The guards, however, were immovable. They had been instructed not to leave my side, and were firm in their obedience to this command. Nothing that I said would dissuade them. 'If we disobey the Seneschal, he will flay us,' they pointed out, inaccurately. (Roger Descalquencs has never flayed anyone, to my knowledge.) At last they agreed to evacuate the bailey, leaving only one of their number at the door of the house, while the rest defended the gate – which was almost indefensible. With this I had to be satisfied.

'If your daughter is still frightened,' I told Johanna, 'then we shall all leave. But I hope that she returns, for I am anxious to meet her.'

Having said as much, I felt that I had demonstrated my own good intentions. What more could I have done? The widow, however, seemed to expect a good deal more – indeed, she looked at me with an expression of such anxious entreaty that I was discomforted. So I left her, and went into the house, where Alcaya was removing books from her friend's wedding chest.

She handled them lovingly, with great reverence, and placed them into my hands as a mother might place her newborn infant into the arms of a baptising priest.

She was beaming with love and pride.

There were two books: St Bernard of Clairvaux's treatise 'On loving God' and Pierre Jean Olieu's treatise on poverty. Both had been translated into the vernacular, and St Bernard's work was a handsome volume indeed, though very old and in a fragile condition. You will, of course, have read this treatise, and will have rejoiced over that noble commencement: 'You wish me to tell you why and how God should be loved. My answer is that God Himself is the reason why He is to be loved'. Was there ever a more simple, more profound, more exultant *exordium*? (Save that of the Scriptures themselves!) Olieu's work, however, is of an altogether different strain. This dead Franciscan professes himself driven to write it 'because the serpentine cunning of the old Adversary (by which he means the Evil One) continues, as in the past, to stir up trouble against evangelical poverty'. He execrates 'certain pseudo-religious girded with teaching and preaching authority' – namely, Dominicans such as myself – whom he condemns as having abandoned that stringent adherence to poverty which he regards as a requisite for salvation. You may not be familiar with this man's books and pamphlets. You may not be aware that they have inflamed the passions of his fellow Franciscans, in this part of the world. Believe me when I tell you that this obscure southern friar, with his erroneous and extreme notions was, in some small way, responsible for the obduracy of the four Franciscans burned last May in Avignon. Do you recall the case? Like so many other Franciscans, and even lay folk, they were obsessed with the foolish (really, quite unworkable) view that servants of God such as themselves should live as paupers, owning nothing personally nor even in common. They advocated begging in rags, and proclaimed that the Church had become 'Babylon, the great whore, who has ruined and poisoned mankind'! Why did they say this? Because, they maintained, our Holy and Apostolic Church is given over to lust, avarice, pride and concupiscence. Some of their followers even call our Supreme Pontiff the Antichrist, and preach that a new age approaches, in which they themselves will lead Christendom to glory.

Well, I need not remind you of what you must know already; doubtless you are acquainted with the decretal *Gloriosam ecclesiam*, wherein the Holy Father tabulates many of the errors into which 'presumptuous men' have fallen. As an inquisitor of heretical depravity, I was naturally constrained to study this document with great care when it reached the Bishop, for it is a fine distinction that separates those who love poverty and those who worship it above all else – even above proper obedience to apostolic authority. So far, I might add, I had not encountered anyone in Lazet whose beliefs seemed to echo those proscribed by the Holy Father; moreover, none of our Franciscan brethren wore 'short and skimpy' habits (as condemned in that other decretal *Quorundam exigit*, late last year) or testified to the belief that the gospel of Christ had been fulfilled in them alone. Of course, our Franciscan brethren in Lazet are not like many others who dwell in this region. They have not expelled their duly appointed Prior in favour of a candidate more sympathetic to the opinions of Pierre Olieu and his ilk – following the example set by the friars of Narbonne in 1315. Here in Lazet, we are perhaps a little isolated from the passions and new ideas that disturb the peace of other towns. In Lazet, our heresies are very old, and our passions predictable.

But I digress. What I wish to say is that Pierre Jean Olieu's treatise, while it is still read by many worthy folk (increasingly, however, in an attempt to discredit its assertions) ... while it is still widely read, and can be found, for example, in the library of Lazet's own Franciscan friars – it seems to carry a stain, or perhaps exude a dark cloud, especially since the Holy Father commissioned eight theologians to investigate the author's *Lectura*, not long ago. In any event, the treatise now requires an excuse, or explanation.

So I sought one from Alcaya de Rasiers.

'The treatise on poverty,' I muttered, turning over its well-thumbed pages. 'Have you read his commentary on the Apocalypse?'

'The Apocalypse?' said Alcaya, with a blank look.

'Pierre Jean Olieu wrote other books on other subjects. Have you read them?'

'No, alas.' She shook her head, smiling. 'I once heard someone reading from another book which was said to be his. On Evangelical Perfection?'

'*Questions on Evangelical Perfection*. Yes, that would have been his. I have not read it myself.'

'Father Augustin had. He said that it contained many false-hoods.'

'Did he?' Once again, I felt myself to be stumbling about in Father Augustin's footsteps. Naturally, he would have examined Alcaya's soul with great attention. Naturally, he would have had her arrested, if her beliefs were in any way unorthodox.

Or would he?

I found it difficult to accept that Father Augustin would have neglected his religious duty for the sake of his daughter's happiness. On the other hand, I found it just as difficult to imagine him conceiving a daughter in the first place.

'And what did Father Augustin say about *this* book?' I

inquired, indicating the treatise in my hand. 'Did he say that it contained many falsehoods?'

'Oh yes,' the woman replied cheerfully.

'And yet you treasure it, still?'

'He did not say that it was *all* false. Only some things.' She reflected, for an instant. 'He said that it could not be proven that Christ was so poor, from birth to death, that he left nothing to his mother.'

'Ah.'

'I asked him if it could be proven that Christ was *not* poor, from his birth to his death,' Alcaya continued, still smiling, as at a fond memory. 'He said no. We had a fine old talk. He was a very wise man, Father Augustin. A very wise and holy man.'

The thought of my superior debating the *usus pauper* with this dubious old woman – constrained, I doubt not, by the knowledge of how much his daughter loved her – almost brought a smile to *my* face. How frigid his manner would have been! How repellent he would have found the whole act! And how, I am sure, he would have delighted in condemning Alcaya to a formal interrogation, if there had been any reason for doing so. The complacency with which she discussed their 'fine old talk', as if describing an exchange between two washerwomen, set my own teeth on edge.

Nevertheless, it behoved me to allay any doubts that I might have possessed – as carefully as possible.

'Tell me,' I said, reviewing the text of the decretal *Gloriosam ecclesiam* in my mind (for I had no other authority to consult, on this subject), 'did you discuss any other falsehoods with Father Augustin? Did you discuss the Church, and whether she has fallen from the way of Christ, because she is overflowing with riches?'

'Oh yes!' This time Alcaya laughed out loud. 'Father Augustin said to me: "Has anyone ever told you that the Roman Church is a harlot, and that her priests have no authority?" And I said to him: "Yes, Father – *you* just did! Surely you cannot believe such a thing?" He turned as red as bacon! But I meant it in jest,' she added, as if to reassure me. 'Of course he would not believe such a thing.'

'And *you* do not?'

'Oh no.' A placid rejoinder. 'I am a faithful daughter of the Roman Church. I do what the priests tell me to do.'

'But surely the priests did not tell you to leave your husband, or beg in the streets, or come here to live? I must confess, Alcaya, that your life does not appear to be the life of a good Christian woman. It appears to be somewhat perverse – the life of a mendicant. A fugitive.'

For the first time, Alcaya's serenity was shaken. She sighed, and looked sad. Then she placed a hand on my arm, confidingly.

'Father, I have been searching for a way to serve God,' she revealed. 'I did not leave my husband – he threw me out. I had no money, so I was forced to beg. I wanted to join a religious community, but who would take me? Only the Beguines, Father, and what they preached there was wrong.'

'In what way, wrong?'

'Oh, Father, they were very good, very poor folk, who loved Christ and St Francis, but they said terrible things about the Pope. The Pope and the bishops. It made me quite angry.'

'What a sin,' I replied, my pulse racing. 'And did you tell Father Augustin about these people?'

'Oh, yes, Father.'

'And did you tell him their names?'

'Oh, yes.' Upon being questioned further, Alcaya described the community in detail, so that I was able to identify it as a group of Franciscan tertiaries (most of them women) under the protection of a friar who, if he had not been counted among the forty-three required to recant their errors in Avignon last year, certainly should have been. Alcaya also informed me that she had alerted a local priest to what was being preached, among these people, and had deserted them forthwith. 'Then I joined some women connected with *your* Order, Father, but they did not like me. None of them could read, you see, and they feared me and plotted against me.' There followed a long and tedious digression regarding the sort of communal conspiracies, mutual slander and evil-minded retaliations that one so often encounters in families, courts and monastic foundations. Though related to me in accents of sorrow and amazement rather than bitterness and choler, the details were unedifying, and I disregarded them. Suffice it to say that there appeared to be a profound antagonism between Alcaya and a woman called Agnes. 'I was thrown into the street,' Alcaya continued, 'and there I met Babilonia. I saw at once that she was close to God. I thought: could this be God's purpose for me? Should I take these people – like Babilonia and poor Vitalia – and should I lead them to a place where they will be happy in God's love?' Alcaya's voice quickened and became more animated; her expression grew brighter. 'You see, Father, these dear virgins are moved by the purest love of God; they are like those shining daughters of Zion, standing about serene Virginity, wonderfully adorned with gold and gems, as witnessed by Abbess Hildegard. I have spoken to them of their desires, and they wish – so strongly, Father! – they *long* to embrace Christ with a chaste love, they sigh deeply for His presence, they rest peacefully when thinking of Him. They have forsaken the pangs of the flesh, I assure you; I tell them: "The flesh is no use, it is the spirit that gives life," and they know it. I speak to them of their heavenly Bridegroom, who will enter willingly the chamber of their heart if it is decked with the flowers of grace and the fruits of the Passion, picked from the tree of the Cross. We praise him together – we talk of that sweet moment when "His left hand is under my head and his right hand has embraced me". And Babilonia has felt the caress of those hands, Father, she has immersed herself in the love of God. She has seen The Cloud of Living Light, like the Abbess Hildegard.' By now Alcaya's tone was rapturous; her eyes were filled with tears. 'When I read to her the visions of the Abbess's book, she cried out in astonishment.

She recognised the Light within the Light. She had experienced the moment of eternal harmony that dwelt within it. Oh, Father, she has known union with Christ! She has been blinded by the light of Divine Love, she has lost her will, and her soul has come into God. What a blessing, Father! What joy, for all of us!'

'Yes indeed,' I stammered, stunned by this flow of words. Many of them I recognised: they were the words of St Bernard, and Abbess Hildegard. But they were imbued with a certain ecstasy, an ardent passion, which cannot be counterfeited. I saw that Alcaya was moved by a true and overwhelming love of God, a longing for the divine presence, and this was admirable.

But such passion can be dangerous. It can lead to excess. Only the strongest and wisest of women, moved by such fervour, can be trusted to follow God's path without careful guidance. (As Jacques de Vitry says of the *mulier sancta*, Marie d'Oignes: 'she never bent either to the right or the left but trod the middle and blessed path with a wondrous moderation'.)

'Father, when I was a little girl,' Alcaya continued – more quietly, now, 'I went up onto that mountain out there, and I heard angels. It was the only time in my life that I have ever heard them. So when Johanna spoke to me of her fears for her child, I knew that Babilonia would be happy here, where the angels sing. I knew that no one would grudge us this roof, which sheltered me as an infant. I knew that, with Johanna's assistance, we could come here and live, happily and piously, in the sight of God.' Leaning forward, Alcaya took my hands in hers, and looked up into my face, and her own face was suffused with a shining, smiling contentment. 'Have you felt God's love here, Father? Has the perfect peace of His glory filled your heart?'

What could I say? That God's love was a boon for which I had striven all my life, but had rarely attained to my satisfaction? That my soul was weighed down by my corruptible body, so that (in the words of St Bernard) earthly dwelling preoccupied the mind, busy with many thoughts? That I was a man of a practical, rather than a spiritual, nature, unable to lose myself in contemplation of the Divine?

'When I look at that mountain,' I replied bluntly, 'my heart is filled, not with peace, but with pictures of Father Augustin's butchered limbs.'

God forgive me for that. It was said with a vicious intent, and it drove the joy from Alcaya's eyes.

God forgive me that I should have shut my heart to His presence.

I did not meet Babilonia that evening. She would not return while the soldiers remained, and the soldiers refused to leave unless I accompanied them. For some time I waited, conversing with Alcaya as I watched Johanna (whose subtle shifts of expression hinted at thoughts that I would have liked to share). But at last I was obliged to quit the forcia while there was still light in the sky – for my guards were anxious that Casseras should be reached before darkness fell.

I went back with them resolving that, when the sun rose again, I would secretly retrace my steps to the forcia alone. By this means I would gain a short time with Babilonia before my escort found me and frightened her away. I would also see the women in the perfection of their undisturbed peace, and judge whether, as Alcaya had insisted, it was truly the peace of God. Such an arrogant assumption – that I had it within me to judge what was, and what was not, the peace that passeth all under-standing! I know better now. But even then, I was affected by Alcaya's fervour. I had felt its warmth, and was curious to discover the fire from which it sprang. I wanted to meet Babi-lonia, and decide whether she was indeed 'close to God', or whether she was possessed by a demon; I wanted to examine her features for a trace of those other features, once so familiar to me, now already fading from my remembrance.

It must be admitted, too, that I felt the need to finish my conversation with Johanna, which had been interrupted before my curiosity was satisfied. This is what I truly believed, though I was, perhaps, more carnally minded in my desires than my conscience would allow – who knows? Only God. I was drawn to Johanna and admitted as much to myself that night as I lay on my pallet in the priest's house. But I resolved to follow my reason, and not my heart. I banished from my mind any thoughts of her (as I have so often done, with so many impious reflections), and sought God's forgiveness, and meditated upon His love, which I had not sought as unavailingly as I should have, or known as I would have wished. Of course, I knew God's love as we all know it: namely, in the gifts that He has bestowed (... *wine that maketh glad the heart of man, and oil to make his face to shine, and bread which strengtheneth man's heart* ...), but above all, in the gift of His only-begotten Son. I had read, and been told, and knew it to be true in my heart, that God loves the world. But I had read also of His love as it has touched the saints. I had read of St Bernard, 'inwardly embraced, as it were, by the arms of wisdom' and receiving 'the sweet inpouring of the Divine Love'. I had read of St Augustin, rejoicing 'when that light shineth into my soul' and when 'that embracement is enjoyed which is not divorced by satiety'. This was divine love in its purity, in its very essence; I recognised it as one would recognise a distant and lovely mountain, forever unreachable.

Yet Babilonia may have reached it. Alcaya believed that she had; Father Augustin, that she had not. I was more inclined to trust Father Augustin's judgement, naturally – he had been a man of wisdom, of education, of great experience and virtue. Yet Alcaya had somehow stirred my soul, and I asked myself: had Father Augustin, for all his wisdom, education and virtue, ever truly felt the inpouring of Divine Love? Would he have recognised its manifestation in another? Would he, like Jacques de Vitry, have acknowledged God's presence in the uncontrolled weeping of Marie d'Oignes, or would he have been as those other men, condemned by the aforesaid Jacques, who maliciously slandered the ascetic life of such women and, like mad dogs, railed against customs which were contrary to theirs?

But I chastised myself. Father Augustin had been no mad dog, and Marie d'Oignes was never stoned in the streets. I realised that my mind was clouded by weariness, and turned my thoughts to other matters. I thought of Pierre Jean Olieu's treatise, which had been given to Alcaya during her brief sojourn with the unorthodox Franciscan tertiaries. I was troubled by the fear that I had not questioned her as thoroughly as I should have, regarding her views on the poverty of Christ. Of course, she had described herself as a 'faithful daughter of the Roman Church', who did what the priests told her to do – and thus did not reject their authority, on the grounds that such priests were neither cleansed by frugality nor devoted to senseless error. Furthermore, I knew that Father Augustin had passed this way before me, and failed to identify Alcaya as being enamoured of Holy Poverty to the extent that it endangered her soul.

Nevertheless, I should have settled my doubts on this point, and resolved to do so.

I also thought about the other people who had to be questioned: the Provost of Rasiers; the children, Guillaume and Guido; the local shepherds who grazed their sheep near the forcia. It would be a difficult task, because this was no formal inquisition, with set procedures such as those laid out in Guillaume Durant's *Speculum judiciale* (have you consulted his work, at all?), and those established, over the years, by custom and papal decree. Testimony given to the Holy Office is always transcribed by a notary, in the presence of two impartial observers – such as the two Dominicans, Simon and Berengar, usually present at my interrogations. Oaths must be taken and registered; charges must be revealed or withheld, according to what seems expedient; permission for a delay must be granted or denied – again, according to what seems expedient. There are rules, and the rules must be followed.

But in this case the inquisition was an informal one, and I had no rules to guide me. To begin with, my authority extended only to the extirpation of heretics: it was not my place to hunt down Father Augustin's murderers unless they were motivated by, or infused with, heretical beliefs. Another man might well have arrested the entire population of Casseras, reasoning (perhaps justly – who knows?) that anyone to be found within the vicinity of such a crime must, by this very fact, be implicated as leaven of the Pharisees. I was not, however, convinced that such an action would be the best course. In any case, where would the people of Casseras be held when our prison was already bursting with the people of Saint-Fiacre?

How I wished that Father Augustin was at my side! He would have known what to do. I felt myself to be insufficiently experienced, sinking into a morass of unrelated yet somehow important information: Bernard de Pibraux and his three young friends, the scattered limbs and the missing horses, Pierre Jean Olieu's treatise, Father Augustin's letter to the Bishop of Pamiers. Father Augustin had written that Babilonia was possessed by a demon; if I met her, would I find myself confronting the Inveterate Enemy of the Human Race? St Dominic had done so many times, and had triumphed, but I was no saint – the prospect made me tremble.

I remember that I was praying devoutly for a new superior when I suddenly fell asleep. Whereupon I dreamed, not of angels or demons, but of candles, many hundreds of them, in a place that was huge and dark. No sooner had I lit one of these candles than another was extinguished by some mysterious means (for there was not a breath of wind), and I was obliged to turn back once more with my taper. All night, it seemed, I ran from candle to candle. And I woke before sunrise – as was my custom – horrified to see that for all my ceaseless toil, I was still surrounded by darkness!

I should tell you that I had spoken to Father Paul before retiring, but had not asked him if he would accompany me to the forcia. Over a humble meal of bread and cheese we had discussed Father Augustin and his death, but I had not mentioned that I wished to visit the women again – knowing that, in his concern for my safety, Father Paul undoubtedly would have alerted my bodyguards. Therefore I was obliged to quit his house as quietly as possible. The fact that a sergeant had been accommodated in the kitchen, for the specific purpose of protecting me from nocturnal attack, made this difficult; although I crept from my room barefoot I nevertheless woke him, and was forced to whisper some lie about relieving myself. He barely acknowledged this remark before closing his eyes once more. Even so, I knew that when I failed to return, his watchman's instinct would rouse him. Consequently I proceeded with all haste, stopping only to pull on the boots which I had been carrying.

I could not saddle my horse because it was sharing a barn with my bodyguards. Instead I had to set out on foot, like a true mendicant, my path illumined by the very faintest dawn light. This radiance naturally grew brighter as I walked; then the sun rose, the stars faded, the birds awoke, and doubtless I should have reflected, as did St Francis, on the beautiful variety of these creatures, who received the word of God with such joy when he preached to them. But I was blinded by my own fear. In truth, my courage in attempting this journey had been founded on fear. The more afraid I was, the more stubbornly I desired to prove myself courageous – manly – undaunted. *Fear not*, I had written, in my missive to Father Paul. *I have taken a stroll to the forcia, and shall return soon.* God forgive my vanity! But I was beginning to regret it, let me assure you: the air was so still, the road so empty, the light so dim. A rustle in the bushes to my left caused me to halt, then redouble my pace, then halt again. I recall uttering the words, 'What am I doing?' and would have retraced my steps willingly, if not for the fact that I had communicated my intentions to Father Paul. By returning, I would also be admitting that I had been afraid to advance. Again, what vanity!

So I pushed on, repeating to myself certain psalms, as well

as those requirements once listed by Bernard Gui as being necessary to a good inquisitor (for we had, over the years, corresponded a great deal on this very subject). According to Bernard – and who is better placed to judge? – the inquisitor should be constant, persevering amidst dangers and adversities even unto death. He should be willing to suffer for the sake of justice, neither rashly precipitating danger nor shamefully retreating in fear, for such cowardice weakens moral stability. I wondered if I had rashly precipitated danger, in leaving Casseras alone, and decided that I probably had. Almost with longing I began to listen for the sound of pursuing hoofbeats. Why did my escort not come to rescue me?

Then, all at once, I reached the site of Father Augustin's murder. I saw the dark stains on the pale earth; I smelled the corruption; I felt the weight of encroaching, shadowy foliage. It was truly a cursed place. And doubtless it would have driven me back, if not for the little patch of gold that seemed to glow near one of the most horribly defiled rocks. Upon drawing closer, I was able to identify this gleaming object as a spray of yellow flowers. They seemed fresh, and they were tied with a string of plaited grass.

In their simple and delicate beauty, I recognised an offering of devotion.

My first act was to pick them up, but feeling that this was somehow wrong, I quickly replaced them. In some mysterious way, they rendered the clearing less terrible. Much of my fear was dispelled when I regarded them; I found myself smiling. And my smile widened as the melody of a song reached my ears, for what can move our hearts like music? Shall not the very mountains and hills break forth into singing? (*O sing unto the Lord a new song: sing unto the Lord, all the earth.*) Of course, this song was not a psalm, but some low composition written in the local tongue – nevertheless, it possessed a certain poetry. You will forgive me if, in my attempt to reproduce and translate it, I do not succeed in conveying its gentle charm: to the best of my recollection, it ran as follows.

Little lark, I sing with you
For I, too, greet the sun!
Little lark, tell my lover
That he is the one.
Little lark, do not linger
Let me watch you flee.
Tell my love that I will have him
And he will have me.

Not praiseworthy sentiments, by any means, but the tune was sweet and joyful. It was sung by a woman whose voice I did not recognise. Nevertheless, I followed this Siren song, disregarding any possible danger; I pursued it through the trees, my boots slipping on rough ground and my skirts catching on twigs and thorns, until I emerged onto a gentle, sloping pasture that was warmed by the rising sun. And if only I were a poet, that I might convey to you the glory spread at my feet.

In the freshness of that morning the air was as clear as the chime of a tenor bell. Therefore I viewed the scene before me with an eagle's eyes: I saw distant valleys, and mountains that cast long, misty shadows; I saw Rasiers, so small that I could have cupped it in my hands; I saw the gleam of a river and the sparkle of dew in the sunlight. Sheer cliffs, like the walls of a mighty castle, seemed to be dyed a tender pink. Larks and swallows wove intricate patterns against the cloudless sky. I felt that I saw the world as God must see it, in all its majesty and all its intricacy. (*But the very hairs on your head are all numbered . . .*) I felt as if I stood on the crest of creation, and my heart swelled, and I thought to myself: O Lord my God, Thou art very great; Thou art clothed with honour and majesty, who coverest Thyself with light as with a garment: who stretchest out the heavens like a curtain: who layeth the beams of His chambers in the waters: who maketh the clouds His chariot: who walketh upon the wings of the wind. And as the warmth of the sun caressed my face, and the pure air filled my nostrils, and the sweet, faint melody of that base but beautiful song enchanted my ear, I heard another voice join the first in grace-ful harmony, and I saw the two women who sang, moving out of a thicket that lay below me on the hillside. They were carrying baskets on their heads, and they walked in perfect accord, the one holding the hand of the other. I recognised the taller of the two as Johanna de Caussade. She recognised me, I think, at the same instant, but she did not pause in her song or gait.

Instead she smiled, and saluted me with a free and careless joy, as one might salute a dear friend, or an acquaintance met in some rapturous circumstance – at a festival, perhaps, or a victory celebration. Then she spoke to the girl beside her, still smiling, and they both looked up at me, and suddenly my heart was filled to overflowing. How can I describe this extraordi-nary sensation, almost painful in its pleasure, as warm as new milk, as wide as the sea, infinitely wondrous? I wanted to weep and I wanted to laugh. My weary limbs were made vigorous, yet curiously languid. I felt that I would live for all eternity, yet I was happy to die where I stood, knowing that my death was unimportant. I looked with equal love on the yellow grass, the white butterflies, the nettles, the sheep's dung, the women below: I wanted to cradle creation in my arms. My love was all-encompassing, so that I felt it was not truly mine, but was flowing through me, around me, into me, and then I looked into the sun, and was blinded by a great light. For a moment which barely extended beyond the span of a single breath, yet which was infinitely prolonged, I was as an infant suspended in its mother's womb. I felt Christ enfolding me, and He was peace, and He was joy, and He was as terrible as death, and I knew His unending love for me, because I saw it and clasped it and felt it in my own heart.

God, how can I show you these things with only words to help me? I have no words. No words are sufficient. Was not the Angelic Doctor himself, when overcome by a mystic rev-elation in his later years, unable to speak for some time after-wards? Doubtless his revelation was of a higher order than mine; certainly he displayed a genius in his use of words that I can never hope to equal. And this being the case – if God's presence deprived him of his agile tongue – then how can I find the words which eluded him?

I know that God was with me, on that hillside. I know that Christ embraced me, though I cannot tell you why, since I did nothing, said nothing and thought nothing which merited such a precious gift. Perhaps He was simply there, in the perfection of the morning, and took pity on me as I stumbled into His presence. Perhaps He was in Johanna's heart, and her smile was the key which unlocked my own soul, so that at last the Divine Love found a way into it. How can I know? I am no saint. I am a sinful and slothful man, who, by some wondrous act of mercy, reached beyond the cloud by which all the earth is covered.

St Augustin once said that, when a man's soul does pierce the carnal darkness which enfolds terrestrial life, it is as if he were touched with a swift coruscation, only to sink back into his natural infirmity, the desire surviving by which he may again be raised to the heights, but his impurity being insufficient to establish him there. According to St Augustin, the more anyone can do this, the greater is he.

This suggests that a man must work to gain such blessedness. But did St Paul work anything but evil, before he received the Light on his way to Damascus? It was God's work, and not his own, which brought him to the Truth. Thus it was God's love, and not my own, which brought me so close to Him.

Doubtless He knew that, left to my own devices, I would never have lifted my eyes from the ground. Perhaps I never will again; perhaps I do not have the strength or the purity.

But I do have it within me to love God. I love God now, not as my Father, who provides gifts and instructions, but as my lover, as my heart's ease, as my faith and hope, as the food and wine which nourishes my soul. To love like this requires work, without question: fortunately, I can always attain such heights by meditating upon that immeasurable moment when

I languished with love, on the couch of the hillside, in Christ's joyous and sorrowful embrace.

I can also find it by meditating upon Johanna de Caussade's smile. For just as that smile first unlocked my heart, I found that it continued to do so.

'Father?'

It was Johanna's voice which opened my earthly eyes again and drew me back into myself, pulling me like a fish on a line. The eternity of my divine communion had endured for just an instant; the two women were still striding towards me when my soul was released from rapt contemplation, and I was left, still dazzled, with the tide of love receding from my heart. I looked for a while without seeing, without speaking. Then my vision seemed to clear, and the first object which impressed itself upon my eyes was the face of Johanna's companion.

I saw the face of a young woman, perfectly formed and as fair as a lily (though slightly scarred about the chin and temples). If I were a troubadour, I could sing her praises as they should be sung, comparing her skin to roses, her softness to a fledgling's, her russet hair to apples and silk. But I am no poet of the heart, so I shall simply say that she was beautiful. In all my years, I have never seen a woman of such tender beauty. And because her eyes held, not even the innocence of a child, but the innocence of a baby animal – because my heart was still engorged with love, too much love to contain – I smiled at her lovingly. I would have smiled with equal fondness at any fly or tree or wolf which might have presented itself to my gaze at that moment, because I loved the world. But as luck would have it, she was the first object that my vision encountered, so she it was who received the smile which God Himself had formed.

Then she smiled back, with a smile as sweet as honey.

'You are Father Bernard,' she said.

'And you are Babilonia.'

'Yes.' She seemed delighted. 'I am Babilonia!'

'Are you well, Father?' Johanna inquired, for – as I later learned – my voice was unnaturally slow and breathless. In effect, I gave the appearance of being either drunk or ill.

Realising this, I hastened to reassure her.

'I am well,' I said. 'Quite well. And you? What are you doing? Collecting more wood?'

'Mushrooms,' said Johanna.

'And snails,' her daughter added.

'Mushrooms and snails!' For all this meant to me, they might have said 'wool grease and fly eggs'. I was still almost dizzy with elation, and had to fight the urge to laugh out loud, or weep unrestrainedly. Seeing the puzzled expression on Johanna's face, however, I forced myself, with all the strength of my mind and spirit, to speak quietly and act with decorum. 'Any luck?' I asked.

'A little,' Johanna replied.

'I find the snails, but I do not eat them,' Babilonia added. 'They make me choke.'

'Indeed?'

'Have you brought the soldiers, Father?' Johanna spoke easily, without fear or concern, but I saw her daughter blink several times. 'Are they with you, today?'

'Not today. Not yet.' Some inner hilarity prompted me to append: 'I crept out this morning. I managed to escape. But they will come after me, soon.'

'Then we must hide you, quickly!' Poor Babilonia was manifestly dismayed. I realised that she was innocent in all things – perhaps even simple – and must never be mocked or teased, because she saw only what was in front of her.

'The soldiers do not want to hurt him, rosebud,' Johanna remarked. 'They want to protect him. From the men who killed Father Augustin.'

'Oh no!' Babilonia's eyes filled with tears. 'Then you should go back! Now!'

'My dear child, I am in no danger, here. God is with us.'

In my divinely inspired serenity, I conveyed a warmth and a confidence which calmed her, somewhat; I even touched her arm (an action that I would not normally attempt, let me assure you). Then I asked the two women if they had completed their search for God's bounty.

'We have done enough for today,' Johanna replied.

'May I accompany you home? I wish to speak to Alcaya.'

'Father, you may do anything you choose. You are an inquisitor and an important man. Father Paul told us so.'

It seemed that Johanna was speaking with gentle irony, but I was not offended.

'I may not do quite *everything* I choose, Madame. There are certain rules and laws that I must obey.' Feeling unnaturally light-hearted, I continued in a manner which was probably unwise, as we began our climb back to the forcia. 'For example, I must not break my vows of chastity and obedience, no matter how dearly I might wish to.'

'Is that so?' Johanna was walking beside me as she made this remark, and I saw her cast in my direction a sidelong glance which was (I can find no other words to describe it) of a speculative, even flirtatious, character. Rather than ignite my passions, however, it had the opposite effect: I felt a cold shock, as if doused with water, and shook my head as if this water had entered my ears.

'Forgive me,' I mumbled. 'Forgive me, I am not myself.'

'No,' said Johanna, almost with amusement. 'I can see that. Are you sick?'

'Not sick, no, I – a strange spell.'

'Did you walk here from Casseras?'

'Yes.'

'And do you often walk such distances uphill?'

'No,' I said, 'but I am not Father Augustin, Madame! I am not infirm!'

'Of course not.'

Her tone made me laugh.

'How well you soothe my tender vanity. Did you practise

145

this skill on Father Augustin, or is it the natural endowment of every mother?'

This time it was Johanna's turn to laugh, but she did so quietly, without opening her mouth. 'Oh Father,' she said, 'we all have our vanities.'

'How very true.'

'For example, I pride myself on being able to find good people, who will be of use to me.'

'Like Alcaya?'

'Like Alcaya. And like you, Father.'

'Indeed? But I fear that you are sadly mistaken.'

'Perhaps,' Johanna admitted. 'Perhaps you are not so good.'

At this we *both* laughed, and in so doing seemed to share an understanding of our mutual thoughts and intentions which I have shared with no other human being. Let me explain this, for I know you will say: 'Here is a monk and a woman. What can they know of each other's hearts and minds, save the promptings of carnal desire?' And you would be right, to a degree, for we were both subject to the stirrings of the flesh, being sinners in the sight of God. But I believe that, because we *were* sinners – culpably vain, disobedient, headstrong, even irreverent – because we shared so many sins, we saw each other clearly. We seemed to know each other because we knew ourselves.

Suffice it to say that we were of sympathetic temperaments. A curious conjunction, when you consider that she was an illiterate merchant's daughter. But God is the fount of far greater mysteries.

'There were some yellow flowers on the road,' I observed, when it became clear to me that we had avoided the site of Father Augustin's death, by some tortuous circuit. 'Did you pick them, or did Babilonia?'

'I picked them,' was Johanna's response. 'I doubt that I shall ever visit his grave, so I had to leave them where he died.'

'He will be buried at Lazet. You can always visit Lazet.'

'No.'

'Why not? You cannot stay here in winter. Why not go to Lazet?'

'Why not go to Casseras? It is much closer.'

'They may not welcome you, in Casseras.'

'They may not welcome us in Lazet. Babilonia is never welcomed anywhere.'

'I find that hard to believe.' Glancing ahead to where Babilonia was mounting the steep road, I was struck afresh by her beauty. 'She is an ornament, and as gentle as a dove.'

'To you, she has been as gentle as a dove. To others, she will be like a wolf. You would not recognise her.' Johanna delivered this remark with a singular absence of deeply felt emotion. It was as if she regarded such a transformation as commonplace. But her tone became more animated when she continued. 'You were like Alcaya, when you greeted her. If only everyone was as gentle! Augustin smiled at her as if his guts were paining him.'

'Perhaps they were. He was not a well man.'

'He was afraid of her,' Johanna continued, ignoring my comment. 'He loved her, but he was afraid of her. She attacked him once, and I had to pull her off. He sat there shaking. There were tears in his eyes. He was ashamed, because he was so afraid.' Suddenly she frowned, and her dark brows snapped together, so that she wore a formidable look. 'He told me that she was cursed through our sin – his and mine. I told him nonsense. Do you think he was right, Father?'

It seemed to me that Father Augustin had spoken out of shock and despair, but I replied cautiously. 'The Scriptures would not have it so. "What mean ye, that ye use this proverb concerning the land of Israel, saying, The fathers have eaten sour grapes, and the children's teeth are set on edge? As I live, saith the Lord God, ye shall not have occasion to use this proverb in Israel."'

'Then Augustin was wrong. I knew he was wrong.'

'Johanna, we cannot know what the Lord intended. Only

147

one thing is sure – that we are all sinners, every one of us. Even Babilonia.'

'Babilonia's sins are not her own,' the widow retorted, stubbornly.

'But Man has been born in sin ever since the Fall. It is God's plan for us, as human beings, that we should transcend this sin by attaining salvation. Are you telling me that Babilonia has the soul of an animal – that she is less than human?'

The widow opened her mouth, and shut it again. She seemed to think deeply. Because we had reached the last and steepest portion of our climb, we were unable to converse until we had gained those pastures which surrounded the forcia. Then, still panting from her exertions, she turned to me with a grave and sorrowful look.

'Father, you are a very wise man,' she said. 'I knew that you were merciful, and a pleasant companion, because Augustin made it clear to me. I knew that I would like you even before we met, from the way he talked of you. But I did not understand that you had so much wisdom in your heart.'

'Johanna – '

'What you say is true, perhaps. To believe that my daughter's sins are not her own is to believe that she is an animal. But Father, sometimes she *is* an animal. She makes animal noises, and tries to rend me apart. How can a mother accept that her own child wants to kill her? How can a human being lie in her own filth? How can Babilonia's sins be hers, when she has no memory of them? How, Father?'

What could I say? To Father Augustin, clearly, Babilonia's degraded acts had been inflicted upon her by the presence of demons, as punishment for his own sins. But I wondered if he was correct. I wondered if the loathing which he felt for his moral and physical frailty had misdirected him, in this instance.

'Remember,' I said, after some hesitation, 'that Job, being perfect and upright, was tested by God and Satan with every imaginable misfortune. Perhaps it is Babilonia's virtue, and not her sin, which draws down this wrath upon her. Perhaps she, too, is being tested.'

Johanna's eyes filled with tears.

'Oh, Father,' she murmured, 'could that be true?'

'As I said, we cannot know what the Lord intended. We only know that He is good.'

'Oh, Father, what a comfort you are.' Her voice was tremulous, but she smiled, and swallowed, and wiped her eyes firmly. 'How kind you are.'

'That was not my intention.' Although it was, of course. The charity of Christ's love was still in my heart, and I was moved to make the whole world happy. 'Inquisitors are not kind.'

'True. But perhaps you are not a very *good* inquisitor.'

Smiling, we both then proceeded to the forcia, where Alcaya greeted me joyfully. She was sitting by Vitalia's bed, reading to the old woman from St Bernard's treatise. I observed (in a jovial manner) that it was reassuring to see her with St Bernard in her hand, rather than Pierre Jean Olieu. And she shook her head at me fondly, like an aunt.

'How you Dominicans hate that poor man,' she said.

'Not the man, but his ideas,' was my response. 'He was too ardent in his pursuit of poverty.'

'That is what Father Augustin said.'

'And did you agree with him?'

'Of course. It made him too angry if I disagreed.'

'Alcaya,' the widow protested, 'you argued with him all the time!'

'Yes, but he always defeated me in the end,' Alcaya pointed out. 'He was very wise.'

'Alcaya,' I said, thinking that I would be frank as to my concerns, rather than veiling them in seemingly harmless and amiable chatter, as was my custom, 'did you know that Olieu's books are regarded with great disfavour by the Pope, and many important men of the Church?'

She gazed at me wonderingly.

'So much so,' I went on, 'that to possess a copy is to invite suspicion of heretical beliefs. Did you know that?'

I heard Johanna snort, but I did not look at her. I fixed my attention on Alcaya, who simply smiled.

'Oh Father,' she said, 'I am not a heretic.'

'In that case, you should read other books. And you should burn Pierre Jean Olieu's treatise.'

'*Burn that book!*' Alcaya cried. She seemed amused, rather than shocked, and I was puzzled until she explained that Father Augustin had bidden her, in the heat of argument, to burn the treatise on several occasions. 'I said to him: "Father, this is my book. I have so few. I love them so dearly. Would you rob me of my own child?"'

'Alcaya, you are courting peril.'

'Father, I am a poor woman. I know where the book is wrong, so what harm can it do?' Presenting St Bernard's treatise for my inspection, she caressed it lovingly, first the binding, then the vellum pages. 'Father, see how beautiful they are, these books. They open like the wings of a white dove. They smell of wisdom. How could you burn even one of them, when they are so beautiful and innocent? Father, they are my friends.'

Merciful God, and what could I say to that? I am a Dominican. I have slept with St Augustin's *Confessions* clasped to my bosom. I have wept to see pages turn to dust in my hand, beneath the cruel sentence of bookworm. I have kissed the Holy Scriptures. Every word of Alcaya's speech made tender flowers bloom in my heart – already well watered by the love of God, that day.

And I thought of my own books (my own, yet not my own), which had been bestowed upon me by the Order and by certain people who had loved me, in the past. My father had given me two books upon my profession: Jacobus de Voragine's *The Golden Legend*, which he revered, and Gratian's *Decretum*, which he consulted. From one of the lectors at Carcassonne, an old and very wise brother called Guilabert, I had received a copy of Donatus's *Ars Grammatica*. (In it he had written: *I am old, and you are my best student. Take this, use it wisely, and pray for me when you do*. God knows, I treasured this book!) There was a noble woman in one of my congregations, when I was preacher ordinary, who had pressed upon me her Book of Hours, saying that my eloquence had moved her to give many of her possessions away – and although made somewhat uneasy by her enthusiasm, I could not bring myself to reject the volume, which was exquisitely decorated and embellished with gold.

Finally, Father Jacques had left with me one of his books when he died: Cicero's *Ad Herrenium de arte rhetorica*. Thinking about this work, and about the others in my cell, I was shamed – as ever – by the possessive nature of my love for them. (*No man can serve two masters . . .*) Of course they were not truly mine, but I had the use of them for as long as I lived, and so regarded them as my own hands or feet. Was this not sin, for a monk of St Dominic? Was I no better than Alcaya, who spoke of her books as children, both beautiful and innocent?

'Alcaya,' I said – and God knows, I was making a terrible sacrifice – 'if you give me Pierre Jean Olieu's treatise, I shall give you another book in its place. I shall give you the *Life* of St Francis, from a book called *The Golden Legend*, which is a greater work by far. Have you ever read *The Golden Legend*?'

Alcaya shook her head.

'Well,' I continued, 'it contains the stories of many saints, St Francis among them. And he, as you know, was wedded to Lady Poverty with all his heart and soul. Will you take this blessed work, in exchange for the other? It is of much finer quality.'

Now, I had made such a generous offer to test Alcaya's faith. If she was infected by Olieu's errors, she would be reluctant to surrender his work no matter what the reward. But even as I spoke her eyes grew bright; she touched her mouth, then her breast.

'St Francis!' she cried. 'Oh, I ... oh, what a blessing ...'

'Do you have this book with you?' Johanna inquired of me.

'No. But I shall send for it. You will have it before I leave Casseras. Come.' I placed my hand on Alcaya's shoulder, and stooped so that my face was level with hers. 'Give me Olieu's book, and put my mind at rest. Will you do that for me? It is my father's book I offer you, Alcaya.'

To my profound astonishment, she stroked my cheek, causing me to pull away sharply. Later Prior Hugues admonished me for allowing this to occur, saying that my cordial – even affectionate – behaviour had encouraged such intimate actions. Perhaps he was correct. Or perhaps God's love still shone in my eyes, drawing from Alcaya the natural response.

In any case, she stroked my cheek, and smiled.

'You need not give me your father's book,' she said. 'If this other book troubles your spirit, then you may have it with my love. I know that you wish me nothing but good, for you have been enlightened by rays of heavenly wisdom.'

As you may imagine, I was lost for a reply. But I had no need of one, because at that moment Babilonia (who was outside the house) uttered the most terrible scream.

'*Mama!*' she cried. '*Mama, the men! The men!*'

I cannot recall moving. All I can recollect is that I was suddenly in the bailey, advancing on Babilonia, who was running hither and yon like a caged rabbit. I caught her, and held her, and was rewarded with bites and scratches for my pains.

'Be easy,' I said. 'Be easy, my child, I will not let them hurt you. Come, be easy.'

'Mama is here, rosebud. Mama is here.' Johanna had reached us. She tried to embrace her daughter, but Babilonia pulled away; she began to sway in my arms, swinging her head and making strange noises – noises like a demonic language. I was astonished at her strength. Indeed, I barely had enough strength in my own arms to restrain her, though she was so small and slight.

Then she began to scream again, and this was the screaming of a damned soul, and when I looked into her face I saw another face entirely, red and contorted, with a blue, extruded tongue and gnashing teeth, tumid eyes, swelling veins. I saw the face of a devil, and it frightened me so much that I blasphemed (to my eternal shame), whereupon Babilonia began to repeat the blasphemy, at inhuman speed.

'Let her go!' cried Alcaya. 'You are afraid, Father, let her go!'

'But she will hurt you!' I gasped.

'Let her go!'

As it happened, I was given no choice, for at that very instant Babilonia and I were wrenched apart by one of my sergeants. Although I had not been aware of their presence, my bodyguards had arrived at the forcia; they had been welcomed by fearsome screams, and had seen me wrestling with a Fury, my face white beneath streaks of blood.

It is perhaps not surprising that they responded with unnecessary force.

'Father! Father, are you hurt?'

'Let her go! You – stop it – let her go! *Stop it!*' I was very angry, for they had taken Babilonia, and thrown her to the ground, and one of the soldiers (a large, unwieldy person) was kneeling on her back. Shaking off my attendants, I gave this man a mighty push, and toppled him sideways. Be assured that he would never have yielded, if he had been in any way prepared.

'My love. Oh, my love, Christ is here. Lord Jesus is here.' Swooping down upon the young woman's prostrate form, Alcaya cradled in her arms Babilonia's bloody and dusty head. 'Can you taste His sweetness? Can you feel His embrace? Drink His wine, dearest, and forget your sorrows.'

'Is she hurt?' I was bent over this strange couple, anxiously trying to judge Babilonia's condition, when I felt more hands pulling me back. Once again I was forced to extricate myself from the grip of concerned soldiers, who appeared to want me out of harm's way. 'Let *go*, if you please, I am in no danger! Look!'

And I indicated the unfortunate girl at my feet, who was lying still, and moaning, with her eyes shut. The sergeant beside me gazed down at her as one might gaze at dead vermin.

'Did she do it, Father?' he inquired.

'What?'

'Did she kill Father Augustin?'

'Kill . . .?' It was a moment before I understood. 'Imbecile!' I snapped, and turned back to Alcaya. 'Is she hurt?' I repeated. 'Did they hurt her?'

'No.'

'I am very sorry.'

'You are not to blame,' said Johanna. 'But I think – forgive me, Father, I think you had better go.'

'Yes.' My escort agreed with her. 'You come with us. That mad woman will scratch your eyes out.'

So I departed, then and there. I thought it best, though I was sorry that my leavetaking should have been attended by such unpleasantness. As I withdrew from the bailey I turned, and saw that Babilonia was on her feet again, neither screaming nor struggling but standing quietly, like a woman fully possessed of her faculties – and I was reassured. Johanna, I noticed, lifted her hand to me, and this was also reassuring. (The memory of that gesture, faltering and apologetic, remained with me for some time.)

Alcaya appeared to have forgotten my existence; she never looked up to watch me go.

In other circumstances, I might have berated my bodyguards all the way back to Casseras, and earned their sullen disapproval. But at first I was too shaken to speak. I was thinking of Babilonia's transformation, and the satanic forces which must have unleashed it. Then, as we passed Johanna's flowers, the peace of God re-entered my soul. It calmed me and silenced me; I was as a sheep beside still waters. Therefore remove sorrow from thy heart, I told myself, and put away evil from thy flesh. For who knoweth what is good for man in this life, all the days of his vain life which he spendeth as a shadow?

'My friends,' I said to the men riding with me, 'I have a suggestion to make. If you forget to tell the Seneschal that I visited the forcia alone, I shall neglect to tell him that no one stopped me from doing so. Does that seem fair to you?'

It seemed very fair to them. Indeed, their fears were assuaged instantly, and their mood was lightened. For the remainder of the journey we talked of pleasant things such as food, and mad people, and wounds that we had witnessed in the past.

And none of them knew that my heart yearned for the company that we had left behind.

Ye that are heavy laden

I remained with Father Paul for two days.

On the first day, after leaving the forcia, I went to Rasiers and spoke to the Provost. A self-important little man with a pompous manner, he nevertheless provided me with a very full account of his investigation into Father Augustin's death, an investigation which was, I must admit, quite faultlessly conducted. Then I retraced my steps to Casseras, and interviewed the two boys, Guillaume and Guido, about their discovery of the remains. Although I sensed that their parents were somewhat alarmed to see me conversing with these children, the boys themselves were only too happy to oblige me, because I had possessed enough foresight to arm myself with certain cakes and sweetmeats, cooked at my request in the priory kitchens. Indeed, I was soon attended by all of the youngest villagers: they would wait for me on doorsteps, and peer at me through windows. But I raised no objection to this pursuit, for children are not practised liars. If one is patient, and friendly, and eager to confess oneself astonished, one can learn a great deal from children. They will often notice things which escape the attention of grown men.

For example, after inquiring into the movements of Father Augustin and his bodyguards, I went on to ask about any other strangers who might have passed through the village. Any men in blue robes, perhaps? Men who might have lived in the woods, and come to the village at night? No? What about armed men, on horseback?

'The Seneschal came,' said Guillaume. (A clever boy, Guillaume.) 'He came with his men.'

'Ah yes.'

'He asked us the same question. He called the whole village together, and he asked us: ' "Have you seen any armed men on horseback?" '

'And had you?'

'Oh no.'

'No.'

'No one had.'

'Except Lili,' one of the smaller children observed, and Guillaume frowned.

'Lili?' he said, addressing a tiny girl well endowed with curly dark hair. 'What have you been saying?'

But Lili simply stared at him, blankly.

'She saw a man with arrows,' Lili's friend hastened to assure us. 'But no horse.'

'Arrows?' Once again, Guillaume took it upon himself to question the witness. 'Where was this, Lili? You should have told the Seneschal!'

'But she saw no horse. The Seneschal talked about horses.'

'Prima, you fool! As if it mattered! Lili, when did you see this man? What did he look like? Did he have a sword? Lili?' No reply being proffered, Guillaume abruptly lost patience with the little maid. 'Oh, she saw nothing. She is so stupid. She made it up.'

'Lili, come here.' After allowing Guillaume to interrogate her – in the belief that she might respond more openly to a friend – I decided that I would lose nothing by addressing her myself. 'Lili, I have something for you. See? A delicious dumpling. It has nuts in it. Do you like that? Yes? I have another . . . is it in here? No, nothing in here. Is it in my sleeve?

Shall we look? No. Perhaps we might find it if we go to that place where you saw the man with the arrows. I think it might be there. Will you show me? Yes? Come, then.'

Thus it transpired that I marched out of the village hand-in-hand with a three-year-old child, pursued by many other children. They accompanied me to the edge of a wheat field, beyond which lay a rocky and overgrown hillside, largely denuded of trees. Nevertheless, there was sufficient cover to provide any lurking assassin with the means by which he might pass close to Casseras without being detected – except, perhaps, by a child too small to be detected herself.

I examined the area which Lili identified, pretending to find there a honeyed almond. She accepted this in a graceless fashion, but was not forthcoming when I pressed her for a date or time.

'She told me about it a long time ago,' Prima volunteered.

'How long?'

'A long time ... days and days ...'

'It must have been before we found Father Augustin,' Guillaume interjected, 'because none of us have been allowed out of the village by ourselves since then.'

As I have already remarked, Guillaume was a clever boy.

'Were you frightened, Lili? When you saw the man?' I asked, and she shook her head. 'Why not? Did he smile at you? Did you know him?' Again she shook her head, and I began to despair of extracting from her a single, coherent word. 'I think that this girl has lost her tongue. Can you speak, Lili, or have you lost your tongue?'

In response, her tongue was offered up for my inspection.

'Oh!' Prima suddenly exclaimed. 'I know! She told me that she had seen one of Father Augustin's soldiers! And I said that she was lying, because they had already gone to the forcia!'

'You mean this happened on the *same day*?'

'Yes.'

'Lili – look at me. Was there blood on the man? No? No

blood? What colour was his hair, was it black? Brown? What about his tunic? Lili? Look at me, now.'

My tone, however, was too urgent; her lip trembled, and she began to wail. I could have hit her, God forgive me.

'She is so stupid,' Guillaume sympathised. 'Give her another almond.'

'And me! And me!'

'Give me one, too!'

After expending a great deal of time and energy, I was able to establish that the armed man had possessed black hair, a green tunic, and a blue cloak. When asked if he had ridden into Casseras with Father Augustin, earlier that day, Lili was unhelpful. It soon became apparent that she was unable to distinguish between one armed man and another.

Nevertheless, I had enlarged the sum of my knowledge considerably. And I was pleased, very pleased, because none of Father Augustin's bodyguards had been seen wearing a green tunic, or carrying a quiver of arrows. It seemed that the man encountered near the wheat field was not a familiar, and therefore might well have been an assassin, although I could not be sure of this.

Even today, I am still unsure, for after sedulously pursuing the matter, I was unable to find one more scrap of information. Although I urged Lili's parents to question her themselves, they were simple folk, as inarticulate as their offspring, and I did not anticipate much help from that quarter. Nor did their neighbours yield any useful gossip or speculation; as Roger Descalquencs had discovered, the inhabitants of Casseras had seen nothing, heard nothing, suspected nothing. Furthermore, they professed themselves to be good Catholics, compliment-ing Father Augustin as one who kept his nose out of their business. Naturally, I was very delicate and circumspect in my questioning – I even listened outside a few closed shutters. But after two days spent endearing myself to one and all, with cakes and sympathy and a few carefully placed promises, Lili's unre-liable description was still my only triumph. I could detect not a single trace of heresy (if one discounts – as I usually do – the endless complaints about tithing). Nobody had even made a false accusation, and this surprised me, for it is rare to investigate a village without prompting at least one inhabitant to defame his or her enemy with a vague lie about refusing meat, or spitting out the host during Mass.

Therefore my hopes were disappointed, though my spirits were not cast down. It was as if the great blaze of Divine Love, ignited in my heart on that dewy hillside, had left warm embers which illumined all the dark corners of my soul, and would not allow my temper to grow stiff and chilly. Be assured that I devoted twice as much thought to my mystical communion with God as I did to my investigation of Casseras; nevertheless, my mind was not clouded by such a holy distraction, but made clear and sharp and strong.

It must also be admitted that I thought a good deal about the women in the forcia, and this perhaps was not so commendable. I even sent one of my bodyguards back to Lazet for the *The Golden Legend* (or at least, that codex dealing with St Francis) – which I was unable to bestow on Alcaya in person, being reluctant to invade Babilonia's peace once again with my large and clumsy escort. Instead I left the book with Father Paul, securing from him a promise that he would deliver it at the earliest opportunity. Inside it I wrote: *May the teachings of St Francis guide you like a star and comfort you in times of trouble. I hope to see you in Lazet this winter. The Lord bless and keep you; you shall hear from me again.*

Naturally, I employed the vulgar tongue for this inscription, and hoped that Alcaya would read it to her friends.

When I returned to Lazet, I found that many events had occurred during my absence. The severed head had arrived, and – despite its advanced state of corruption – had been identified as belonging to Father Augustin. Consequently, Prior Hugues had ruled that the remains be interred, and with all speed: a modest burial and funeral Mass had been conducted. The Bishop's horse had also arrived, to the very great joy of its owner. Roger Descalquencs had received a report, from one of the local castellans, that two children from Bricaux had seen a naked stranger swilling himself down in the local stream, but had been frightened away when he waved a sword at them. According to the children, there had been a horse tethered nearby, but no sign of any other men.

The date of this sighting had been difficult to fix with any certainty, but the Seneschal was convinced that it had taken place on the day of Father Augustin's death. The description of the man sighted was also somewhat vague. 'Big and hairy, with huge teeth and red eyes' was how Roger paraphrased it. Nevertheless, he sent it to all the royal officials in the region – together with Lili's account of the man near the wheat field. I was not sanguine as to the usefulness of such an incomplete *effictio*, but Roger was quite pleased.

'Little by little,' he said. 'Step by step. We know that there were at least three: one went over the mountains into Catalonia; one went east, towards the coast; one headed north. The one who headed north was big and hairy. The one who went east abandoned his horse – '

'Abandoned the *Bishop's* horse,' I corrected. 'Was he riding his own? Lili saw no horse. Did the horse by the stream look like one of the Bishop's, or did the assassins arrive at Casseras on foot, and depart on stolen horses?'

Roger frowned. 'To attack five mounted men . . .' he muttered. 'It would be so dangerous, if you were not mounted yourself.'

'They had arrows,' I pointed out.

'Even so . . .'

It was then that I acquainted the Seneschal with my theory regarding a possible traitor in Father Augustin's retinue. We agreed that, distracted by an assault from outside their ranks, the honest familiars may not have noticed any threat from within – until it was too late. Effectively, they might have been stabbed in the back. And in these circumstances, it might have been possible to attack them without the assistance of horses.

'Father, you have the mind of a brigand,' Roger said admiringly. 'This would explain everything.'

'Almost everything.'

'Give me a description of the two men you suspect – Jordan and Maurand, are those the names? Give me a full description, and I will notify everyone I can.'

'We must also examine their recent activities, the people they consorted with, the houses they might have frequented – '

'Exactly.' The Seneschal thumped my shoulders in a gesture of goodfellowship. 'Ask their comrades, and if they give you any names, bring them to me.'

In this way I was burdened with yet another heavy task, at a time when Lazet's Holy Office had practically ceased to function. Fortunately, I had received word from Bishop Anselm that the Inquisitor of France had been informed of Father Augustin's death, and was assiduously seeking a replacement. I knew that this would be a slow and difficult exercise, in view of the fate that had befallen my slain superior; indeed, I had little hope of securing assistance before the new year. But it reassured me that the matter was being addressed, and that my plight was known to those people well placed to do something about it.

You will agree, I think, that with so much to occupy my thoughts, I was justified in turning away Grimaud Sobacca when he requested an interview on the morning after my return from Casseras. Do you remember Grimaud? He was the familiar to whom Father Jacques had entrusted certain unpalatable duties – the man who had erroneously defamed Johanna and her friends as 'heretics'. I was, therefore, loath to indulge him, and refused him admittance to the Holy Office.

With his usual persistence, however, he confronted me in the street as I returned to the priory.

'My lord!' he said. 'I must speak to you!'

'I am not interested in your lies, Grimaud. Get out of my way.'

'Not lies, my lord, no! Only what I have heard! You will thank me for this, on my honour!'

Though reluctant to distinguish this verminous creature with an *effictio*, I believe that such a description may serve to illustrate the wickedness of his soul, for his appearance was as repellent as his moral depravity. His greasy and pustulent skin, his purple nose, his corpulence – all were indicative of gluttony, intemperance, excess. Sloth made him flabby; envy caused him to whine. He was like an ibis, which cleans out its bowels with its own beak.

'My lord,' he exclaimed, as I moved to pass him, 'I have news about Father Augustin's death! I must speak to you *in private!*'

On hearing these words, I was naturally forced to accommodate him, for I did not wish to discuss the matter in a place where others might hear. So I took him back to the Holy Office, seated him in my superior's room, and stood over him in a threatening fashion.

'If I were not so busy, Grimaud, I would arrest you for bearing false witness,' I said. 'Those women in Casseras are not heretics, and never were. So if I were you, I would think very, very carefully before defaming anyone else, because next time I shall not be merciful. Do you understand?'

'Oh, yes, my lord.' The man was unashamed. 'But I only tell you what I hear.'

'Then your ears are full of dung,' I snapped, whereupon he laughed desperately, thinking to endear himself with a false show of appreciation. 'Be quiet! Stop braying, and say what you have to say.'

'My lord, a friend was in Crieux, two days ago – at the inn there – when he saw Bernard de Pibraux's father, brother and nephew at the next table. As he passed, he heard them talking. The father, Pierre, said: "It makes no difference. Kill one, and Paris sends another." Then his nephew said: "But at least we avenged my cousin." And Pierre said: "Hush, you fool – they have spies everywhere!" And then they were silent.'

Having delivered this information Grimaud himself fell silent, looking into my face expectantly. He was like a dog under a table, waiting for a bone. I folded my arms.

'And you expect payment for this?' I said, whereupon his brow puckered.

'My lord, they said: "Paris sends another!" '

'Grimaud, who is this "friend" of whom you speak?'

'A man called Barthelemy.'

'And where may I find him?'

'In the hospital of St-Etienne. He cooks the food there.'

This reply startled me somewhat for I had expected to hear that the aforesaid Barthelemy had departed on a pilgrimage, or died of a fever. But then I reflected that he might have agreed to support Grimaud's testimony for a cut of the anticipated fee – especially if he was ignorant of the penalties inflicted for bearing false witness.

On the other hand, there was a chance, just the faintest chance, that the story was true. Grimaud, though generally a liar, was not invariably so. Herein lay the difficulty in rejecting all his claims outright (especially in light of the fact that Pierre de Pibraux was high on my list of suspects).

'I shall speak to your friend, and to the innkeeper at Crieux,' I said. 'If I am satisfied that there is some truth in what you say, then you shall receive payment.'

'Oh, *thank* you, my lord!'

'Come back in two weeks.'

'*Two weeks?*' An expression of horror was written upon Grimaud's face. 'But my lord ... two weeks ...'

'I am busy. Very busy.'

'But I need help now – '

'I am *busy*, Grimaud! I have no time for you! No time! Now get out, and come back in two weeks!'

It must be confessed that I raised my voice, and my friends will tell you that I do not often forsake my equanimity in this manner. But I was daunted by the number of tasks confronting me. To begin with, I was expected to investigate Jordan and

Maurand, the two bodyguards under suspicion, together with their habits and their associates. I had to interview Bernard de Pibraux, his three young friends, his father and his brother. Raymond Maury, the baker, had been summoned to appear before me on the following day, and I had not made preparation for this, nor for my interrogation of his father-in-law. As for the other possible suspects (such as Bruna d'Aguilar), I had been ignoring them completely. Raymond Donatus and Durand Fogasset were pestering me for work, and Brother Lucius was sitting idle. Pons, the gaoler, had informed me that one of the Saint-Fiacre villagers had died, and that others were ill; he said that such deaths were to be expected in an overcrowded prison. When would I be able to question the prisoners from Saint-Fiacre?

I could not say. I did not know. It seemed to me that I would be obliged to appoint one of my brethren as a vicar – although as a vicar myself, I had no authority to do such a thing. If Bishop Anselm had been like Bishop Jacques of Pamiers, I might have persuaded him to establish an episcopal inquisition, but I despaired of securing any useful assistance from Bishop Anselm. Indeed, I was consumed with despair, and not simply on account of the labour that stretched before me like a wilderness.

My heart was sore troubled, for Prior Hugues had counselled me with harsh words concerning my days in Casseras.

Upon my return from Casseras, I went to the Prior and requested a hearing. Chiefly, I desired to acquaint him with that transforming and ecstatic experience which had overtaken me on the hillside. I wanted to ask him how I might cleanse my soul further, and what steps I should follow so as to reach once more that exalted state. Possibly I was ineffectual in my attempts to describe it, however, for he appeared concerned as to Johanna's role in what he deemed a 'lustful episode'.

'You said that she smiled at you, and your heart was filled

with love,' he said reprovingly. 'My son, I fear that you were subject to the allurements of bodily passions.'

'But it was an *all-embracing* love. I loved everything I saw.'

'You loved creation.'

'Yes. I loved creation.'

'And what did St Augustin say about such love? "It is true that He created everything exceedingly well, but He, not the creation, is my good." '

This remark caused me to reflect, and the Prior, seeing my consternation, continued.

'You speak of the flowers that calmed your fears with their beauty and their perfume. You speak of the music that ravished you, and the vista that enthralled you. My son, these are sensual delights only.'

'But they led me to God!'

'Again, I turn to St Augustin. "Love, but take heed what you love. The love of God, the love of our neighbour, is called charity; the love of the world, the love of this life, is called concupiscence." '

But I was having none of this. 'Father,' I said, 'if we are turning to St Augustin, we must consider everything he says. "Let the root of love be within, of this root can nothing spring but what is good"; "Because thou dost not yet see God, thou dost earn the seeing of Him by loving thy neighbour." '

'My son, my son.' The Prior lifted his hand. 'Contain your passions.'

'Forgive me, but – '

'I am familiar with the authorities who would support your argument. St Paul says: "Not what is spiritual comes first, but what is animal, then what is spiritual". St Bernard says: "Since we are carnal and born of concupiscence of the flesh, our cupidity or love must begin with the flesh, and when this is set in order, our love advances by fixed degrees, led on by grace, until it is consummated in the spirit". But what else does St Bernard say? He says that, when the Lord has been sought in watching and prayers, with strenuous effort, with showers of tears, He will at length present Himself to the soul. Where was your effort, Bernard? Where were your tears?'

'There were none,' I admitted. 'But I feel that God perhaps bestowed on me the blessing of His divine love so as to spur me on to effort of this kind. By allowing me to taste of His sweetness, He ensured that I would be filled with a longing for more.'

The Prior grunted.

'Father,' I went on, sensing that he was unconvinced, 'I have been filled with just such a longing. I am a better man for what I saw and felt. I am humbler. More charitable – '

'Oh, come now, Bernard, we both know that this means nothing. Even Andreas Capellanus points out that profane love can ennoble. What is it he says? Something about love making man shine with so many virtues, and teaching everyone, no matter how lowly, so many good traits of character?'

I was amused to discover that my old friend had read *The Art of Courtly Love* at some time in his life, and had even committed portions of it to memory. I myself had never encountered the work; it is not one generally found among Dominican friars.

'Why Father, I have not consulted this authority,' was my somewhat ironical response. 'But there is a song I once heard – how did it go?

All that Venus bids me do
Do I with erection,
For she ne'er in heart of man
Dwelt with dull dejection – '

'For shame!' Prior Hugues expostulated. 'Bernard, you are irreverent. We talk of love, not sensual excesses.'

'I know. I am at fault. But Father, I have loved women before this (I am sorry to say), and not one of them has ever bathed my heart in divine radiance. This was different.'

'Because the woman was different.'

'Oh, Father, have you no respect for my judgement?'

'Have you no respect for *mine*? Bernard, you came to me. I have given you my opinion: if there is a woman involved, you are courting peril. All the Masters of the Church tell us this. Now, if you would disregard your vows of obedience, and wish to contest my position, then turn to a greater authority. Seek out the symptoms of divine and profane love – learn to distinguish them. Consult the Angelic Doctor. Consult the *Etymologies*. Then prostrate yourself before God, you who are not worthy to receive His blessings in any form, owing to your profound arrogance of spirit.'

Having delivered himself of this reprimand, the Prior imposed a series of penitential exercises upon me, and dismissed me from his presence. It was a bitter moment, I must confess. Whereas I should have eaten ashes and embraced dunghills, I was moved to stubborn rebelliousness; the arrows of choler were within me, the poison whereof drank up my spirit. For a time, my temper was inflamed. My brethren shrank from me because, in such a state of repressed fury, I was like a basilisk: my voice, though never raised, could burn and blister. My penances were conducted with ill-concealed disdain. I believed that the Prior had turned judgement into gall, and the fruit of righteousness into hemlock.

Naturally I prayed, but my prayers were like slippery ways in the darkness. Naturally I consulted such authorities as the librarian recommended, but with a view to discrediting the Prior, and demonstrating the justice of my own cause. The more I read, however, the more uncertain I became as to the true nature of that moment on the hillside. When studying theology, I had done so – how shall I put it? – in a manner somewhat detached and theoretical. Although I had considered the union of the soul with God, and other related matters, to know in your head that to be present in God is to be nothing in oneself, to abandon whatever is distinctive in oneself – to know this in your head is different from knowing it in your heart. In other words, I seemed to read with freshly opened eyes that, to dwell in God, one must renounce oneself and all things, including creatures that exist in time or eternity; that one must not love this good or that good, but the good from which all good flows. It is a strange experience, using such wisdom to interpret an incident in one's own life. (Previously, I had employed my philosophical and theological knowledge merely to debate propositions with learned interlocutors.) It was like taking testimony from a witness, and measuring it against the errors anathematised in a papal decree. I was forced to ask: had I indeed abandoned myself, and everything around me? Was my soul completely dissolved in God?

As my anger dissipated, I saw what I should have seen from the first (and you will shake your head at my fatuity): that to make the claims which I had been making was a perilous thing to do. Consider, for example, how I, as an inquisitor of heretical depravity, would have regarded such a story if presented to me as evidence of heretical beliefs. Would I not have wondered what ungodly insolence could possess a man who claimed communion with God Himself, though nothing in his life or works seemed to justify such beatitude?

How troubled I was! Plunged into uncertainty, I was like a leaf in a strong wind, tossed this way and that. I would remember my timeless joy on the hillside, and be certain that my soul had reached God. Then I would read further, and begin to doubt. I considered St Paul's journey to Damascus: I reflected on the light that shone around him, and the voice that spoke to him, and the fact that, when he arose, he saw nothing. Many masters teach that in nothing, he saw God, for God is nothing. Dionysius wrote of God: 'He is above being, He is above life, He is above light.' In the *Celestial Hierarchies*, he says: 'Whoever speaks of God through a simile speaks of Him in an impure fashion, but whoever speaks of God by using the term *nothing* speaks of Him properly.' Therefore, when the soul comes into the One and there enters into a pure rejection of itself, it finds God in nothing.

And so I asked myself: is that what I found on the hillside? Nothing? It seemed to me that I had found love, and we all know that God is love. But what *kind* of love? And if I had indeed experienced God's love, then perhaps, because *I* had experienced it (for I believe that I was conscious of my own being, throughout), I did not become truly unformed, informed, and transformed in the divine uniformity which makes us one with God. Oh, I was so confused! I prayed for enlightenment, but none came. I sought the grace of God's presence, but remained untouched by divine love – or at least, by that love which had filled me on the hillside. I spent a good deal of time on my knees, but not enough, perhaps; my duties interfered with my spiritual quest. All the peace had fled from my soul. Burdened with work, condemned by my superior, spiritually troubled, I had no rest. Even on my bed, like Job, I was full of tossings to and fro unto the dawning of the day.

Once, I spent a whole night prostrate before the altar, earnest in my desire to reach God. I did not move, and after a time the pain was very great. I offered it up to our Lord; I besought Him that He should make me an instrument of His peace. How strenuously, how passionately I strove to dismiss myself from myself! How intensely I wanted Him there in my heart! But the more desperately I sought Him, the more distant He seemed, until at last I felt alone in all creation, cast adrift from the love that informs all love, and I wept in despair. *My God, my God, why hast thou forsaken me?* I was as a lost sheep, and a sheep that merited little, for even in these depths I questioned His infinite mercy. Why, on that hillside, had He seemed to touch me with His divine love when I had done nothing to secure it – and now withheld the same, when I sought it with such fervour?

You will agree, I think, that this inquiry shows how far I was from my goal. Indeed, I was most unworthy, for my nature is far from mystical, and my understanding is limited. I would even go so far as to say that my desire for God's love was in some measure promoted by my desire to prove that I had known it once before. Weak, degraded hypocrite! Suffer as I did, I deserved to suffer even greater agonies – for mark where I sought relief. Mark where my tormented spirit found rest. In Christ's bosom? Alas, no.

In the midst of my vexation, I would turn, not to prayer, but to Johanna de Caussade.

I would picture her smile, and feel comforted. I would review in my mind our dialogue, and laugh. I would set her image before me, in my cell at night, and regale it, silently, with descriptions of my torments, my struggles, my confusion. Admirable conduct in a friar of St Dominic! *But I am a worm, and no man; a reproach of men, and despised of the people.* I was ashamed, but at the same time obdurate; I would argue with myself that she was perhaps God's instrument, a lamp and a star. Of course she was not in any way an example, as was Marie d'Oignes – whom Jacques de Vitry called his 'spiritual mother' – or St Margaret of Scotland, who influenced King Malcolm to goodness and piety. ('What she rejected, he rejected ... what she loved, he for love of her, loved too.') But perhaps the love so manifest between Johanna and her daughter had shown me the path of love. Or perhaps it was Alcaya's path – and Johanna, a fellow sinner, had taken my hand to lead me down it.

Shameful thoughts! Only regard my elaborate and ingenious postulations – my tortuous attempts to justify the culpable longings I nurtured. Prior Hugues knew me well. He knew that I was affected by Johanna, to the extent that my vows were endangered. (A common occurrence among brethren who must go out into the world.) Doubtless Father Augustin's role in the widow's life had encouraged me to indulge my emotions, for if he, the perfect inquisitor, had succumbed to her charms, who was I to resist them? Not that my interest was purely or even largely salacious. Recall, if you will, my response to her flirtatious look – my shock and my fear; I entertained no visions of a carnal nature. I wanted only to talk with her, to laugh with her, to share with her my thoughts and my troubles.

I wanted her to love me, and not as we should love all our neighbours, but with a love that distinguished me as much as it excluded other men. *Have mercy upon me, O God, in Your goodness, in the greatness of Your compassion wipe out my offence.* I remembered a proposition put to me, once, which had been derived from the teachings of an infidel: namely, that profane love reunites parts of souls which were separated in the creation. A pestiferous error, without doubt, but one that seemed a poetic *translatio* for my own condition. I felt that Johanna and I were perfectly matched, like the two sides of a broken seal. I felt that we were in some ways like brother and sister.

But not in all ways, I fear. For one day, as I was walking in the street, I saw the back of a woman whom I mistakenly identified as Johanna de Caussade. I stopped abruptly; my heart seemed to spin around in my chest. Then I saw that I had been mistaken, and my disappointment was so profound that I recognised the full width and depth of my sin. Aghast, I realised how far I had fallen from grace.

Whereupon I turned on my heel and went straight to the Prior, who patiently heard my confession.

I told him that I was in love with Johanna. I told him that this love was clouding my judgement. I begged his forgiveness, and upbraided myself for my vanity, my stupidity, my stubbornness. How obstinate I had been! How wilful! My neck was an iron sinew, my brow brass.

'You must curb your pride,' my superior agreed.

'I must extinguish it.'

'Make that your purpose this month, then. Practise obedience. Mortify your flesh. Be silent during chapter (I know you will find that a great trial) and tell yourself, over and over again, "Brother Aeldred is right; I am wrong".'

I burst out laughing, for Brother Aeldred, our Master of Students, was a man with whom I had little sympathy. He and

I differed greatly in our opinions, his being based on insufficient knowledge and faulty powers of reasoning.

'This is a heavy cross,' I bantered.

'And therefore the most efficacious.'

'I would rather wash his feet.'

'Your desires, Bernard, are exactly what we are trying to overthrow.'

'Perhaps I should begin with a more attainable goal. Perhaps I should tell myself: "Brother Aeldred has a right to open his mouth; I am wrong to expect him to understand."'

'My son, I am quite serious.' The Prior spoke gravely. 'You are an intelligent man; no one doubts that. But you pride yourself too much on your intellect. What merit does it hold, if it is accompanied by sloth and vanity and disobedience? This is not Rome or Paris – you will not find the world's greatest minds gathered in Lazet. Perhaps if you did, you would acknowledge that you are not among them.'

'Well ... *perhaps* ...' I replied, with a false and exaggerated air of reluctance.

'Bernard!'

'Forgive me.'

'Will you be laughing at the gates of Hell, I wonder? It seems to me that if you truly recognised the sinfulness of your actions, you would be weeping, not laughing. You have been disobedient. You have given way to the desires of the flesh, and loved your own will. You have been presumptuous – more than presumptuous, irreverent, even obscene! – in equating the lust of concupiscence with the ecstasy of divine love. God forgive you, my son, is such an unholy error that of an intelligent man?'

Perhaps it was the faint note of scorn in his tone which prompted me to speak at this point. Or perhaps it was the knowledge that, in making confession, one must reveal every thought and feeling.

'Father, I have sinned in my love of Johanna de Caussade,' I said. 'I have sinned in my anger and my pride. But I am not convinced that what I felt, on that hillside, was of earthly origin. I am not satisfied that it was *not* the love of God.'

'Bernard, you are in error.'

'Perhaps. Perhaps not.'

'Is this humility? Is this repentance?'

'Would you have me deny Christ?'

'Would you have *me* accept such a blasphemy?'

'Father, I have searched my soul – '

'– and succumbed to conceit.'

At this, I must confess, I was angered – though I had promised to eschew anger, and abandon pride.

'It is not conceit,' I protested.

'You are vainglorious.'

'You think me incapable of reason? Incapable of distinguishing between one kind of love and the other?'

'Because you are blinded by pride.'

'Father,' I said, and I was trying to stay calm, 'have *you* ever known divine love?'

'It is not your place to ask such a question.'

'I know for a fact that you have never known a *woman's* love.'

'Be silent!' All at once, he was very angry. I had rarely seen the Prior angry – certainly not since his election. Throughout his life he had cultivated serenity, and even as a youth had presented a tranquil face to the world. Moved by some demon of mischief, I had often worked, in those far-off days, to undermine his equanimity, teasing and taunting him – but with little success. Even so, there was no one else as capable of disturbing his peace of mind.

And although we were old men, he still remained the slow, plump former oblate with no experience of the world, while I remained the quick, lean graduate of dissipation.

'Be silent!' he repeated. 'Or I will have you scourged for your insolence!'

'I do not mean to be insolent, Father, I simply wished to

point out that I am somewhat familiar with love, both profane and perhaps divine – '

'*Hold your tongue!*'

'Hugues, hear me on this. I am not attempting to challenge your authority – I am in earnest, I swear. You know me, I am such a worldly man, but this is something different – I have been wrestling with demons – '

'You are *guided* by demons. You are inflamed with pride and ignorant of God's will.' He spoke breathlessly, brokenly, and stood up to deliver his *conclusio*. 'I see no profit in further congress. You will fast on bread and water, you will remain silent in this priory, and you will prostrate yourself at chapter for a month – or risk expulsion. If you come to me again, let it be on your hands and knees, for I will not see you otherwise. God have mercy on your soul.'

And so it was that I lost the Prior's friendship. I had not understood, until that moment, how profoundly his election had inflated his sense of dignity. I had not understood that in challenging him, I had seemed, in his eyes, to disparage his abilities, and question his right to the office.

Perhaps, if I had understood this, I might not be in my present position.

September passed; Lent began; summer drew to a close. In the priory, we celebrated Michaelmas and the feast of St Francis. In the mountains, the shepherds drove their flocks south. In the vineyards, grapes were trampled. The world continued as God has ordained *(He appointed the moon for seasons: the sun knoweth his going down)* while Father Augustin slowly rotted, unavenged. For I acknowledge, to my shame, that I advanced not one step towards a true understanding of his murder.

After exerting myself in that direction for several days, I had collected a good many facts about Jordan Sicre and Maurand d'Alzen. I was already aware that Jordan had come to Lazet from the garrison of Puilaurens. Born in Limoux, he had family

175

there of whom he rarely spoke: his comrades believed that he had broken with all his relatives. He was more highly trained than many of our familiars, and possessed a short sword which he employed with 'much skill'. Before his appointment to the Holy Office he had served in the town garrison, and I discovered that the transfer had been carried out at his own request. (A familiar's pay is better than a garrison sergeant's, and his duties are less onerous, though his standing is perhaps not as high.) Jordan lived with four other familiars in a room behind a shop, which was owned by Raymond Donatus. He was not married. He rarely, if ever, went to church.

These facts were known to me. But after speaking to the men who shared his room, and the sergeants who had worked with him in the city garrison – some of whom, having accompanied me to Casseras, were eager to be of assistance – I gained a more thorough appreciation of Jordan Sicre. He was a hard-headed, rather morose fellow who despised incompetence. He liked to gamble, and indulged this passion freely without often falling into debt. He spoke knowledgeably about shearing and pasturage. He patronised harlots. He was respected, but not loved; I was told that he had no close friends. Most of his free time was spent gambling with a few like-minded associates, all of them familiars or garrison sergeants. His effects (such as they were) had been shared out among the remaining inhabitants of his room. He had been thirty years old, or thereabouts, when he had volunteered to accompany Father Augustin on that fateful journey.

Maurand d'Alzen had also volunteered for Father Augustin's guard. He had been younger than Jordan by three or four years, a native of Lazet, whose father was a smith in the St-Etienne quarter. He had lived with his family, but did not appear to be greatly missed. Upon first hearing his name in connection with the massacre, I had recalled often chiding him for blasphemy or excessive violence; on one occasion, he had even been accused of breaking a prisoner's ribs, though this charge was never proven. (There had been bad blood between

Maurand and his alleged victim, but the prisoner had died without regaining consciousness, and no one had actually witnessed the assault.) Consequently, I knew Maurand as a vicious youth of little apparent merit – an impression which was confirmed in my conversations with his family, with his comrades, and with the woman described as his 'mistress'.

This unfortunate girl, a poor cousin, had worked for Maurand's father from an early age. At sixteen she had given birth to Maurand's illegitimate son, who was now three years old. On her face and arms she bore the scars of her lover's attentions, for he had possessed a heavy hand; indeed, it appeared that she had first known him carnally not long after her thirteenth birthday, when he had raped her and deprived her of her virginity. She resented him, not so much for her own sake as for the sake of her little son, who had also suffered beatings. On several occasions her lover had been banished from the house, but had always been welcomed back by his family.

Although she did not say as much, I assumed, from her demeanour, that she was not at all saddened by his death.

It appeared that Maurand's other relatives had also turned against him, owing to the frequency and violence of his rages. They described him as lazy, disrespectful, intemperate. He was always short of money. An uncle had accused him of stealing a belt and cloak, but could furnish no proof; nevertheless, Maurand's father had replaced these items. Many of the neighbouring women complained to me of Maurand's lewd and suggestive remarks. Oddly enough, he had attended church diligently, and was regarded by the canons of St-Etienne as 'a simple lad, rough but devout'. Nevertheless, I asked myself: is this the kind of man we employ at the Holy Office? And I vowed that, at the earliest opportunity, I would review the current hiring procedures. Clearly such a responsibility could not be entrusted to Pons alone.

Maurand's fellow familiars were a little more generous in their estimates of him. They called him 'jovial', and commended him for his humorous anecdotes. He had been a big, strong, solid fellow, not a trained fighter, but capable of throwing a powerful punch (together with any table, staff or helmet that might come to hand). They admitted that he had possessed a quick temper, and had never been known to repay money lent to him. For this reason, no one had ever lent him money twice.

'He had no money for whores,' I was told, 'so he was always getting into trouble with the women. He was so big and strong, some of them were glad to go with him. But most of them were afraid.'

'Where did he spend his time?' I queried. 'When he was not working, or at home, where did he go?'

'Oh – the inn at the market. We most of us go there.'

'Of course.' I was familiar with the lounging clusters of sergeants who sat by the door of that establishment, spitting at young men and making obscene gestures at young women. 'Who were his friends there? Aside from yourselves?'

I received a long list of names – a list so long that I was obliged to write it down. Apparently Maurand had been known (and doubtless abhorred) by half the population of Lazet. Although I recognised none of the names as belonging to family or associates of Bernard de Pibraux, I did recognise the name of Aimery Ribaudin's son-in-law, Matthieu Martin. And as you will recall, Aimery Ribaudin was one of the six people suspected of bribing Father Jacques.

'*Aimery Ribaudin*?' the Seneschal exclaimed, when I consulted him on this matter. 'Impossible.'

'Father Augustin had been questioning his friends and relatives,' I replied. 'If Aimery knew about that, he had a reason for killing Father Augustin.'

'But how could Aimery Ribaudin be a heretic in the first place? Why, look how much he donates to St Polycarpe!'

Certainly, the case against Aimery was not strong. Some eight years previously, a weaver had been convicted of bringing a Perfect to the deathbed of his wife, so that she might be hereticated with the *consolamentum*. One witness interrogated about this incident remembered having seen Aimery speaking to the accused man two or three years after the death of his aforesaid wife (the weaver having left his family's village for Lazet, during the intervening period), and giving the accused man some money.

I was reluctant, however, to supply the Seneschal with these details, which were not publicly known.

'Aimery Ribaudin is under investigation,' I said firmly, whereupon Roger, shaking his head, muttered something to the effect that if *he* had been Aimery, he would have been tempted to kill Father Augustin himself. Fortunately for Roger, I chose to ignore this remark. Instead I proceeded to inform him of Grimaud's accusation regarding Pierre de Pibraux, and the inn at Crieux. 'I have not yet spoken to Grimaud's friend, Barthelemy, or the innkeeper,' I finished, 'but I shall do so before Bernard de Pibraux's three friends come to Lazet. I summoned them here some time ago. Even then, I had my suspicions.'

'By God, it sounds promising!'

'Perhaps. As I said, Grimaud is very unreliable.'

'But I know Bernard de Pibraux's father,' the Seneschal revealed, rising and pacing the floor. (I had decided to consult him at headquarters, because I was doubtful as to the degree of privacy available at the Chateau Comtal.) 'I know him well, and he has a temper. They all do, in that family. By God, Father, they could have done it!'

'Perhaps.'

'And if they did, we can bring them to justice! And the King will stop hounding me about this thing!'

'Perhaps.' My tone must have been somewhat listless, for at the time I was still wrestling with certain spiritual questions raised by my visit to Casseras, and had been sleeping very little. The Seneschal looked at me in a puzzled way.

'I thought that you would be more excited,' he observed. 'Are you ill, Father?'

'I? Oh no.'

'You seem ... your colour is bad.'

'I am fasting.'

'Oh.'

'And there has been so much work to do.'

'Listen.' The Seneschal sat down again, leaned forward, and placed both hands on my knees. He was flushed, and I sensed that, with our quarry barely out of reach (or so it appeared), his hunter's instincts had been roused. 'Let me talk to this Barthelemy fellow. If he seems to be telling the truth, let me go to Pibraux and find out what Pierre and his family were doing on the day of Father Augustin's death. I can even stop at Crieux on the way. Talk to that innkeeper. Take a load off your shoulders. What do you say?'

I said nothing for a while. I was reviewing his offer, and the phrasing of Pierre's alleged conversation at the inn. At last I said: 'There was no suggestion that Pierre and his nephew killed Father Augustin with their own hands. If they hired mercenaries, all of them would have been safely in Pibraux on the day of the murder.'

The Seneschal's face fell.

'But,' I continued, thinking hard, '*Barthelemy* may not realise that. If you go to him, and tell him what you intend to do at Pibraux, and warn him of the penalties incurred by those who bear false witness, you may frighten him into admitting that he lied — if he *does* lie to you. Tell him that if Pierre was in Pibraux on the day of the murder, you will know that someone has been lying — '

'And if he clings to his story, then he is probably telling the truth!' Roger finished. He slapped my knee in delight, and with such vigour that he almost crippled me. 'What a mind you have, Father! As cunning as a fox!'

'Thank you so much.'

'I shall go straight to Barthelemy. And if he gives me satisfaction, I shall ride to Pibraux this afternoon. By God, if I could get this thing off my back — what a relief it would be!

And for you too, Father, of course,' he hastened to add. 'You will be able to rest easy, once the killers have been punished.'

It shamed me that I seemed to be suffering on account of Father Augustin's death, when in fact my sleepless nights were the result of matters unrelated. It shamed me that I should be thought more devoted to his memory than I really was. Therefore, once the Seneschal had gone, I addressed my duties with a renewed sense of purpose. That very afternoon, an interview had been scheduled with Raymond Maury's father-in-law (who was, as you may recollect, a wealthy furrier); with the assistance of Raymond Donatus, I questioned this man about his son-in-law's alleged heretical opinions, and – since I was not satisfied with his answers – questioned him again. Drawing on depositions extracted from various other witnesses by Father Augustin, I pointed out that in some cases they contradicted the furrier. They named him as being present during an episode of which he denied any knowledge. They quoted him as saying: 'My son-in-law is a damned heretic!'. How could he deny his complicity, when it was so very clear?

Be assured that I was implacable. And after a long and tiring interview, the furrier at last capitulated. He confessed that he had been trying to protect Raymond Maury. He begged me, weeping, to forgive him. I told him that I forgave him with all my heart, but that he must and would be punished for his sins. The sentence would be formulated at the next *auto de fé*, and although various learned authorities would have to be consulted, the usual penance for the crime of concealing a heretic was compounded of prayer, fasting, flagellation and pilgrimage.

The furrier continued to weep.

'Of course,' I told him, 'if it should be found, from the testimony of other witnesses, that you actually shared Raymond's beliefs – '

'Oh no, Father, no!'

'A repentant heretic will receive mercy. An obdurate heretic will receive none.'

'Father, I am not a heretic, I swear! I would never, *never* –
I am a good Catholic! I love the Church!'

Having discovered no evidence to the contrary, I believed
him; one begins to develop a certain instinct for lies when one
is an inquisitor of heretical depravity. Although the truth might
be concealed, one can often smell it, just as a pig can smell
buried truffles. Besides which, the furrier had sworn an oath
to tell the pure, simple and full truth – and Cathar believers
will not, under any circumstances, take an oath.

Nevertheless I continued to pretend that I was suspicious,
for I had a notion that Father Jacques had been well rewarded
for disregarding Raymond Maury – and if that was the case,
then the payment had very probably come from Raymond's
father-in-law.

In any event, I decided to proceed on that assumption.

'How can I believe you,' I said, 'when you persist in hiding
things from me?'

'No! Never!'

'Never? What of the money you paid, to ensure that your
son-in-law escaped punishment?'

The furrier looked at me through his tears. Slowly, he
changed colour. I saw his throat move as he swallowed.

'Oh,' he said faintly. 'I forgot about that – '

'You *forgot*?'

'It was so long ago! He asked me for it!'

'Who did? Father Jacques?'

'Father Jacques?' The furrier stared in astonishment. 'No.
My son-in-law asked me. Raymond asked me.'

'For how much?'

'Fifty livres tournois.'

'And you gave them to him?'

'I love my daughter – she is my only child – I would do
anything – '

'Would you kill for her?' I inquired, and the look he gave
me was so pitifully confused – so afflicted and drunken, but
not with wine – that I almost laughed aloud. 'It has been

suggested,' I said falsely, 'that when Father Augustin began to pursue Raymond, you hired assassins to kill him.'

'*I?*' the man screeched. Then he became angry. 'Who says this?' he demanded. 'This is a lie! I never killed the Inquisitor!'

'If you did, you should confess to it now. For I shall find you out in the end.'

'*No!*' he shouted. 'I told you I lied! I told you I paid money! I told you everything! But I *did not kill the inquisitor!*'

Despite all my efforts, I could not persuade the furrier to retract this statement. Only torture would have changed his mind, and I had no wish to employ torture. For there is a point past which a man will admit to anything, and I had never really entertained the belief that Raymond Maury's father-in-law had been responsible for Father Augustin's death. Naturally, I was prepared to check his testimony. I was prepared to recall many of those witnesses already interviewed by Father Augustin, and inquire as to the furrier's recent habits, expenditures and associates. But I did not expect to find that he had been frequenting the inn at the market, or playing dice with Jordan Sicre. I did not expect to find that he had been bribing the Bishop's stablehands.

I simply wanted to eliminate him from my list of suspects.

So I dismissed him, thanked my 'impartials' (the aforementioned Brothers Simon and Berengar), and concluded the interrogation. Then I took Raymond Donatus aside to instruct him as to the drawing up of the finished protocol. He was eager to express his views on the furrier, whom he regarded as 'almost certainly responsible for the murder of Father Augustin'. But he said nothing about Father Jacques.

It surprised me that he was able to resist the temptation. Indeed, I was so surprised that I raised the subject myself.

'You knew, of course, that Father Augustin was investigating his predecessor's virtue,' I remarked.

'Yes, Father.'

'Have you formed any opinions as to the justice of this inquiry?'

'I ... it is not for me to say.'

As you may imagine, I was most amused by his uncharacteristic reticence. 'But my friend,' I observed, 'you have never been silent before.'

'It is a very delicate matter.'

'True.'

'And Father Augustin instructed me not to talk about it.'

'I see.'

'And if you think that *I* may be implicated, be assured that I am *not!*' the notary exclaimed, making me start. 'Father Augustin was quite satisfied on this point! He questioned me several times – '

'My son – '

'– and I told him that I *trusted* Father Jacques – it was not *my* place to keep a tally of the people named in all those hundreds of inquisitions – '

'Raymond, please, I was not accusing you.'

'If he had suspected me, Father, he would have dismissed me – or worse!'

'I know. Of course. Calm yourself.' I would have said more, if I had not been interrupted by a familiar who approached me with a sealed letter from Bishop Anselm. This functionary also bore a verbal message from the Seneschal, which he related to me word for word. Barthelemy, it appeared, had indeed encountered Pierre de Pibraux at Crieux, but had heard him say nothing sinister or suspicious.

'I am to tell you, Father, that your little ruse worked,' the familiar announced.

'Thank you, sergeant.'

'I am also to tell you that another one of the prisoners has died. An infant. The gaoler wants to talk to you.'

'God save us. Very well.'

'Also, I am asked to inform you that the familiars have not been paid this month. Of course we know that you have been very busy – '

'Yes, sergeant, I shall look into it. Apologise to your comrades for me, and tell them that I shall visit the Royal Steward of Confiscations tomorrow. As you say, I have been very busy.'

Cheerful tidings, were they not? Little wonder I found no comfort in life, beset as I was with doubt, failure and frustration. But I had yet to receive the cruellest blow. For when I opened the Bishop's letter, I found enclosed within it a missive from the Inquisitor of France.

It appeared that my new superior had been appointed – and that he was Pierre-Julien Fauré.

He cometh with clouds

I know that you must be acquainted with Pierre-Julien Fauré. I know that you must have met him while he was in Paris, for he attracts one's attention, does he not? Or rather, he forces himself upon one's notice. He is a noisy man, and always has been; I can testify to this because I have known him myself for a very long time. You see, he is a native of this region.

We first encountered each other when I was still a preacher ordinary, before the encouragement of my superiors had prompted me to assume the mantle of a student, once more, so that I might become a lector of great fame and influence. (Laughable, is it not?) During my travels with Father Dominic, I passed through Toulouse, stopping long enough to acquaint myself with the Provincial House of Studies – where Pierre-Julien had been resident for just a year. In those days he was a pasty youth enamoured of St Thomas Aquinas, whose entire *Summa* he appeared to have committed to memory. It was this feat, I think, rather than any brilliance of delivery or insight, which recommended him to his teachers – for when I attended one of the lectures there, I was impressed by the remarkable fatuity of his questions.

I did not expend much thought on his character at the time,

seeing him merely as a boy of no great distinction, pale and sickly from his studious life (or so I believed, although I now know that his pallid complexion is natural to him), possessed of an enthusiasm which somehow repelled me, and a voice that was apt to become shrill if ignored. We only spoke once: he asked me if I found it difficult to resist the temptations of the world, now that I was moving freely among them.

'No,' I replied – not yet having become entangled with the aforementioned young widow whose charms compelled me to break my vows.

'Do you see many women?' he inquired.

'Yes.'

'That must be very hard.'

'Indeed? Why so?'

Of course I knew exactly what he was trying to say, but gained some satisfaction in seeing him blush, and falter, and withdraw. I was in many ways a vicious young man, and often acted cruelly; in this instance, however, I was punished for my arrogance. What greater punishment could there be than to find myself vicar to a man I snubbed so long ago – a man who has reached far loftier heights than I shall ever attain, despite possessing a lower degree of intelligence?

At any rate, we parted, and I did not meet him again until we were both studying at Montpellier Studium Generale. Here we moved in different circles; I gathered that he was struggling (while I soared), but that he had mastered a fund of gossip which caused him to be much pursued by those interested in the debates of Paris, or the politics of the Papal court. He had filled out, by then, though he was already losing his hair. I once positively *destroyed* him during an informal disputation, for his position was untenable, and his rhetorical skills were undeveloped; again, however, I have come to regret the vigour with which I demolished his arguments. One's meanness of spirit always overthrows one, eventually.

I knew nothing of his subsequent career until I began to encounter him at the provincial chapters, from about 1310. By this time he was a Prior; I, a Preacher General and Master of Students (but not in his priory, thanks be to God!). It became clear that we differed on many subjects, including the works of Durand de Saint Pourcain – which were not, as you may recall, *utterly* banned from the schools, but permitted as long as they contained suitable glosses. Pierre-Julien, I think, would have preferred it that his students read nothing but Pierre Lombard and the Angelic Doctor. He chided me, in offensively avuncular tones, for possessing an 'undisciplined intellect'.

I fear that we did not cherish each other with a fraternal affection.

It has been several years since my last appearance at a provincial chapter, owing to the demands of the Holy Office, and – I must speak frankly – to the fact that I am not a favourite with the Provincial himself. But correspondence with other brethren has kept me informed as to Pierre-Julien's advancement. I learned that he was teaching in Paris, then moved to Avignon, where he was well regarded at the Papal court. I learned that he had been sent to assist Michael le Moine, the Inquisitor of Heretical Depravity at Marseilles, with the task of persuading those obstinate Franciscans of Narbonne to recant. And now, after apparently distinguishing himself in the holy task of extirpating heresy, he had been appointed Inquisitor of Lazet, 'in place of Father Augustin Duese'.

I must confess that I laughed (albeit gloomily) when I noted the Bishop's use of words, for in no manner could Pierre-Julien be regarded as a 'replacement' for Father Augustin. The two were cast from entirely different moulds. And if you are unable to appreciate their differences – not, perhaps, having known either man very well – let me recount the activities of my new superior during his first two days in office.

He arrived approximately three weeks after I was notified of his appointment, but was preceded by several letters alerting me to the date of his intended arrival. Having set the date, he twice changed it, then reverted to the original just three days before his appearance. (If only he had been residing in Paris, instead of Avignon, I would have had longer to wait!) Naturally, he expected to be greeted by the usual solemn reception – a reception eschewed by Father Augustin – so I was kept very busy arranging matters with the Bishop, the Seneschal, the Prior, the canons of St Polycarpe, the consuls ... well, you will understand how many people must be consulted on these occasions. The new Inquisitor wished to be greeted by a party of high officials at the city gate; then, accompanied by a troup of soldiers and a band of musicians, he wished to proceed to St Polycarpe, where he intended to address the entire population of Lazet regarding 'God's great and spreading vine, which was planted by the hand of the Lord, redeemed by His blood, watered by His word, propagated by His grace, and rendered fruitful by His spirit'. After a large part of the congregation had dispersed, he would greet the leaders of the city one by one, that he might 'come to know as a good shepherd the finest sheep in his flock'.

One could only conclude, from reading these instructions, that Pierre-Julien regarded the post of Inquisitor as one fairly elevated in the hierarchy of Angels. Certainly, when he arrived, this impression was confirmed by the paternal air with which he blessed everyone save the Bishop, who received instead a warm and reverent kiss. (The Seneschal, I am sure, was not entranced by Pierre-Julien's manner.) I derived great satisfaction from noting that my old friend no longer needed a razor to keep his tonsure in place; he was almost completely bald, save for a few wispy hairs still clinging to the scalp around his ears. For the rest, he was largely unchanged – shrill, vehement, sweaty and as pale as congealed fat. When he saw me he merely nodded, but I expected nothing more. If he had kissed me, it would have turned my stomach.

I shall not weary you with an exhaustive account of his reception, though I will say that, as I had anticipated, the *translatio* of the Lord's vine was extended to the very limits of endurance – until, in fact, it was longer than the vine itself. He spoke of us all as 'grapes', our cities as 'bunches', our doubts as 'burrowing worms within the grapes'. He spoke of 'catching the foxes in the vineyard'. He spoke of the Apocalypse as 'the treading of the grapes' and Judgement Day as 'the tasting of the wine'. (Some wine would be imbibed by God, you see, and some expectorated.) I must confess that I was almost helpless with laughter by the end of his sermon, and had to pretend that I was greatly moved — that my snorts and tears were evidence of affliction, rather than of suppressed hilarity. Even so, I believe that Pierre-Julien was unconvinced. Doubtless he did not regard me as one of the world's juicier grapes.

Nevertheless, when we finally spoke (and this was on the second day, after he had conversed privately with the Bishop, the Seneschal, the Prior, the Royal Treasurer, and the Royal Steward of Confiscations), he greeted me in a genial fashion, as one might greet a fondly indulged, if somewhat wayward and stupid, lay brother.

'My son,' he said, 'what a time it is since we last met! You look well. Clearly the life here agrees with you.'

Although he did not add 'out on the edge of civilisation', his meaning was apparent.

'It has, in the past,' I replied, 'although I cannot speak for the future.'

'And yet this place seems to be forsaken by God,' he continued, abandoning pleasantries. 'Such wickedness! I wept when I heard of Brother Augustin's horrible fate. I thought: "Satan came also among them". Little did I know that I would be bidden to rise up and cleanse the lepers myself.'

'Oh, we are not *all* lepers, here,' I said, inwardly enraged. 'Some of us still follow the Lord's statutes.'

'Of course. But it is a deep mire, is it not? The floods overflow. I am told that the prison is full, and Father Augustin's assailants are not yet captured.'

'As you may imagine, *Brother*, I have been overwhelmed with work — '

'Yes. And now I have come to your aid. Tell me about the investigation so far. Have you advanced, at all?'

I assured him that we had. I described Father Augustin's death, taking care not to dwell on Johanna or her friends, whom I dismissed as being 'pious and humble'; I described the Provost's inquiry, the Seneschal's investigation, and my own visit to Casseras (with certain important omissions); I described the list of suspects and my efforts to determine the extent of their guilt. I also aired my theory regarding a traitorous familiar, whom I had not, as yet, identified.

'Both Jordan and Maurand could be culpable,' I said. 'Jordan, because he was a gambler, a trained mercenary, and a highly efficient man; Maurand, because he was in almost every respect violent and depraved.'

'But why do you think it likely that someone betrayed Brother Augustin?'

'Because the bodies were dismembered, and scattered abroad. It would make sense if the purpose of such a strange action were to conceal the absence of one body.'

'But you said that most of the remains were found on the road.'

'Yes, they were. But several heads, which are the most distinctive members, were carried away – '

'Describe the site to me. You said the massacre took place in a clearing?'

'A sort of clearing.'

'And the road passes through it?'

'I believe the term "path" is more apt than "road".'

'Is this path crossed by other paths, when it reaches the clearing?'

Puzzled by his inquiry, I had to reflect for a moment before I could respond to it.

'As I recall, there are a number of goat tracks which converge there.'

'Ah!' Pierre-Julien threw up his hands. 'There you have it. A crossroads.'

'A crossroads?' I repeated, mystified.

'You are not aware of the importance of crossroads?'

'Importance?'

'Come.' Pierre-Julien rose from the bed. We were sitting in his cell, which was cluttered with what I can only describe as 'possessions', most of them books. He had a great many books, together with two or three astronomical instruments, a collection of ointments in glass phials, a portable altar, a jewel-encrusted reliquary and a carved box full of letters. From the midst of these earthly impediments he extracted a small book, which he held almost gingerly, as if it might at any moment burst into flame. 'Observe,' he said. 'You are doubtless unfamiliar with this work. It is entitled *The Book of the Offices of the Spirits*, and was derived from that ancient and mystical text, *The Testament of Solomon*. Because it is in many ways dangerous, you will only find it circulated among learned men whose strength of piety is unchallenged.'

At this point I might well have said: 'Then how did you secure it?' But I forbore. Indeed, I was curious about this dangerous book.

'It concerns the hosts of hell,' Pierre-Julien continued. 'In it you will find all the evil angels − their names, their manifestations and their skills. Regard this page, for example: "Berith has three names. By some he is called Beall; by the Jews, Berith; by necromancers, Bolfry: he cometh forth as a red soldier, with red clothing, on a red horse. He answereth truly of things past, present and future. He is also a liar, he turneth all metals into gold."'

'Show me,' I demanded, reaching for the book. But Pierre-Julien would not relinquish it.

'Of course these are only the *principal* demons,' he said. 'Demons such as Purson, Leraie, Glasya Labolas, Malaphas, Shax, Focalor, Sitrael, and the rest. Many of them have unnamed regiments of lower demons beneath them.'

'Brother, I pray you, let me see.'

Once again, however, the book was withheld.

'As you may imagine, knowledge of this kind is perilous enough,' Pierre-Julien declaimed. 'But the book also contains formulae for conjuring and invoking the demons named herein. Rites for harnessing their powers.'

'No!' I had heard of such texts, but had never beheld one. Indeed, I had always suspected that they might exist only in the febrile imaginings of senility. 'It is a magical book, then!'

'It is. And if you turn to the prescriptions for invocation, you will read the following: that, in order to conjure up the five demons Sitrael, Malantha, Thamaor, Falaur and Sitrami, after first preparing oneself with chaste fasting and prayer, one must fumigate, asperge and consecrate the black-handled and white-handled knives – '

'Brother – '

'One moment, please. And therefore, having prepared oneself in various ways, one must take a living black virgin hen to a crossroads at midnight, cut it into pieces and scatter it, all the while chanting, "I conjure, charge and command you, Sitrael, Malantha, Thamaor, Falaur and Sitrami, you infernal kings, in the name and by the power and dignity of the Omnipotent and Immortal Lord God of Hosts – "'

'Brother, are you trying to say – '

' – although of course, in the case of Brother Augustin's death, the conjurers, being heretics, would have employed the name of their own foul deity – '

'Brother, are you in *earnest*?' I could scarcely believe my ears. 'Are you trying to tell me that Father Augustin was sacrificed to conjure up *demons*?'

'It is very probable.'

'But he was not a virgin hen!'

'No. But if you examine books such as this, you will see that human limbs are occasionally sacrificed. And if you are familiar with the prosecution of Guichard, Bishop of Troyes – which is probably not the case, but let me assure you that when I was in Paris I consulted copies of witnesses' depositions held by the Inquisitor of France – if you are familiar with this sad affair, you will know that when Guichard and the friar Jean le Fay read from their book of incantations, a form appeared like

193

a black monk with horns, and when Guichard enjoined it to make his peace with Queen Joan, this demon demanded one of his limbs in return.'

I assure you, I stood there with my mouth hanging open. Of course I remembered the persecution of Guichard, which took place ten years ago. I remembered the tales of Guichard's infamies: that he was the son of an incubus, that he kept a private demon in a flask, that he had poisoned Queen Joan with a mixture of adders, scorpions, toads and spiders. And I remember thinking at the time that if these tales were not distorted by distance, they were so monstrous as to be laughable. But ten years ago everyone was talking about the iniquities of the Knights Templar – do you recall? The knights were accused of worshipping Satan with acts of blasphemy and sodomy, with the murder of infants, and with the invocation of demons. Whether or not these allegations were true, I have no way of confirming: I was not an Inquisitor of heretical depravity at the time, for which I am profoundly thankful, and now know how easy it is to extract a confession with live coals. I also know that many knights withdrew the confessions which they had made under torture, and were burned to death still protesting their innocence. But you must have drawn your own conclusions regarding the Order's activities in France, so I shall not be diverted. Suffice it to say that when I heard the charges against Bishop Guichard, I could not help wondering if certain people had used the fear of demonic forces, then so prevalent, to destroy his reputation. And I was justified, I think – for was he not released from custody four years ago, and sent as a suffragan bishop to Germany? This, I believe, was after certain witnesses, once hostile to him, had testified to his innocence on their deathbeds.

Not that I would deny the existence of demons, or the necromancers who would seek to summon them from the depths. St Thomas Aquinas has pointed out that when a magician invokes a demon, the demon is not truly coerced; though it may appear to be subject to the wishes of the conjurer, it is in fact leading the man more deeply into sin. But if Guichard had been guilty of such a sin, why was he now a suffragan bishop, with the blessing of the Holy Father?

In effect, I could not believe that Pierre-Julien was using the example of Bishop Guichard seriously. Perhaps, too, I was thinking of that notorious attack on Pope Boniface VIII, made by the same forces behind the persecution of Bishop Guichard and the Knights Templar: namely, the forces of King Philippe. You will undoubtedly recollect how violently the King and Pope Boniface were opposed to each other. It is probably not surprising that, after the Holy Father's death, the King charged him with all manner of heretical and diabolical practices. In fact I seem to recall that Boniface too was accused of harbouring a private demon, which he is alleged to have conjured up by killing a cock and throwing its blood on the fire. Perhaps, like Guichard, he was employing a book similar to that in Pierre-Julien's hand. But if he was indeed guilty, then why were the proceedings against him suddenly suspended, when Pope Clement (may he rest in peace) at last acceded to the King's various demands regarding bulls passed by the aforesaid Boniface?

Oh, I am a mistrustful and irreverent soul. The Provincial used to say as much, when we disagreed on this very matter. But I believe that I am not alone in my doubts. Others I know have questioned the King's reasons for pursuing Pope Boniface and Bishop Guichard.

Pierre-Julien, however, was clearly not among them.

'It was my impression that the charges against Bishop Guichard were never proven,' I said.

'They were indeed! He was imprisoned!'

'But his accusers surely recanted.'

Pierre-Julien made a dismissive gesture. 'Mercy extended to a sinner does not make him any less a sinner, as you know. Now as to Father Augustin, it seems to me that certain sprouts of depravity, in their desire to serve the devil and deny God's truth, may have done so by sacrificing one of the Lord's most zealous defenders in a way that would conjure up all the hosts of hell.'

'Brother – '

'When I was first told about this assassination, I wondered if it was an act of sorcery. I said as much to the Holy Father, and he was most concerned.'

'He was?' I found this hard to believe. Personally, I would have laughed out loud. 'But why?'

Pierre-Julien looked at me with a pitying, patronising air. He placed a hand on my arm, and pulled me back down onto the bed, where we both sat side by side.

'You are a long way from Avignon, here in Lazet,' he consoled me. 'Of course you would have no understanding of the latest attack on Christendom. I mean the deadly contagion of sorceries, divination and invocation of demons. Are you aware that the Holy Father has appointed a commission to investigate sorcery *within his own court*?'

I shook my head, speechless.

'It is so. He himself, in fear of this pestiferous society of men and evil angels, has been driven to employ a magical snakeskin, to detect the presence of poison in his food and drink.'

'But surely . . .' I swear to you, I could not find the words. 'Surely the Holy Father would not fall into the same sin . . .?'

'My son, are you ignorant of past conspiracies against Pope John? Are you unaware that Bishop Hugh Geraud of Cahors and his fellow conspirators last year attempted to kill the Holy Father?'

'Yes, of course, but – '

'They bought from a Jew three wax figures to which they attached three strips of parchment bearing the names of the Pope and his two most loyal supporters. Then they concealed these figures, together with poisons procured from Toulouse, in a loaf which they dispatched to Avignon.'

'Really?' Although I knew of the plot, I knew nothing of wax figures. 'Did you see them?'

'What?'

'The figures.'

'No. But I have spoken to people who did.'

'Oh.' Confused, I held my peace. It seemed that there was some campaign afoot of which I was utterly ignorant. Of course, necromancy was not in the domain of an inquisitor of heretical depravity, so I could not have been expected to concern myself with it. Nevertheless, I felt for the first time that I had lost my grasp of the world. I felt like a mountain peasant, confronted by an invading army for which nothing has prepared him.

'I think that you should read this,' Pierre-Julien advised, at last relinquishing *The Book of the Offices of the Spirits*. 'I also have here another book that you should read, called *Lemegeton*. Treat them as manuals for the detection of sorcerers and diviners. Armed with this knowledge, you will be better equipped to overcome the forces of evil.'

'But it is not my job to investigate magicians. I am not enjoined to do so.'

'Perhaps you soon will be,' Pierre-Julien observed, 'if the Holy Father has his way. Besides, you are investigating Father Augustin's death, are you not?'

I held up my hand. 'Brother,' I said, 'Father Augustin was *not* sacrificed.'

'How can you know this?'

'Because he was not a hen, because he was not killed at midnight, and because he was not scattered around a cross-roads. Father Augustin was scattered across the length and breadth of this country.'

'My son, we cannot know how many other books of this kind there are – books full of unknown rites and incantations. Books that we have never seen, containing unimaginable blasphemies.'

'Perhaps. But if *you* have never seen them, Brother, I will swear on the Holy Scriptures that no one here has seen them either. As you say, we are a long way from Avignon.'

Pierre-Julien began to shake his head. 'Alas, would it were

so!' he sighed. ' "And when He is come, He will reprove the world of sin." There is no corner of the earth free from Satan's pestilence.'

All at once I was overcome by a terrible fatigue. I felt that, struggle as I might, Pierre-Julien would never be suppressed. He was indefatigable – imbued by a fervour that no man of moderate passions could hope to match. It had become apparent to me that this energy, this tenacious enthusiasm, was the means by which he had advanced so steadily, outfacing all opposition. After a while, one simply gave up.

'For example, was Casseras searched for magical texts?' he inquired, with unflagging zeal.

'It was searched. Nothing of a suspicious nature was found.'

'Nothing? No concealed knives, hooks, sickles or needles? No black cocks or cats?'

'I have no idea. Roger Descalquencs conducted the search.'

'And the villagers – did you question them regarding their knowledge of sorcery?'

'How could I?' Once again, my anger was kindled. 'Brother, the Holy Office has not been enjoined to concern itself with divination!'

'Even so, I feel that the time has come,' Pierre-Julien replied. He seemed to think for a moment. 'When next you question any suspects or witnesses concerning this matter, ask them what substances they have eaten, or given to be eaten – claws, hair, blood and suchlike. Ask them what they know in respect of enabling the barren to conceive, or discord between husbands and wives, or children either dying or miraculously being cured.'

'Brother – '

'Ask them if they have seen or used any images of wax or lead; also, about methods of gathering herbs, and any thefts, within their village, of chrism or holy oil or the sacrament of the body of Christ – '

'Brother, perhaps *you* should ask them these things.' I could not envisage myself conducting such an interrogatory to Pierre-Julien's satisfaction. 'You are clearly more knowledgeable than I am. It is more fitting that you should investigate Father Augustin's death, while I attend to other business.'

Again, Pierre-Julien pondered, while I offered up a silent prayer to the Lord. But the Lord had cast me off. 'No,' my superior said at last, 'you have advanced too far down the road. You have been to Casseras, and know the people. It will be better if you continue your investigation, while I commence inquiries into that village you arrested – what is it called?'

'Saint-Fiacre.'

'Saint-Fiacre. Precisely. Of course, I shall scrutinise your progress, and make suggestions as to how it might be improved. In fact, and you will find this very helpful, I shall transcribe the questions that you should be asking, with regard to magic and invocations. Not being acquainted with the relevant literature, you will probably need guidance in the pursuit of necromancers.'

Why standest Thou afar off, O Lord? Why hidest Thou Thyself in times of trouble? You can imagine how meekly I endured this trial – with what patient humility I bowed to the will of God. Like Job, I cursed the day. But I did it silently, in my heart; by some miracle, I found the strength to refrain from speech. For if I had spoken, I would have wailed like the dragons, and mourned as the owls.

Truly, the Lord had punished me for my sinfulness. And like the increase of His governance and peace, the punishment would have no end.

Soon after Pierre-Julien's arrival, an *auto de fé* was held. I had arranged it so, for there were many prisoners waiting to be sentenced. I had also wanted to impress upon my new superior that, despite my many faults and shortcomings, I had nonetheless succeeded in apprehending at least some ravaging wolves. Therefore, amidst all my other duties, I had summoned together an assembly of judges to pass sentence, and had caused to be announced from every local pulpit the days on which the public ceremony was to be performed. I also took care to ensure that this announcement included notice of the single execution scheduled to take place – for I have found that, unless one promises a death, one can rarely attract the numbers required for such an occasion.

The judges were Bishop Anselm, Prior Hugues, the Seneschal, the Royal Steward of Confiscations, a representative of the Bishop of Pamiers (learned in canon law), a local notary of impeccable reputation, and, of course, Pierre-Julien Fauré. For a day and a half they debated the various cases presented to them amidst the luxurious appointments of the Bishop's palace; then, having agreed on suitable punishments, they had these sentences recorded. When they dispersed, it was with great relief, for their dispositions were not well matched. Privately, I was informed by the notary that Bishop Anselm was 'an impediment' and the canon from Pamiers 'too narrow in his understanding'. ('All he knows is out of Penafort's *Summa iuris*! There is more to the law than Penafort, Father.') Roger complained to me that the aforesaid notary 'had made no sense, with his long words' and that Prior Hugues was 'too soft'. As for the canon, he referred to the Seneschal as 'ignorant and rough'.

No one had anything complimentary to say about Pierre-Julien. Even the Bishop, in strict confidence, asked me if my superior 'thought that *he* was a bishop'. And the Seneschal was driven to observe, during the proceedings, that if 'that greasy maggot mentions his papal commission one more time, I shall stuff it down his throat'.

Assemblies of this nature will often expose latent antagonisms, I have found.

Once the sentences had been decided upon, a large wooden platform was erected in the nave of St Polycarpe. Here, on the appointed day, sixteen penitents congregated, together with those notables required to be present: various consuls, the Seneschal, the Bishop, Pierre-Julien Fauré and myself. Pierre-Julien delivered the sermon, which was such a tangle of *translatio* that it was virtually incomprehensible. (What, I still wonder, could he have meant by 'drinking cockle from the cup of Christ's blood in the same measure that ye mete withal it shall be measured to you again'?) Then an oath of obedience was administered to the Seneschal, and to other representatives of the secular arm; a solemn decree of excommunication was fulminated against all who hindered the Holy Office; and Raymond Donatus was bidden to read aloud the confessions of each penitent, in the vulgar tongue.

I generally bestowed this task on Raymond Donatus, because he carried it out with such verve and passion. Even in summary, these confessions can be long, unwieldy statements, full of dull and petty offences, but Raymond Donatus could move his audience to tears, or stir it to a fury, simply by relating the humblest of sins. (Blessing bread in the heretical manner, for instance.) On this occasion he outdid himself; even the penitents wept, and could barely be heard when they acknowledged that the confessions were true. Having abjured, they were subsequently absolved from the excommunication which they had incurred, and promised mercy if they conducted themselves with obedience, piety and humility under the sentences about to be imposed upon them.

The sentences were in some cases harsher than I had anticipated. Usually, although the Seneschal is quite merciless, Prior Hugues will argue for clemency, and the result is moderate and reasonable. In this instance, however, Pierre-Julien endorsed the Seneschal's point of view, and no one opposed to his severity had the strength to withstand that unquenchable zeal which I have elsewhere deplored.

Thus Grimaud Sobacca, for the sin of bearing false witness, received life imprisonment, where I would have recommended red tongues on his clothes, scourging with a rod every Sunday in church, fasting from the Friday after Michaelmas until Easter, and a very large fine. Similarly, Raymond Maury's father-in-law was sentenced to five years in prison, where I would have imposed only a series of pilgrimages: say, to St Marie of Roche-amour, to St Rufus of Aliscamp, to St Gilles of Vauverte, to St Guillaume of the Desert, and to Santiago de Compostella – all within a space of five years.

Indeed, Pierre-Julien seemed to favour imprisonment above the penance of pilgrimage. (I knew that Pons would raise some objections to this, but resolved that whatever he had to say, he would say to Pierre-Julien.) Only one penitent was sentenced to pilgrimage, and this a young woman whose offence was simply that, as a child, she had seen a Cathar Perfect at her uncle's house without knowing what he was. She was condemned to perform seventeen of the minor pilgrimages, and to bring back from each shrine, as is customary, letters confirming her visit. It was specified that she need not wear the cross, or submit to scourging at any of the shrines, but in my opinion she merited a much lighter penance. I would have imposed a series of observances: daily mass, the paternoster to be recited ten times a day, abstention from meat, eggs, cheese, and so forth.

You will remember the Perfect Ademar de Roaxio, of whom I spoke earlier in this narrative. As an obdurate heretic, he certainly would have been executed, if he had not perished in prison; instead, his remains were condemned to the pyre, along with those of another man who had received the *consolomentum* on his deathbed. This man's wife – who, though not a heretic herself, had allowed the heretication – was sentenced to imprisonment. The libidinous Bertrand Gasco of Seyrac, also mentioned previously, was sentenced to three years in prison, after which he would be required to wear crosses for life. One of the women seduced by him, Raymonda Vitalis, received an identical punishment. In all, only three of the penitents were not sentenced to a prison term; of these three, one was the aforementioned young woman fated to perform seventeen pilgrimages, one was absent, and one was relaxed *debita animadversione puniendum* – that is, abandoned to the secular authorities for punishment.

This third penitent was a lapsed heretic, a former shepherd and a beast in human form. Convicted for adoring a Perfect some twelve years previously, he had abjured and been reconciled, had submitted to a six-year prison sentence, and had been released on the condition that he wore the crosses. This he did, and proudly, too; on several occasions he was fined and flogged for assaulting good Catholics who taunted him as a bearer of that infamous brand. He even carved a cross on his breast, and was heard to brag that he had been to hell, and it was here on earth – a belief derived from the Cathar teachings. When he was defamed for being a lapsed heretic, he claimed that his accusers were bearing false witness against him, yet for all that he cursed the Holy Office, the Church and the Seneschal when he was arrested; he spat on Father Jacques and called him a devil; he said that Christ was dead, and that we had killed Him with our sins. In prison, awaiting sentence, he had howled like a wolf and bitten Pons on the leg, eaten his own ordure, prophesied that all of Lazet would be destroyed by God on the day of his death. Yet I do not believe that he was mad. We conversed three times, and he spoke coherently – logically – although his intention always was to offend and infuriate with insults, curses, depraved conduct. Once, when I was unaccompanied (and let me assure you that I never again entered his cell without an escort!), he pulled me to the floor, held me down in a painful grip, and threatened to know me carnally. I do not doubt that he might even have carried out this threat, for all that he was manacled, because his strength was astonishing. Fortunately, however, my cries alerted one of the guards, who whipped him with a chain until my release was secured.

The name of this irredeemable sinner was Jacob Galaubi. Everyone who knew him feared him, and I feared him most of all. For I had looked into his eyes, as he held me down, and I had seen there such hate that I seemed to be looking into the bottomless pit itself. Indeed, when he appeared in St Polycarpe for the *auto de fé*, he seemed to have issued forth from that very same pit, for he was scarred by the wounds that he had inflicted upon himself, and crooked from the weight of the chains that bound him, and he gnashed his teeth, and rolled his eyes, and would have uttered threats and blasphemies if his tongue had not been burned with a hot coal. (This cruelly original punishment had been devised by Pons, who professed himself 'tired of that bastard's foul mouth'.) Therefore, instead of blaspheming, Jacob drooled like a hungry wolf, and all who saw him shuddered.

Since he had made no confession, he was not required to confirm its truth; his sins having been recited, he was led back to prison. Here he was given one more day to repent, that his soul might not pass from temporal to eternal flames – but it surprised no one that he remained obdurate in his contempt for the Holy and Apostolic Church. Indeed, when I approached him on this matter, he refused to acknowledge my presence at all. Of course he could not speak; his tongue was too swollen. But upon my asking him if he solemnly confessed and recanted his sins, he made no gesture of assent. He simply stared through me, and yawned, and turned away – abandoned by the Holy Spirit.

The following day he was tied to a post in the marketplace; faggots mixed with straw and vine branches were piled up to his chin; then he was asked, by the Seneschal, if he would renounce the works of the Evil One. I am doubtful as to whether he even heard this query, for he had resisted with great energy his removal from prison, and his guards – as a result – had been somewhat heavy-handed. In effect, he was only half conscious, and I have to admit that I was relieved. Not that I would have advocated mercy, for Jacob deserved to die. There are some lapsed heretics who, when they approach death, do so in a proper spirit of humility, weeping and submissive, reconciled to the Church – and although their penitence might be feigned, I am unable to witness their final agony without remorse. Jacob, however, was a festering sore on the body of the Church; his poison was like the poison of a serpent. He shall drink the wine of the wrath of God, and he shall be tormented with fire and brimstone in the presence of the holy angels.

Yet, for all this, I had to turn away when the pyre was ignited. I had to recite prayers in a loud voice, not, I confess with shame, to honour Christ, but to ensure that Jacob's last, terrible cries would not reach my ears. It is my weakness, this shrinking. A man convinced as to the justice of an execution should have the strength to watch the results of his work. Father Augustin, I know, would not have shielded his eyes, or stopped his ears.

Father Augustin would even have watched the final indignity, when the half-burned body was retrieved from the pyre, broken up, and put on a fresh fire of logs until it was reduced to ashes. Many citizens stay to watch this procedure, but it has always made me feel quite ill. Again, I can offer no excuse. My hands are feeble, and my knees as weak as water.

You may be wondering, as you read my description of this *auto de fé*, why I have neglected to recount the fates of certain people such as Raymond Maury and Bernard de Pibraux. You may be asking: were they not present? In summary, they were not, for reasons that I shall herewith tabulate.

Upon being questioned, Raymond Maury had freely confessed to his sins. He was a deeply frightened man, and anxious to be reconciled. He even confessed to offering Father Jacques what he called 'mercy money' – fifty livres tournois. He told me that, in view of his large and dependent family, Father Jacques had chosen to be lenient.

Now, this confession had presented me with a serious difficulty. For while it would be easy enough to sentence Raymond Maury for his other crimes, the sin of bribing an inquisitor of heretical depravity was not one which I had heretofore encountered. I did not know what to do. Should

Raymond be tried for this error? Should Father Jacques? I had no one to consult, for Father Augustin was dead, and Pierre-Julien had not, at that time, arrived from Avignon. Therefore I resolved to write to the Inquisitor of France for guidance, suspecting that he might not want such a shameful secret to be generally known, and to keep Raymond in custody, awaiting sentence, until I received a reply.

Pierre-Julien, when he was was notified of this decision, agreed that we should wait for a ruling from Paris before proceeding against Raymond Maury.

The case of Bernard de Pibraux was different, for he admitted nothing. I had finally found the time to interrogate him, and had been struck by his great beauty, already somewhat faded, after several months in prison, and by his very appealing character. Suffering had stripped away his wild, irresponsible tendencies, his lustfulness and his drunkard's temper, until what lay beneath was clearly visible: a quiet yet steely resolution; a pure, confused young soul. He was a lion cub, that boy, and his spine was as rigid as a hyena's. My heart softened when I beheld him; I understood at once, completely and without disapprobation, why Father Jacques had never cited him to appear before the Holy Office.

Not that Father Augustin had been wrong to pursue the matter. Were not the pharisees compared to whited sepulchres? A beautiful face may conceal a degenerate soul, for many heretics, as St Bernard points out, are crafty in the extreme – skilled in dissimulation. Who knows but that I was wrong in my estimate of Bernard de Pibraux? Father Augustin, after all, was more virtuous than I.

Yet once again, my weakness betrayed me. I looked upon Bernard de Pibraux, I listened to his earnest, halting, resolute testimony, and oh! How I yearned to be in another place, another time, another vocation! I found myself rising and pacing the floor, while Raymond Donatus stared, and Bernard faltered.

'My friend,' I said to the prisoner, 'let me be frank with

you. You were seen bowing and giving food to a heretic. That is the sum of the evidence so far. Now, I will agree, the suspicion against you is not vehement. Therefore, I have decided to ask your father to gather twenty compurgators in your oath of denial. This is not often done, but I think your case merits it. If your father can find twenty people of your own station, people of good repute, who are personally known to you and who will swear to your orthodoxy, then I should be able to present to my new superior, when he arrives, a reasonable argument for your release.'

'Oh Father – !'

'Wait. Listen to me. You will not be proclaimed innocent, Bernard. The charge will simply be declared "not proven". You will still be expected to abjure the heresy of which you clear yourself. And if I find any further evidence implicating you, I shall not be merciful. Understand that.'

'Father, I am not a heretic. I am not. It was all a mistake.'

'So you say. It might be true. But I cannot speak for my superior. He may be unconvinced.'

And he was, of course. Pierre-Julien scoffed at my suggestion that I call for compurgators – at least until Bernard had endured a prolonged diet of bread and water. If fasting failed to induce him to confess, there were always more vigorous methods of extracting the truth. Only when these methods had failed could we begin to consider the possibility of his innocence. 'A rod is for the back of him that is void of understanding,' my superior observed.

I was disappointed, but hardly surprised. Torture has always been the mark of incompetence, in my view. Upon informing Bernard de Pibraux of my superior's decision, I pointed out that confessing would result in a lenient sentence, whereas persevering on his present course would lead to ruin, misery, despair. I pleaded with him: he was, I said, a fine and noble youth, the pride of his father and the joy of his mother. Would a pilgrimage, or perhaps a year or so in captivity, not be preferable to the rack?

'It would be a lie, not a confession,' he answered, as pale as the moon.

'Bernard, you are not attending.'

'I am innocent!'

'Listen.' I put to him one last proposal. 'You may be innocent, but your family may not be. If your father was behind the death of Father Augustin, then you should tell us so. Because if you do, I can assure you, your sentence will be as light as a feather.'

Impressed as I was with the dignity of his bearing, I almost expected him to spit in my face. But he had learned restraint in captivity: his only response was a sick expression, and a few reproachful words.

'I thought you were a good man,' he said. 'But you are just like the others.'

Sighing, I told him to consider his options very carefully. I also told him that he could appeal to the Pope, but that the appeal would have to be made before a sentence was passed. (I did *not* tell him that the Holy Father was unlikely to grant him his freedom.) Then I left his cell, consoling myself with the thought that a few weeks on bread and water might induce him to change his mind – for I did not want to see him on the rack.

This, then, was the reason why Bernard made no appearance at the *auto de fé*; he was still immured, and fasting. Nor were Bruna d'Aguilar or Petrona Capdenier obliged to abjure their errors in public, for I had not yet had time to investigate them. As for Aimery Ribaudin, I had summoned him to appear before the tribunal, and when he came he had brought with him, unprompted, testimonials of his orthodoxy from fifty compurgators – including Bishop Anselm – together with two notaries and twelve witnesses who were willing to support his version of events. According to Aimery, the money he had given to the heretical weaver had been payment for cloth, nothing more. He had been ignorant as to the weaver's delinquent past. Father Jacques, he said frankly, had accepted his word on this. And in gratitude, he had endowed the Dominican priory with a vineyard, four shops and a very beautiful reliquary containing a portion of St Sebastian's fingerbone.

In the circumstances, I was only too willing to declare the charge against him 'not proven'. However, I knew that the final decision rested with Pierre-Julien. So I arranged that the two men should meet, and was wryly amused when my superior approached me afterwards, singing the armourer's praises. A good Catholic, he said, and a model citizen. Modest, upright and devout. Yet even good men can have enemies with vipers' tongues.

'So you believe this to be a case of false witness?' I inquired.

'Undoubtedly. Whoever is responsible for slandering such a civic ornament should be dealt with.'

'He has been. He died in prison two years ago.'

'Ah.'

'Brother, if you regard Aimery Ribaudin as having been falsely accused, perhaps you should reconsider the case against Bernard de Pibraux, which is almost identical — '

'Nonsense.'

'He too claims that he was ignorant of the heretic's identity — '

'He is not of good character.'

When Pierre-Julien said 'character', he was, of course, referring to wealth and influence. It was ever so in this world. But I was not offended, for there can be no doubt that the rich and powerful *do* beget enemies, and Aimery's reputation was otherwise without blemish. Furthermore, I had become privy to certain facts which effectively removed from Maurand d'Alzen, and therefore Aimery's son-in-law, any suspicion of complicity in Father Augustin's death. I had learned, in brief, that Jordan Sicre was still living.

This information was brought to me in the priory less than a week before the *auto de fé*. One evening after discipline was administered, in that short space of time before the brethren retired, I was approached by a lay brother who supervised the kitchen staff. He requested my permission to speak, and I gave it to him, although I had been reciting to myself the seven penitential psalms. (Let it not be forgotten that I was still in the midst of a spiritual dilemma – of which I shall speak again, in this narrative.)

The lay brother, whose name was Arnaud, apologised for intruding. He had spoken to the Subprior, who had advised him to speak to me. He himself was speaking not on his own behalf, but on behalf of one of the kitchen hands. He would not have disturbed me for a matter of trivial import –

'Get to the point, Brother, please,' I said.

But when Arnaud flinched, I immediately regretted my impatience, and drew him into my cell, and addressed him sympathetically. The tale he told was a curious one. Every day, after our chief refection, the scraps remaining were distributed to the poor – along with certain loaves baked specifically for this purpose. The food was taken to the priory gate by a kitchen hand, one Thomas, who was entrusted with the duty of ensuring that all the hungry people waiting there received at least a small portion of the day's bounty. Most of these supplicants were regular in their attendance; Thomas knew them by name. Several days previously, however, a man had appeared who was unknown to him – who had refused a piece of bread because it was 'defiled by gravy' and therefore by 'meat, which is sinful'.

Thinking that this was a reference to the Lenten fast, Thomas had ignored it. But two days afterwards, the same beggar had chided another with 'partaking of food begotten by coition'. Being unfamiliar with the term 'coition', Thomas had turned for clarification to Arnaud.

'I remember that you once spoke of the sins of the heretics,' Arnaud observed hesitantly. 'You told us that they will not eat meat, because they will not kill any bird or animal.'

'That is correct.'

'You also told us that they wear blue, and this man was not wearing blue. But I felt that I should alert you even so.'

'Brother, you were right to come to me.' I took his hand. 'You are a watchdog at the gates of the vineyard. Thank you.'

He flushed, and looked gratified. I asked him to notify me when it was next time to feed the poor, and I would question this strange beggar. Although I found it difficult to believe that an ardent heretic would seek help on the very doorstep of a Dominican priory, I was impelled to investigate nonetheless. If I did not, I would run the risk of being defamed as a fautor and concealer of heresy.

The following day, before Nones, Arnaud once more approached me and took me to view the aforesaid supplicants. They were clustered around the priory entrance, about a score of them; some were mere children, others old and sick. But one, at least, was in his prime – a slender man with a sallow complexion, honey-coloured eyes, and delicate hands.

I recognised him instantly.

You will recall the peerless familiar described at the beginning of this narrative. I referred to him only as 'S'. At the time of which I speak, 'S' had been absent from Lazet for five months, condemned as a contumacious heretic. By giving him a key, and summoning a guard to my side when this key was scheduled to be employed, I had secured his 'escape' from prison. Our agreement had been that he would go south, and infiltrate a band of heretics living in the mountains of Catalonia. One year hence, he would lure some of them back across the mountains; a date had been set on which they were expected to be found – and arrested – in a village near Rasiers.

So what, I asked myself, was he doing in Lazet?

'My friend,' I said to him, as if he were a stranger, and thinking furiously all the while, 'is it true that you will not eat meat?'

'It is true,' he replied, in his silken voice.

'And why is that, pray?'

'Because fasting is good for the soul.'

'Surely, if you come here, you are too hungry to fast.' As I spoke I was wondering: where shall we go? For I could not take him to headquarters, where he would be recognised. On the other hand, questions would be asked if I introduced such an alien figure into the priory.

'My soul is more hungry than my flesh,' 'S' remarked, turning to go. Whereupon I took Arnaud aside, and whispered to him that I would follow this sprout of infidelity, in order that I might discover his lair. Why, he could have issued from a veritable *nest* of heretics! And I left at once, before Arnaud could question me further.

Loitering some distance behind my quarry, I pursued him past the Chateau Comtal and to the other side of the market-place. His pace was steady; he never looked back. All the same, I sensed that he was aware of my presence. At last I was led, not to the corner of a fowlyard or a shadowy church doorway, but to a hospitum. Although the upper floor was inhabited, the lower – a warehouse – was locked up like a prison. As I walked past, however, I saw my familiar produce a key from his garments, and enter the building through a side door.

Having completed a circuit of the quarter, I returned to this door, which was opened to admit me.

'Welcome,' my familiar softly remarked. Then he closed the door just as softly, so that the only light illumining the space wherein we stood was admitted by two small, high windows. Looking around, I saw that the warehouse was filled with bales of wool, and piles of lumber. But I also discerned a heap of straw not far from my feet – and placed near it were certain items (a wineskin, a heel of bread, a knife, a blanket) which led me to conclude that someone was in residence.

'Do you live here?' I asked.

'For the moment.'

'Does anyone know?'

'I think not.'

'Then where did you get the key?' I demanded, and my familiar smiled.

'Father, I own this building,' he said. 'Thanks to your generosity.'

'Ah.' I was aware that 'S' had acquired a vineyard, under a false name, but not that he possessed a hospitum in the heart of Lazet. 'Do you own the contents as well?'

'No. The goods you see belong to my tenants.' He gestured at the ceiling, and I studied him curiously, because he seemed less at ease within his own warehouse than he did in a prison cell. He looked tired, yet oddly alert. His movements were uncharacteristically abrupt.

'Why have you come here?' I inquired. 'To collect rent? You are running a very grave risk, my son.'

'I know that,' he rejoined. 'I came here to help you.'

'To help me?'

'I heard that the Inquisitor of Lazet had been killed.' Sitting on one of the wool bales, he invited me to join him. 'I thought that you might be the one, but I was told that it was somebody else. Father Jacques's replacement.'

'Augustin Duese.'

'Yes. My new friends were eager to find out more. They learned that four guards had been killed, also. Four familiars. Is that true?'

'Perhaps.' Meeting his clear, intent gaze, I was driven to provide a fuller explanation. 'The bodies were hacked to pieces, and widely scattered. It is difficult to say with certainty whether all the guards were killed or not.'

'You have your doubts?'

'I have my doubts.'

'About Jordan Sicre?'

I gasped.

'You have seen him!' I exclaimed, whereupon he put his finger to his lips.

'Hush!' he murmured. 'My tenants will hear you.'

'You have seen him!' I was careful to whisper. 'Where? When?'

'Not far from where I have been living. He has bought a little farm, and is known by a different name. But I recognised him from that pleasant period I last spent in your custody,

213

Father. He used to stamp on my food.' Once again, my familiar smiled. It was a disturbing smile. 'He recognised me, of course. He came to me, and warned me that as an escaped Perfect, I would be a fool to inform the Inquisition – or anyone else – of his identity. And he was right. For an escaped Perfect, it would be a foolish thing to do.'

'Even if it meant securing a lighter sentence?'

'He could not be sure of that.'

'True. But he might be wondering where you are now.'

'Father, I often go preaching. I can be away for days at a time.'

'So he should still be there?'

'I think so.'

'And if he is arrested? What if he mentions you?'

'Oh Father,' 'S' said gently, 'if he is arrested, I cannot return there. Of course he will mention me. Therefore you must decide: what is more important? Jordan Sicre, or my new friends?'

'Jordan.' I had no doubt of that. 'We must get Jordan. But surely, after all this time, you can give me *some* names? *Some* deeds?'

'Oh yes. A few.'

'Then they must suffice. And I must commit them to memory, because we have no pen – '

'Here.' My familiar rose. From behind a wool bale he produced ink, pen, parchment. I was awed by his prescience.

'You write,' I said, but he raised a hand, as if to repel the suggestion.

'Oh, no, Father,' was his reply. 'If I did that, it could be proven that I was the informant.'

Only consider the craft of the man! Truly, he was inimitable. Matchless. I said as much, and he replied that, like most people, he worked for payment.

Whereupon I was quick to assure him that he would receive the sum promised for the Catalan heretics, although there would, perhaps, be fewer heretics than had been anticipated.

But the sum would be paid on the agreed date, to the agreed recipient.

'No matter what I do in the meantime?' he asked.

'No matter what you do.'

'Then you should look for me in eighteen months, in Alet-les-Bains. I have been meaning to visit certain friends there.'

He would say nothing more on the subject. Consequently, after writing down the information which he carried in his head (and his memory, I should emphasise, was astounding), I bade him farewell.

'If I am long absent, questions will be asked,' I appended.

'Of course.'

'You will leave, now?'

'Immediately.'

'Be careful.'

'I am always careful.'

'I shall look for you in Alet-les-Bains.' With this, I turned to go. But before I could open the door, my familiar tugged at my habit – and I was startled, because he had never before made any attempt to touch me.

'You should be careful too, Father,' he said.

'I?'

'Watch your back. Jordan must have been paid to kill your friend. Whoever paid him might still have money.'

'Oh, I know.' Unreasonably, I felt almost honoured that 'S' should have been concerned about my welfare. He had always impressed me as a man of narrow and bitter passions, impervious to the softer sentiments engendered by love, friendship and gratitude. Beneath his placid exterior, one sensed a hard and chilly core. 'Believe me,' I told him, 'every possibility has been taken into account.'

He nodded, as if to say: that is to be expected, from an inquisitor. Then he opened the door, and shut it behind me.

I have not seen him since.

And when He had taken the book

give thanks unto the Lord, for He is good: because His mercy endureth forever. At last God had come to my aid; He had put off my sackcloth, and girdled me with gladness. For I knew that if Jordan were apprehended, the great mystery would be solved. Father Augustin's killers would be named, caught and punished. Justice would be done. And I would no longer be afraid to leave the city.

Be assured, I was in no doubt that Jordan would name the killers. If the rack was required, then so be it. I would have been prepared to turn the windlasses myself, if such a thing had not been prohibited. I would have felt as much compunction as Jordan had displayed when he took part in the murder of a defenceless old man.

As you may imagine, I was eager to interrogate him personally. But I feared lest Pierre-Julien should regard this inquisition as his own. I was afraid because I knew, by then, that his interrogations were clumsy, disorganised and inadequate, replete with strange references to cock's blood, buttock hairs and thieves' skulls. In the middle of a prescribed interrogatory – 'Have you ever seen anyone receive the *consolamentum*? When and where? Who was present? Have you ever adored heretics? Have you ever guided them or arranged to have them escorted from place to place?' – he would inject irrelevant and confusing questions about demonic visitations, sacrifices, sorcery. He would ask: 'Have you ever cut a man to pieces, and scattered his limbs around a crossroads? Have you ever made any kind of sacrifice, to conjure up a demon? Have you ever employed any strange instrument to do so? Have you ever concocted any potion with vile ingredients such as the nails cut from dead bodies, or the hairs from a black cat, in order to cast spells on good Catholics?'

I know that he often asked these questions, because he wanted me to ask them also. He even went so far as to review Durand Fogasset's transcript of my interview with Bruna d'Aguilar – who, as you may recall, was suspected of bribing Father Jacques. And when he discovered that I had never once referred to sorcery or conjuration, he chastised me angrily in front of Durand, Brother Lucius and Raymond Donatus.

'You must interrogate her again!' he ordered. 'You must ask her if she has sacrificed to demons – '

'But there is no *need* to ask her. When Jordan comes, we shall find out soon enough who the culprit is.'

'When Jordan comes? Are you telling me that you have received a reply from Catalonia?'

'Of course not. It is barely a week since I wrote.'

'Then kindly proceed with the investigation. If Jordan *is* caught, well and good. If he is not, we must find the assassins regardless. And we shall only do that if we pursue the sorcerers in our midst.'

I was a derision to all my people, and their song all the day. Glancing around the scriptorium, at the avid face of Raymond, the downcast eyes of Brother Lucius, the wryly sympathetic grimace of Durand, I restrained my wrath, and spoke evenly. Calmly. Politely.

'Brother,' I said to Pierre-Julien, 'might I speak to you downstairs? In private?'

'Now?'

'If you please.'

'Very well.' Together, we descended to his room, which had by then become the receptacle of many books, among them at least six concerned with sorcery and invocation. Closing the door, I turned to him, and was moved to thank God in my heart that He had seen fit to grace me with a lofty stature. For I towered over Pierre-Julien, who, while not exactly stunted, was of an insignificant height. Consequently, my demeanour was all the more menacing.

'In the first place, Brother,' I said, 'I would be grateful if, when you wish to upbraid me for any perceived fault, you do *not* attempt it in front of the staff.'

'You – '

'In the second place, Bruna d'Aguilar is not a sorceress. I shall tell you about Bruna. Bruna is sixty-three years old, she has five living children and has been married twice. She owns a house and a vineyard, a donkey and several pigs, regularly attends church, gives alms to the poor, is a devotee of the Holy Virgin, and is slightly deaf in one ear. She will not eat turnips, claiming that they disagree with her.'

'What – '

'Bruna is also an irascible, unreasonable, repellent old woman. She is engaged in a long-running dispute with the family of one daughter-in-law, accusing them of not paying the agreed dowry. She has fought with all of her neighbours, her youngest son, her two brothers and the families of *both* former husbands. I could tell you about these quarrels, if you had half a day to spare. She is accused of killing her neighbours' chickens – which mysteriously disappeared, not long ago – of emptying slops onto her brother's doorstep, of giving her daughter-in-law the flux with poisoned dried figs. Most importantly, she is accused of giving the Holy Sacrament to one of her pigs, to cure it of a digestive disorder. She is exceedingly fond of her pigs, you see.'

'This is not – '

'I have spoken to every member of her family, her neighbours, her children, her siblings, her few friends. I know what

218

she eats every day, when she defecates, when she ceased to have issue of the bloody flux, what she keeps in her wedding chest, why her husbands died – I could almost tell you when she scratches her nose. So I do think that if Bruna d'Aguilar were sacrificing inquisitors, I would have learned about it. In fact her enemies would have been only too pleased to accuse her of such a crime.'

'You cannot believe that she would do it openly? In front of witnesses?'

'Brother, let me tell you something.' I was fatigued, rather than amazed, by his blind obstinacy. 'I have been working in the Holy Office for eight years. Not once have I, or either of my former superiors, encountered anyone involved with demons, divination, or magic – save perhaps one or two old women accused of possessing the evil eye. But, as I have already pointed out, evil doing of this kind does not concern the Holy Office. Our concern is with heresy.'

'You do not regard it as heresy to consort with the devil? To employ the Holy Sacrament in perverse circumstances?'

'Bruna will be punished for feeding the Holy Sacrament to her pig. She freely admits that she did it, on the advice of a friend who will also be punished. But it was a sin of ignorance, not an act of sorcery. She is a stupid old woman.'

'You say her pigs are all named,' said Pierre-Julien. 'Are they black in hue? Have they ever changed form to your knowledge?'

'Brother!' He was not even listening to me. 'There are *no sorcerers* in Lazet!'

'How can you know this, when you have not asked the right questions?'

'Because I know this city. Because I know the people. And because *you* have been asking these questions, and *you* have not found any sorcerers!'

'Oh, but I have,' he replied smugly.

I stared.

'One of the men from Saint-Fiacre has confessed to

conjuring a demon,' my superior continued. 'He said that he tried to obtain carnal possession of a married woman by offering a doll made of wax, saliva and toad's blood to the devil. He placed the doll under the threshold of her house, ensuring that, if she did not yeld, she would be tormented by a demon. Therefore she did yield, and he subsequently sacrificed a butterfly to the aforesaid demon, which manifested itself in a breath of air.'

As you can imagine, I was profoundly shocked – though not for the reasons which Pierre-Julien might have anticipated.

'He – he has *confessed* to this?' I queried.

'The deposition is being copied now.'

'Then you must have taken him to the lower dunjon.' All at once, I understood. 'You employed the rack.'

'I did not.'

'The *strappado*.'

'Not at all. He was not tortured.' Seeing me speechless, Pierre-Julien made full use of his momentary advantage. 'You will agree, I think, that faced with such incontrovertible proof, it behoves us to seek out and destroy the pestiferous and heretical infection of necromancy among our flock. "For rebellion is as the sin of witchcraft, and stubborness is as iniquity and idolatry." You are a stubborn man, my son – you must submit to my superior understanding of these matters, and ask the questions which I require you to ask.'

Having delivered himself of this insult, he requested that I leave the room, for he had another interrogation to prepare. Puzzled, I did as he bade me. There was no display of anger. I did not even slam the door, being too preoccupied with this unforeseen development. How, I asked myself, could this have occurred? What could have prompted such a strange confession? Was it true? Or could Pierre-Julien be *lying*?

I sought out Raymond Donatus, who was still at work in the scriptorium. When I entered, I was immediately able to deduce, from Durand's embarrassment, Raymond's confiding posture, and the manner in which Brother Lucius hastily picked up his pen, that they had been talking about me. But I was not discomposed. It was only to be expected.

'Raymond,' I said, without preamble, 'did you transcribe a confession about wax dolls for Father Pierre-Julien?'

'Yes, Father. This morning.'

'Was torture employed during that inquisition?'

'No, Father.'

'None at all?'

'No, Father. But Father Pierre-Julien did threaten to use the rack.'

'Ah.'

'He explained how it worked, and how the joints would be separated – '

'I see. Thank you, Raymond.'

'We even went down to look at it.'

'Yes. Thank you. I understand.' I did, too. Pondering, I slowly became aware of Durand's speculative gaze, and the scratch of the canon's pen as he copied what was undoubtedly the relevant deposition. He was hunched so low over his desk that his nose was almost touching it.

'Father?' Raymond cleared his throat, and held up the finished protocol of Bruna's confession. 'Father, forgive me, but shall I give this to Brother Lucius to copy? Or shall I wait until you have interviewed her again?'

'I shall not be interviewing her again.'

The two notaries exchanged glances.

'There is no reason why I should interview her again. I have quite enough to do already. Raymond, when Father Augustin was searching through the old registers, he discovered that one of them was missing. Do you remember?'

Raymond appeared to be somewhat taken aback by this shift in the subject of our conversation. As expected, it had served to distract him from the question of whether I should, or should not, interrogate Bruna d'Aguilar once more. He blinked, and gaped, and made uncertain noises.

'Do you remember?' I reiterated. 'He asked you to look in

the Bishop's library, in case both copies were there. Did you do as he instructed?'

'Yes, Father.'

'And were both copies there?'

'No, Father.'

'Just the one?'

'No, Father.'

'*No?*' I peered at him, as he shifted uneasily. 'What do you mean, *no?*'

'Th-there were no copies. None at all.'

'None at *all?* You mean *both* registers are missing?'

'Yes, Father.'

How can I convey to you my astonishment? My disbelief? Truly I was as the people of Isaiah, who heard indeed, but understood not.

'This is incredible,' I protested. 'Are you sure? Did you look?'

'Father, I went and I looked – '

'How *well* did you look? You must look again. You must go back and search the Bishop's library.'

'Yes, Father.'

'And if you cannot find them, I shall look myself. I shall ask the Bishop for an explanation. This is very important, Raymond, we must find those books.'

'Yes, Father.'

'Did you alert Father Augustin? No? Not at *all?* But why not?'

'Father, he was dead!' Flustered, Raymond was beginning to assume a defensive tone. 'Then you went off to Casseras! I forgot! You never asked!'

'But why should I have asked, when – ? Oh, let it be,' I expostulated, waving my hand at him. 'Go on. Go and find them. Now. Go on!'

'Father, I cannot. There is – I am – '

'Father Pierre-Julien needs him for another inquisition,' Durand interjected.

'When?'

'Very soon.'

'Then you must take his place,' I informed Durand. 'And you, Raymond – off you go. I want you to examine every register in the Bishop's library. Understand?'

Raymond nodded. Then he took his leave, still apparently dazed, and I was left to deal with Durand's objections. These were not vociferous and plaintive, as Raymond's would have been in similar circumstances. (Indeed, it surprised me that Raymond had obeyed so willingly a command which, by its very nature, must have contributed to his general discomfort.) On the contrary, Durand's disapproval was normally expressed in his silences, which could be remarkably emphatic.

On this occasion, however, he was moved to voice his discontent.

'Father, am I to understand that Father Pierre-Julien has been threatening to put prisoners on the rack?'

This was not so much a question as a protest. I understood what he was trying to say.

'We can only hope that the threat suffices,' was my response.

'Father, forgive me, but you may recall that when I agreed to work for the Holy Office – '

'You aired your feelings on certain topics. Yes, Durand, I recall that very well. And you may have observed that, when working with me, those feelings have never been offended. Unfortunately, you are obliged to work with Father Pierre-Julien now. And if you disapprove of his methods, then I suggest you take it up with him – as I have.'

Perhaps I was too blunt, too harsh. Certainly I was expelling my own ire, to the relief of a heart overburdened with sorrows. Turning, I stormed downstairs to my desk, where I began to rummage through Father Augustin's papers. But it occurs to me that you may not comprehend the reason behind this activity. You may have forgotten that Bruna d'Aguilar's was not the final name on Father Augustin's list of bribery suspects. Have you, in effect, been keeping count?

Oldric Capiscol was dead. Raymond Maury had been sentenced. Bernard de Pibraux was starving in captivity. Aimery Ribaudin had skilfully avoided prosecution. Bruna d'Aguilar had been thoroughly investigated. The only suspect still remaining was Petrona Capdenier.

She had been identified, in the testimony of a Perfect examined by Father Jacques, as having fed and housed the said Perfect many years previously. Like Oldric's, her sin had been committed long before Father Jacques's time in office. Yet, while the register containing Oldric's deposition (marked and heavily glossed) was among Father Augustin's papers, I had found there no register in which Petrona's deposition or sentence had been recorded. Apparently she had not been arrested by Father Jacques – and if the reason for this lay in the fact that she had already been condemned, no proof of such a condemnation seemed to exist.

Remembering Father Augustin's search for a missing register, I wondered if the book in question might pertain to Petrona Capdenier's case. This deduction was facilitated by a marginal note, made beside the aforesaid Perfect's testimony in Father Augustin's hand, which designated a period of time and a former, long-deceased, inquisitor of Lazet. Clearly, Father Augustin had inferred from the available information that he should be examining registers dealing with prosecutions undertaken at that time. Clearly, he had been looking for the said registers. And clearly, the fact that not one of them was to be found among his papers indicated either that the search for Petrona's name within these books had been fruitless, or that the book which did contain it was missing.

I searched through Father Augustin's notes once more, but found no other reference to missing books. Knowing that he undoubtedly would have pursued the matter diligently, I was forced to conclude that he had, indeed, died before he was able to do so. The question now was: had the missing register and its copy been mislaid, or had somebody stolen them?

If a theft had been committed, it could have occurred at any time during the past forty years. But it could only have been carried out by a select number of people, for access to inquisitorial records had always been restricted. Naturally, every inquisitor had been permitted to consult them at will. So, too, had various notaries employed by the Holy Office. Recently, the Bishop had been entrusted with copies of the registers, and, before the creation of the Lazet diocese, these same copies had been kept in the priory. As far as I could recall, only the Prior and the librarian had possessed keys to the chest in which the documents were contained.

Having identified possible culprits, I reflected on possible motives for stealing the registers. Father Jacques might have done so, in order to conceal the crime of a woman who had paid him for this very service. (Or had her descendants provided the money?) On the other hand, if he *had* destroyed the register, why had he not expunged Petrona's name from the Perfect's confession also? Indeed, why had he allowed Raymond Maury's name to appear in the records at all?

It seemed to me that there were two far more likely reasons for stealing a register. Firstly, if someone whose conviction was noted therein had lapsed into error once more, years later, that same heretic would certainly have been executed *unless the record of his earlier crime had not been found*. I recalled a case in Toulouse, where one Sibylla Borrell, having confessed and abjured heretical beliefs some ten years previously, had been arrested about five years later for similar practices. Undoubtedly, she would have gone to the stake, if her original abjuration had not been lost. But since it could not be found, she could only be prosecuted as if for a first offence, and had escaped with life imprisonment.

Alternatively, it must be remembered that heretical ancestors are a blight on one's prosperity. One cannot serve as a notary or public official if one suffers from this hereditary stain. Could it be possible, I asked myself, that one of the inquisitorial notaries had discovered the name of his grandfather in this missing book? Could it be possible that *Raymond* had? I straightened as this thought occurred to me, for it was a terrible one. A traitor in our midst! *Another* traitor! And I speculated, with horror, on the possibility that Raymond might have had Father Augustin killed simply because he was searching for the register which had been stolen.

But then I shook my head abruptly. I knew that postulations of this kind were unfounded and extreme, when the evidence was so minimal, and the possible culprits so numerous. Why, the register might never have been copied at all, through some oversight. It may have been lost as the document in Toulouse had been lost. There were any number of reasonable explanations.

Nevertheless, if Raymond Donatus failed to find the book, I resolved to question him as soon as possible. I also resolved to search for the missing register myself. In fact I returned to the scriptorium as soon as I had made this decision, and began to look through the two great chests in which the records were accommodated. No one asked me what I was doing. Durand had already joined my superior in the lower dunjon, and Brother Lucius never uttered a word. He scribbled away assiduously, occasionally sniffing or rubbing his eyes, as I sifted through nearly one hundred years of depravity.

It was a laborious task, for the books were not arranged in any particular order, although the ones on top tended to be of a more recent vintage. Furthermore, as is customary, the depositions within each register were grouped according to the accused's place of residence, rather than the dates on which the depositions had been transcribed. As I struggled with this disorganised mass of testimony, I became more and more furious with Raymond Donatus. It seemed to me that he had not been doing his job – and this I considered to be almost as great a sin as murdering Father Augustin. Indeed, it became quite clear that the missing register had probably been mislaid. I began to regard it as wondrous that a great many more books had not disappeared, under the notary's stewardship.

'Lucius,' I said, and he peered at me over the top of his quill, 'do you know your way around these records?'

'Why – no, Father. I am not permitted to consult them.'

'Well, it might interest you to know that they are a complete *mess*. What does Raymond do all day? Talk, I suppose. Talk and talk and talk.'

The scrivener said nothing.

'And there are loose folios everywhere. And see – bookworm! Abominable. Unforgivable.' I decided that I would have to rearrange all the documents myself – a task in which I was still engaged when, towards Compline, Pierre-Julien suddenly entered the scriptorium. He was out of breath and perspiring heavily, as if he had run up the stairs. His face was uncharacteristically flushed.

'Ah! My son,' he panted. 'There you are.'

'As you see.'

'Yes. Good. Uh – come this way, if you please, I wish to speak to you.'

Mystified, I followed him back downstairs. He was extremely agitated. When we reached my desk he turned to me, and folded his arms. His voice quivered with suppressed emotion.

'I have been informed,' he said, 'that you have no intention of following my advice, as regards the interrogation of prisoners on the subject of sorcery. Is that true?'

Startled, I was for a moment at a loss as to how I should reply. But Pierre-Julien did not wait for me to formulate a rejoinder.

'In the circumstances,' he went on, 'I have decided to assume control of the investigation into Father Augustin's death.'

'But – '

'Kindly surrender to me all of the relevant documents.'

'As you wish.' I told myself that, rather than employ his ludicrous interrogatory, I would prefer to abandon the task altogether. 'But you should know what I have discovered – '

'I am also considering your future in the Holy Office. It seems to me that you do not approach this work in the proper spirit.'

'I *beg* your pardon?'

'I have decided to discuss the matter with the Bishop, and Prior Hugues. In the meantime, you should occupy yourself with correspondence and other minor duties – '

'Wait. Stop.' I held up my hand. 'Are you actually attempting to dismiss me from this post?'

'It is my prerogative.'

'Surely even *you* are not misguided enough to believe that you can function here without my assistance?'

'You are a vain and insolent man.'

'And you are a blockhead. An empty wineskin.' Suddenly, I lost control of my temper. 'How dare you presume to instruct me in anything? You, who cannot conduct a simple interrogatory without resorting to the clumsy weapons required by utter ineptitude?'

' "Let the lying lips be put to silence, which speak grievous things proudly and contemptuously against the righteous." '

'I was about to say the very same thing myself.'

'You are dismissed.' The man's lips were trembling. 'I do not want to see you here any more.'

'Good. Because the sight of *you* makes me sick to my stomach.'

And so I left, that he might not witness the depth of my anger. For I did not wish to show him how bitter the blow had been – how profoundly he had hurt my pride. As I walked back to the priory, I showered him with curses. 'May the dust of your land become lice. May you be as dung upon the face of the earth. May your blood be poured out by the force of the sword. May your wheat and rye be smitten . . .', all the while telling myself that I was glad to break his yoke from off my neck. To be free of his feeble tyranny – why, that was a blessing! I should be offering thanks to the Lord! And without my help, would he not flounder into a morass of bafflement and frustration? Would he not be compelled to come crawling back, seeking deliverance?

I told myself this, but it was no balm to my troubled spirit. Only see how far I had strayed from perfect humility! I could have called down the fires of hell upon him. I could have smitten him with the botch of Egypt, and with the scab, and with the itch whereof thou canst not be healed. And in this I was no servant of Christ, for what saith the high and lofty One that inhabiteth eternity? *I dwell in the high and holy place, with him also that is of a contrite and humble spirit.*

When you reflect on my anger, you might ask yourself: is this a man who has known divine love? Is this a man who has communed with the Lord, and tasted of His infinite mercy? Perhaps, you might think, you should revise your position. And assuredly you would be justified, because I too had begun to doubt. My heart was now as cold as stone; I burned incense to vanity; mine iniquities were gone over mine head. My soul was embroiled in earthly matters, when it should have been seeking that city whose river's current is a source of joy, and whose gates the Lord loves more than all the tents of Jacob. I had turned away from God's embrace − or perhaps that embrace had never truly been offered to me.

My stony heart, warmed with the fever of anguish, rather than the blaze of love, slowly cooled as I lay in bed that night. I thought with despair of all my sins, and of the enemies who had spread a net by the wayside. Silently I pleaded: O deliver me from the deceitful and unjust man! Then I thought about Johanna, and found a comfort which I could not derive from contemplation of the Lord − for in contemplating Johanna, I felt no shame for my faults and frailties. (God forgive my sins!) I wondered what she was doing, and whether she had yet departed for her winter abode, and whether she thought about me, as she lay in the dark. Knowingly, I ate of the forbidden fruit, and it tasted sweet, though it left me hungry for more. I reflected on my promise that she should hear from me again; for some weeks I had been struggling with the composition of a letter wherein I desired to confess my blameworthy attachment to her, and declare my intention that we should never meet again. Of course, it would be a difficult letter to write, and almost impossible to send without arousing suspicion. After all, why should a monk be corresponding with a woman? And how could I express myself openly to a person who was unable to read?

Then I sat up. The letter! Thoughts of one letter had led me to thoughts of another: the letter from the Bishop of Pamiers – the letter concerning Babilonia's demonic possession. It still lay among Father Augustin's papers. If Pierre-Julien happened upon it, the results might be terrible indeed. Who could say what foolish and erroneous fancies it might spawn within that block of wood on his shoulders?

I knew that I must retrieve it. I vowed that I would. And then I lay awake all night, tormented by the fear that I might not reach my goal before Pierre-Julien did.

The next morning, I did not attend the Prime service. I hastened at once to headquarters, chilled by the first breath of winter. Knocking on the outer door, I was surprised to receive no immediate response, for a guard was usually stationed just inside this door during the night. Then it occurred to me that Brother Lucius, who was renowned for his early arrivals, might have been admitted already. So I pounded with greater force, and at last was rewarded by the voice of the scrivener.

'Who is it?' he said.

'Father Bernard. Open up.'

'Oh.' There was a scraping sound as he unbarred the door. Then his face appeared. 'Come in, Father.'

'Sometimes I wonder why you go back to St Polycarpe of an evening,' I observed, brushing past him. 'You should sleep here and have done.' While he barred the door again, I hurried to my desk – but it had been cleared of Father Augustin's papers. Cursing inwardly, I went to look in the inquisitor's room. Still I found nothing.

It appeared that Pierre-Julien had taken the papers back to his cell.

Winded by this harsh blow, I sank into a chair and considered my options. To retrieve the letter from his cell would not be difficult, as long as he himself was absent. But if he intended to drag the papers around with him, I would have little hope of recovering the said letter. And what would be the use, if he had found it already? There was every reason to believe that he had spent at least some of the previous night consulting these documents, or why carry them to the priory at all?

I decided that my best hope, if he would not relinquish the papers, was to gain access to them in his presence, and remove the letter while drawing his attention to something else. To the problem of the missing register, for example.

I rose.

'Lucius!' I called. 'Lucius!'

'Yes, Father?'

Entering the anteroom, I saw that he was halfway up the stairs.

'Will Raymond be here soon, Brother? He generally seems to arrive before I do.'

Brother Lucius pondered for a moment.

'Sometimes he is early, sometimes late,' was the cautious reply. 'But he is not often this early.'

I resolved, then and there, to visit the notary's house and inquire as to whether Raymond had found the missing register in the Bishop's library. If he had not, I would immediately present this troubling information to Pierre-Julien, who might find it so remarkable that he would relax his grip on the letter I so desired. Not wishing to waste any time, for time would give Pierre-Julien a chance to read the selfsame letter, I thanked Brother Lucius and withdrew, my course set for the noble residence of Raymond Donatus. I knew where it was, though I had never crossed its threshold. Once the hospitum of a flour merchant, it had been purchased by Raymond five years previously, and its vaulted warehouse turned into stables. (I should point out that the notary possessed two horses, which were as dear to him as his vineyards; he talked more about them than he did about his son and daughter.) The dwelling was very big, and boasted carved stone lintels above the windows. Inside, the beams of the roof had been painted with red and yellow stripes. There were even some chairs around the table, and a crucifix placed over the front door.

But when Raymond's wife answered my knock, she was dressed in rags, like a servant, and her face was filthy.

'Oh!' she said. 'Father Bernard!'

'Ricarda.'

'I have been cleaning. Forgive me, these are my old clothes.' Inviting me in, she offered food and drink, but I declined with thanks. Looking around the kitchen, with its mighty hearth and dangling hams, I said that I wanted to speak to Raymond.

'Raymond?'

'Your husband.' Noting her blank gaze, I added: 'Is he here?'

'Why no, Father. He is at the Holy Office, surely?'

'Not as far as I know.'

'But he must be. He was there all night.'

'All *night*?' I said, not thinking with sufficient speed. The poor, flustered woman began to exhibit symptoms of distress.

'He – he often has to work all night,' she stammered. 'He told me so.'

'Ah.' Of course, I then realised – all too late – what Raymond had been doing. He had been spending nights with harlots, and lying about it afterwards. I was angry to think that the Holy Office had provided him with an excuse.

'Ricarda,' I said, determined not to lie on his behalf, 'your husband was not at headquarters when I left. The only person there was Brother Lucius.'

'But – '

232

'If your husband did not come home last night, you must seek another explanation.'

'He has been abducted! Something has happened to him!'

'I doubt it.'

'Oh, Father, what am I going to do? Maria, what am I going to do?'

Maria appeared to be a wetnurse; she was sitting by the hearth with an infant clasped to her bosom, and she was as ample as Ricarda was wizened.

'You should mull yourself some wine, *Domina*,' she advised her mistress. 'He will come to no harm.'

'But he is missing!'

'No one can lose himself in this town,' the wetnurse replied, and we exchanged glances. Although she had a slow and placid way of speaking, there was nothing sluggish about Maria's intellect.

'Father, you must help me,' the bereft wife pleaded. 'We must find him.'

'I am attempting to find him – '

'Perhaps the heretics have killed him, the way they killed Father Augustin! Oh, Father, what shall I do?'

'Nothing,' I said decisively. 'Just sit here and wait. And when he does come home, I want you to give him a tongue-lashing for his dissolute behaviour. Doubtless he is gambling somewhere, and no longer knows if it is day or night.'

'Oh, *never*! He would never do such a thing!'

Seeing Ricarda dissolve into tears, and feeling unequal to them, I assured her that I would find her husband. Then I took my leave, stricken with guilt that I had been the agent of such distress, yet hoping at the same time that Raymond should suffer for his impudence. To claim that he was working all night! It surpassed belief.

I decided that I should return to headquarters, report the notary's disappearance, and use this opportunity to ascertain the whereabouts of Father Augustin's papers – for I knew that Pierre-Julien always started his day's work after Prime. While retracing my steps, however, I happened upon Roger Descalquencs in the marketplace, and stopped to address him. He was engaged in some minor dispute about taxes (for market tolls are the subject of as many complaints as tithes), but broke off his argument with an irate cheese vendor when he saw me waiting.

'Greetings, Father,' he said. 'Were you looking for me?'

'No,' I replied. 'But now that I have found you, there is something I wish to discuss.'

Nodding, he took me aside, and we conversed in low voices as around us sheep bleated and buyers haggled and wandering vendors chanted praise of their wares. I told him that Raymond Donatus had vanished overnight – that he seemed to be missing. I offered him my suspicions that the notary was sleeping off his debauchery in some harlot's bed. And I requested that the Seneschal's garrison, well known, as it was, among the more sinful elements of Lazet, should keep watch for the notary as it went about its business.

'Gone all night?' said Roger, thoughtfully. 'Yes. That is worrying.'

'Oh, I am not *concerned*. Clearly it has happened before. Why, he could be at the Holy Office now.'

'But he might also be lying in a dung-heap with his throat cut.'

Taken aback, I queried this speculation. Why should it have crossed the Seneschal's mind?

'Because mixing with whores means mixing with thieves,' he retorted. 'Down by the river, among the beggars and boatmen, there are people who would cut your throat for a pair of shoes.'

'But I am not aware that Raymond found his pleasures among such people. As far as I can ascertain, he favoured servant girls and widows.'

'A whore is a whore.' The Seneschal clapped me on the back. 'Rest easy, Father, I shall find him for you, even if he was dumped in the river. No one escapes me in this town.'

And having made this pledge he returned to his debate with the cheese vendor, securing my promise that if Raymond *was* at headquarters, I should alert one of the garrison guards as soon as I could. Although he seemed quite cheerful, it will come as no surprise to you that his dire predictions discomposed me. As I returned to headquarters, I was plagued by unhappy thoughts: I considered the possibility that Raymond had, indeed, been killed for his purse, and thrown into the river. Or that, as an employee of the Holy Office, he had met a fate similar to Father Augustin's. Of course these fears were irrational, for there was a more likely explanation, and it was the one which I had given to Roger in the first place. But still my soul was troubled.

When I reached headquarters, I was admitted by Pierre-Julien himself. To judge from his bruised and puffy countenance, he too had spent a sleepless night – and now seemed less than enchanted to see me. Before he could object to my arrival, however, I asked him if Raymond Donatus was in the building.

'No,' he rejoined, 'and I have an inquisition scheduled. I was about to send a familiar to his home.'

'You will not find him there,' I interrupted. 'Raymond has been missing all night.'

'What?'

'His wife has not seen him since yesterday morning. I have not seen him since yesterday afternoon.' And the fact that he should have been present, to record testimony, concerned me a great deal. Although it was not his first night away from home, it was the first time that he had failed to attend a planned interrogation. 'I suspect that he habitually devotes his nights to harlots, and I worry that he may have fallen among thieves. Of course, it may simply be a case of over-indulgence – '

'I must go,' Pierre-Julien announced. I was still on the threshold, for he had been blocking my path, and was almost knocked down as he brushed past me. 'Send for Durand

Fogasset,' he continued, tossing this command over his shoulder. 'Tell Pons that the inquisition is cancelled.'

'But – '

'Stay here until I return.'

Astonished, I gazed after his retreating form. Such an extraordinary departure admitted of no explanation. But then it occurred to me that his room was now vacant, and I went to look at his desk.

Sure enough, Father Augustin's papers were there – and among them I found the Bishop of Pamiers' letter. *Rejoice in the Lord always, and again I say, Rejoice!* Here indeed was proof of God's mercy.

I concealed the document in my garments, thinking that later, perhaps, I would destroy it. Then, in obedience to Pierre-Julien's command, I proceeded to the prison, where I asked Pons to send for Durand Fogasset. I also notified him of Raymond's absence. We agreed that by means of a whorish woman, a man is brought to a piece of bread; Raymond, said Pons, should have 'kept his wick out of strange tallow'.

'If you ask me,' he added, 'that fool started bedding somebody's wife, and talked about it once too often. I always said he would.'

'Do you know the name of his most recent conquests?' I queried.

'If I did, I would tell you. I was always too busy for Raymond's filth. But the scrivener might have a notion – or that young lad, Durand.'

It was good advice. When I spoke to Brother Lucius in the scriptorium, however, he was vague, and not very helpful. Women? There had been so many women.

'But recently,' I pressed him. 'In the last few weeks.'

'Oh ...' The poor canon flushed. 'Father, I try not to listen ... it is such an occasion of sin.'

'Yes, of course. I realise that. And dull, too, I daresay. But can you recall any names, Brother? Or characteristics?'

'They all seem to be of a very lascivious nature,' he

mumbled, as scarlet as sin. 'With an ample ... an ample bosom.'

'All?'

'Raymond calls them "udders". He likes "big udders".'

'Ah.'

'There was one called Clara,' Brother Lucius continued. 'I remember her because I thought to myself: how can a woman who bears the name of that blessed saint be the fount of such iniquities?'

'Yes. It is a great sin.'

'But he does not often tell me their names,' the scrivener concluded. 'He likes to identify them according to their appearance.'

I could imagine. I could also sympathise. Indeed, my pity for Brother Lucius was profound, and I could not find it within me to inquire further. He was sufficiently mortified already, I thought. There are some monks who will discuss coition and female flesh without flinching, freely and happily, but Lucius was not one of them. He was a man of great modesty, raised by a widowed mother (now blind) and cloistered from the age of ten.

'Tell me,' I said, 'did you see Raymond yesterday afternoon? He went to St Polycarpe, but did he come back here after I left?'

'Yes, Father.'

'Oh, he did?'

'Yes, Father. He was still here when I went to Compline.'

'And did he say anything to you? About the Bishop's library? About where he was going last night?'

'No, Father.'

'Did he say anything at *all*?'

Again, Brother Lucius flushed. Nervously he rearranged the articles on his desk, and wiped his hands on his habit.

'He – he talked about you, Father.'

'Did he, indeed?' It was only to be expected. 'And what did he say?'

'He was angry with you. He said that you insulted him, and ordered him about like a servant.'

'Anything else?'

'He said that pride goeth before destruction.'

'Indisputable,' I said, and thanked Brother Lucius for his help. Having decided to wait for Durand, I returned to my desk, where I sat idly, reviewing the information which I had collected. It amounted to very little. I wondered, for the first time, if it was Raymond who had informed Pierre-Julien that I did not intend to follow his advice regarding interrogations. Durand, I felt sure, would not have repeated my comment about questioning Bruna d'Aguilar. And Lucius would only have answered a direct question; he would never have raised the subject without encouragement.

Doubtless Raymond was responsible. In the heat of his anger, on his way to the Bishop's palace, he had probably alerted Pierre-Julien to my flagrant disobedience. *Pride goeth before destruction.* Raymond's own pride had always been very tender.

I was still ruminating when Durand Fogasset knocked on the outer door. Rising, I went to unbar it for him.

'Raymond Donatus is missing,' I announced, as he entered.

'So I heard.'

'Have you seen him since yesterday? Because no one else has. Not even his wife.'

Durand's appearance suggested that he had been dragged out of bed, for his gaze was bleary, his face creased, his attire rumpled. He peered at me from under his shock of black hair.

'I told Father Pierre-Julien that you should look in a few beds,' he replied. 'You know Lothaire Carbonel? The consul? I saw Raymond with one of his servants a few weeks ago.'

'Wait a moment.' I was startled by this reference to my superior. 'When did you speak to Father Pierre-Julien about this?'

'Just now.' Collapsing onto a bench, Durand sat with his grasshopper legs stretched out in front of him, rubbing his eyes and yawning. 'I pass Raymond's house on my way here – as you know.'

'You mean that Father Pierre-Julien was at Raymond's *house*?'

'Everyone was at Raymond's house. The Seneschal. Most of the garrison . . .'

'The *Seneschal*?'

'He and Father Pierre-Julien were having an argument on the doorstep.'

I sat down. My knees would no longer support me, for I had received too many shocks that day.

'They were arguing about registers,' Durand continued, in a lazy, but slightly puzzled, fashion. 'Father Pierre-Julien was insisting that if any had been found, they were the property of the Holy Office, and should be surrendered to him unopened. The Seneschal told him that none had been found – only Raymond's personal registers.'

'The *Seneschal* was looking for *registers*?'

'Oh no. He was looking for Raymond's corpse.'

'*What*?'

Durand laughed. He even patted my hand.

'Forgive me,' he said, 'but the look on your face! Father, I was told that, when a man or woman is killed, the Seneschal always suspects the spouse above all others.'

'But there is no evidence that – '

' – Raymond is dead? True. Personally, I believe that he has drunk too much wine and is sleeping it off somewhere. Perhaps I am wrong. The Seneschal has more experience of these things.'

I shook my head, sinking in deep mire, where there was no standing.

'Of course, one must ask oneself: where *has* he been bedding these women?' the notary went on. 'He owns a couple of shops, hereabouts, but they are fully occupied. Perhaps there is a tenant who allows him use of the floor for a reduced rent? Or perhaps he just employs dung-heaps, like everyone else.'

Slowly my thoughts were becoming more coherent. I rose to my feet, and told Durand that I was going to visit Raymond's house. Before I had reached the door, however, he called me back.

'Father – one question.'

'Yes? What is it?'

'If Raymond is alive, and I have no doubt that he is, what will happen to me?'

'To you?'

'With only one inquisitor, there will not be work enough for two notaries.'

I met his gaze, and something in my own eyes, or in the set of my mouth, must have answered his question. He smiled, and shrugged, and spread his hands.

'You have done me a great service, Father,' he said. 'This post was becoming too bloody for my taste.'

'Stay here,' I rejoined, 'until Father Pierre-Julien returns. He summoned you specifically.'

Then I took my leave, distracted by all the questions that I wanted to ask. Had Raymond Donatus taken Holy Office registers home with him, in the full knowledge that such an act was forbidden to all but inquisitors of heretical depravity? Was Pierre-Julien aware of this breach of regulations? And which registers had been singled out? Seeking enlightenment, I flew towards Raymond's house on winged feet, only to be met, within sight of headquarters, by a frantic Pierre-Julien.

'So!' he exclaimed.

'Ah!' I said.

Although we were standing in the street, under the eyes of many curious citizens, he began to upbraid me in a voice as shrill as a shepherd's pipe. He was even whiter than usual.

'What do you mean by going to the Seneschal without my permission?' he ranted. 'How dare you take it upon yourself to approach the secular arm? You are wilful and disobedient!'

'I no longer owe you my obedience, Brother. I have left the Holy Office.'

'True! So kindly refrain from interfering in Holy Office affairs!'

He moved to pass me, but I caught his elbow.

'To which affairs are you referring?' I inquired. 'To the missing registers, perhaps?'

'Let go.'

'Durand heard you tell the Seneschal to give up any registers found among Raymond's effects. You said that they were the property of the Holy Office.'

'You have no right to interrogate me.'

'On the contrary, I have every right! Do you know that Raymond has reported two of the registers missing? Can it be that he has them in his possession, and that you are *aware* of it? Can you be ignorant of the rule laid down by the first Inquisitor of Lazet, that inquisitorial registers should never leave the confines of the Holy Office unless in the custody of an inquisitor?'

'I gave Raymond permission to take a register home,' Pierre-Julien said hurriedly. 'It was needed for a task that I set him.'

'And where is it now? In the hands of the Seneschal?'

'It may be on Raymond's desk. He may not have taken it after all – '

'You gave him custody of an inquisitorial register, and now you do not know where it *is*?'

'Stand aside.'

'Brother,' I declared, with reckless disregard for all the people listening, 'it seems to me that you are unworthy of the post which you occupy! To flout the rules in this manner, to run such risks – '

' "He that is without sin among you, let him first cast a stone!" ' Pierre-Julien cried. 'You are hardly in a position to condemn me, Brother – you, whose obtuseness prevents you from identifying heretics who are directly under your nose!'

'Indeed?'

'Yes, indeed! Do you mean to say that you missed the letter

from the Bishop of Pamiers, which lies among Father Augustin's papers?'

I swear to you, my heart stopped. Then it began to pound like a smith at his anvil.

'Somewhere in this diocese is a girl possessed by a demon,' Pierre-Julien continued wildly, 'and where there are demons, there are surely necromancers. Truly, Brother, you are one of the blind that have eyes. You are not fit to be my vicar.'

And he walked off before I could formulate a response.

The waters of Nimrin

onsider my position. Effectively, I had been forbidden the precincts of the Holy Office. My love for Johanna de Caussade, whether starved or nourished by her absence (and I believe the authorities differ on this question), was strong enough nonetheless to keep me awake at night. I knew Pierre-Julien Fauré, and I knew how his mind worked; once he had equated the possessed girl in the letter with Babilonia de Caussade, he would stop at nothing to secure a confession of sorcery from her – and from her associates, also. Furthermore, although he was in no way sharp-witted, even he must suspect Babilonia eventually, if only through a process of elimination. I could not base my hopes on his want of intellect.

Out of the depths have I cried unto Thee, O Lord! Like St Augustin, I bore about a shattered and bleeding soul; my heart was utterly darkened and whatever I beheld was death. Indeed, after Pierre-Julien had walked away from me, I stood for a while without seeing or hearing. I was, as he had declared, like the blind people that have eyes and the deaf that have ears. I ate the bread of sorrow, for I knew the ways of the Holy Office. Once you have caught its attention, there can be no escape. Its net is wide, and its memory long. I understood this:

who better? So it was that I mourned, and saw in front of me only nettles and saltpits – the desolation of hopelessness.

For some time I wandered the streets without a destination, and to this day I cannot tell you if I was greeted as I walked. My gaze was turned away from the world; I saw nothing but the scourge of my sorrows. Then, as I wearied, I became more conscious of my flesh and surroundings. I began to consider the protests of my belly, for it was after Nones, and I should have been eating. So I returned to the priory, where, on account of my late appearance at refection, I was the recipient of many reproving looks. Doubtless I would be chastised for my tardiness at the chapter of faults, but this did not concern me; I was already feeble and sore broken beneath the rod of my own conscience. Any penances placed upon me would be well deserved, for in my pride and conceit I had banished myself from the Holy Office. I was prevented from helping Johanna because I was excluded from any decisions made regarding her fate. I had crippled my own arms and cut out my own tongue.

I had been a fool, for a fool uttereth all his mind, but a wise man keepeth it in till afterwards.

God of mercy, how I suffered! I went to my cell, and I prayed. Fighting the despair which repeatedly overwhelmed me – and which hampered my faculties whenever it did so – I struggled to formulate a solution. But only one presented itself. Somehow, I would have to find my way back into the Holy Office, though it would be easier for a camel to go through the eye of a needle. Somehow, I would have to recover my position there.

I realised that my admittance would be purchased at a high price. Pierre-Julien would force me to spread dung upon my face, and lick the dust like a serpent. Let me assure you, however, that I was willing to eat ashes like bread, if it was necessary. My pride was as nothing, next to my love for Johanna.

You may think it unaccountable that I should have

succumbed to such a reckless, carnal passion so swiftly, after only two brief encounters. You may wonder at the strength of those chains, so newly forged, that bound me so tightly to the distant object of my desire. But was not Jonathon's soul knit with the soul of David, upon their first meeting? Has it not been attested, by many authorities, that love, entering through the eye, is very often instantaneous in its effect? There are countless examples, both in the present and in the past – and mine, I must confess, is another. With little encouragement, despite all objections, I would have sucked the poison from a leper's sores to save Johanna from harm.

So perhaps it was God's will, that I should have suffered such reverses. Perhaps it was His plan that I should be made humble and contrite. Having failed to transform me with His divine love, He might have been seeking the same result with chastening and displeasure. *It is good for me that I have been afflicted, that I might learn Thy statutes.*

Therefore I washed my face, considered my strategy, and returned to headquarters with the intention of embracing dunghills. By now it was almost Vespers, and the shadows were long; while I had been engaged in prayer and self-condemnation, the greater part of the day had fled. But it seemed that Raymond Donatus was still missing, for when Brother Lucius answered my knock, he told me as much.

'And Father Pierre-Julien?' I queried. 'Where is he?'

'He is upstairs, in the scriptorium. He is consulting the registers.'

'Would you tell him that I come, in a humble and contrite spirit, to seek his forgiveness?' I said, ignoring the canon's dumbfounded look. 'Please ask him if he will condescend to grant me an interview. Tell him that I am in earnest, Brother.'

Obediently, Brother Lucius went to deliver my message. As soon as he was out of sight, I slipped into Pierre-Julien's room, and restored Bishop Jacques Fournier's letter to its rightful place, having no wish to be condemned as a thief, in addition to my other sins. Needless to say, I did not linger. By the time

Brother Lucius had returned, I was standing once again by the outer door, my demeanour one of innocence and humility.

'Father Pierre-Julien says that he will not speak to you,' I was informed.

'Tell him that I come only to listen and accept. I was in error, and seek his guidance.'

Again, Brother Lucius trudged up the stairs. After a brief interval, he descended once more, with a cold and graceless reply.

'Father Pierre-Julien says that he is busy.'

'Then I shall await his convenience. Tell him so, will you, Brother? I am here, when I am required.'

Whereupon I sat down on one of the benches, and began to recite the penitential psalms. As I had anticipated, the sound of my voice (which is well trained, though I say it myself) brought Pierre-Julien out of the scriptorium as quickly as smoke will drive a rat out of a hole.

'Be silent!' he spluttered, from the top of the staircase. 'What do you want? You are not welcome here!'

'Father, I have come to you in supplication. I have been ignorant and disobedient. I have scorned wisdom and burned incense to vanity. Father, I ask your forgiveness.'

'I cannot discuss this now,' he replied, and indeed he seemed quite distraught, rumpled and sweaty and tremulous. 'There are too many things – Raymond is still missing – '

'Father, let me be your staff. Your footstool. Let me only be of service.'

'You are mocking me.'

'No!' Moved as I was by a profound apprehension, anxious as to the safety of Johanna and disgusted at my own pitiful conceit, my tone was absolutely convincing. 'Believe me when I tell you that I wish to forsake my self-will. I am lowly and inferior, poured out like milk and curdled like cheese. Father, forgive me. I go about puffed up with pride, when I should be thinking only of my sins, and of the dread judgement of the Lord. I am like the enemies of the cross of Christ, whose

God is their belly, and who mind earthly things. Your judge-ment is my law, Father. Command me, and I shall obey – for I am unworthy in the sight of God. I am a fool, and a fool's mouth is his destruction.'

How shall I explain the tears that rose to my eyes then? Perhaps they were tears of abhorrence, though whether this loathing was directed at my numerous sins, or at Pierre-Julien, or at my horrible predicament, or at all three, I cannot decide from this distant vantage. At any rate, they had the desired effect. Pierre-Julien appeared to hesitate; he looked up to the scriptorium, then back down at me. He advanced a few steps.

'You are truly contrite?' he asked, with evident suspicion, though with less force than I would have expected.

In reply, I sank to my knees and covered my face with my hands.

'Have mercy upon me, O God, according to Thy loving kindness,' I intoned, 'according unto the multitude of Thy tender mercies, wipe out my offence. Wash me thoroughly from mine iniquity, and cleanse me from my sin. For I acknowledge my transgressions, and my sin is ever before me.'

Pierre-Julien grunted. He descended to my side, and laid a clammy hand on my tonsure.

'If you are truly aware of your errors,' he said, 'then I freely forgive you for your obstinate arrogance.' (Coals of fire, let me assure you!) 'But it is God's mercy you should be seeking, my son. It is God who knows your heart, and who would restore unto you the joy of your salvation. For the sacrifices of God are a broken spirit. Is your spirit sufficiently broken, my son?'

'It is,' I answered, and I was not lying. For whereas once I would have gritted my teeth under such pompous benevo-lence, now I thought simply: It is as much as I deserve.

'Then come.' Clearly, my compunction tasted sweet to Pierre-Julien. It revived him like wine, bringing colour to his cheeks and a smile to his face. 'Come, let us exchange the kiss of peace, and may the Lord bless our union with the extirpa-tion of many heretics.'

For my sins, he embraced me; I accepted his kiss as I would have accepted a scourging, as penance for my presumption. Then I followed him into his room, where he discoursed for a while on the virtue of humility, which purified the soul like a refiner's fire and like fuller's soap. I listened in silence. At last, having satisfied himself that I did not intend to challenge him, he bade me return to my duties 'in a spirit of obedience', remembering always that the meek shall inherit the earth.

'Father,' I said, before he could return to the scriptorium, 'regarding the letter you mentioned, the one from the Bishop of Pamiers – '

'Oh yes.' He nodded. 'I believe it to be an important piece of evidence.'

'Against whom, Father?'

'Why, against the girl in question, of course!'

'Of course.' I had to proceed with great care, for I did not wish to appear recalcitrant. 'Have you identified her?'

'Not yet,' he admitted. 'But I will ask Pons if there are any beautiful young girls in prison who appear to be possessed by a devil.' Suddenly he frowned, and fixed me with a faintly suspicious look. '*You* have been reviewing all of the inquisitions undertaken by Father Augustin,' he said. 'Have you not encountered anyone fitting this description? Anyone whom he might have interviewed? The date of the letter should help.'

Here I was in some difficulty. I did not want to alert Pierre-Julien to Babilonia's existence. On the other hand, it would be awkward if he discovered her by some alternative means, and accused me of trying to deceive him. Therefore I answered his question with another question, designed to throw him off the scent.

'If Father Augustin never mentioned this girl, and never had her charged or even investigated,' I said, 'surely he was convinced of her innocence?'

'Not at all. It only means that he died before he could commence the inquisition.'

'But, Father, if she is indeed a sorceress, why would he call her possessed, and seek to free her from her bondage?'

'It could be that she is simply a victim of sorcery,' Pierre-Julien admitted. 'Even so, she will lead us to the culprit. And recollect, too, what the Angelic Doctor has to say about conjuration. Though it might appear that the demon is in the sorcerer's power, this is never the case. Perhaps the girl invoked a demon, and was then possessed by it. She is a woman, remember. A woman is naturally weaker than a man.'

'But Father Augustin described this girl as being of great spiritual worth,' I pointed out. 'Surely he would not have done so, if he believed her to be a sorceress?'

'My son, Father Augustin was not infallible,' my superior rejoined, somewhat impatiently. 'Did he ever instruct you as to the methods and characteristics of a sorceress?'

'No, Father.'

'No. Then perhaps he was as ignorant of the subject as you are, though doubtless learned in other matters. Remember, too, that he is dead, now. We must proceed alone.' Rising, Pierre-Julien indicated that our discussion was at an end; he told me that, as a gesture of contrition, I should interview Bruna d'Aguilar once more, and use the interrogatory that he himself had supplied. 'You can do it before Compline, if you wish,' he added. 'I am very busy at present, so I have no need of Durand.'

'Yes, Father,' I meekly concurred. 'And on the subject of notaries – '

'I shall make my decision in a day or two,' he interrupted. 'Of course, if Raymond Donatus continues to absent himself, another notary will have to be appointed.'

Bowing, I stepped aside, that he might pass through the door ahead of me. Although my appearance was grave, I was rejoicing in my heart, for it seemed that he had left the investigation of Bishop Jacques Fournier's letter in my hands. If it were so, then I had a very good chance of shielding Babilonia from his accusatory eye. There was every reason to believe that he might never know of her existence.

Sadly, however, I had underestimated both his wit and his desire for control. Shortly after returning to the scriptorium, he summoned me from my desk by raising his shrill voice and calling my name.

'Bernard!' he cried. 'Brother Bernard!'

Like a faithful servant I hurried to do his bidding, and found him sitting beside an open records chest, surrounded by inquisitorial registers.

'It just occurred to me,' he said. 'Father Augustin was killed on his way to visit some women near Casseras. You called them "pious women". Is that not so?'

'Yes, Father,' I replied, with a sinking heart.

'Did you visit these women, when you were in Casseras?'

'Yes, Father.'

'And are any of them young and beautiful?'

'Father,' I said jovially, though within me I was as desolate as the waters of Nimrin, 'to a monk such as myself, *all* women appear young and beautiful!'

Pierre-Julien frowned. 'Such remarks are unworthy of you, Brother,' he snapped. 'I ask you again: are any of them young and beautiful?'

'Father, I am in earnest. What is beautiful to one man may not be beautiful to another.'

'Are any of them *young*, then?' he insisted, and I knew that I must answer, for he was growing impatient.

'I would not call any of them young,' was my cautious rejoinder. 'They are all mature women.'

'Describe them to me.'

I did so, commencing with Vitalia. Though I was careful not to praise too highly Johanna's flawless complexion, or Babilonia's angelic face, my unemphatic *effictio* of each woman nevertheless interested Pierre-Julien. If only I could have lied! But to do so would have been running a very great risk – a very great risk indeed.

'Did either of these women exhibit any strange character-istics?' he asked. 'Any impiety of speech or disrespect in their demeanour?'

'No, Father, not at all,' I said, hoping that none of the ser-geants had mentioned Babilonia's strange fit.

'They are diligent in their church attendance?'

'When health permits. They live some distance from the village.'

'But the local priest visits them regularly? Every day or so?' As I hesitated, he continued. 'If he does not, Brother, I would regard the position of these women as undesirable. Women should not live together without men, unless they are subject to constant attendance by a priest or monk.'

'Oh, I know.'

'Women cannot be trusted, otherwise. They are likely to stray into error.'

'Of course. Father Augustin was concerned about this very problem. He went there to persuade them that they should become Dominican tertiaries.'

'I do not like it,' Pierre-Julien declared. 'Why should they live in such a remote place? From what are they fleeing?'

'From nothing, Father – they simply wish to serve the Lord.'

'Then they should enter a nunnery. No, it is highly suspi-cious. They were in the vicinity of Father Augustin's death, they are living like Beguines (who have just been condemned by the Holy Father, did you know?), and one of their number is very possibly a sorceress. In the circumstances, I think that they should be summoned for questioning.'

What could I say? If I had argued, he would have taken the matter out of my hands. So I bowed my head, and seemed to submit, all the while thinking: This must be prevented. This *will* be prevented. And it occurred to me that if I was slow in the completion of my superior's directive – if I dawdled in its pursuit – then Johanna and her friends might very well have left the forcia before they could be cited to appear in Lazet.

Of course, one never escapes the Holy Office; by moving

251

around, one simply postpones the inevitable. But as I lay in bed after Compline, reviewing the events of the day, I was struck by another thought. What about the missing register? Being preoccupied with Johanna's peril, I had neglected to ask Pierre-Julien, as he sat in the scriptorium scrabbling through our records, what it was that he sought. I suspected, however, that he had been searching for the same book which had taken him to Raymond's house. It seemed to me that missing registers had figured largely in recent events affecting the Holy Office, and I wondered if I could use this to my advantage.

Perhaps, if I worked hard enough, I might secure Pierre-Julien's dismissal. To lose a register, after all, was an act of gross incompetence. And there were doubtless other ways in which his efforts could be undermined.

You will notice that I did not concern myself with Raymond's disappearance. My thoughts were wholly with Johanna. As Ovid says: 'Love is a thing full of anxious fear': he whom the sword of love has wounded is shaken all the time by the constant thought of his beloved, and his soul is bound in slavery. Nothing else is of any interest, when his love is threatened.

Against Thee only have I sinned, and done this evil in Thy sight.

The next morning I attended Prime, but Pierre-Julien did not. He was not in his cell, when I stopped there on my way out of the priory. And although I expected to find him at headquarters, I was disappointed in that hope, too.

Instead I encountered Raymond's wife, who sat weeping by the door of the Holy Office, like a penitent.

'Ricarda,' I said. 'What are you doing here?'

'Oh ... oh, Father, he did not come home!' she sobbed. 'He is dead, I know it!'

'Ricarda, this is no place for you. Go back to your house.'

'They say he had women! They say I killed him!'

'Nonsense. No one thinks such a thing.'

'The Seneschal does!'

'Then the Seneschal is a fool.' I helped her to her feet, wondering if she was capable of finding her way home unaccompanied. 'We are looking for him, Ricarda,' I said. 'We are doing our best.'

Still she sobbed, and I saw that she was not fit to be left alone. Therefore I decided to escort her back to her residence, and proceed from there to the Chateau Comtal – for I was anxious to meet with Roger Descalquencs. You see, I had undertaken to do three things that day: to question Roger about his search of Raymond's house, to think of some way that I might warn Johanna of my superior's intentions, and to visit the Bishop's palace. It had occurred to me that I would do well to consult Anselm's library, not simply because Raymond had done the same just before his disappearance, but because this library was contained not in chests, but in bookcupboards, with each codex laid out carefully, one beside the next. As a result, I surmised, it might be possible to discern where a book was missing.

Therefore it was no inconvenience to me that I should be required to attend Ricarda. I went with her all the way to her front door and delivered her into the care of her wetnurse (who was well placed, since her poor mistress had been reduced to little more than an infant). From there I walked briskly to the Chateau Comtal, where I was greeted jovially by the guard at the gate. I recognised him as one of the men who had escorted me to Casseras.

'Too late, Father,' he observed. 'Your friend just left.'

'My friend? What friend?'

'The other one. The inquisitor. I can never remember his name.'

'Not Father Pierre-Julien Fauré?'

'The very one.'

'*He* was here?'

'Yes. He went that way, if you want him.'

I replied that I did not, and requested an audience with

the Seneschal. But he, too, had recently departed (off to question a certain provost about certain fines and confiscations), so I took my leave and headed for the Bishop's palace. Here I was obliged, for courtesy's sake, to exchange a few words with the Bishop himself, before securing the keys (and the permission) that would allow me to consult his books. Fortunately, he was engaged in a rather fierce argument when I approached him. Indeed, I could hear angry voices raised as I sought admittance at the front door. It was for this reason that I was spared a long and tedious account of his latest equine purchases.

Not even Bishop Anselm could put horseflesh ahead of a room crowded with glowering combatants – including his chaplain, the Archdeacon, the Dean of St Polycarpe, the Royal Treasurer, and the consul, Lothaire Carbonel.

'Brother Bernard,' the Bishop said, into the sudden silence occasioned by my entrance. 'I am informed that you wish to consult the library?'

'At your convenience, my lord.'

'Oh, you are always welcome. Louis, you have the keys – take Brother Bernard to the library.'

Obediently, his chaplain rose and escorted me upstairs to the Bishop's private chambers. We had barely made our withdrawal before the shouting began again; it was apparent that Bishop Anselm had deeply offended St Polycarpe's chapter of canons. But this was not unprecedented, for they rarely agreed with him on anything – and for good reason, too. He had a tendency to regard the cathedral treasury as his own private cashbox.

Louis, a dour and avaricious glutton, took me to the Bishop's book-cupboards, which were contained in a locked room beside his luxurious sleeping chamber. The light being poor, he lit an oil lamp for me. Then he left as I ran my eye down the shelves, looking for a break in the pattern of tooled leather bindings. What a proliferation of cupboards the Bishop possessed! Instead of being piled up in tottering heaps, each codex had its own space, to facilitate the task of locating and identifying the many volumes in his library.

As a result, it was not difficult to see where books were missing. One space was sharply defined, and the dust lying on the naked shelf thus exposed informed me that the register in question had been missing for several weeks – though not (to judge from the dust on the covers of the flanking books) for several years. The other space was less easily discerned, but a peculiar looseness in the ranks told me that something had recently been extracted.

I was pleased to discover that someone on the Bishop's staff (or perhaps a former employee of the Holy Office) had taken care to arrange all the books in a certain order, thus helping me to deduce the contents of at least one of the two absent volumes. Since the registers on either side of the space left by this book comprised testimony from the inhabitants of Crieux, I inferred that the lost register also covered the sins of this village. It came as no surprise to me that the aforesaid depositions had been recorded under the guidance of the inquisitor mentioned by Father Augustin in his marginal note. Decidedly, Father Augustin had been searching for this lost register. Decidedly, too, it had not been lost for very long.

The other missing register was also an old one – at least forty years old. Unfortunately, I was unable even to hazard a guess as to its contents, owing to the slight rearrangement of the neighbouring records (effected to conceal such an eye-catching vacancy, perhaps?). Even after consulting some of these records, I could not decide which villages were missing. Therefore, since nothing further could be done, I sought out Brother Louis, and found him listening at the door of the Bishop's audience room. He looked annoyed when he saw me.

Clearly, I was interrupting an important part of the debate.

'Finished, Father?' he inquired, and continued, without waiting for a reply: 'I shall lock up, then. You know your way out.'

'Brother, there are two registers missing,' I said, before he could bundle me over the threshold. 'Did you take them? Did the Bishop?'

'Of course not!' Though pitched very low, Louis's voice was infused with both fear and anger. 'We never touch those books! Father Pierre-Julien probably took them.'

'Father Pierre-Julien?'

'He was here this morning. I saw him leave with a register under his arm.'

'Indeed?' This was *most* interesting. 'One register, or two?'

'Father, you must consult Father Pierre-Julien. It is not my place to question his movements.'

'No, no. I understand.' In my most reassuring manner, I asked about Raymond Donatus. He had visited the palace just a day or two previously. Had he taken any registers with him?

Louis frowned.

'Raymond Donatus did not come here,' he said. 'The last time I saw Raymond Donatus was . . . oh, weeks ago. Months.'

'Are you sure?'

'Yes, Father, I am *quite* sure.' Again, I sensed that Louis was torn between fear and fury. 'We have seen no one from the Holy Office except Brother Lucius. Brother Lucius always delivers the new registers directly to me.'

'But he never enters the library himself?'

'No, Father.'

'And when Raymond Donatus was last here – did he take any registers then?'

'Maybe. I cannot recall. It was a long time ago.'

'But you surely would have noticed?'

'Father, I have many things to occupy me! My days are very full!'

'Yes, of course.'

'At present, for example, I should be in there, with Bishop Anselm. He told me to return as soon as you had finished. Are you finished now, Father?'

Recognising that Louis would be of little further use, I said that I was, and left him. Then I set out for headquarters, hoping to find Pierre-Julien.

To my surprise, I encountered him just outside the palace. He was sweaty and flustered, and his face was red. Under his arm, he carried two inquisitorial registers.

'You!' he exclaimed, stopping abruptly. 'What are you doing here?'

I could have asked him the same question. I *wanted* to ask him the same question. But having learned to be cautious, in my exchanges with Pierre-Julien, I responded in a meek and obliging manner.

'Consulting the Bishop's library,' I said.

'Why?'

'Because Raymond told me, before he disappeared, that one of the Bishop's registers was missing. And now I find that two are gone.' Fixing my gaze on the registers under his arm, I could not forbear to ask: 'Are they the two?'

He looked down at the volumes blankly, as if he had never seen them before. When he looked up again, he seemed at a loss – and it was some time before he could answer.

'They are,' he said at last. 'I am returning them.'

'You took one this morning?'

'Yes, I ... I took one this morning.' Suddenly his voice quickened; the words came tumbling out. 'As I told you before, I allowed Raymond to take one of the registers home. Since it had not been found there, I came here this morning to consult the Bishop's copy. As I was doing so, it occurred to me: perhaps the Seneschal, when he searched Raymond's house, mistook our inquisitorial registers for Raymond's own. Therefore I went to him, and asked him to show me the registers which he *had* found. Imagine my joy when I discovered that I was correct!'

'You mean – '

'Raymond had in his possession not only the register I gave to him, but both copies of another volume of testimony which

Father Augustin must have requested.' With a rather unnatural smile, Pierre-Julien flourished his leather-bound burden. 'The mystery is solved!' he declared.

I could not agree with him. As I marshalled my thoughts, various questions occurred to me.

'Raymond told me that those books were missing,' I pointed out. 'The ones requested by Father Augustin.'

'He must have found them after all.'

'Then why not give them to me?'

'Doubtless he ... doubtless his fate overtook him, before he was able to do so.'

It was a reasonable explanation. As I pondered it, Pierre-Julien continued.

'I have just returned our copies to the scriptorium,' he said. 'Now I shall restore these books to the Bishop, and all will be as it should be.'

'And you say that the *Seneschal* had these registers?' I had been struck by another thought. 'Why would he have taken Raymond's registers? For what purpose?'

'Why, to see if they contained any evidence!' Pierre-Julien sounded impatient. 'Really, Brother, you are very slow.'

'But he cannot have looked at them. If he had looked at them, he would have seen that some were not Raymond's.'

'Exactly! The Seneschal is a busy man. He had not studied the documents. If he had, of course, he would have alerted us.'

'And he still has the other registers? Raymond's own notarial registers?'

'I presume so.'

'And he found them all together? In the one place?'

'Brother, why do you ask? Of what importance is it, where he found them? He found them! *That* is what concerns us. Nothing more.'

Pierre-Julien's tone pierced my reverie (for indeed, I had been thinking aloud) and caused me to refrain my lips. For I sensed that my superior was growing agitated, even angry, and

I wanted to give him no cause for dismissing me from my post, again.

So I bowed, and nodded, and appeared to be satisfied. Then we parted (with many congenial words), and I hurried back to headquarters as quickly as the dignity of my position would allow. I banged on the door until Brother Lucius had unbarred it; I pounded upstairs to the scriptorium, fumbling for the keys on my belt.

'Lucius!' I cried. 'Did Father Pierre-Julien just return some registers, to one of these chests?'

'Yes, Father.'

'Which one? Which chest?'

The scrivener was still struggling up the stairs; I had to wait until he was in the room before my curiosity was satisfied. When he pointed to the larger chest I unlocked it, and extracted the topmost book.

'No, Father,' Lucius objected. 'He put them further down.'

'Where? How far down?'

When the scrivener shrugged, I almost stamped my foot in frustration. It seemed that I would be forced to look at every register – and would I have time to do so, before Pierre-Julien returned? But I was lucky, for when I picked up the fifth register I found the testimony for which I (and Father Augustin) had been searching: twenty-year-old testimony from the inhabitants of Crieux.

I did *not*, however, find two of the first five folios. A large portion of the list of deponents, and most of the table of contents, had disappeared. When I opened the next book, I discovered that it had been similarly abused. The two registers were now incomplete.

What an abomination!

Flicking through them, I found more evidence of missing folios. I found irregularities; I found gaps in the depositions. I also found a name familiar to me – the name of a man, now deceased, whose son happened to be Lothaire Carbonel (the very man whose presence I had just left in the Bishop's palace).

Merciful God, I thought, and the father died before sentencing. But I could expend no further time on the matter, for Pierre-Julien was doubtless on his way back to headquarters, and I was reluctant to have him know that I had been checking the records.

Therefore I threw them down, exclaiming 'Oh, I cannot find them!' (for the scrivener's benefit), and locked the chest again with trembling hands. Be assured, I was profoundly agitated. It was apparent to me that Pierre-Julien himself had defaced the registers – for if he had not, he would have mentioned to me that they were damaged. *The Lord preserveth the simple: I was brought low, and He helped me.* How the Lord had helped me! To deface an inquisitorial register was bad enough, but the reason for doing so was even worse. Clearly, having for the first time consulted certain registers that may or may not have been stolen by Raymond Donatus, Pierre-Julien had discovered, and concealed, the identity (or identities) of heretics formerly defamed – heretics to whom he must be in some manner related. Obdurate heretics, who had not made amends and performed penances. Heretics who might very well deprive him of his position, and cover him with shame, if their connection to him was made public.

How I gloried in my discovery! How I gloated! How fervently I thanked God, and praised Him, as I strutted downstairs to my desk! But I also knew that my evidence was incomplete: that it would be unassailable only if I had the names and crimes of the heretics in question. So I hastily sharpened my pen, and sat down to compose a letter.

I addressed it to Jean de Beaune, the Inquisitor of Carcassonne. I gave him as much as I knew about the missing depositions, and asked him if, at any time during the past forty years, he or his predecessors had requested copies of this same testimony. It was quite possible (though not, perhaps, very probable) that such a request had been made. In the event that it had, could the text be copied, and the new copy sent to Lazet? I should be eternally indebted.

Having completed this missive, I wrote an almost identical one, addressing it to the Inquisitor of Toulouse. Then I sealed both documents, and took them to Pons. (For it was Pons who always chose and dispatched familiars when messengers were needed.) If all went well, a response could be expected within three or four days.

Righteous art Thou, O Lord, and upright are Thy judgements! By sacrificing Pierre-Julien, I intended to save Johanna. And I was determined to effect my superior's dismissal, with or without solid evidence. But I shall reveal more of my plans later in this narrative.

Upon returning to my desk, I was surprised (though not grieved) to discover that Pierre-Julien was still absent. I was even more surprised when he missed refection at the priory. In fact, I was beginning to feel somewhat concerned, and would have set out to look for him, if he had not suddenly reappeared at headquarters late that afternoon, smelling strongly of wine. He greeted me in a noisy fashion, and launched into an explanation of his long absence which might have been perfectly convincing, if it had not been so thoroughly confused. Then he put a hand on my arm, and drew me close.

'Did I tell you,' he said, 'that Raymond tore some folios out of the registers he borrowed?'

My evident surprise, I hope, was attributable to the duplicity of such an act. In truth, I was astonished that Pierre-Julien had even raised the subject. But I quickly realised that he was attempting to conceal his own corrupt behaviour, in the event that I had consulted (or intended to consult) the registers. And I muttered an incomprehensible reply.

'He probably did it to protect his own name,' Pierre-Julien continued, 'and then fled the city when he realised that his sin would be discovered. But we shall find him.'

'Could he have done it for somebody else?' I inquired. 'Could he have done it for money?'

'Perhaps. It is very sad.'

261

'Could he have been killed by the person who offered him payment,' I went on, 'to ensure that he would never reveal this fact?' And although I had raised such a possibility almost in a mocking spirit, I suddenly wondered: was I close to the truth? Had Raymond been killed because he had secured the damaged registers *after* they had been damaged, and knew who had damaged them? But this reading of events would preclude my superior's guilt, so I discounted it.

'Oh – I think that is *most* unlikely,' Pierre-Julien exclaimed, in a disconcerted fashion. 'But in any event, Brother, you may leave the problem safely in my hands. You have enough to worry about with your investigation of Father Augustin's terrible fate. Have you summoned those women, yet?'

'No, Father,' I replied, with perfect serenity. 'I have not summoned those women, yet.'

And rest assured, I did not intend to.

That very evening, Raymond Donatus was found.

You will recall the grotto of Galamus in the city market-place. You will also recall that every day, at sundown, a certain canon of St Polycarpe collects from this holy depression such offerings as have been placed there. He puts the offerings in a large sack and takes them back to the cathedral kitchens, for they are mostly herbs, loaves, fruit and suchlike. Sometimes there is salted fish, and sometimes a little bacon, but only once, on the aforesaid evening, was there a generous quantity of meat – joints of meat heavily wrapped in layers of bloody cloth.

Surprised at such abundance, the canon on duty dropped each irregular parcel into his sack. The weight of his burden was such that he was forced to drag it, rather than carry it, all the way to the kitchens. Among the kitchen staff there was much rejoicing: God was good to bestow such largesse upon His faithful servants. But when the first bundle was unwrapped, rejoicing turned to horror.

For the meat was human: a severed arm, bent at the elbow.

Naturally, the Dean was summoned, then the Bishop, then the Seneschal. By Matins, every bundle had been unwrapped, and the constituent parts of Raymond Donatus had been revealed. Observing the identity of the corpse, Roger Descalquencs had at once sent for Pierre-Julien, who was, consequently, absent from the priory during Matins.

Now consider, if you please, my superior's subsequent behaviour. I do not know if he was told why the Seneschal wanted him, but even if he was only enlightened upon reaching St Polycarpe, he neglected to inform me of the horrible discovery which had been made there. I was told, after Matins, that the Seneschal had required Pierre-Julien's attendance (for I was quick to query his vacant seat in the choir); I was forbidden, however, to leave the priory myself. Therefore I returned to my bed in a state of profound disquiet, barely able to sleep.

Upon rising again I encountered Pierre-Julien at Lauds, and spoke to him in his cell immediately afterwards. He told me that Raymond's dismembered corpse had been found in the grotto of Galamus; that heralds would publish the news around the city, and seek out witnesses who may have seen the remains being deposited; that someone would have to inform the unfortunate widow.

'Perhaps you could do that, Brother,' Pierre-Julien suggested. He was looking very tired and ill. 'With the help of her parish priest, or ... or some friend or relative ...'

'Yes, of course.' I was too shocked to object. 'Where – where is he?'

'At St Polycarpe. They have put him in the crypt. The widow may have her own wishes ...'

'God forgive us all,' I murmured, genuflecting. 'How long has he been – that is to say – are the remains quite fresh, or – ?'

Pierre-Julien swallowed, and winced. 'Brother, I really cannot speculate,' he replied. 'My expertise is not sufficient.' Then he rose, and I rose with him. 'Durand must be notified,' he continued. 'I shall do that myself. I shall also write to the Inquisitor General, informing him that Satan is still among us. The Holy Office is besieged, but we shall fight and we shall triumph. For God is our refuge and our strength.'

'Besieged?' I echoed, without comprehension. Then suddenly I understood. 'Oh. Yes. The same fate as Father Augustin. But not the same culprits, Father.'

'The very same,' he said firmly.

'Father, Jordan Sicre is in Catalonia. Or at least, he is on his way from there.'

'Jordan Sicre was only an agent of evil.'

'But Father Augustin and his escort were dismembered so as to hide the absence of Jordan's body. Raymond's death is quite different – '

'It is the same. A sacrifice at a crossroads – exactly the same. An act of sorcery.'

I would have contested this position, if I had not been afraid to arouse Pierre-Julien's ire. Instead, concerned that he would at any moment raise the subject of Johanna and her friends, I quickly left him. I left the priory altogether and, knowing that Ricarda's parish was served by the church of St Antonin, I directed my steps towards this church – all the while thinking: What is the answer? Who is to blame? Why standest Thou afar off, O Lord? But before reaching St Antonin, I passed a herald declaiming in the street, and stopped to listen.

Although it was still early, he had drawn a sizeable audience: people were hanging out of their bedroom windows, bleary-eyed, in an effort to hear his strange tidings. Because I knew some of these people, and had no wish to converse with them (or I would never get to St Antonin), I hung back, keeping just close enough to hear what the herald had to say. It was this: that Raymond Donatus, public notary, had been found in the grotto of Galamus, cut to pieces. That the Seneschal wished to interview the perpetrator of this foul act, or anyone who might have witnessed it, or anyone who might have cleaned up copious amounts of blood in the past two days, or anyone who might have seen several large, cloth-wrapped bundles being placed in the grotto of Galamus. Also, that the Seneschal wanted to hear of, or from, anyone who had been salting meat recently. Also, that he wanted to talk to anyone who had seen Raymond Donatus within the last three days. Also, that anyone missing a cloak, or cloaks, should be reported to the Seneschal at once.

The punishment for this pernicious and bloody crime would be terrible, and the Lord's vengeance would be even more terrible. By the order of Roger Descalquencs, Royal Seneschal of Lazet.

Having delivered this message, the herald drummed his heels on his horse's flanks, and passed on. Immediately, the air was abuzz with exclamations. If I had lingered, I undoubtedly would have been noticed, and questioned – but I fled before the herald's last words had even fallen from his lips. I fled as soon as he mentioned the salting of meat. I fled, not to St Antonin, but to St Polycarpe, where I demanded access to the crypt.

Here, amidst the sepulchres, the Sacristan showed me Raymond's mutilated corpse. I shall not defile this parchment with a description. Suffice it to say that the body was partly clothed, discoloured, and almost unrecognisable. Laid out in a lidless stone sarcophagus, each severed portion occupied its proper place. And every portion smelled strongly of brine.

'This corpse has been salted,' I gasped, through my sleeve. 'Yes.'

'What was it wrapped in? Where is the cloth?'

'It was wrapped in four cloaks, which were torn into pieces,' the Sacristan replied, his voice muffled by his own sleeve. 'They were taken by the Seneschal.'

'And the clothing was not removed from the body,' I muttered, thinking aloud. As you may recollect, Father Augustin's clothing *had* been removed. 'What were the Seneschal's comments? Does he suspect anyone?'

'Brother, I know not. I was not present when he examined

the remains.' After a slight hesitation, the Sacristan went on to ask me, in his gentle way, if Ricarda Donatus would soon send for the corpse. 'It should be buried, Brother. The flies – '

'Yes. I shall see to that as soon as possible.'

Thanking him, I left St Polycarpe – but did not proceed from there to Ricarda's house. In this, I think, I failed in my duty to her (but it must be confessed that another woman reigned in my heart and mind, that day). Cruelly, I allowed poor Ricarda to hear of her husband's terrible fate from a herald in the street, rather than from the lips of a sympathetic friend – for I went straight to headquarters, where Brother Lucius unbarred the door to admit me.

Pierre-Julien was in his room, talking to Durand Fogasset; I could hear their voices. Brother Lucius looked more insubstantial than ever as he blinked up at me like an owl in the sunlight. I asked him if he recalled his last encounter with Raymond Donatus, and he nodded, mutely.

'You said that you left these premises before he did,' I observed. 'Is that correct?'

'Yes, Father.'

'So you cannot tell me which guard was on duty here, that night? On the night shift, I mean – not the morning shift.'

'No, Father.'

'Then go and ask Pons.' I moved towards the staircase. 'Ask Pons who was on the night shift in here, and tell him to send that guard to me. I want to question him.'

'Yes, Father.'

'Oh – and Lucius! Are your lamps alight, upstairs?'

'Yes, Father.'

'Good.'

As the scrivener went to do my bidding, I fetched one of his lamps and took it down to the door of the stables. You will recall that this door was at the bottom of the staircase; I carefully examined the wooden plank which barred it, but could see no dust on the plank, nor any marks of recent use left in that dust. The floor, similarly, was swept clean of both dust and footprints. It seemed strange to me that the floor should be so clean. Who would think to clean it, and why? As far as I was aware, no one had entered the stables since the removal of Father Augustin's remains.

Lifting the bar, I laid it to one side and pushed the door open. Immediately, my nostrils were assailed by a putrid odour which was almost entirely attributable to my own incompetence. You see, I had forgotten to notify the inhabitants of Casseras about their brine barrels. For weeks they had stood, unsealed and full of the brine in which rotten flesh had been suspended. Not that the stables had ever been sweet-smelling, since the advent (and slaughter) of Pons' swine. Nevertheless, this stench was more noisome than any pig. It was noxious – suffocating. It made my eyes water.

Holding my breath, I peered into the first barrel, and saw only the dark, oily surface of the brine. The floor around the barrels was damp, but it was damp everywhere, permanently damp, and as slick as melting ice. The horse-trough was dark with blood, whether of man or pig I could not say; although the stains looked old, they were at the same time sticky – perhaps from all the moisture thereabouts. I have neglected to point out that it had been raining a good deal over the previous week or so, and rain always had a deleterious effect on those stables. Indeed, I would never have kept a horse of mine in there. Milk, perhaps, and fish – but not a horse.

To my immense frustration, I could not see any irrefutable evidence that Raymond Donatus had been butchered or salted in this malodorous cavern. Something certainly had been, but it might have been the pigs. On the other hand, there was nothing to suggest that Raymond had *not* been slaughtered there, and I thought it more than possible that he had. Possible? I thought it probable. I looked around at the weeping walls, the dense shadows, the slimy, blackened stone floor, and I thought: this is a den of evil. Almost I could hear the bat's wings of conjured demons.

Hastily, I climbed the stairs again.

'Oh! Brother Bernard!' Pierre-Julien was now in the ante-room, and looked surprised to see me. 'You have informed Ricarda?'

'I have smelled her husband's corpse,' was my response. 'It has been salted.'

'Salted? Why, yes. It was in brine.'

'And were you aware of the brine barrels, downstairs?'

'Brine barrels?' Again, he seemed surprised. But I was not entirely convinced that the surprise was genuine. 'No. Why are there brine barrels?'

'They came from Casseras, with Father Augustin's remains. Did not the Seneschal mention this to you?'

'Not at all.'

'Then he was remiss. Ah.' At the sound of creaking hinges I turned, and saw Brother Lucius enter from the prison, with one of the familiars close behind him. This man was a long-time employee of the Holy Office – a former mercenary called Jean-Pierre. I recognised his yellow, pock-marked face, cres-cent-shaped like a slice of cored apple, and the dispirited slope of his shoulders. He was small and wiry, with a great deal of hair. 'Jean-Pierre,' I said, noting the wary set of his counte-nance, 'were you on duty when Raymond Donatus left here, three nights ago?'

'Yes, Father.'

'You saw him leave? You barred that door behind him?'

'Yes, Father.'

'And he did not return? No one returned?'

'No, Father.'

'You are lying.'

The familiar blinked; around me, I could sense a certain tension, or stiffening. My next words had an even more notice-able effect, as was my intention. For it seemed to me that if Raymond's corpse had been kept in the stables – a likely con-clusion, since it must be asked: where else could one secretly salt a corpse? – then Jean-Pierre (who had been alone in the building, on the night of the notary's disappearance) may very well have put it there. Who else would have had the time to perform such butchery?

'I know that you are lying, Jean-Pierre. I know that Raymond Donatus was murdered in this building. And I know that you did it.'

'What?' Pierre-Julien exclaimed. Durand gasped, and the familiar reeled as if struck by a blow.

'No!' he cried. 'No, Father!'

'Yes.'

'He left! I saw him leave!'

'You did *not* see him leave. He did not leave here. He was killed downstairs, and his body was kept for two days in the brine barrels. We know this. We have evidence. Who else could have done it, but you?'

'The woman!' Jean-Pierre wildly claimed. 'The woman must have!'

'What woman?'

'Father, I – I – it was a lie, I was – the notary did leave, but he came back. With a woman. Late.'

'And you let him in?'

The familiar was no longer yellow, but red; he looked as if he might burst into tears. 'Father, I was paid,' he spluttered. 'Raymond Donatus paid me.'

'So when he knocked on the door, you demanded payment for entry.'

'No, no, he offered it! Earlier!'

'And had this happened before?'

'No, Father. At least ... not with me.' Jean-Pierre's voice was barely more than a croak. 'He said that Jordan Sicre used to help him, before Jordan was – before he disappeared. He used to bring many women, Father, and I know that it was wrong, but I never killed him. I never did. He offered me money once, to kill Jordan, but I turned him down. I could never do something like that, never.'

'Describe the woman – ' Pierre-Julien began, only to be interrupted. As you may imagine, I wanted to hear more about Jordan Sicre.

'How were you to kill Jordan?' I demanded. 'When? Why?'

'Father, he told me that Jordan had killed Father Augustin, and was being brought back to Lazet. He told me that Jordan must be poisoned, or he would reveal that Raymond had been bringing bad women into the Holy Office. He said: If they find out about me, Jean-Pierre, then they will find out about you, too. But I would not do it, Father. Murder is a sin.'

'Describe the woman,' Pierre-Julien repeated. 'How old was she? Did she have reddish-brown hair?'

'There *was* no woman!' I snapped. 'He is lying!'

'No, Father, no!'

'Of course you are!' I turned on the accused. 'Are you trying to tell me that a mysterious woman killed Raymond Donatus, dragged him down to the stables, cut him to pieces, and left through the door that you were guarding? Do you think me a *fool*, Jean-Pierre?'

'Father, hear me out!' The familiar, now weeping, was very, very frightened. 'He took her upstairs, Father, and then sent her down to me! We – we went in there ...' He gestured at Pierre-Julien's room. '... because the chair has a cushion on it – '

'You fornicated in *my chair*?'

' – and then she went out – she went back upstairs, for her money. Later, I heard the door close – I was still in your room, my lord – she must have left with him, Father, she *must* have.'

'Did you actually see them leave? Both of them?' Durand suddenly asked, before remembering that he should have been silent. But it was a good question.

'I heard them leave,' the familiar replied. 'I heard footsteps, and the door closing. It was unbarred. And nothing else happened the whole night. Father, I *swear* this is the truth! She either killed him in here – perhaps I fell asleep – or they left, and she killed him after!'

'You are lying. You killed him yourself. You were paid to kill him.'

'*No!*' Wailing, the familiar fell to his knees. '*No, Father, no . . .*'

'Why should he be lying?' Pierre-Julien said sharply. 'Why should this woman not have been the sorceress from Casseras?'

'Because there *is* no sorceress from Casseras!' I almost spat at him. 'This has nothing to do with the women from Casseras!'

'Raymond's murder was sorcery, Bernard!'

'It was *not* sorcery! It was planned to *look* like sorcery! This man was paid to kill Raymond Donatus, and dispose of the body as a sorcerer would!'

'Nonsense! Who would pay him to do such a thing?'

'You would, Father!' I thrust a finger into his breastbone. '*You* would!'

To make intercession for them

an you understand my reasoning, in this? Perhaps your mind is not trained to unravel the threads of guilt and innocence, as it is undoubtedly trained to pursue more exalted mysteries, such as the meaning of the incarnation. Perhaps you would prefer not to soil your intellect with such base and bloody details, offensive to virtuous men and unacceptable to the Lord.

If so, then allow me to set before you certain propositions. Firstly, it seemed to me that Raymond Donatus was very possibly implicated in the murder of Father Augustin – else why plan to kill Jordan Sicre? One surely does not poison a man to prevent him from revealing one's perverse taste for harlots. At any rate, I found this to be an unconvincing explanation, whereas my own made good sense. Why Raymond should have wanted to kill Father Augustin, on the other hand, was a question to which I could provide no answer. Certainly, I was unable to apply my deductive powers to this problem when it first arose in my mind, engaged as I was in a dispute with Pierre-Julien regarding my second proposition: namely, that he himself was responsible for the murder of Raymond Donatus.

Doubtless you will think such a proposal absurd. But only

reflect on the mutilated registers: they had been in Raymond's possession, had they not? If they had indeed contained testimony damaging to Pierre-Julien (as I suspected), then he would have wanted no one to read them, or convey to others what had been read. And the peculiar disposition of the notary's remains did suggest sorcery. To place them at a crossroads, rather than dumping them in the river, was an act designed to mimic the formulae of demonic invocations.

I ask you: who else, in the entire city, was educated in such obscure and idolatrous practices? Who else would have attempted to implicate a cast of persons – that is, necromancers – held in suspicion by one man and one man only? I thought to myself that if Pierre-Julien had wanted a heretic blamed for Raymond's slaughter, he should not have disposed of the corpse in a manner so elaborately faithful to his own construction of satanic ritual.

These were my thoughts, which sprang partly from reason, partly from emotion. Have no doubt that I *wanted* my superior to be guilty. I wanted him out of the way. Thus I was driven, to some degree, by prejudice, and half blinded by it also. I did not stop to consider what connection there might be, between Raymond's murder of Father Augustin and his own subsequent killing. I did not stop to consider the disappearance of the first register, long before Pierre-Julien's arrival in Lazet. I was too anxious to establish my superior's guilt.

So I accused, and was reviled in turn.

'You are bedevilled!' Pierre-Julien spluttered. 'You are possessed! Insane!'

'And *you* are a descendant of *heretics*.'

'Those women have bewitched you! They have infected your mind! To protect them, you defame me!'

'No, Fauré. To protect yourself, you defame them. Do you deny that you you removed folios from those registers?'

'Get out! Get out of here! Go!'

'Yes – I shall go! I shall go to the Seneschal, and he will arrest you!'

'*You* will be the one arrested! Your contempt for the sacred institution which I represent is sheer contumacy!'

'You represent nothing,' I sneered, moving to the door. 'You are a liar, and a murderer, and a fool. You are a quivering heap of fetid offal. You will be cast into the lake of fire, and I shall stand by singing, in white garments.' Glancing at Durand (who appeared to regard this altercation with feelings compounded equally of shock and delight), I saluted him, and retreated. Then I made for the Chateau Comtal. Undoubtedly I was a source of great astonishment among the citizens of Lazet, for I ran all the way with my skirts hitched up around my knees, so that everyone who saw me pass stared as if at some miraculous vision. It is rare indeed to see a monk in full flight (unless one is a brigand), and to see an inquisitor of heretical depravity pounding along like a hare pursued by a hound – well, that is a sight you may not expect to encounter in the course of three lifespans.

At any rate, I ran. And you can imagine my appearance when I reached my destination. I could barely gasp out a greeting as I stood hunched over, my hands supported on my poor monastic knees (so ill-adapted to strenuous exercise, after years of prayer and fasting), my chest aflame, my limbs tremulous, my heartbeat so loud that it deafened me. Recall, too, that I am not a young man! And the Seneschal, when he saw me thus debilitated, was as concerned by the sight as he would have been by an eclipse of the sun, or a three-headed calf, for it was a sight which presaged many troubles.

'God in heaven!' he blasphemed, before quickly crossing himself. 'What is it, Father? Are you hurt?'

I shook my head, still mute with breathlessness. He had risen, and so too had the Royal Treasurer, with whom he had been closeted. But an inquisitor of heretical depravity will always have precedence over such a minor official; when I dismissed him (with a gesture), he departed, leaving me in sole possession of the Seneschal's company.

'Sit down,' Roger commanded. 'Drink some wine. You have been running.'

I nodded.

'From whom?'

I shook my head.

'Breathe deeply. Again. Now drink this, and talk when you can.'

He gave me wine from the table by his bed, for we sat in the famed room wherein had slumbered King Philippe himself. As ever, I could not help admiring the embroidered damask hangings on this bed, which was decked out like an altar in silver and gold. Roger seemed to lavish on it all the luxurious adornments that he denied his own person.

'So,' he said, when I had recovered myself. 'What is it? Has someone else died?'

'You saw Raymond's corpse,' I responded (brusquely, owing to a shortness of breath). 'You saw that it had been salted.'

'Yes.'

'Do you remember the brine barrels which you brought from Casseras? My lord, they are in our stables, where you left them.'

Roger's eyes narrowed.

'And have they been used lately?' he inquired.

'I know not. It seems likely. My lord, it seems logical. Raymond was the last of us in the building that night. Why not pay the guard on duty to kill him, and put his corpse in the stables, where it would remain, for a time, unnoticed?'

There was a long silence. The Seneschal sat watching me, his solid arms folded across his breast. At last he grunted.

I took this as a signal that I might continue.

'My lord, did Father Pierre-Julien come to you yesterday, and ask for the inquisitorial registers which you had taken from Raymond's house?' I inquired.

'Yes.'

'Registers which you had not yet consulted?'

'Father, I have been very busy.'

'Yes, of course. But when *I* came to look at them, I found that they had been mutilated. Folios had been removed. Yet Father Pierre-Julien had said nothing of this – nothing! – when he first told me of their discovery. Does this not suggest that *he* may have damaged the books, rather than Raymond? For he did accuse Raymond, my lord. He said that Raymond was trying to conceal some heretical antecedents.'

'Father – forgive me ...' The Seneschal ran his fingers through his hair. 'I am lost here. Why would you think that Raymond was innocent? Why is his guilt so hard to believe?'

'Because Father Pierre-Julien did not even *mention* the missing folios when he told me that he had found the books.'

'Yes, but – '

'It should have been the first thing out of his mouth, my lord. To desecrate an inquisitorial register! Why, that is almost as great a crime as murdering Father Augustin!'

'Mmmph.' This time the Seneschal wiped his face, and shifted his shoulders, and generally behaved like a man uncomfortable with a stated proposition. 'Well ...' he said, 'and what follows? Are you saying that Father Pierre-Julien has been trying to hide a heretical grandfather?'

'Or some such thing. But it was Raymond who stumbled on the register which implicated Father Pierre-Julien. So – '

'So Pierre-Julien *killed* him? Oh, Father, is that likely?'

'Raymond was killed in the Holy Office stables! I am sure of it! If you search the brine tubs, you may find evidence – threads from his clothes – remember, my lord, Father Augustin and his escort were found unclad.'

'Father, this guard you mentioned. Has he confessed?'

'No, but – '

'Then he has not explained why, instead of leaving the corpse in brine until the following night, he did not simply carry it to the grotto directly after Raymond was killed?'

I paused. It must be admitted that this question had not yet occurred to me. Again with folded arms, the Seneschal watched . . . and waited.

'Perhaps it was a way of – of ensuring that the blood was not so evident,' I said at last, in faltering tones. 'Perhaps – perhaps – why, perhaps he did not have time, because the morning shift was due to begin! And recollect that he had to clean up all the blood.'

'Father, let me ask you something else.' The Seneschal leaned forward. 'Have you spoken to Father Pierre-Julien about this?'

'I have.'

'And what does he say?'

'What would you expect him to say?' I snapped. 'He denies everything, of course!'

'Did he point out that, even if this guard of yours did kill Raymond Donatus, he could have been paid by the very same people who had Father Augustin killed?'

'My lord, *Raymond* had Father Augustin killed.'

Until this moment, the Seneschal had remained quite calm, if somewhat puzzled, and cautiously sceptical. Now, however, his entire face was contorted into an expression of profound surprise.

'*What?*' he exclaimed, then burst out laughing.

'My lord, hear me! It makes sense! The guard says that Raymond offered him money to poison Jordan Sicre when Jordan was brought back to Lazet!'

'And you believe him?'

I frowned. 'Believe whom?' I said.

'Why, this guard, man!'

'Yes.' I was working very hard to restrain my temper. 'Yes, I believe him.'

'Even though he refuses to admit that he killed Raymond Donatus?'

'Yes . . .'

'So you believe him when he *accuses* Raymond, but not when he refuses to confess that he murdered Raymond?'

I opened my mouth, and shut it again. Seeing me confounded, the Seneschal, who had raised his voice, as if to shout
me down, immediately moderated his tone. He even laid a
friendly hand on my wrist, clasping it tightly.

'Father, you should go away and think this through,' he said
with a smile. 'Father Pierre-Julien might be a horse-fly, but
you cannot let his stings send you mad. You should get more
sleep. You should leave the Holy Office.'

'He has dismissed me from the Holy Office.'

'Just as well. That place is bad for your health, Father, my
wife says so. She saw you in the street the other day, and she
told me that you had lost your looks. Too thin, she said. Your
face all grey, and full of dark lines.'

'Listen to me.' Just as he had grabbed my arm, so I grabbed
his. 'We must question the guard. We must go to headquarters,
and find out the truth. Father Pierre-Julien will not let me in
there without you, and we *must* know what happened that
night, before he extracts some kind of false confession from
the man – '

'But I thought you said that you wanted a confession?'

'A true confession!' My fear for Johanna was by now acute,
and was beginning to affect my judgement. I was finding it
difficult to restrain those passions which drove me; shaking him
off, springing to my feet, I paced up and down as if demented.
'The guard spoke of a woman, blamed a woman. Pierre-Julien
will try to implicate the women at Casseras, with this – this
dubious sighting. This nonsense – '

'Father, be still. Calm yourself. I shall come.'

'Now?' (Not a word of thanks, you will note! How misguided they are, who contend that profane love ennobles!)
'You will come now?'

'As soon as I have finished here.'

'But we must hurry!'

'No. We must *not*.' Again he took my arm, on this occasion
so as to lead me to the door. 'You go to the chapel, and pray,

and calm yourself. I shall come to you when I have finished with the treasurer.'

'But – '

'Be patient.'

'My lord – '

'Easy riding always gets you there in the end, Father.'

Thus was I dismissed from his presence: kindly, but firmly. He was intractable when he had made up his mind. Knowing this, I set a gloomy course for the chapel, which was deserted (thanks be to God) save for the presence of the Holy Spirit. A small but very beautiful room, boasting a glass window above the altar, it has always been one of my favourite places in the world, with its lavishly painted walls and ceiling, its silk, its gold, its shimmering tiles. I enjoy it – God forgive me – because it is like a lady's jewel-box, or a giant, enamelled reliquary, and it makes me feel precious. Fine feelings, for a Dominican monk! But then, I have never claimed to be a particularly distinguished example of monastic virtue.

Certainly I found little comfort in the contemplation of Christ's Agony, as I sat there staring at the German crucifix hanging on the wall. So masterly was its execution that one could almost see every bead of sweat on the contorted body and anguished face. *But He was wounded for our transgressions, He was bruised for our iniquities.* The sight of that precious blood – that holy affliction – disturbed me profoundly, for I saw in it a dire warning of how Johanna might suffer, if placed in Pierre-Julien's custody. I thought of the *murus strictus*, and my inner eye seemed new minted, for it regarded the chains and the cells and the filth with a terrible, sharp-edged clarity that pierced me like a sword. These things had once been acceptable, when inflicted on lapsed and obdurate heretics. But they were awful beyond endurance when Johanna was threatened with them.

As for the lower dunjon – but I was unable to reflect on such a possibility. My mind recoiled; I groaned aloud, and struck my knees with my fists several times. 'O Lord God, to whom vengeance belongeth,' I prayed, 'O God to whom vengeance belongeth, show Thyself. Lift up Thyself, Thou judge of the earth: render a reward to the proud. Lord, how long shall the wicked, how *long* shall the wicked triumph?'

And so I recited various psalms, until at last I began to feel the peace of that still and lovely place. Gradually I was soothed. I reminded myself that, while Jean-Pierre could indeed be questioned as a heretic – having allegedly killed an employee of the Holy Office – torture required the consent and presence of the subject's Bishop, or the Bishop's representative. It required the assistance of special familiars. There could be no torture without much preparation. And there could be no confession, in this instance, without torture.

Fool that I was! As ever, I underestimated Pierre-Julien. Indeed, I comforted myself with delusions, for when at last the Seneschal completed his business, and accompanied me to headquarters, we found – upon arriving – that Durand was outside the prison door, vomiting into the dust.

I did not need to ask why.

'No! God, no!' I blasphemed.

'Father, I cannot.' Durand was weeping. His face was wet, and he looked very young. 'I cannot, I cannot!'

'*He* cannot! It is forbidden!' Grabbing the poor boy's arm, I shook him (when I should have comforted him), made cruel in my rage and anxiety. 'Where is the Bishop? You must know the rules! You should have alerted me!'

'Father, Father,' the Seneschal objected, removing the notary from my grasp. 'Restrain yourself.'

'This is no time for restraint!' I believe that I would have forced my way past the guards, then and there, if Pierre-Julien had not himself appeared, quite suddenly, with a handful of parchment. Clearly he was in search of Durand. This quest had brought him outside, and the altercation that followed consequently took place under the very eyes of the two prison guards, as well as the eyes of a passing farrier, and the woman who lived in the house opposite the prison.

'You are in contravention of the law!' I bellowed, with such force that Pierre-Julien, startled to discover me on the prison's threshold, dropped half of the document that he was carrying. 'Jean-Pierre was not defamed! You cannot question a man as accused who has not been formally defamed!'

'I can if he has already confessed to a delegated judge,' Pierre-Julien retorted, stooping to recover his scattered folios. 'If you consult Pope Boniface's statute, *Postquam*, you will see that I can be regarded as such.'

'And where is the Bishop, pray? Where is his representative? You cannot employ force without one or the other!'

'I have received a commission from Bishop Anselm, in writing, to act for him wherever and whenever his presence is required,' said Pierre-Julien. To my surprise, he was maintaining a dignified demeanour, even in the face of direct attack. 'Everything is quite in order – at least, it would be if Durand had not been taken ill.'

'Am I to understand that you are questioning this guard, this Jean-Pierre?' the Seneschal inquired of him.

'That is correct.'

'Under torture?'

'No.'

'Not any more,' Durand supplied, faintly. 'They burned his feet, but doused the fire when he promised to confess.'

'The prisoner has confessed his sins,' Pierre-Julien interrupted, silencing the notary with a frown. 'His testimony has been recorded, and witnessed. All that remains is the confirmation – which we shall secure as soon as Durand is well enough to read through the deposition.'

'But you must wait for a day!' I protested. 'That is the rule! One whole day before a confession is confirmed!'

My superior waved this objection aside. 'A formality,' he said.

'A formality? *A formality?*'

'Father, you must control yourself.' The Seneschal addressed me in quite severe and repressive tones, before turning to Pierre-Julien. 'And what exactly has this guard confessed to?' he inquired. 'Killing Raymond Donatus?'

'For diabolical purposes.' Pierre-Julien consulted the document in his hand. 'To summon up a certain demon from the humbler levels of the underworld, by sacrificing one of the servants of the Holy Office.'

'This is what he said?'

'Yes, my lord – though not in so many words. Of course, he was assisted and instructed by other, more skilled and abominable idolaters. By this I mean the women from Casseras – '

'No!'

' – one of whom lured Raymond to the slaughter, that night – '

'A fabrication!' My pen falters as I attempt to describe my feelings of outrage and disbelief. 'Those women are not sorcerers! They are not witches! You have put their names into the mouth of that poor wretch!'

'The women *are* witches,' Pierre-Julien replied, 'because I have here testimony confirming the fact. Whether or not they had Father Augustin killed is difficult to establish, but I do know that they defiled his remains.'

'Nonsense!' I might have revealed, at this point, Babilonia's parentage. But I had vowed to tell no one, and could not break my vow except with Johanna's permission. 'They were devoted to Father Augustin!'

'Furthermore,' Pierre-Julien continued, implacably, 'one of their number seduced Jean-Pierre, and with promises of great rewards induced him to admit her into the Holy Office, that he might murder Raymond Donatus while the woman and the notary were carnally engaged.'

'Falsehoods!' I cried, snatching the deposition from Pierre-Julien's grasp. He attempted to retrieve it, and for a short time we grappled, until separated by Roger Descalquencs. Though smaller than I, the Seneschal was powerfully made, and used his force with the economy that is only learned through years of experience in combat.

'Enough!' he said, half angered, half amused. 'I do not allow brawling in the streets.'

'This is a falsification! It is testimony obtained under duress!' I cried.

'He says so because he is bewitched, my lord – the women have infected him with their poison – '

'*Enough*, I said!' Shaking us, the Seneschal then released his grip, so that we both staggered – and Pierre-Julien fell down. 'This cannot be decided here. We shall wait for a day, and see if Jean-Pierre retracts his confession. Meanwhile, the women will be fetched.'

'No, my lord!'

'By *you*, Father Bernard, and some of my garrison sergeants. You will bring them here, and you will *both* question them, and if there is any evidence of sorcery, or murder, or anything else, you will both be satisfied.'

'My lord, when Jordan Sicre arrives, this vile and bloodthirsty man will be proven wrong.'

'Perhaps. But until Jordan does arrive, Father Bernard, I suggest we act carefully, and wisely, and stop losing our tempers. Is that acceptable to you?'

What could I do, but agree? I could expect nothing more favourable to Johanna, who was now firmly under suspicion. At least if she were in my custody, I could ensure that she would be treated well.

So I nodded.

'Good.' The Seneschal turned to Pierre-Julien, who had picked himself up, and was dusting off his mantle. 'Is that acceptable to you, Father?'

'Yes.'

'Then I shall go and arrange your escort, Father Bernard, and you should go and tell your Prior that you will be absent, tonight. How many women are there?'

'Four,' I replied. 'But one is very old and ill.'

'Then she can ride with you. I shall give you Star, again. Or perhaps – well, that can be decided. Coming, Father?'

He was talking to me. Suspecting that he did not wish to leave me with Pierre-Julien (lest we disembowel each other), I again signified my assent, and moved to join him. I was prevented from doing so, however, when Durand caught at my skirts.

'Father ...' he murmured, quietly despairing. I looked into his red-rimmed eyes, and saw there a great horror, so profound that it surprised me. For Durand had never impressed me as a peculiarly gentle soul.

'Courage,' I said, in very subdued tones. 'We shall be rid of all this soon enough.'

'Father, I *cannot.*'

The break in his voice touched my heart, though it was so full, at the time, of Johanna. Patting his cheek with paternal kindness, I made as if to kiss his other cheek, but in fact placed my lips on his ear.

'Keep vomiting,' I whispered. 'Do not restrain yourself. Do it on his shoes, if necessary. He will dismiss you in the end.'

Durand smiled. Later, as I prepared for my journey in a state of unspeakable distress, the thought of that smile was comforting to me. It had been a smile of hope, and complicity, and defiance. It had given me strength, for I knew that in Durand, at least, I had a friend. Not a friend of great influence, perhaps, but one who would help me no matter what course I chose to take.

Two are better than one; because they have a good reward for their labour. For if they fall, the one will lift up his fellow: but woe to him that is alone when he falleth, for he hath not another to help him up.

I had hoped that Johanna and her friends might have departed Casseras. I had hoped that the misty mornings and days of rain might, in presaging the arrival of winter, have urged them to seek a warmer, drier, more secure habitation. But I had not reckoned on Vitalia's poor health. It seemed that the women were awaiting an improvement in her condition (as one might wait for a break in the clouds), so as to take advantage of it, and move her without causing her too much discomfort.

'Is she very ill?' I inquired of Father Paul, from my saddle. He had come out of his home to meet me, as had almost every inhabitant of Casseras; many of them had called my name in accents of pleasure, and the children had presented me with warm, welcoming smiles.

Unhappily, my preoccupation with Johanna was such that I looked on their faces blankly, and barely acknowledged their greetings.

'She is very old,' said Father Paul. 'It is my belief, Father, that her time is at hand. But I may be mistaken.' He glanced with uncertainty at my horse, upon which I remained steadfastly mounted, and at the ten sergeants who attended me. 'Are you going up there now, Father? Or will you stay here until morning?'

'We shall not be sleeping in the village,' was my response. I had thought about the matter carefully on my way to Casseras, and had come to this conclusion: that to bring my prisoners back to the village for the night would mark them unequivocally *as* prisoners, since they would naturally be guarded, and guarded in the sight of all. But by remaining at the forcia I would protect them from such humiliation; they would be able to ride through Casseras proudly, escorted like princesses, not circumscribed like criminals.

'You are staying at the forcia?' Father Paul exclaimed, clearly shocked. 'But why?'

'Because we do not have time to return to Lazet before nightfall!' I snapped. Then I urged my mount forward, unwilling to provide further explanation, and eager to fix my hungry eyes on Johanna's face. How I longed to see her! Yet at the same time I dreaded the meeting. I dreaded the fear that my coming would engender, and the confusion that it would cause. I remembered our last encounter, on the dawn hillside, and my very bowels yearned. That incomparable, that effulgent morning! Surely it had been a gift from God. *Sing unto the Lord with thanksgiving; sing praise upon the harp unto our God: Who covereth the heaven with clouds, Who prepareth rain for the earth, Who maketh grass to grow upon the mountains.*

The mountains were now grey, and wreathed in cloud. There was no radiance in the heavens. As we climbed the rugged path to the forcia a light drizzle began to fall, as softly as duck's down. At the site of Father Augustin's assassination, a small spray of purple flowers lay soaked in the mud.

I would have retrieved it if the soldiers had not been with me. I would have kept it as I should have kept those first golden flowers. But afraid that I would be judged, and taunted, I passed them by.

Though I have lived a very cloistered existence, I have been privy to much discussion on the nature of profane love, sometimes debated in a very proper spirit (as bearing on the essence of divine love), sometimes in a spirit less proper. From these colloquies, and from my reading, I have learned that love is a certain inborn suffering, and that there are symptoms which invariably overtake a man in love. These are, firstly, a tendency to become pale and thin; secondly, a tendency to lose one's appetite; thirdly, a tendency to sigh and weep; fourthly, a tendency to become subject to fits of trembling when in the presence of the beloved. Ovid listed many of these symptoms in ancient times; since then, they have been examined and tabulated over and over again, so often that I had come to regard them as undisputed and inescapable.

I had therefore been alert to any changes in my own sleep and appetite – noting them, when they did occur, as further indications that I was shackled by the chains of desire. (Looking back, I wonder if these symptoms would have been as severe, if my beloved had not been threatened.) Now, as I approached the forcia, I expected to be overcome by tears and trembling, which I was anxious to conceal from the eyes of my escort.

But when I first caught sight of Johanna, I was conscious

only of an overwhelming joy – which flooded my heart like a fountain – and then, on the very heels of this sentiment, intense concern. For the soldiers had refused to hang back; they would not let me enter the forcia alone, ahead of them, lest I be captured, or killed, or otherwise used to effect an escape. Though I had argued vehemently that they insulted me in presuming that I could be overcome by two old women, a mad girl and a slow-moving matron, they had prevailed through sheer force of numbers. As a result, we entered the forcia like a conquering army, causing Babilonia to scream, and run, and hide behind a wall.

'Forgive me,' I gasped, dismounting precipitately, as Johanna gazed at us in consternation. 'This is not my doing. I was sent. There has been – oh, such madness. Such madness.' I went to her, and took both of her hands in mine; her fingers were long and warm and rough. Her face ravished me. I had thought, once, that she was not beautiful. How could I have been so blind? Her skin was pale and lustrous, like a pearl. Her eyes were deep and clear. Her neck was a tower of ivory. 'Do not fear, Johanna, for I shall protect you. But I must explain . . .'

'Father Bernard?' Alcaya now emerged from the house, bearing the *Legend* of St Francis. She smiled at me as if she could imagine no greater joy than the sight of my face; she bowed, and pressed her lips to my hand in a gesture of profound obeisance. My escort might not have existed. 'Oh, Father,' she said fervently, 'how good of you to come here again. How eagerly we have awaited you.'

'Alas, Alcaya, my visit is not an occasion for happiness.'

'But it is!' she insisted, still clutching my hand in one of hers, as she cradled her book in the other. 'At last I may thank you! At last I may tell you how you have transformed our lives with this wondrous gift! Oh, Father, we have been touched by the Holy Spirit!' There were tears in her eyes as she addressed me, and a radiance, too, which shone through the tears like sun through a shower of rain. 'Truly, Father, St

Francis was close to God. Truly we must strive to follow his example, that we may be engulfed by the celestial fire, and eat of the spiritual food.'

'Yes. Unquestionably.' God forgive me, I had no time for St Francis then. 'Alcaya, the soldiers have frightened Babilonia. Will you speak to her, and comfort her? Tell her that I shall not let them harm any of you. Tell her that I am your shield and your fortress. Will you tell her that?'

'With all my heart,' said Alcaya, smiling blissfully. 'And then we shall talk, Father. We shall speak of sublime penitence, and the Holy Spirit, and the contemplation of divine wisdom.'

'Yes. Yes, of course.' I turned to Johanna, who was now watching the garrison sergeants as they dismounted. Some were beginning to unpack their saddlebags. 'We shall be sleeping here tonight,' I quickly explained, 'and escorting you to Lazet tomorrow. Johanna, the new inquisitor has come, and he is a fool – a dangerous man. He believes that you and your friends are heretics and witches – '

'*Witches?*'

' – and that you killed Father Augustin. He will not listen to reason. But I am working hard to dislodge him. I believe that he is implicated in another killing. If I can prove it, if I can speak to the witness who helped to murder Father Augustin, and who still lives . . .' Seeing her colour change, I faltered. I sensed that it was all too much for her to absorb at the one time, and pressed her hands so passionately that she winced. 'Johanna, do not fear. You will be safe,' I said. 'You have my word on that. My promise.'

'Who – who must go, tomorrow?' she asked faintly. 'Not Vitalia?'

'All of you.'

'But Vitalia is sick!'

'Forgive me.'

'She cannot sit on a horse!'

'Not by herself. But I shall ride with her. I shall support her.'

'This is ridiculous.' Now she was growing angry. 'A sick old woman like that! How could a sick old woman kill anyone?'

'As I said, my superior is beyond reason.'

'And you?' she cried, snatching her hands away. 'What about you? You say that you are our friend, yet you come here to take us prisoner!'

'I *am* your friend.' (Friend? I was her slave.) 'Do not condemn me. I came here to protect you. To comfort you.'

She looked at me with her clear, direct, formidable gaze, which pierced me like an arrow, and which was almost level with mine. I had forgotten how tall she was.

'Be calm,' I said softly. 'Have courage. We shall prevail if you follow my advice, and do not lose heart. God is with us – I know He is.'

At this she smiled, and her smile was weary and sceptical. Glancing away, she said: 'It is good that you are so certain in your beliefs.'

Then she went to her daughter.

I wanted to follow her, and persuade her, and touch her again (God forgive my sin), but I could not. Instead I approached the commander of my little retinue, and we discussed the disposition of fires, bedding and horses. There was not sufficient shelter in the bailey for ten men; the sergeants wanted to return to Casseras for the night, where there were barns in which to sleep, and lavish hospitality. I said that they might all return to the village, but that I would stay. Since this was out of the question, six volunteered to remain at the forcia, while the rest rode back to Casseras through the rain and the deepening twilight.

A watch bill was then drawn up. It enabled three of the volunteers to sleep, while two stood guard at the door of the farmhouse, and one minded the horses. The sleeping arrangements were as follows: Vitalia's bed was placed in the bedroom, in order that she might join her three friends there. A bundle of straw was placed in the kitchen (or in the room that now served as a kitchen), and this was to be my bed. One of the sergeants was to sleep on the kitchen table, another by the kitchen fire, a third by my feet. The horses were to be tethered beneath such fragments of wood and thatch as still remained around the bailey.

I insisted that the women's fowl should not be touched, but was overruled. 'Who will feed them while we are gone?' Johanna said. So the five birds were killed, drawn, plucked and eaten by my ravenous escort; I myself ate only bread and leeks – it being Lent – while Alcaya and Babilonia refused to touch the charred remains of their birds (Babilonia because the manner of their death had distressed her greatly, Alcaya because she professed to avoiding meat except on feast days).

For Vitalia, some of the chicken was boiled in a soup, which she ate with softened bread. I could see at a glance that she was in no state to travel. Indeed, she could barely walk, and when I took her hand it felt like a dry leaf, or the hollow carcass of a dead insect. But when I mentioned the coming journey she simply smiled, and nodded, leading me to wonder if she had understood.

'Of course she understands,' Johanna remarked tersely, when I expressed my doubts. We were sitting around the brazier, inhibited by the presence of several guards, for I felt that I could not talk freely while they were listening. 'There is nothing wrong with her mind.'

'Vitalia will bear her cross with courage,' Alcaya declared. 'Christ is with her.'

'I hope so.' It was one of the sergeants who spoke. 'She may not last the trip, otherwise.'

'God's will be done,' said Alcaya, with great tranquillity. I hastened to assure her that I would ride very slowly, so as not to jolt the sick woman, and that for this reason we had to depart at dawn, or at any rate as soon as possible in the morning. Whereupon Johanna asked if she and her companions would be permitted to take their possessions with them. Their clothes, for example. Their books and cooking utensils.

I was distressed by the dry and formal manner of her speech.

'You may take your clothes, and . . . and such possessions as will not impede our progress,' I replied.

'So the chest stays,' she said.

'I fear so.'

'You must know that it will be stolen.'

'I shall ask Father Paul to keep it for you.'

'Until we return?' Though her words were unquestionably selected to comfort her daughter, their tone was ironic, and without hope. It seemed that she had dismissed my assurances, discounted all my claims.

This angered me, I must confess.

'You *will* return,' I said sharply. 'There is no doubt that you will. I have undertaken to accomplish your release.'

'With prayer?' she mocked, though still speaking carefully.

'With prayer, yes! And by other means!'

'We should all pray,' said Alcaya. 'Let us pray now.' She had been holding Babilonia's hand, and murmuring into her ear; only with constant attendance had she contrived to keep the younger woman relatively calm. 'Father, will you say a prayer for us?'

I did so, intoning psalms until the sergeants, rising, declared that we should now go to sleep, if we were to depart early. (I had hoped to drive them from the room, with my recitations, but was disappointed in this desire – perhaps because it was still raining.) The women agreed, and retreated to their beds. The sergeants, after consulting with one another, split into two groups, the one withdrawing, the other staying. As the three who remained rolled themselves up in their cloaks, I whispered the office of Compline to myself, distracted by my aching limbs and worldly obsessions. Johanna's behaviour had tormented me; it appeared that she did not regard me as a close friend after all. How coldly her gaze had rested on my countenance! How wounded I had been by her lack of faith, and her sardonic remarks! Yet still there had been a common understanding between us – I had sensed her feelings, even as I had deplored them.

Lying on my pile of straw (which was almost as uncomfortable as the priory beds), I found no peace in the contemplation of Johanna. I wanted to go to her, and demand an explanation. By turns I was angry, fearful, and distressed. I told myself that she too was afraid – and more so than I – but my heart was turned within me. Though exhausted by the day's exertions, I was unable to sleep on that clammy floor. *Now is my soul troubled; and what shall I say? Father, save me from this hour.* As the long night unfolded, I resigned myself to wakefulness, listening to the snores of the sergeants, the moans of Babilonia (doubtless a victim of harrowing dreams), and the patter of rain on the roof. I prayed, I cursed, I despaired. Truly, I walked in darkness, and had no light.

But it was God's plan that I should be sleepless. For I was awake when Babilonia slipped out of the bedroom and passed me on noiseless feet, making for the door. I heard her challenged by the guards stationed there; I heard her explain, in trembling accents, that she wished to empty her bladder. And I heard them reply that she might do so around the corner of the house, but that if she did not return forthwith, she would suffer a terrible fate indeed.

Listening with great concentration, I heard nothing more, and for a brief time was unconcerned. I knew that the guards would not allow her to stray. As her absence continued, however, I grew worried. Why did the men not hail her? Why did they remain silent? I would have questioned them from my bed, if I had not been reluctant to rouse Vitalia and her companions. As it was, I threw off my mantle and went to the door, surprised to discover (when I reached it) that the guards had left their post. Their lamp had also disappeared. But since it was no longer raining, I was able to hear a faint noise, a kind of grunt, followed by a squeak, accompanying some form of activity which was taking place on the other side of the house.

On reflection, I behaved very foolishly. There was nothing to indicate that the sounds I heard were not the sounds of ambush, and silent slaughter. Even the muffled laugh could have been that of a cut-throat. But my instant assumption proved to be correct, for rounding the corner, with a cry of outrage, I stumbled upon the two missing guards on their knees in the dirt.

They were attempting to rape Babilonia.

Believe me when I tell you that I am not a violent man. Blessed are the peacemakers, are they not? Sinful I might be, but not a shedder of blood. For me, the words of St Paul have always served as a guide and commandment: *Let your moderation be known unto all men.* To strike a blow is not the way of moderation. Violence begets violence, whereas peace is the reward of those who love God's law. And he that is slow to anger is better than the mighty.

Yet the sight that I beheld seemed to deprive me of all reason. I need only have requested that the two men sheathe their weapons, and release their captive, for they were shocked at my sudden appearance, and would have obeyed without demur. Instead, I drove my heel into the head of one (which was level with my knee), and planted my fist in the face of the other. I grabbed the knives which they had dropped, threatening to use them. I shouted, and pummelled the writhing, mail-clad body which lay at my feet. I behaved like one demented.

Undoubtedly I was a fool. I was also fortunate, because though taller, and blessed with the advantage of surprise, I was not as skilled in combat as my armoured foe, who would have triumphed easily if given the chance to retaliate. As it transpired, however, they were not. For Babilonia's screams, and my own noisy indignation, had roused the sleepers. They came running, some of them with drawn swords, whereupon there followed a period of great confusion.

Babilonia howled and wept in Alcaya's arms. I reviled the would-be rapists at the top of my voice. The sergeant in command, who had been sleeping, vainly besought us to be calm. He demanded an explanation. I gave him one. The accused men denied it.

'She was trying to escape!' they insisted. 'We went after her!'

'With your leggings around your knees?' I cried.

'I was passing water!' The older of the two stepped forward. 'If I had been at my post, she would have slipped away from us!'

'*Liar*! I saw you! Her skirts were up!'

'Father, that is not true.'

'It *is* true! Ask the girl! Babilonia, tell us!'

But Babilonia was beyond speech; she had retreated into a world of demons. As Alcaya held her she jerked and writhed, and flailed her arms, and struck her head on the ground, and howled like a dog. Seeing this, several of the sergeants crossed themselves.

'My daughter would not try to escape,' Johanna said hoarsely. She was kneeling; in the feeble lamplight her eyes glittered. 'My daughter has been attacked.'

Still there were doubts among the comrades of the accused men. They looked at Babilonia and saw, not a beautiful woman, but a mad or possessed creature. Besides which, they were disposed to be lenient with their fellow mercenaries. I felt that, if I had not been present, they might very well have turned their backs, and allowed the assault to continue.

Debased wretches! I told them that the Seneschal would be informed. I insisted that they remove their bedding from the kitchen; no longer, I said, would they be permitted to sleep in comfort there. They must remain outside the house, whether or not they were on guard duty. I warned them that I, too, would be on duty, that I would guard the bedroom door like a watchdog. 'Beware my teeth!' I exclaimed. 'Beware the wrath of the Holy Office! These women are in my care! If you harm any one of them, you will suffer for your contumacy!'

With threats of this kind, I impressed upon my glowering escort the need for restraint. Certainly I was in some peril, for I stood alone, unarmed save for my rank and reputation; if all six guards had acted in accord, unleashing their lusts upon the defenceless women, I could not have prevented them. Nor could I have condemned them afterwards, if they had chosen to kill me first. Doubtless a convincing story could have been concocted: a lurking band of armed heretics could have been blamed, and my death attributed to the same forces responsible for Father Augustin's death.

All this crossed my mind as I stood there. But I knew that as an inquisitor of heretical depravity, I was endowed with a terrible and awe-inspiring distinction. The ubiquity of the Holy Office is such that only the simplest of souls would dare to defy it. Everyone knows that to offend an inquisitor is to invite calamity.

Therefore, although the sergeants glared, and scowled, and muttered, they did not resist. They obeyed my instructions, vacating the house as requested, so that I was left in sole command of the kitchen and all its contents. While Babilonia was divested of her wet and dirty clothes, dried, calmed, dressed, embraced and finally given some kind of herbal infusion to drink, I remained in the bedroom with Vitalia, to whom I related a somewhat expurgated account of the incident which had taken place outside. When Babilonia was put to bed, however, the kitchen was restored to me. I was able to warm myself at the brazier. I was able to remove my own outer garments and dry them as I listened to the moans and murmurs from the bedroom, together with the rougher, though equally muffled, tones of the guards by the door, who were doubtless condemning my character, sentiments and actions in the very harshest terms.

Presently the men fell silent. Babilonia continued to moan, and occasionally to cry out; I could hear Johanna singing to her, very softly, as if trying to lull an infant to sleep. Otherwise there was no sound except for the crackling of the fire, which I fed with handful upon handful of dry faggots. After a while even this was too much for me. I let the flames burn low, unable to rise from the table, for I was weary beyond words. I felt that, like an elephant, if I were to lie down I would never rise again. So I stayed upright, looking at my hand, which was throbbing from its violent collision with that foul lecher's cheekbone. I was not thinking about anything in particular. I was too tired to think. Indeed, I would very probably have fallen asleep where I sat, if I had not been roused by Johanna's sudden appearance.

She was standing beside me before I noticed her. When I looked up, I saw that she was clad in some kind of under-garment, or night-attire – at any rate, in something thin and grey and formless. Her hair was loose. For a long time we looked at each other, and my mind was empty.

At last she said, in the faintest of whispers: 'I thought that you had betrayed us. But I was wrong.'

'Yes.'

'I was so frightened.'

'I know.'

'I am still frightened.' Although her voice broke on this, she summoned up the strength to continue. 'I am still frightened, but I have come to my senses. Forgive me. I know that you are a true friend.'

Again we looked at each other. How can I account for my silence at this point? Dazed with fatigue, stupid with surprise, my senses reeling at the sight and the sound of her, I was struck dumb. I could say nothing. I could not even move.

'Thank you,' she said. And when I failed to respond, she put her hands over her eyes and burst into tears.

Like a clarion, those tears awakened me from my trance. I leapt up. I embraced her, and she clung to me, as her daughter whimpered in the next room.

'I am not brave,' she sobbed, against my shoulder. 'I saw them burn ... I saw them die, when I was young ...'

'Hush.'

'Alcaya is brave. Vitalia is brave.'

'You are brave.'

'I am frightened! Babilonia knows it.'

'Shh.'

'She knows it!' A mere thread of sound. 'I cannot comfort her. We are lost.'

'No.'

'We are dead!'

'*No*.'

God forgive me, for I am a sinner. I am counted with them that go down into the pit: I am as a man that hath no strength. But Thou, O Lord, art a God full of compassion, and gracious, long-suffering, and plenteous in mercy and truth. Do not the Scriptures tell us that love covereth all sins? My gracious Lord, I loved her. Every one of her tears smote my heart, wounding me sorely. My very liver was poured upon the earth. I would have done anything to comfort her, anything to bear away her sorrows. But what could I do? In an agony of remorse, I pressed her to my bosom, kissing the crown of her head, her ear, her neck, her shoulder. Then she turned her face up to me, and my kisses rained down upon her closed eyelids, her silken cheeks, her temples. I tasted salt. I smelled her hair. *Because of the savour of Thy ointments, Thy name is as ointment poured forth.* As I staggered, overcome, she pulled my head down and planted her lips firmly on mine.

O Lord, rebuke me not in Thy wrath: neither chasten me in Thy hot displeasure. For her kiss was not honey and milk – it was a bombardment. A flaming arrow. It did not invite me to linger in an orchard of pomegranates, with pleasant fruits; it siezed and bound me, like a warrior. The heat of it seemed to ignite my blood, and dissolve my joints. I found myself unable to breathe.

So I turned my head away, abruptly.

'What?' she said, and looked around. Perhaps, for an instant, she expected to see someone else in the room. But there was no one.

Meanwhile, I had stepped back a pace, and this small retreat told her everything. As she gazed at me, her expression changed. She released her grip on my neck.

'Forgive me,' she whispered.

I shook my head, panting.

'Forgive me.' Her hair fell over her face as she wiped it; suddenly we were standing apart, and I felt cold again. 'Forgive me, Father,' she echoed, weary and contrite, her voice dull, her manner dejected. Then she looked up once more, with the faintest glint in her eye. 'I did not mean to frighten you,' she added.

Now, here it was that I sinned most grievously. For my pride was offended, my indestructible pride, which was as tender as burned flesh and as vast as a mountain. I said to myself: Am I man? Am I as a lion among the beasts of the forest, or do I drink from the cup of trembling? And, in the most profound vanity of spirit, disregarding my vows, moved by lust and insolence, I drew her back to me with a jerk, even as she turned away; I enfolded her in my arms, so that I might impress upon her lips the proof of my adoration.

Remember, if you will, that I was lightly clad. So too was Johanna, and in this, perhaps, we were unfortunate. But I doubt that a barrier less permeable than chain mail would have prevented us from consummating our desires. We were deaf to Babilonia's moans and Alcaya's murmurs (though always conscious that we ourselves must remain silent). We ignored the proximity of the guards, as if the flimsy woollen curtain which shielded the door was made of solid stone. Without speaking, without releasing one another, we moved from the table and fell upon my humble bed.

What followed is not a fit subject for scrutiny. As St Paul said, the body is not for fornication, but for the Lord. Nevertheless, he also said: 'I see another law in my members, warring against the law in my mind, and bringing me into captivity to the law of sin which is in my members. O wretched man that I am! who shall deliver me from the body of this death?'

Thus wrote St Paul, and if *his* flesh was subject to the law of sin, then who was I to resist the lures of concupiscence – the bondage of corruption? For I am carnal, and sold under sin. I have obeyed unrighteousnes, indignation and wrath. I made Johanna's body my temple, and I worshipped it. Believe me when I say that I was culpable. For I sinned freely, with all my heart.

Yet I sinned through love, and the Scriptures tell us that love is as strong as death; many waters cannot quench it, neither can the floods drown it. Why, it is itself a flood! It carried me along like a twig, and I was drowning – striving – gasping for breath, while Johanna, with her arms around me, seemed to be pulling me down, down, down into a mindless and liquescent state of rapture.

It was she who led, I who followed. It hurts my pride to say as much, but Eve, after all, was Adam's guide when it came to the pursuit of iniquity. Or was I driven, like a sheep? Certainly she was as terrible as an army with banners, her touch strong and sure, her passion fierce.

'You are so beautiful,' was all that she said (or breathed, for our conjunction was of necessity extremely quiet). I almost laughed when she said this, for she was as fair as the moon and as clear as the sun, while I – what am I but a weathered, sapless, balding, attenuated haunter of libraries?

It puzzles me still that she should have desired this old monk's frame.

I would like to say that I feasted upon lilies, gathered my myrrh with my spice, and went down into the garden of nuts to see the fruits of the valley. But there was no time for languid enjoyment. The act with which we defiled ourselves was short, sharp and ungraceful – and I shall not sully your eyes with another word on the subject. Suffice it to say that we were soon on our feet again, fumbling with our garments; all at once the noises from the bedroom seemed threatening, and very near.

We said little. There was no need for speech. My soul was knit with hers – we spoke with kisses and glances. But I did remark, softly, that she could sleep in peace, for I would be watching over her.

'No you will *not*,' she whispered. 'You will sleep too.' And when I shook my head, smiling ruefully, she put her hand to my cheek, fixing me with her clear, intelligent gaze.

'This was not your sin,' she said. 'If it was anyone's, it was mine. Do not let it fester. Do not be like Augustin.'

'Alas, there is no danger of that. I am not like Father Augustin.'

'No.' Though her voice was quiet, it was also emphatic. 'You are not like him. You are all here. You are complete. I love you.'

O God, Thou knowest my foolishness; and my sins are not hid from Thee. Her words filled me with a joy that was like pain. I bowed my head, fighting back tears, and felt her lips on my temple.

Then she went back to her bed. As for me, I obeyed her injunction; I slept, though my heart was full. I slept and dreamed of perfumed gardens.

Ye shall know the truth

here was no opportunity for dalliance the following day: too much had to be accomplished. The horses had to be fed, watered and harnessed; a sketchy repast had to be consumed; Vitalia had to be clothed, and carried from the house. Then, after the other women had packed into leather and fustian bags such possessions as could be transported easily, it was discovered that Alcaya had never mounted a horse in her life. Faced with the difficult and treacherous ride to Casseras, we therefore decided that she should accompany one of the sergeants, while the horse set aside for her use should be employed to carry luggage.

It was still raining fitfully; the path to the forcia was a river of mud. Few words were exchanged as we picked our way down slipperly inclines, each step as perilous as the last. I was particularly hampered, for Vitalia was sitting in front of me (she would have slid off the crupper, if placed behind), blocking my view and interfering with my mastery of the reins, such as it was. I do not believe that Star even felt her weight, for she was like a bundle of tinder – a breath would have blown her away. Nevertheless, the terrain, the weather, and her occupation of my saddle, served to slow our progress. It was broad daylight when at last we reached Casseras.

Here we were joined by the other sergeants, as cheerful as their comrades were moody and dour. These four happy men had spent a dry night in Bruno Pelfort's barn; it was apparent, from their satisfied demeanour, that no sanctimonious Dominican had interfered with *their* lecherous activities. The village, indeed, had treated them well, but when urged by Father Paul to stay for a while – or at least until the rain eased – they would not hear of it. They had received their orders, and their orders were to return forthwith. A little rain never hurt anyone, they declared.

I took exception to this remark, for it was quite evident that the rain was not having a salutory effect on Vitalia. Her lungs squeaked and rattled; her lips were blue; her hands were stone cold. Most of the time I had been obliged to support her, holding her upright with one arm around her waist, as I guided my mount with the other. The farther we had travelled, the more deathly afraid I had been that she would die on the journey. And although I did not reveal this fear (being mindful of Babilonia's presence), I expressed my strong belief that the trip should be acomplished in stages, even if it took several days.

But I was overruled.

'The longer it takes, the more risky it is,' my escort insisted. 'The women might escape. Besides, we are not equipped for a long journey. And the rain will clear, soon. We should press on.'

So we did. Riding ahead of Johanna, I was barely afforded a glimpse of her; although I glanced back, once or twice, I saw only the top of her head, for she was watching the road for potholes and other obstacles. Happily, we had completed the most difficult portion of our route upon gaining Casseras, and from Rasiers onward we travelled with comparative ease. We had nothing to fear from brigands, of course. As for the rain, it stopped before midday. Only Vitalia did not improve with time; her colour became very bad, her breathing became even worse, and as we approached the gates of Lazet, just after

Vespers, she lost consciousness, slumping forward onto Star's neck as I struggled to keep her in the saddle.

It was not a pleasant homecoming. Babilonia, convinced that her friend was dead, began to wail, flinging herself from her horse in a dangerous manner which left her with an injured knee. Alcaya also tried to dismount, but was prevented by the sergeant who rode with her. Another sergeant helped me to lower Vitalia to the ground, while a passing pair of Franciscans – visitors, it transpired, from Narbonne – stopped to give aid. Then, as Alcaya argued, and Babilonia sobbed, and the two friars assured me that one of them was a priest, able to perform the last rites if they were required, a blanket was extracted from one of Johanna's leather bags. Carried between four sergeants, it was used to support Vitalia during the final leg of her journey to prison.

Slowly, we approached the towers of Narbonne gate. Slowly, we passed beneath its cavernous vaulting. Since Babilonia could no longer ride, she joined me on my horse, where she sat with her face buried between my shoulders, weeping until my mantle and tunic and scapular, barely dry from the morning's rain, were again wet through. As we entered the city, our procession attracted many curious stares, not least from the garrison sergeants and citizens on watch duty who were stationed along the walls. Some of them flung questions at my escort regarding the number of riderless horses in our cavalcade – eliciting short and blasphemous replies. Some offered to lead the horses, while some made crude observations about our prisoners. Because the women disregarded these comments, I too held my peace, reluctant to disturb Babilonia. But I took note of the men who had sullied the air with such filth. Later, perhaps, I would see them punished.

Although we encountered many people known to me, on our way to headquarters, my grim and dirty visage repelled inquiry; indeed, it repelled remarks of any sort. Johanna rode with her head bowed, regally upright, even after such a long and difficult journey. At the southern well a small crowd of matrons, beggars, children and old men stopped talking to watch us go by; one, having identified me, asked her neighbour if the woman riding with me was a heretic. A small boy spat at Vitalia. A carpenter called Astro genuflected.

We reached our destination just as the windows of heaven were opened. Dismounting in the rain, I called for Pons and demanded immediate assistance. Then I delivered Babilonia into her mother's care, before proceeding to instruct the gaoler, who had been inspecting a prisoner's corpse, as to the manner and quality of my prisoners' confinement.

'These women will remain together,' I said, leading him back inside. 'You will put them in the guardroom on the top floor.'

'The guardroom?' Pons protested. 'But where will the familiars go?'

'If the familiars wish to eat or sleep, they can do it with you.' I had climbed the stairs to his quarters, which comprised a large kitchen and two bedrooms, lavishly furnished. Looking around, I saw no evidence that more people could not be accommodated. 'Any blankets or linen which the women might require are to be given freely. I want them fed from your own table – '

'What!' the gaoler's wife exclaimed.

' – and if possible,' I continued, ignoring her, 'I shall have food sent over from the priory. These women are not your prisoners, Pons, they are your guests. If they suffer any ill-treatment, you may expect the same.'

'From whom?' the gaoler inquired, moved to insolence by my demands. 'I hear that you are no longer with the Holy Office.'

'Would I be sent on Holy Office business, if I were no longer with the Holy Office? Now, one of the women is very ill, so I want you to provide her with broth, and suchlike. Invalid food. And if her condition should be the cause of any grave fears – you understand? – then I am to be notified at once. No matter how late it might be. Oh – and if any of the women want to consult me, I should also be notified.'

Pons snorted. His wife glared. Perhaps I should have been less abrupt, and more tender with their dignity. Perhaps I should have been mindful of the questions that would be asked, regarding my concern for Johanna's welfare. But I was anxious that the women should be restored to comfort with all haste. I was determined that Vitalia should not die at the prison door. I was afraid lest Pierre-Julien should appear, and contradict my instructions.

'There are weapons in the guardroom,' Pons pointed out. 'Pikes. Fuel. Spare manacles.'

'Remove them.'

'But where should they be put?'

'In the lower dunjon.'

'There is a prisoner in the lower dunjon.'

'A prisoner?'

'A new prisoner. I *told* you we were overcrowded!'

Such were the obstacles placed in my path. Nevertheless, I prevailed; the guardroom was cleared of every item save for its table, benches, beds and slop-bucket. Two pallets were installed, and clean linen was laid out. Only my wishes regarding the brazier were contested; having brought it all the way from Casseras, I had hoped to place it near Vitalia's bed. But Pons warned me that it would be employed to burn down the prison.

'It will not,' I said.

'Father, it is against the rules!'

'Vitalia must be kept warm during the night.'

'Then her friends can sleep with her.'

He refused to allow the brazier to be lit. Father Pierre-Julien, he said, would not permit such a breach of regulations. And knowing that this was almost certainly true, I capitulated. At all costs, I was determined that Pierre-Julien should remain ignorant of my orders regarding Johanna de Caussade.

'There can be no fire,' I told her, when she was led into

the guardroom. 'But if you need more blankets, the gaoler will bring them.'

'Thank you,' she murmured, gazing at the hooks on the wall. She was clasping Babilonia, who clung to her like an infant.

'The nights are not too cold.' This assurance was for my own sake, as much as hers. 'When you are dry, you will feel warmer.'

'Yes.'

Then Alcaya entered.

'Why, this is a palace!' she exclaimed. She had remained cheerful throughout the journey, except when moved to anger by the actions of her guards. 'As dry as old bones, and big enough for ten! Father, surely your own monastery cannot offer such comfort?'

Reassured, Babilonia looked up. Even Johanna's expression changed. Only Vitalia, who was asleep, and the familiars bearing her between them, who resented losing their guard-room, were not affected by Alcaya's buoyant spirits. Truly, this woman possessed a joyous soul. With great delight she brought to our attention the twittering of birds, which were to be found in large numbers around the city wall, nesting and feeding among the towers.

'Our little sisters will sing to us,' she beamed. 'And how good it is to hear bells again! This room is very light. I shall be able to read if I sit under the window.'

'Lamps are not permitted,' I told her. 'Forgive me. But the corridors are always illuminated, so there will be some light, even when night has fallen. Are you hungry? Would you care to eat?'

'We need water,' Johanna replied.

'Of course.'

'We need our baggage.'

'And you shall have it.'

'Where are *you* going to be?' she asked, misery and longing in her gaze. I wanted to kiss her, but had to be content with placing a hand on her arm.

'If you need me, I shall come. They will send for me. And I shall visit you often.'

'Perhaps you can lend us some more books,' Alcaya said brightly. It was an insolent request, but it made us all smile. Doubtless it had been formulated for this very purpose.

'Perhaps,' I retorted. 'Perhaps I should ask the Bishop to call on you.'

'Oh, yes. That would be pleasant. Bishops are always good company.'

'Not Bishop Anselm. But I shall do my best. And now I must see to your luggage, and the water. Is there anything else? No? Try to rest. You will see me again, before Compline.'

'Father ...' It was Johanna who spoke. She touched my hand, and let her fingers rest there. I could feel that touch throughout my body. 'Father, what will happen now?'

'Sleep,' I said, knowing that she was only trying to detain me. How I wished that I could have stayed! 'A meal first, then sleep. Tomorrow I shall return.'

'And Vitalia ...?'

'If you need me, the gaoler will have me summoned. If you need a priest, I shall bring one.'

And having soothed her with many other assurances, I left. I found the missing baggage in Pons' quarters; it was dispatched to the guardroom, along with a pail of water and a bowl of soup. I spoke with every familiar on duty, making it clear that if the women were hurt, offended, or merely inconvenienced during the night, God's wrath would descend upon the agent of their discomfort. Then I visited headquarters, where I found Durand and Brother Lucius in the scriptorium.

'Father!' Durand exclaimed. He was slumped at Raymond's desk, supporting his head with one hand as he languidly turned the pages of the register in front of him.

Lucius was sharpening a pen.

'Where is Father Pierre-Julien?' I inquired, brushing aside their greetings. 'Has he left for Compline?'

'Father, we have not seen him all day,' was Durand's response. 'He told me that I should always be on hand, but he is not available himself.'

'Where is he?'

Durand shrugged.

'Is he ill? Have you heard from him?'

'Yes, Father.' The notary seemed to be examining my face; perhaps the stains of travel were holding his attention. 'When Jordan arrived, I sent a message to the priory, and the reply was from Father Pierre-Julien. He told us to have patience.'

'When *Jordan* arrived?' I could hardly believe my ears. 'You mean Jordan *Sicre*?'

'Yes,' said Durand.

'He is here?'

'Yes, Father. He arrived this morning. But no one has spoken to him.'

'Then I shall be the first. Brother, will you kindly fetch Brothers Simon and Berengar? Durand, will you prepare your equipment? I shall need you to transcribe.' Glancing at the window, I saw how late it was, and wondered what excuse I would proffer for missing Compline. 'Jordan can be interrogated in Father Pierre-Julien's room,' I went on to observe, 'since it is not occupied at present. I shall speak to Pons. This is *most* opportune.'

'Father – '

'What?'

Durand looked at me, his brow furrowed. At last he said: 'Are you still – that is to say – I thought – '

'Well?'

'You have not relinquished your duties?'

I hastened to assure him that, if I were dismissed from the Holy Office, he would be the first to know. And having reassured him thus, I went to ask Pons about Jordan Sicre.

The gaoler informed me, with sullen disrespect, that Jordan

was the prisoner in the lower dunjon. A letter had accompanied him, and it was addressed to me. The letter was now with Brother Lucius. Jordan's escort – four Catalan mercenaries – had already departed from Lazet. Pons had received no orders from Father Pierre-Julien concerning the new prisoner.

If I wanted him, I was welcome to him. And here were the keys.

'I shall need a guard, as well.'

'Not with Jordan. He is wearing manacles on his hands and feet.'

'Is that necessary?'

'He knows this prison, Father. Some of the guards are his comrades. But you know best, of course.'

How angry he was! I thought him unreasonable, and turned away without thanking him. But upon remembering one final matter of importance, I quickly turned back.

'Has anyone been speaking to Jordan?' I inquired.

'I told him that he was a louse.'

'But there have been no lengthy exchanges? No recounting of gossip?'

'Not as far as I know.'

'Good.'

I was aware that my interrogation would more readily succeed if its subject was ignorant of recent events affecting the Holy Office. I also knew that fewer risks would be run if I conducted this interrogation in the lower dunjon. Therefore I went back to the scriptorium, told Durand of my change of heart, and searched Brother Lucius's desk for the Catalan letter.

It had been penned by the Bishop of Lerida, who, together with a local bailiff, had arrested Jordan Sicre and confiscated his property. I was informed that the prisoner had been using a false name; also, that he had accused some of his neighbours of being heretics; also, that he had mentioned a Perfect, an escapee of my own prison, formerly a resident of the Lerida diocese but now, regrettably, absconded.

Briefly, I wondered where 'S' might be. Wherever he was, I wished him well.

'Father?'

I looked up. Durand was still slouched at his desk, pens and parchment laid out neatly in front of him. He scratched his scrubby jaw as I waited.

'Father, I have to tell you,' he said. 'Brother Lucius's work has become very sloppy.'

'His work?'

'Look.' Drawing my attention to the folios piled on the floor, in preparation for binding, Durand indicated the size and unevenness of the text, together with certain mistakes therein. 'You see – *hoc* for *haec*, as if he cannot distinguish between them.'

'Yes. I see.' I saw, and was astonished. 'But it used to be so fine!'

'No longer.'

'No. That much is evident.' Ashamed, I returned the offending document to my companion. 'This is very humbling. I should have noticed before.'

'You have been occupied with other matters,' Durand replied (a trifle magnanimously, I thought). 'Only when you work with him does it become evident.'

'Even so ...' I pondered, for an instant. 'Have you any notion why this change might have occurred?'

'None.'

'Has his mother – do you know if his mother has become ill, or ...?'

'Perhaps.'

'And have you notified Father Pierre-Julien of this problem?'

Durand hesitated. 'No, Father,' he said at last. 'Brother Lucius is a good fellow. And Father Pierre-Julien is so ... well ...'

'Tactless,' I finished. 'Insensitive.'

'He might reveal that I was instrumental – '

'Quite.' I understood perfectly. 'Have no fear, my friend. I shall deal with the matter myself, and your name will not be mentioned.'

'Thank you, Father,' Durand said quietly. At which point Lucius himself returned with Simon and Berengar, cutting short our dialogue.

It was time to interrogate Jordan Sicre.

You must understand that there is a procedure to be followed, when examining a witness or suspect, whether cited or appearing of his own free will. In the first place, after he has been quietly and unostentatiously summoned and warned by the inquisitor or the inquisitor's deputy, he is made to swear upon the Holy Gospels to tell the whole truth and nothing but the truth in the matter of heresy and whatever touches thereupon, or is connected in any way with the office of the Inquisition. He is to do this both in respect of himself as a principal, and as a witness in the case of other persons, living or dead.

Once the oath has been taken and registered, the subject is urgently exhorted to tell the truth. If, however, he requests time or opportunity for deliberation in order to give a more carefully considered response, that may be granted if it seems expedient to the inquisitor – especially if he appears to be seeking it in good faith, not guilefully. Otherwise, he is required to testify at once.

Now, Jordan Sicre did not ask for such a delay – not knowing, perhaps, that it was his right to request one. Similarly, he did not ask for proof of infamy, nor for the charges laid against him. (It is thus with many illiterate defendants, who thereby allow me a great deal of latitude in my proceedings.) Nevertheless, he struck me as an intelligent man, for he was wise enough to refrain his lips and volunteer nothing until questioned. From his corner of the lower dunjon, where he had been shackled to the wall not far from that instrument of torment known as the rack, he watched silently as Durand,

Simon and Berengar seated themselves in those places reserved for them.

He was a squat, broad-shouldered man, with a dun complexion, high cheekbones, and very small eyes. There was a large bruise blossoming on his temple. I recognised him instantly.

'Of course!' I said. 'I remember you. You were the one who saved me from Jacob Galaubi.'

No reply.

'I am very grateful to you for preserving my virtue. Very grateful indeed. But I fear that it can have no bearing on our present circumstances. What a pity that you should have yielded to temptation! Of course, I am told that the reward was considerable. A handsome farm, three dozen sheep, a mule. Am I correct?'

'Two dozen,' he amended, hoarsely. 'But – '

'Ah. Even two dozen, though – even they would have required some help.'

'I hired a man. And a maidservant.'

'A maidservant! Riches. Are there any outbuildings?'

'Yes.'

'Describe them to me.'

He did so. As I questioned him about the arrangement of rooms in his house, the tools and cooking utensils kept there, the surrounding pasturage and the contents of his vegetable garden, he became more loquacious, losing his stiff, wary manner in the joy of reminiscence. It was apparent that this farm had been the summit of his ambitions – his heart's desire – his single weakness. It was the crack in his stony carapace.

I let him talk until the crack had widened, a little. Then I inserted the point of my knife.

'So you paid, I think, some fifty livres tournois for this desirable property?' I said.

'Forty-eight.'

'A large sum.'

'I inherited the money. From an uncle.'

'Truly? But Raymond Donatus maintains that he gave it to you.'

This falsehood was designed to shatter Jordan's defences, and it certainly shook him. For although his expression remained blank, an involuntary movement of his eyes told me that I had struck a tender spot.

'Raymond Donatus has never given me any money,' he said. Noticing his use of the present tense, I rejoiced. It was clear that he knew nothing of Raymond's recent demise.

'Then you received no payment for admitting his women into headquarters?' I queried.

Again, his eyes shifted. He blinked several times. Was it anxiety I saw, or relief?

'These are all lies,' he said. 'I never let any women into headquarters.'

'Then you are falsely accused?'

'Yes.'

'One of your comrades confirms Raymond's testimony. He himself was paid to admit Raymond's women, and says that you were also.'

'Lies.'

'Why should he lie?'

'Because I could not defend myself.'

'So you were easy to blame because you were absent?'

'Yes.'

I pressed him on this matter of prohibited entry, as if it were of great importance. I lingered on it, talked around it, and appeared as if outraged that fornication had occurred on Holy Office premises. I spoke of proof: of 'vile and impure stains', of women's intimate garments, of certain herbs which prevent a woman from conceiving. With various equivocal remarks, I even seemed to suggest that the money used to buy Jordan's farm was the money paid to him for assisting in Raymond's seduction of servant girls.

By such means I delivered him into a state of confusion:

firstly, because talk of carnal union is bound to distract any man in the prime of life; secondly, because he had been expecting accusations of murder, and was instead required to defend himself against more petty charges. Having denied complicity from the beginning, he was forced to stand his ground, tiring himself over a minor infringement when he should have been husbanding his strength. For make no mistake: lying is a wearisome business. One needs to be alert and vigorous, if one is to lie convincingly again and again. As the interrogation drags on, it becomes less easy to concentrate, and therefore more difficult to present a faultless arrangement of lies.

Jordan made his first mistake beneath the pressure of my prurient speculation. There are certain priests who profess to deplore the many diabolical and degenerate varieties of copulation, but whose relish, as they extract descriptions of these acts, and publically tabulate and condemn them, suggests that they derive a reprehensible enjoyment from the contemplation of lascivious immorality. Imitating such priests, I dwelt on the benefits that Jordan might have received from the women pursued by Raymond Donatus. I inflicted upon him a perfectly obscene interrogatory, replete with gross acts which, I assure you, beggared belief – acts which I once encountered, with great shock, in an Irish penitential.

I asked, for instance, if Jordan had employed certain objects when fornicating with Raymond's women. I asked if he had expelled his seed in any place other than a womb. I asked if he had required the women to perform any perverse caresses, to eat or suck or excrete anything, to recite any holy words or foul suggestions while engaged in these depravities ...

Oh, but they are best passed over. Suffice it to say that Jordan strenuously defended himself, and with mounting annoyance, as I poisoned the air with my lewd remarks. (Poor Simon and Berengar were as red as the blood of grapes, and even Durand looked uncomfortable.) Finally, when I falsely asserted that I had spoken to one of the aforesaid women, who had accused Jordan of sodomy, the subject of this unfounded accusation lost his temper.

'That is not true!' he cried. 'I never did! I never did any of those things!'

'Just virile copulation as ordained by the laws of nature?'

'Yes!'

'With no defilement of the inquisitor's chair, or obscene use of Holy Office quills or parchment – '

'No!'

'Just simple fornication on the floor of Father Augustin's room.'

'Yes,' he snapped, then paused, as he realised what he had said. 'I mean – '

'Do not attempt to deny what you just affirmed,' I interrupted. 'Your shame is understandable, but lying under oath is a greater sin than fornication. If you are truly repentant, God will forgive you. And the Holy Office, too, will forgive you. Now – did you, or did you not, introduce salacious women onto Holy Office premises for payment?'

Jordan sighed. He no longer had the strength to resist in a matter of such trivial import. Besides, I had given him a small gift of hope.

'Yes,' he admitted.

'And you used these payments to buy a farm in Catalonia?'

'Yes.'

'Was that before or after your disappearance?'

He thought for a moment. Evidently, it occurred to him that the dates of his purchase could be checked. 'After,' he said at last.

'So you were carrying forty-eight livres tournois on your person when you went to Casseras with Father Augustin?'

'Yes.'

'Why?'

'Because I used to carry them everywhere. Otherwise they might have been stolen.'

'I see.' Although I found this explanation preposterous, no trace of disbelief appeared in my voice, or on my face. 'Tell me what happened that day,' I continued. 'The day of Father Augustin's death.'

How long had he been expecting such an inquiry? Almost with relief he launched into his account, speaking quickly and without inflection.

'I was feeling ill,' he said. 'Something I ate at the forcia, perhaps – I wanted to vomit. So I dropped behind, and told the others to wait at Casseras for me – '

'Wait!' I held up my hand. 'From the beginning, please. When were you instructed to join Father Augustin's escort?'

Once again, my purpose was to weary him – and to reassure him. I listened pleasantly to his recital, uttering no sharp objections, but only encouraging noises. Occasionally I would ask him for more details, or to repeat himself regarding the chronology of events, and he did so easily, carelessly, until we reached the moment at which he had 'dropped behind'. Then his narrative became somewhat more laboured, though in a fashion which few people might readily discern. You see, when a story is not true, but fabricated, it is more difficult for the narrator to isolate spontaneously any particular part of it. Because he did not experience what he professes to have experienced, he cannot draw on his memory. Therefore if his testimony is interrupted, he will repeat it from the beginning, so as to keep the logical sequence of events in order. A person telling the truth does not have to concern himself with logical coherence. He will simply recite what he remembers, untroubled by inconsistencies.

According to the prisoner, he had been taken ill, and was obliged to dismount shortly after leaving the forcia on his return journey to Casseras. Then, having rested for a while, he had proceeded. (At this point, I inquired as to where Jordan had voided his previous meal, and was told that he had been careful to vomit into a patch of undergrowth, where it might have gone unnoticed. He was an intelligent man, was Jordan.)

Presently, he had heard a faint scream, and various other frightening sounds which told him that Father Augustin's party was being attacked somewhere on the road ahead. As he advanced, however, the sounds had diminished, suggesting that the contest was over. But who had won? Uneasy, Jordan had concealed his horse and hidden behind a rock, waiting for enlightenment.

'You did not want to walk into an ambush yourself,' I said sympathetically.

'I did not.'

'Knowing that, if the others had been killed, you yourself would have no chance.'

'Exactly.'

'And what happened then?'

Then Father Augustin's mare had galloped past with an empty saddle. She had been followed by a man mounted on Maurand's horse, who had caught the runaway and guided her back down the hill.

Upon witnessing this event, Jordan realised that his comrades had been defeated, and very probably slaughtered. So he had waited for a while before approaching the scene of the massacre, surreptitiously, on foot. In doing so, he had kept as close to the path as possible, and had therefore witnessed the escape of two men who had ridden up the hill on stolen horses.

Naturally, I requested a full description of these men. Jordan replied that one had been wearing green, and one a red cap, but that they had passed too quickly for him to see anything more.

'Was there nothing unusual about them?' I inquired. 'Nothing that impressed you particularly?'

'No.'

'Nothing at all that caught your attention? Even in that fleeting instant?'

'No.'

'So the fact that they were covered in blood did not strike you as being especially noteworthy?'

317

Foolish creature! He hesitated, and I thought to myself: 'This man is lying'. For if he had truly seen the assassins, he would have noticed the gore before anything else. 'Wearing green', indeed!

However, I forbore to comment, and retained my sympathetic demeanour.

'I thought you meant their height, or ... or the colour of their hair,' he stammered, after a brief pause. 'Naturally, they were covered in blood.'

'Naturally. And then what did you do?'

'I went on until I came to the clearing. Where the bodies were. It was a terrible sight.' (Nevertheless, Jordan's voice was calm as he described it.) 'Everyone hacked to pieces. I looked around, but I saw that nobody was left alive, so I went away again.'

'Did you vomit?'

'No.'

'Your gut was restored to health at this point? I must confess, a sight like that would have turned *my* stomach.'

There was a long silence. Upon reflection, Jordan remarked: 'You are not a soldier. Soldiers must be strong.'

'I see. Well, go on. What next?'

Next Jordan had spent some time thinking. It occurred to him that, as the only survivor, he would undoubtedly be suspected of complicity in this horrible crime. The Holy Office would want to blame somebody. Perhaps it would be best if he disappeared, if he escaped to the mountains and bought a farm. After all, he had the money on him.

'So I did,' he concluded.

'So you did. But it was a foolish thing to do, my friend. If you are innocent, you need have no fear of the Holy Office.'

A snort was his only reply.

'On my honour, we would not condemn without cause,' I insisted. 'Durand, will you kindly read out your transcription of this man's testimony? We must be sure that it is correct.'

If Durand was surprised (for it is customary to wait a day,

and read to the prisoner a more finished transcript, before cofirmation is secured), he did not allow his surprise to show. His voice was almost expressionless as he read through the deposition, and the effect was very tedious. Jordan evidently found it so, for he yawned several times, and wiped his weary face with his hands. When I asked him, at the close of the reading, if there were any amendments that he wished to make, he shook his head.

'None at all?'

'No.'

'Nothing you may have missed?'

'No, Father.'

'For example, the fact that Raymond Donatus paid you to kill Father Augustin's party and dismember the corpses so that your own absence would escape comment?'

Jordan swallowed.

'I never did that,' he sighed.

'My friend, I do not *believe* that you did it. I *know* that you did it. I have Raymond's confession here, in front of me.' I was lying, of course; the document in front of me was a set of notes made during my interviews with the inhabitants of Casseras. But it is often the case that the written word will strike fear into the hearts of illiterate people, when the spoken word will not. 'Would you care to peruse it?' I added, knowing full well that Jordan could not read. He was eyeing the document as if it were a snake about to bite him. 'You do realise, do you not, that Raymond planned to have you poisoned when you returned here? It was this plan which alerted me to his guilt. It surprises me that he did not have you killed in Catalonia.'

'Raymond is – ' He stopped, and cleared his throat. There were beads of sweat on his brow. 'Raymond is lying,' he said.

'Jordan, listen to me.' I adopted a persuasive tone. 'I have enough evidence to have you buried alive – whether or not you confess. You must see that. And if you refuse to confess, that is the best you can hope for. The worst is that you will fall into the hands of my superior, Father Pierre-Julien. You see, when you killed Father Augustin, you did us all a great disservice, because Father Pierre-Julien came to replace him. And Father Pierre-Julien is a violent man. You should have seen what he did to Jean-Pierre, to induce him to admit that he took your place in Raymond's service. If you wish, I can have Jean-Pierre brought down here. He has to be carried, because he cannot walk. His feet have been burned.'

Perceptibly, Jordan winced.

'Now, what you may not realise,' I continued, 'is that for true repentance, there will always be mercy. Have you heard of St Pierre the Martyr? He was a Dominican inquisitor just like me, and he was murdered by a band of assassins, just like Father Augustin. One of the assassins was a Pierre Balsamo, who was caught almost in the act, and later escaped from prison. Yet when recaptured, he repented, was forgiven, and was allowed to enter the Dominican Order. Did you know that?'

Jordan shook his head, frowning. 'Is it true?' he said.

'Of course it is true! I can show you any number of books which recount the story. Ask Brother Simon. Ask Brother Berengar. They will tell you the same.'

My impartials indicated that they would, indeed, testify to the truth of my assertions.

Of course,' I continued, 'there is no reason to think that *you* would be accepted into the Dominican Order. But unless you confess to your sins, and abjure them, there can be only one outcome. Do you understand?'

To my disappointment, Jordan did not reply. He sat staring down at his knees, as if they and they alone could provide him with an answer to his problems.

'Jordan,' I said, trying another tactic, 'have you ever been received into a heretical sect?'

'I?' His head jerked up. 'No!'

'You have never believed as true another faith than that which the Roman Church holds to be true?'

'I am not a heretic!'

'Then why did you kill Father Augustin?'

'I did not kill Father Augustin!'

'Perhaps not,' I conceded. 'Perhaps you yourself did not strike the blow. But at the very least, you stood by while he was butchered like a pig. Now, why was that? Was it simply for gain? Or was it because you are a believer and fautor of heresy?' Consulting my transcription of the report made to me by 'S', I read aloud the list of names therein recorded. 'All these people are defamed heretics,' I said. 'You were seen associating with them in Catalonia. Yet you did not alert the Holy Office.'

Jordan's eyes narrowed; his breathing became quite ragged. It is possible that he had been hoping to bargain for his life with these very names – and now he had discovered that I already possessed them!

'The Perfect!' he said abruptly (obviously referring to 'S'). 'You got him!'

'Why did you fail to alert the Holy Office?' I repeated, ignoring his exclamation.

'Because I was in hiding!' he barked. 'How could I say a word? And if that Perfect is calling me a heretic, he is lying to save his skin. Did he tell you where to find me? I should have – '

He broke off, suddenly.

'What?' I said. 'What should you have done? Killed him, too?'

Jordan remained speechless.

'My friend, if you were a good Catholic, you would confess to your sins, and repent,' I told him. 'I think that you are Godless. And being a Godless murderer, you will suffer a punishment far greater than any decreed by the Holy Office. You will be cast into a lake of fire, for all eternity, if you do not atone. Think hard, now. Perhaps Raymond told you a lie. Perhaps he told you that Father Augustin was visiting female heretics for heretical purposes, and therefore deserved to perish. If he told you such things, your crime can be understood, and readily forgiven.'

321

At last my words had a noticeable effect. I sensed that Jordan was considering them, examining them.

'Did Raymond tell you that Father Augustin was an enemy of God?' I said softly. 'Jordan? What did he tell you?'

Jordan looked up, took a deep breath, and announced, without meeting my gaze: 'He told me that *you* wanted Father Augustin dead.'

'*I?*' Startled, I did what no inquisitor should ever do: I let the prisoner see my consternation.

'He told me that you hated Father Augustin. He told me that you would arrange it so that I would never be blamed.' Turning to Durand, the vile butcher declared: 'Father Bernard is the killer, not I!'

At this point I had recovered my equanimity, and laughed out loud. 'Jordan, you are a fool!' I said. 'If I had arranged this murder, do you think that I would have let you come back here? Do you think that you would be sitting before me, alive and well, denouncing me in front of witnesses? Come, now, tell me what happened. You have just admitted complicity.'

I have said that Jordan was intelligent. Only a man with a certain degree of intelligence would have sought to attack me, thereby hoping, perhaps, to gain some advantage. But he had not given sufficient thought to his offensive, and had walked into a trap of his own devising.

He sat there mutely, wondering, no doubt, how he had come to such a pass. But I knew better than to give him time for thought.

'You have no choice. We have your confession. Who else was implicated? Tell me, and repent, and you may yet escape death. Remain silent, and you will be regarded as obdurate. What do you have to lose, Jordan? Perhaps a little wine will help you to remember.'

I have often found that wine on an empty stomach will loosen the tongue. But even as I gestured to Brother Berengar, signifying that he should bring me some of the wine poured out for this very purpose, Jordan began to speak.

He admitted that Raymond Donatus had often fornicated with women in the Holy Office, under his very eyes. He told me that one day, the notary had come to him with a further proposal: for fifty livres tournois, Jordan should kill Father Augustin. It should be done, not on the premises of the Holy Office, where everyone who frequented the building would be under suspicion, but in the mountains, which were commonly known to be infested with heretics. According to Raymond, it was important that heretics should be blamed.

The plan was a good one, but would require four other people trained in combat. Each would be paid thirty livres tournois for a successful assassination.

'I have worked in a lot of garrison towns,' Jordan revealed. 'I knew mercenaries who had done such things before. So when I was sent to these towns, carrying messages from the Holy Office, I spoke to four men who were happy to earn thirty livres tournois.'

'Kindly give me their names,' I said, and Jordan obliged. He recounted the movements of the four men: how they had come to Lazet, had been provided with half their fee together with daily expenses, and had waited until Father Augustin left for Casseras.

'I was told the day before,' said Jordan. 'So I told the others, and they set off before the gates shut, sleeping that night in Crieux.'

'They had no horses?'

'None. They had to walk to Casseras. But they arrived in good time. And I knew the path to the forcia. I could tell them where to wait.'

As he described, in a gruff and unapologetic manner, the device by which he had forced his party to stop in the appointed clearing, I felt cold rage growing in my heart. He had claimed to be dizzy and nauseous, all but falling from his horse. He had then been joined on the ground by one of his comrades. This man, while in the act of tending him, had been stabbed in the gut, an action designed to unleash a shower of arrows from the undergrowth.

It was of prime importance that the two mounted familiars receive the brunt of the attack. By the time Father Augustin had recovered from his shock, it was too late to flee; his guards had been cut down, his horse's bridle seized.

He had witnessed the deaths of all his companions, before he too was murdered. I was compelled to look away, when Jordan pointed out that my superior had been killed with a single blow, as if this was somehow an act of mercy. I had to concentrate all my resources on retaining a tranquil demeanour, when I wanted to snatch up a stool and break it across Jordan's skull. The man deserved to be flayed alive. He was something less than a man, for his soul was dead. And his heart was blackened with the smoke of sin.

'We undressed the bodies before we cut them up,' he related. 'We had been told to do that. And to take the heads with us. The heads and some of the other parts, to hide the fact that I was missing. Then we all went in different directions. You see, we only had half of the money. I had to go to Berga, and wait there until Raymond heard that Father Augustin was dead. When he did, he sent the other half of my fee to a notary in Berga, who paid it over to me.'

'The name of the notary?' I inquired.

'Bertrand de Gaillac. But he knew nothing. He was Raymond's friend.'

'And what about the blood? The blood on your clothes?'

'We had all brought spare clothes. As soon as we were clear of Casseras, as soon as we had reached water or a place to hide, we were supposed to wash and change. Then we were supposed to get rid of the horses.' After a brief pause, the prisoner added: 'I killed mine. It was safer. Out there in the mountains, the crows and wolves would have found it first.'

This, then, was the substance of Jordan Sicre's confession. A bloody tale, without the leaven of redeeming sorrow. At its conclusion, I had Durand read it aloud once more, and my impartials witnessed it as being correct and complete. Jordan, too, was given that privilege. Having derived all that I needed from the man, I did not waste any more kind words or assurances on him. He merited no such gentle usage.

'What will happen now?' he asked me, as I moved to depart.

'Now you will await sentencing,' I replied. 'Unless you have anything further to add.'

'Only that I am very sorry.' (He sounded more anxious than apologetic.) 'Did you write that down?'

'I shall make a note of your penitence,' was my response. I was very, very tired. Perhaps I should have been congratulating myself on a deed well done – for it had been, though I say it myself, an exceptionally fine piece of work – but I felt little desire to rejoice. It was all I could do to mount the stairs to the trapdoor; Durand had to help me through it. The prison was dark, with lamps burning. I had no idea how late it was.

'Will you need a familiar to escort you home?' I inquired of the impartials, who assured me that they required only a lamp, or torch. Having secured one for them, I bade them farewell, and turned to Durand. We were standing near my desk, at the time, with one lamp between us; the shadows around us were dense, chilly, and faintly menacing. It was very quiet.

'I want you to guard that protocol,' I instructed. 'Do not let it out of your sight, until a copy has been made.'

'Shall *I* make the copy?'

'Perhaps that would be best.'

'Any amendments?'

'You can ignore the farm, of course. Most of the journey to Casseras can be omitted.'

'The apology?'

Our eyes met, and I saw in his (which were a very fine colour – gold and green, like a sunlit glade) the same ferocious disgust as that which still lurked in my own heart. It warmed me, somehow. It gave me relief.

'I leave that to your discretion, Durand. You always say that I discard too much exculpatory material.'

At this we both paused, perhaps to reflect on the horror of the deeds that had been narrated to us. Gradually, the silence lengthened. Numb with fatigue, I found that I had nothing more to say.

'You are a great man,' Durand remarked abruptly. He was not looking at me; he was frowning at the floor. 'A very great man, in your own particular way.' Then, after another, briefer silence, he added: 'But I would not describe it as God's way.'

'No.' I was able to speak only after exerting myself enormously. 'No, neither would I.'

This concluded our dialogue. Durand left the building, with his head bowed and Jordan's testimony clasped to his breast; I went back into the prison, so that I might say goodnight to Johanna. Though it was very late, I could not return to the priory without saying goodnight, if only because I had made her a promise. To break such a promise would have been unthinkable, though it concerned a trivial greeting. For a lover, even the most minor infraction is invested with a vast and terrible importance.

You know that love gets its name from the word for hook, which means 'to capture' or 'to be captured'. I was captured in the chains of desire, and could not stray far from my beloved. All that day, in fact, while supporting Vitalia, and reassuring Babilonia, and interrogating Jordan, I had remained captive to thoughts of my nocturnal impurity. Unchaste visions would persistently enter my mind, causing great flushes of heat to overwhelm my body, and suffuse my cheeks. Yet while I thrust these memories away, I found them irresistible, returning to them repeatedly, although they filled me with shame – just as a dog returneth to his vomit. How true it is, as Ovid says, that 'We strive for what is forbidden, and always want what is denied us'!

I had broken my vow of chastity. In following the enticements of the flesh, rather than that eternal heritage which the heavenly King, with His own blood, restored to all men, I had delivered myself to the flames of Gehenna. Did not Pierre Lombard himself point out that 'Other sins stain the soul alone ... fornication stains not only the soul but the body'? *For behold I was shapen in iniquity; and in sin did my mother conceive me.* Furthermore, I was in thrall to a woman, and it is commonly known that women are founts of duplicity, vainglory, avarice, lust. Samson was betrayed by a woman. Solomon was unable to find a single good woman. Mankind was condemned by the sin of a woman. I knew all this in my head, yet my heart would not be convinced.

So it was that I went to the guardroom, alone and unchallenged. Because it was not a cell, there was no hatch in the door; I had to content myself with a gentle knock, and a murmured greeting, rather than a glimpse of my beloved's face.

It was she who returned my salutation, her voice muffled by the thickness of wood between us.

'The others are asleep,' she said softly.

'As you should be, also.'

'But I was waiting for you.'

'Forgive me. I should have come earlier. There were matters I had to attend to.'

'Oh, my dear, it was not a complaint.'

This fond endearment set my pulse racing, and I pressed my brow against the door, as if endeavouring to penetrate it. At the same time I was filled with despair, for the corporeal barrier between us seemed to represent all those other, less surmountable impediments to our love. Even Heloise and Pierre Abelard were more favoured in their conjunction – yet the Lord had dealt with them very harshly indeed. The future held no hope, as far as I could judge. The best outcome to be expected was that Johanna should be given a minor penance, released with her daughter, and permitted to flee from Pierre-Julien's sphere of influence. But such an escape, of course, would also necessitate leaving me behind.

I told myself that this would be a good thing. Love was a

kind of madness — an illness that would pass. *A time to love, and a time to hate.* What would it profit me, to abandon my life's work for a woman I hardly knew? For a love that was as much anguish as joy?

'It cannot happen again,' I whispered. 'Johanna, we cannot allow it to happen again.'

'My dear, what chance is there?' she replied sadly. 'It was my last taste of love.'

'No. You will remain here only a short time, I promise.'

'Bernard, do not put yourself at risk.'

'I? I am not at risk.'

'You are. The gaoler's wife said so.'

'The gaoler's *wife?*' I almost laughed. 'Not a widely respected authority, hereabouts.'

'Bernard, be careful.' Her tone was urgent. 'You favour us too much. People will guess. Oh, my dear, it is not for my own sake, but for yours.'

Her voice broke, and I myself was torn between tears and laughter — astonished, dismayed laughter.

'How can this be?' I said. 'How can this have happened? I hardly know you. You hardly know me.'

'I know you as well as I know my own soul.'

'Oh, God.' I wanted to drive my head through the door. I wanted to expire in her arms. O Lord, I thought, all my desire is before Thee; and my groaning is not hid from Thee. My heart panteth, my strength faileth me ...

Make haste to help me, O Lord my salvation.

'Bernard?' she said. 'Bernard, hear me out. This is my doing. When Augustin talked of you — of the things you said, and the way you laughed — I thought to myself: This is a man I want to know. Then, when you appeared, and when you smiled at me, you were so tall and so beautiful, and your eyes were like stars. How could I resist? But I should have resisted. For your sake, I should have resisted. It was so wrong of me.'

'No.'

'It was! It was cruel! You would have helped us without

this. You would have remained strong, and clear, and happy, but now I have shaken you. And I did it because I wanted to have you, before it was too late. I am so wretched. I am not worthy. I have made you miserable and unclean.'

'This is nonsense. You flatter yourself. Do you think that I have no will of my own? Do you truly believe that I am faultless?' To reassure her, and also to punish her (for she seemed to think that I had been driven like a sheep, in all things), I revealed my encounter with the other widow, during my years as a preacher ordinary. 'I have strayed from the path before this. I have been disobedient and unchaste. It is my nature.' Then, as she remained silent, I began to fear that I had caused her deep offence. 'But the widow was nothing,' I hastened on. 'It was vanity and boredom that drove me into her bed. This is different.'

'For me, also.'

'In some way,' I said desperately, 'in some way, I feel sure, God has brought us together. For some reason ...'

'So that we must suffer when we part,' Johanna sighed. 'You should go, my love, before anyone sees you. We should not talk like this again – unless it is to say goodbye.'

'God forbid.'

'Go now. Go. It is too late. There are too many people nearby.'

'Do you think I care?'

'You are like a boy when you say that. Go to bed, now. Pray for me. You are in my thoughts.'

Was she stronger than I, or was her love weaker? I would be there still, if she had not banished me from her presence. And I felt that I had left part of me outside the guardroom, as I staggered downstairs: I felt dizzy and ill, as if my heart's blood was draining away.

Nevertheless, I had the presence of mind to glance at my desk, in the hope that a letter might have arrived from Toulouse, or Carcassonne, regarding the missing registers. (Now, of course, no longer missing, but incomplete.) To my sorrow,

329

there was nothing of interest – and Pierre-Julien's desk, similarly, offered up no pleasurable surprises. It was at this point, however, that God granted me a brief and brilliant clarity of vision. I suddenly thought: 'Why wait for help that might never come? Why not use what is at hand?' Whereupon I attacked the sheafs of my more recent correspondence

After a quick search, I found what I had been seeking. It was a commonplace letter from Jean de Beune, in which the inquisitor had, without excessive elaboration, referred to my request for copies of a deposition implicating the inhabitants of Saint-Fiacre. (This was the witness from Tarascon, do you recall?) '*As to the copies that you require,*' he had written, '*I shall see to it that they are made, and dispatched to you forthwith.*'

The date at the close of the letter was easily defaced: one minor blot was enough.

'O give thanks unto the Lord, for He is good: for His mercy endureth forever,' I prayed. 'For the redeemed of the Lord say so, whom He hath redeemed from the hands of the enemy.'

Then I tucked the letter into my belt, and departed for the priory in a fiercely sanguine state of mind.

Forgers of lies

As you may imagine, I was a clumsy and inattentive participant in the office of Matins that night. Roused after only a short and fitful sleep, I was too dazed with exhaustion to acquit myself well. I remained standing when I should have been seated – remained seated when I should have been standing. I missed signals, and dozed off while reciting my *pater* and *credo*. But in the normal course of events, I am as unlikely to fail at my office as St Dominic himself, so I was surprised at the hostility which my blunders seemed to provoke. Even in my half-conscious state, I noticed the glares and grimaces.

At Lauds, however, I was, as always, punctilious. Even so, I observed many scowls directed at me – and just as many lingering looks which appeared to be sympathetic, in a somewhat pointed and particular way. The only brother who refused to acknowledge my existence at all was Pierre-Julien. Though seated almost directly opposite me in the choir, he contrived to avoid even glancing in my direction.

Only when I approached him directly, after Prime, was he forced to recognise me. He nodded. I nodded. Then, after an exchange of hand signals, we retired to his cell, where conversation was permitted if conducted discreetly and without excessive noise. I began to speak before he could establish the subject of our dialogue himself.

'Yesterday, Jordan Sicre arrived,' I said abruptly.

'Yes, but – '

'I interrogated him, with all formalities observed.'

'*You?*'

'And he told me that Raymond Donatus had paid him to kill Father Augustin. He could not tell me why. He did not know.'

'But you are no longer an inquisitor of heretical depravity!' Pierre-Julien exclaimed, then quickly lowered his voice, as he remembered where he was. 'You have no right to question suspects!' he hissed. 'You are forbidden the premises of the Holy Office!'

'The women from Casseras are therefore not implicated in Father Augustin's murder.'

'This is unacceptable! I shall speak to the Abbot – '

'Hear me out, Pierre-Julien. I know more than you think.' Catching his arm, I pulled him back down onto the bed from which he had risen. 'Just hear me out, before you make any foolish mistakes. I know that this entire mystery revolves around the inquisitorial registers. Father Augustin asked Raymond to find a missing register, then Augustin was killed. When Raymond was killed in turn, you went looking for certain registers that were in his possession. Upon examining them, I found that they were mutilated. That folios were missing.'

'I fail to see – '

'Wait. Listen. When I first realised that there were registers missing – and this was before you recovered them – I wrote to Carcassonne and Toulouse. I asked if any copies had been made of these registers for the use of inquisitors outside Lazet. Yesterday, a letter arrived from Brother Jean de Beune, informing me that copies *had* been made. He promised to arrange that the copies among his records would be copied again, and returned to me here. I have the letter. Do you wish to consult it?'

Pierre-Julien did not reply. He simply stared, and his eyes were blank, and his face was as white as the twelve gates of the Heavenly Jerusalem.

Seeing him at a loss, I pressed my advantage.

'I know that you are implicated in this, Pierre-Julien. I know that you removed those folios. And when I receive the copies from Carcassonne, I shall know why.' Leaning close to him, I continued very quietly, but with great clarity and force. 'Perhaps you are thinking: "I shall write to Brother Jean, and tell him not to trouble himself." Alas! Brother Jean and I are good friends, and you have been the subject of our recent correspondence. He does not hold you in very high esteem, Brother. If you revoke my request, he is bound to question your motives.'

Still Pierre-Julien remained silent – from shock, I believe. Therefore I became more encouraging, and less menacing.

'Brother, I have no wish to see the Holy Office succumb to scandal and recrimination,' I said. 'There may still be time to prevent it. If we act now, if I write to Brother Jean, and tell him that the copies are not needed after all.'

'Yes! Write now!' Pierre-Julien's voice was high and urgent. 'Write to him now!'

'Brother – '

'He must not read them! No one must read them!'

'Why?'

Gasping, gaping, my companion seemed unable to formulate a response. He put his hand to his heart, as if it were threatening to fail him.

I saw that one more push was required.

'If you tell me why, I shall write the letter,' I promised. 'If you order the release of the women from Casseras, and assure me that they will never be held responsible for a crime which they did not commit, I shall write the letter. More than that,

I shall desist from taking any further action. I shall withdraw from the Holy Office. I shall leave Lazet. All I want is a confession, Brother. A confession and an undertaking. I want to know what this is all about.'

'Where is the letter?' he suddenly demanded. 'Show me!'

Offering up a private prayer, I produced from my purse the document which I had defaced, and thereby falsified, the night before. He took it, and held it in his trembling hands, as I indicated the relevant paragraph. But although he stared, his eyes failed to move. He was not reading. Apparently, he was unable to read. His fear and amazement were too profound; he was unable to exercise all of his faculties.

'It is an ancestor, is it not?' I inquired, watching the sweat trickle down from his naked scalp. I spoke gently, without the slightest hint of accusation. 'You have heretical antecedents. But you know, Brother, I have never approved of the practice, so often pursued in the Holy Office, whereby a man must suffer for the sins of his father. "As I live, saith the Lord, ye shall not have occasion any more to use this proverb in Israel." Such ferocious and implacable pursuit seems to me excessive. It seems misguided. St Paul said: "Let your moderation be known unto all men". I do not condemn you as being tainted by your grandfather's heresy, Brother. I believe that all of your sins are your own.'

Hardly the most gentle reassurance, you must agree. A veiled insult, in fact. But it appeared to move Pierre-Julien for, to my eternal surprise, he burst into tears.

'Bless me Brother, for I have sinned!' he sobbed, covering his face with his hands. 'Bless me Brother, for I have sinned! It is a week since my last confession . . .'

Now, having said that I wanted a confession, I did *not*, be assured, want this kind of confession. It was bound by too many restraints. It was certain to hamper me. But although I demurred, Pierre-Julien remained adamant, and I was concerned lest he decide to withhold his story altogether. In any event, no matter how freely given, a confession is practically worthless unless recorded in the presence of a witness or witnesses. So I agreed to his demands, and waited for his confession.

It was not forthcoming.

'Brother,' I said impatiently, as he snivelled into the skirts of his tunic, 'compose yourself. This benefits no one.'

'You hate me! You always hated me!'

'My feelings are irrelevant.'

'God cursed me when He brought me here!'

'Why? Tell me why.' When he refused to answer, I asked him bluntly: 'Did you kill Raymond Donatus?'

'*No!*' he cried, looking up, and shrinking back as I waved an admonitory finger.

'Hush!' I murmured. 'Do you want everyone to hear?'

'I did not kill Raymond Donatus! You keep accusing me, but *I did not kill Raymond Donatus!*'

'Very well. What *did* you do?'

Pierre-Julien sighed. Once again, he buried his face in his hands. 'I removed the folios,' he admitted, in a muffled voice. 'I burned them.'

'Why?'

'Because my great-uncle was a heretic. He died before he was sentenced. I never knew. The people in my family hardly ever spoke of him. "Your Uncle Isarn was a bad man," they said. "He died in prison. He was a shame to this family." I thought that he must have been a thief, or a murderer. He had no children, you see. He had lived outside Lazet. It was difficult to trace the connection.'

'But you did, in the end.'

'No. Not I. Raymond Donatus.'

'Raymond?'

'He came to me, just – oh, not long ago.' Hesitantly, my witness put his hand to his brow. 'I could not believe – he had an old book with him. He showed me a deposition that defamed my great-uncle.'

'When was this?' I demanded. 'When exactly did he come to you?'

'It was after you told him to look for a missing register.' Turning his head, Pierre-Julien gazed at me in a hapless, hopeless fashion. 'This was the register. It had my great-uncle's name in it.'

'Wait,' I said, lifting my hand. 'The register that I wanted was the same register that Father Augustin wanted. I wanted it because *he* wanted it. So why did Raymond want it?'

'I think – I think because there was a name inside. Not my great-uncle's. Another name.' Before I could ask him to elucidate, he did so. 'Raymond said to me: "Father Bernard is looking for this register. If he finds it, the whole world will know that you come from heretical stock. You will be reviled. Your family will be shamed. Perhaps your brother will lose his property, and you will lose your position." ' Pierre-Julien's voice broke, at this juncture, but valiantly he strove to control himself. Finally, he succeeded. 'Raymond told me to remove you from the investigation into Father Augustin's death, and I did. Perhaps he would have asked for more, if he had not been killed. Perhaps he would have asked for money – '

'And he was hiding the register in his own house!' I exclaimed, unable to help myself. 'The register and the Bishop's copy! And when you heard that he was missing – '

'I went there to find them. But the Seneschal was there already. He was looking for registers too.'

'The *Seneschal?*'

'Oh – not the same ones that I was looking for. He wanted the registers with his aunt's name. His aunt was burned as a lapsed heretic.'

Imagine my disbelief. Imagine my astonishment. I swear to you, I would have been no more dumbfounded if the great mountain burning with fire had been cast into the sea before my very eyes.

'The Seneschal found two inquisitorial registers in Raymond's house, but they were the wrong ones,' Pierre-Julien continued, apparently oblivious to my dropped jaw and stupefied demeanour. 'They did not contain his aunt's name.

336

He looked through them, and when he saw the name "Fauré", he approached me at once. He told me that some years before, Raymond had asked him for money. The two men were in Raymond's house at the time, and the notary had produced from some concealed place a register which contained the deposition and sentence of Roger's heretical aunt. Raymond had said that he was only a messenger for Father Jacques. But when Father Jacques died, Raymond had continued to demand money. The Seneschal thought that I must have been in the same position as he was.'

According to Pierre-Julien, the Seneschal had also accused him of killing Raymond Donatus. On being told that this was not the case, Lord Roger had shrugged, and delivered himself of the opinion that Raymond had doubtless been receiving payments from any number of unfortunate people, whose convicted ancestors were scattered throughout the inquisitorial records. One of the notary's victims, he thought, had probably been pushed a little too far.

'If Raymond is dead, I should not be surprised,' was the Seneschal's conclusion. 'On the contrary, I should be delighted.'

Having failed to uncover, within Raymond's house, the registers that contained his aunt's name, Roger had instructed Pierre-Julien to look for them in the Bishop's library and the scriptorium of the Holy Office. When found, these codices were to be brought to the Chateau Comtal. The Seneschal would then produce the registers that he had discovered in Raymond's house, and there would be a formal exchange of documents. After that, certain folios were to be destroyed.

'It took me *such* a long time to find his aunt's name,' my witness remarked fretfully. 'I missed Compline, one evening – you remember? – looking through those miserable chests in the scriptorium. But I found the books at last. And I took them to the Seneschal. And we did what we had to do. When Raymond was found dead, I thought that we were safe.'

I pondered this account of my superior's movements. If what

he said was true (and I had no reaon to doubt it), then I must have searched the Bishop's library just a short time after Pierre-Julien had extracted, on the Seneschal's behalf, the copy of that register containing his aunt's name. While I was scrutinising the gaps left by the two missing books, these volumes were being defaced in the Chateau Comtal. And while I was preparing to leave the Bishop's palace, Pierre-Julien had been restoring the two originals to the records chest in the scriptorium.

Strange, how I had dogged his footsteps that morning.

'So you did not kill Raymond yourself?' I said.

'No.' Pierre-Julien spoke dully. 'I could never do such a thing.'

'Then who could?'

'A sorceress. Jean-Pierre confessed – '

'What nonsense!' I was angry that he should have revived such an unfounded accusation. 'That is utter nonsense, and you know it!'

'The women – '

'Brother, do not waste my time. The Seneschal had a better motive for killing Raymond than any one of those women – and more opportunity, withall. Forget the women. They are irrelevant.'

'Not to you, it seems,' Pierre-Julien observed, maliciously, and with obvious resentment. I ignored him.

'The mystery is almost solved,' I said. 'Raymond Donatus was using the Holy Office records to extract money from people with heretical pasts, or predecessors. When Father Augustin began to consult some of the old registers, Raymond grew nervous. He knew that Father Augustin favoured the prosecution of deceased heretics, and others who had never completed their sentences – the very people whose descendants, also left unpunished, were the natural targets for black-mail. He worried that if Father Augustin were allowed to proceed, some of the people who had been paying him would be cited. He was concerned that they would denounce him to the Holy Office. Finally, Father Augustin demanded a register which *did* contain one of the names that Raymond wished to conceal. So he had Father Augustin killed, hoping that heretics would be blamed.

'Meanwhile, he had hidden in his house that register sought by Father Augustin. Perhaps, while handling it, he had noticed the name "Fauré". So when you arrived, he had a weapon against you. And when I began to look for the same register, he made use of this weapon.' A fearful notion occurred to me, and I considered it. Would Raymond have killed me if I had persisted? Perhaps so. 'Lucky for all of us that one of his other victims decided to take matters into his own hands,' I finished.

'You think that likely?'

'I think it highly probable. Perhaps the body was dismembered in the hope that the same person responsible for Father Augustin's death would be blamed for the second murder.' I liked this supposition. It was tidy and elegant. It satisfied most of my requirements. 'Perhaps I was wrong, in assuming that Raymond was killed on Holy Office premises. Perhaps Jean-Pierre was telling the truth, and had nothing to do with it. Of course, if we questioned all the other staff, we might discover something more. But do we want to? Raymond was an assassin. He suffered the proper penalty. Perhaps we can leave the punishment of his killer in the hands of God.'

At that instant I recalled Lothaire Carbonel, whose father had been defamed in one of the mutilated registers. Could he, perhaps, have been the killer? Certainly he was a prime candidate for Raymond's peculiar form of iniquity.

I promised myself that I would speak to Lothaire in confidence, when the opportunity presented itself. I then gave Pierre-Julien absolution, and a mighty penance which he accepted without a blink. He cared nothing for penances, or justice, or guilt. He desired only one thing, and that with the passion of profound alarm.

'Will you write the letter now?' he said. 'Write it now. Here.'

'Very well. But it must not be sent until the women have been released.'

'Yes, yes! Just write it!'

God forgive me, I enjoyed his desperation. I savoured his pleas like honey, and tormented him with my languid pace, with the painstaking manner in which I sharpened my pen, with the careful exactitude that I employed in the ruling of lines, and the forming of letters.

I am brutish among the people. I am an empty vessel, and a blot upon the book of the living. On account of the wickedness of my heart, and the poverty of my soul, I merited everything that followed.

Be sure your sin will find you out.

'Release them?' said Pons, in disbelief.

'Release them,' Pierre-Julien insisted.

'But – '

'*Release* them!' Frantic with concern that I should dispatch my letter, Pierre-Julien would brook no opposition. He spoke very sharply indeed. 'You heard what I said! Do it now! Give the keys to Father Bernard!'

'They will require horses,' I remarked, as Pons, shaking his head, sorted through the keys that hung from his belt. 'Four horses.'

'I shall go to the Bishop,' Pierre-Julien said quickly. 'I shall go now. Bring them to the Bishop's stables.'

'There might be a delay.'

But Pierre-Julien had already departed. I heard his footsteps on the stairs. Pons, scowling, said that he would unlock the guardroom door himself.

'I never surrender my keys,' he said gruffly.

'A wise precept.'

'How have you done this?'

'What?'

'You have gone too far. There will be a reckoning. You are not unconquerable, Father.'

Astonished, I opened my mouth to demand an explanation. But he was already on his way to the guardroom, jingling his keys so loudly that I could not have hoped to be heard.

'Here is your *friend*,' he barked, as he unlocked the guardroom door. 'Here is your *friend* to save you. Out! Everybody out! You are not welcome here!'

Sensing dismay in the rustles and murmurs which greeted this announcement, I was greatly angered, and told the gaoler to go. He obeyed me willingly, muttering something to the effect that he wanted 'nothing to do with it'. Only when he had left did it occur to me that another strong back might be needed to carry the luggage.

I was annoyed at my own lack of foresight.

'Johanna,' I said, upon entering the guardroom. 'Alcaya. You have all been released. You can go, now.'

'Released?' Johanna was sitting on the floor near Vitalia's bed. She was holding an earthenware cup. 'From this room?'

'From this prison. Come.' I went to her, and held out my hand. 'There are horses waiting. You must pack up your possessions.'

'But where are we going?' Babilonia inquired. Against the grimy stone walls and dusty shadows, her face seemed to glow like an ember. 'Are we going home?'

'You cannot return to the forcia, little one,' I said. 'But you can go anywhere else. Anywhere at all.'

'Not at present, Father.' It was Alcaya who contradicted me. 'Vitalia is too ill.'

I peered at Vitalia, and saw a woman whose strength was dried up like a potsherd, who was all but brought into the dust of death. Withered and sapless, corrupt of breath and grey of skin, she seemed as frangible as fine glass, and I could understand Alcaya's reluctance to have her moved.

'Is she very bad?' I murmured.

'As bad as can be,' Johanna replied.

'Nevertheless, she cannot stay here. It is too dangerous.'

'Father, if she has to move, she may die,' Alcaya pointed out, very gently.

'And if she stays here, she *will* die,' I retorted. 'Forgive me, but there is no choice. If nothing else, she must at least be carried to a hospital. The nearest is Saint-Remezy. It belongs to the Hospitallers.'

'But will they take us all?' Johanna queried, and I had to suppress a surge of impatience. Though I had no wish to frighten her, or her daughter, it seemed to me that none of the women fully appreciated the perils confronting them.

'Listen,' I said, speaking slowly and carefully. 'What I have done here is nothing short of miraculous. And I cannot be sure that our luck will hold. If you do not leave Lazet as quickly as possible, there is no guarantee that you will retain your freedom.'

'But – '

'I *know* that Vitalia is incapable of travelling. I realise how ill she is. So she will go the hospital of Saint-Remezy, while the rest of you establish a home together far away. Perhaps one day she will join you.'

'But Father,' Alcaya protested, speaking as one who wishes to explain something to a dearly beloved child, rather than in tones of passion and outrage, 'I cannot leave my friend. She is my sister in Christ.'

'You have no choice.'

'Forgive me, Father, but that is not so. I may choose to run risks, for the sake of a sister.'

I gritted my teeth. 'A day from now, your sister may not be in a position to appreciate what you have done for her,' I said carefully, conscious always of Babilonia's uncomprehending stare. 'The reward will not be worth the sacrifice.'

'Oh, I think that the reward will be the peace in my own heart.'

342

'Alcaya!' I could no longer restrain myself. 'Have some *sense!*'

'Father – '

'You have no *right* to endanger your other sisters!'

My tone was too angry; it frightened Babilonia, who appealed to her mother in a shrill voice. 'Mama? Mama!'

Johanna went to her quickly, and embraced her, and said to me: 'Alcaya is speaking only for herself. We can each of us make a choice.'

'Yes, yes! Only one of us need stay.' Lovingly, Alcaya smiled at Johanna, at Babilonia. 'I am an old woman; my sisters are young. They have the strength to make a new home, in the way of the Lord.'

Johanna's eyes filled with tears.

'But not without you, Alcaya,' she said, her voice catching.

'With or without me. Dearest, you have sought God's love with a pure heart; He will not desert you now. And I shall pray for you, always.'

'Babilonia needs you.'

'Vitalia needs me, also. And she has no mother to care for her. Forgive me, dearest child. My heart bleeds, but our sister must not be alone.'

Suddenly, I felt as if I did not belong in that room. Like an owl in the desert I watched; I was as a sparrow alone upon the housetop. Excluded. Unremarked.

'Pack up your clothes, now,' I mumbled, conscious that my words went largely unheeded. 'Be ready to leave when I return. I am going to Saint-Remezy, to arrange a bed for Vitalia.'

And that is what I did. Having informed Pons of my intention, I went (on feet that were swifter than a weaver's shuttle) to the hospital of Saint-Remezy, where I spoke to Brother Michael. A glum and weary man, with whom I was distantly acquainted, he sighed at the prospect of succouring another penniless old vagrant, as if the hospital had been established for some nobler, happier purpose. Or perhaps he simply regretted that there was no possibility of a rich bequest.

'But we always have room for a dying woman,' he said to me, surveying a dormitory full of the maimed and the sick. 'After all, she will not be here for very long.'

'She will bring some possessions with her. Naturally, they will fall to the hospital when she dies.'

'Are you sure of that? So often there are relatives who appear at the last moment.'

'There are no relatives.'

With Vitalia's bed thus secured, I returned to the prison, where I was told by an irate Pons that 'the mad girl' had thrown 'some sort of a fit', and would I kindly remove all four women from his guardroom before he kicked them out into the street. As I had fearfully anticipated, the sorrow attendant upon parting from Alcaya had disturbed Babilonia profoundly. I discovered her lying on the floor with red eyes and a bloody face; according to Johanna, she had been pounding her head against the wall.

'She will not leave Alcaya,' my beloved observed, her own voice hoarse with emotion as she raised it above her daughter's rhythmic moaning. 'What are we to do? She will not leave Alcaya, and I cannot leave her.'

'Then Alcaya *must* leave Vitalia.'

'Father, how can I?'

'Listen to me.' I took the stubborn old fool by her arm (God forgive me, but that is how I thought of her, at the time!) and pushed her into the corridor. Then, fixing her with a baleful yet supplicatory eye, in subdued yet forceful accents audible only to ourselves, I presented my case to her.

'Do you trust me, Alcaya?' I said.

'Oh, Father, with my life.'

'Have I cared for you? Have I cherished you all like sisters?'

'You have. Indeed you have.'

'Then will you trust me to look after Vitalia? Will you trust me to attend her, and comfort her? Will you do that for me?'

Her guileless blue gaze seemed to absorb my words, and weigh each according to its merits. I sensed that she was still unconvinced. I sensed that she was searching for another way of describing and explaining to me the depth of her commitment to Vitalia.

So I made my final plea.

'Alcaya,' I said softly, 'you must look after Johanna. You must promise me that. How can I let her go, unless you are there to love and protect her? I beg you. I *entreat* you. Do not abandon her now, just as I am forced to turn away! I cannot – I am not – it is too much bear. It is too much. Alcaya, only grant me this. Please.'

Whether it was on account of my coming loss, or the extent of my fear, or the radiant, tender, sorrowful comprehension that informed Johanna's face, I know not, but tears gathered in my eyes, at that moment. As I wiped them away, I saw that Alcaya, too, was tearful. She took my hand, and nursed it against her cheek like a kitten.

'Oh, my dear son,' she whispered, 'your heart is too full. Lay your burden on me. I will take your love, and I will use it wisely. Your love is my love, Father. Rest your soul, for Johanna will not be alone.'

And suddenly there was peace. There was peace like the peace with which I had been blessed, that morning, on the hillside near Casseras. This time it did not fill me as if I were a cup, or dazzle me like the sun. It touched me as gently as a passing zephyr, and departed again. It warmed my aching heart with a feather-light kiss.

Strengthened, I was nonetheless dazed and speechless. I thought: Christ, are you here? Even today, I cannot tell you if the Holy Spirit came to me then. Perhaps His love was as one with Alcaya's, for her love was pure and true, ardent and selfless, transcending her sex, her sins, and her errors of judgement. She was, I believe, very close to God in her love. Although she was misguided in many things, her love was great. I know this now. I felt it then. I saw why Babilonia was soothed and transformed by Alcaya's love, for it allowed her, perhaps, to taste of that immeasurably greater, deeper, sweeter love which is God's, and His alone.

I am an ignorant and sinful man. I know only that I know nothing. In all the world, there is no one worthy of the Lord, and if His peace passeth all understanding, how could I have hoped to recognise it with my unworthy senses, my stumbling intellect, my sinful heart? Perhaps I was honoured beyond the praise of men and angels. Perhaps I was led astray by weakness and desire. I know not. I cannot say.

But I was comforted with an exultant sorrow – with a yielding strength (I can find no words to describe my sensations) – and found relief when I rested my forehead, briefly, on Alcaya's shoulder. I was obliged to stoop low to accomplish this, and as I did so she embraced me. The smell of her was by no means sweet, but it was not corrupt or fleshly either. Her bones felt as small and brittle as a hen's.

'Take *The Little Flowers*,' she said. 'Read it to Vitalia. I know it by heart now. She will need it more than I.'

Nodding, I signified my assent. Then we went back into the guardroom without exchanging another word. And it was she who subsequently took charge of the evacuation, deciding what should be carried by whom. At her gentle bidding, I went to find the men who would carry Vitalia.

I was still somewhat disoriented, you see, and distracted by questions loftier than the disposition of luggage. I was still drunk with love.

In the gaoler's kitchen, where the familiars, when not on duty, were now obliged to congregate, I found two men willing to hurry the women on their way – if only because they were eager to reclaim their guardroom. No more than two men were needed, for Vitalia was as light and insubstantial as dry grass; we wrapped her in a blanket, and put her on another blanket, which was then employed as a sort of litter. With great difficulty she was carried downstairs, while I walked ahead of her bearing the brazier, and her friends walked behind with their clothes, pots, books, blankets and suchlike. The procession was greeted by many wondering remarks from both staff and prisoners. You will not often see an inquisitor of heretical depravity toting someone else's luggage; be assured, it is a sight worthy of comment.

We went first to Saint-Remezy. Here a pallet had been prepared to receive the sick woman, among scenes of such misery, such blood and pus and filth, such groans and stenches, that we all turned pale, men and women alike. On my previous visit, I had not been introduced to that part of the hospital reserved for the dying. I had not realised that it was a place without hope. I have seen leprosaries more cheerful; catacombs less crowded. The smoky air seemed to taste like rotting flesh.

'We cannot leave her here,' Johanna muttered, too shocked to be discreet. 'Bernard, we cannot leave her here.'

'We must,' I said desperately. 'Look, her bed is in an alcove. It lies apart from the others. And I shall visit her often.'

'Dearest, Vitalia will not suffer.' To my surprise, it was Alcaya who spoke. She dropped one of her bags, so that she might put an arm around Babilonia. 'The world means nothing to her now. Her eyes are fixed on the Eternal Light. She is deaf to this tower of Babel. All she needs is a friend to hold her hand, and feed her broth.'

Looking at Vitalia, I saw that she was indeed barely conscious, and beyond caring about her fate. Nevertheless, it seemed horrible that she should meet her Maker in such surroundings, redolent of death and disease. And how could I possibly ensure that I would be present to bid her goodbye, when she set out on her final journey?

Tormented by such questions, I might have reconsidered my plans then and there, if we had not been approached by a brother who introduced himself as Leo. Smiling and gentle, he touched Vitalia's face, and called her 'my daughter'. He spoke to her as if she could hear him. He spoke to her as if she were more important than any of us.

'My daughter,' he said, 'you are welcome. The Lord is with

you. His angels walk among us, here; I have seen them in the night. Have no fear, my weary soul. I shall pray with you, and you will find peace.'

I knew then that she had come to a safe harbour.

Let me say that in Brother Leo, the hospital of Saint-Remezy possesses a priceless jewel. I spoke to him as the women said goodbye to their friend (and I shall pass over this leavetaking, for it was painful beyond words); he told me that he loved to tend the dying, for they were so close to God. 'It is an honour,' he insisted. 'An honour. Every day, I feel blessed.' To feel blessed amidst such pain, such despair, requires a faith to move mountains; it shamed me to witness his contentment and his tranquil joy, though I also believe that he was a man of – how shall I put it? – limited intelligence. A simple man, but devout. And assured of salvation. Oh yes, there can be no doubt of that. Sometimes, he confessed, he would have to walk outside and scream and rant – but even Christ, after all, prayed to God that the cup might pass from Him.

When we finally departed, I asked Brother Leo for his blessing (much to his surprise), and received it in great humility of spirit. Even now, I think of him often. May the Lord deal bountifully with him, for he is truly a pearl of great price.

But I must proceed with my narrative. Red-eyed and sobbing, the three women followed me to the Bishop's palace, where I was expecting to find four horses saddled and waiting. In this, however, I was unduly optimistic. Instead of being escorted to the stables, my party was brought to Bishop Anselm's audience room; here we found, not only the Bishop, but the Seneschal, Prior Hugues and Pierre-Julien. I knew at once that this gathering boded ill. There was about it the demeanour of a tribunal. There were even soldiers posted at the door. And the Bishop's notary was present, sitting with a quill in his hand. He was, perhaps, the most ominous sight of all.

You must strive to picture the assembly, for it was to have

far-reaching consequences. The Bishop, coruscating with gem-stones, occupied the largest and most beautiful chair. He seemed preoccupied with bodily matters, occasionally belching, or stroking his belly, or gripping the bridge of his nose between a thumb and forefinger as he winced. If I am not mistaken, he was suffering from the effects of too much wine. Certainly he displayed an uncharacteristically sullen temper which appeared to support this premise.

Prior Hugues was manifestly ill at ease. Though his expression was impassive in a doughy sort of way, his hands were never still, moving from his knees to his belt to the arms of his chair. Pierre-Julien sat with his head thrown back and his chin jutting forward, in an attitude doubtless intended to impress me as indomitable. Only Roger Descalquencs was standing, and he alone was calm – though perhaps unusually alert.

Faced with such an array of jewellery and weapons and lowering, formidable looks, the women acquitted themselves with a great deal of courage. Babilonia, though she buried her face in her mother's bosom, did not scream or run mad. Alcaya surveyed the men before her with innocent blue eyes, exhibiting no fear, but only intense and respectful interest. Johanna was afraid. I deduced this from her bloodless complexion, and the compression of her soft lips. Nevertheless, pride kept her back straight, and her shoulders squared. From her considerable height, she was able to look down her nose at Bishop Anselm and Pierre-Julien.

She was even able to meet the Seneschal's eye with a level gaze.

'Ah. Brother Bernard.' Wearily, the Bishop pronounced my name as I entered the room; he spoke as if it were a considerable effort to remember who I was, and why I was present. The women he dismissed with a single glance, as too unimportant to acknowledge. 'At last we can proceed. Brother Pierre-Julien?'

Pierre-Julien cleared his throat. 'Bernard Peyre de Prouille,' he said, in a squeaky voice, 'you are hereby charged as a heretical believer, and a concealer and hider of heretics, on the basis of public infamy.'

'*What?*'

'Do you swear upon the Holy Gospels to tell the truth, the whole truth, and nothing but the truth in regard to the crime of heresy?'

Speechless, I regarded the Gospels presented to me by Roger Descalquencs. Limply, I allowed him to place my hand upon it. Shock had deprived me of my faculties (foolishly, perhaps, I had not anticipated such a development), and I swore my oath without conscious collaboration, as if my will had departed. But then my wandering gaze found the Prior, and I saw in his eye a discomfort which roused me.

'Father!' I exclaimed. 'What *is* this nonsense?'

'How do you plead?' This time, Pierre-Julien's voice was stronger and harsher. He would not be deflected. 'How do you plead, Brother Bernard?'

I was on the point of shouting 'Not guilty!' when my wits were suddenly restored, and I realised that I had very nearly fallen into a trap. You see, in the *ordo juris* of inquisition, a defendant can only be charged formally if he has either confessed or been defamed. If he has been defamed, and that by trustworthy citizens, his judge must offer up proof of infamy before requiring him to plead. And if he pleads not guilty, proof of his guilt must then be forthcoming.

However, since the *Liber sextus* of Boniface VIII, judges have been permitted to proceed without establishing infamy if the defendant does not object. Very nearly, I had neglected to do so.

But I remembered my rights before the fatal plea was announced and, turning to Pierre-Julien, said: 'Where is the public infamy? What are the charges?'

'You ask me what the charges are? When you come before us with these heretics, whose escape you were effecting?'

'*Escape?*' I cried. 'You gave your permission!'

350

'Which you secured through lies and trickery,' the Seneschal broke in. I looked up, and saw an old friend who was a stranger: a man whose small, dark eyes surveyed me coolly, as implacable as stones. 'You spoke of a letter from Jean de Beune. No letter arrived from Carcassonne yesterday. No letter has come from there in a week, and Pons has confirmed this. Your plans are thwarted.'

It occurred to me, then, that the Seneschal was my real enemy. If Pierre-Julien was exposed, then he too was threatened. And he was a strong man, cunning, a fighter accustomed to battles both on and off the field. Doubtless Pierre-Julien had fled to seek his help at the first opportunity; doubtless it was Roger Descalquencs who had first asked of my falsified letter: 'Is it genuine?' And while I wasted time at the hospital, Roger had quickly established that my letter was not, in fact, what I had professed it to be.

I stared at him, and for the first time felt something like fear.

'My lord,' I said, swinging around to face the Bishop, 'these charges are the result of a conspiracy between the Inquisitor and the Seneschal. They are unfounded. Brother Pierre-Julien admitted to me, this very morning, that he and the Seneschal destroyed parts of inquisitorial registers which implicated their families as heretical – '

But the Bishop raised his hand. 'Brother Pierre-Julien claims differently,' he said. 'Brother Pierre-Julien claims that you came to him threatening to expose his heredity as tainted, unless he released the women who stand before us. He claims that you fabricated a letter in which false accusations were made concerning his family. In his initial despair, he bowed to your wishes. But he soon realised that he was imperilling his soul by doing so.'

'My lord, if you consult the registers, you will see that they are damaged – ' I began. At which point Pierre-Julien interrupted me, gabbling something to the effect that these registers had been mutilated when recovered from Raymond's possession.

'Brother Bernard is attacking me in order to defend himself!' the vile man finished. 'But it can be proven that he is a believer, a concealer and a hider – '

'Prove it, then!' I expostulated. 'Where is your proof? What are the charges? And what are you doing here – ' I pointed to the Seneschal ' – and you, Father Hugues, if this is a formal hearing of the tribunal?'

'They are here as impartial observers,' Pierre-Julien supplied. 'As to the proof, it stands here before us, in female form. *These* are the heretics whom you have sought to conceal and defend!'

Whereupon he indicated the three women. Johanna uttered a low moan, and I was distracted, for an instant, as I sought to reassure her with a glance. I was therefore unable to quell Alcaya as she stepped forward. In her cheerful, undaunted way she said: 'Oh, no, Father. We are not heretics.' And the whole assembly stared at her in surprise.

No one had anticipated such boldness from a woman. No one could believe her audacity. It was the Bishop who, upon recovering, bade her irritably to remain silent – and like a good daughter of the Church, she obeyed his command.

Consequently, I was obliged to defend her claim myself.

'They are not heretics,' I insisted. 'They have been neither charged nor defamed. Therefore I cannot be accused of concealing them.'

'They *have* been defamed,' Pierre-Julien replied. 'Jean-Pierre has accused them of sorcery, and plotting against the Holy Office.'

'His testimony has not been confirmed.'

'He confirmed it yesterday.'

'It was extracted under torture.'

There is nothing wrong with that, Brother Bernard,' the Seneschal remarked. Whereupon I turned on him.

'Impartial observers have no right to comment on an inquisition!' I snapped. 'If you open your mouth again, you will be expelled from this assembly! My lord, hear me out.' Once again I addressed the Bishop. 'Last night, Jordan Sicre, one of the familiars presumed to have been murdered alongside Father Augustin, confessed that he had arranged this assassination at the behest of Raymond Donatus. No mention was made of the women you see here. They had nothing to do with Father Augustin's death.'

'Jean-Pierre's testimony concerned the death of Raymond Donatus not Father Augustin,' Pierre-Julien interjected.

'But the two are linked! My lord, Raymond had Father Augustin killed because Father Augustin was consulting old registers. And Raymond was using these registers to extract money from people with heretical antecedents. Whoever killed Raymond was perhaps sick of paying, and frightened of being exposed – '

'As a heretic?' said the Bishop.

'Or as a descendant of heretics.'

'Then these women are still implicated,' the Bishop declared. 'Their motive is unimportant.'

'My lord – '

'You see how he defends them!' Pierre-Julien suddenly cried. 'He himself is charged, yet he seeks to secure their safety before his!'

'My safety is assured,' I rejoined. 'If they are cleared, I am cleared, for who can believe that I am a heretic? Who? Who can possibly defame me? Father, you know that I am a good Catholic.' And I appealed to the Prior, who was so old a friend, and so well acquainted with the furnishings of my heart. 'You must know that this is nonsense.'

But the Prior shifted uneasily in his chair. 'I know nothing,' he murmured. 'There is other evidence ...'

'What? What evidence?'

'Pierre Olieu's treatise on poverty!' Pierre-Julien exclaimed. 'Do you deny that this unholy book is to be found in your cell?'

Now it became apparent to me, at this juncture, that I had been investigated. My cell had been searched; questions, perhaps, had been asked. And I realised that an inquiry into my orthodoxy must have been made while I was in Casseras.

It no longer surprised me that Pierre-Julien had been 'too busy' to interview Jordan Sicre. Without question he had been occupied with weightier matters: namely, the blackening of my reputation.

'There are books concerned with the invocation of demons in *your* cell, Brother Pierre-Julien,' I said, remaining outwardly calm, though inwardly I trembled. 'No one, however, assumes that you are engaged in such practices.'

'The works of Pierre Olieu have been condemned as heretical.'

'Some of his *ideas* have been condemned – not all of his work. Besides, you will find this book in the library of the Franciscans.'

'And in the hands of many Beguines.'

'True. That is why I intended to burn it. I do not agree with its arguments.'

'Indeed?' Pierre-Julien's tone was sceptical. 'Then why was the book in your cell, Brother? Was it given to you?'

'I confiscated it.'

'From whom?'

Knowing that the truth would further condemn Alcaya, I prevaricated. 'From a misguided soul,' I said.

'From a heretic? From the heretic you allowed to escape, not long ago, when you let him walk away from the priory unchallenged?'

Mystified, I glanced at Prior Hugues. He was looking down at his hands.

'Heretic?' I said. 'What heretic?'

'Brother Thomas claims that he brought to your attention a heretic who was begging at the gate of the priory.' Pierre-Julien leaned forward. 'He claims that you pursued the man. But according to Pons, you did not have him arrested, charged or imprisoned. You allowed him to escape.'

'Because he was not a heretic.' Doubtless you will have

identified the 'heretic' of this description; I was eager to protect his anonymity, while at the same time protecting myself. 'He was a familiar, disguised as a heretic.'

'A *familiar*?' said Pierre-Julien, scornfully. 'And who is this familiar, pray? Where can we find him?

'You cannot find him. I cannot find him. He is a spy, and his life would be worth nothing if it became generally known that he had frequent intercourse with an inquisitor of heretical depravity.' Conscious of how inadequate an explanation this appeared to be, I tried to make it more convincing. 'It was he who informed me of Jordan Sicre's whereabouts. He had been spying for me in Catalonia, and knew Jordan from a previous imprisonment. He took a great risk coming here. Then he left, and ... in all honesty, I know only that he will be in Alet-les-Bains eighteen months from now.'

There was a short silence as the gathering digested this information. Prior Hugues looked bewildered; the Bishop, confused; the Seneschal, frankly unimpressed. 'Eighteen months,' he murmured to no one in particular. 'How convenient.'

'Very convenient,' Pierre-Julien agreed. 'And may we have the name of this mysterious confederate?'

'It will do you no good. He goes by many names.'

'Then give us all of them.'

I hesitated. Truly, I had no wish to involve my valued familiar. But knowing that a failure to comply might very well be regarded as contumacy, I reluctantly surrendered the names. After all, it was an act carried out in the man's defence; better that he be publically identified as a servant of the Holy Office than condemned as a heretic.

I also furnished Pierre-Julien with an *effictio*, and urged him to proceed carefully if he intended to question the elusive 'S' as a witness.

'If you must detain this fellow, tell no one the reason,' I said. 'He must be arrested as a Perfect, not a spy.'

'He is a *Perfect*?'

'He pretends to be a Perfect.'

'And he gave you the treatise on poverty?'

'Of course not. Why would a Cathar Perfect possess a book by Pierre Jean Olieu?'

'Aha! So you admit that he *is* a Perfect!'

'Augh!' I was losing patience. 'Father Hugues, this foolishness has gone far enough. You must know that the charges are without foundation. Will you act as my compurgator? You will be one of many.'

The Prior fixed me with a sombre gaze. For a short time he was silent. Then he frowned, and sighed, and said obliquely: 'Bernard, I know where this treatise came from. You told me, remember? And I know where your passions have taken you.' As I stared at him, horrified, he added: 'Perhaps they have taken you farther than I thought. I did warn you, Bernard. We spoke of this at length.'

'Have you – ?'

'No. I have not broken the seal of confession. I have only expressed my doubts.'

'Your *doubts*?' I was furious. No – that term insufficiently conveys my anger. I was transported with rage. I was incensed. I could have killed him. 'How *dare* you! How *dare* you even *consider* passing judgement on me, you brainless, bulbous, spineless illiterate? What makes you think that you have the capacity to comprehend anything I say or do?'

'Brother – '

'And to think that I voted you in! So you could betray me to a man with a head full of wet wool! You will answer for this, Hugues – you will answer before God and the Grand Master!'

'You have always been wayward!' the Prior shouted. 'In the matter of Durand de Saint Pourcain and his work – '

'Oh, are you *mad*? Durand de Saint Pourcain! A disagreement about definitions!'

'You can be unorthodox! Do not deny it!'

'I deny it *utterly*!'

'And that is your plea?' Pierre-Julien suddenly remarked. 'Shall we enter a plea of not guilty, Brother Bernard?'

I stared at him, momentarily confused. Then I saw the notary waiting, and spat out my reply.

'Not guilty! Yes, I am not guilty! And there are others who will act as compurgators for me! Inquisitors! Priors! Canons! I am not entirely friendless, and I shall appeal to the Pope if necessary! The whole *world* will hear of this corrupt conjuration!'

I said as much, but already I knew that these were empty threats. To rally such supporters would take time, and my time was limited. While letters were written and dispatched, my beloved would be in acute danger; Pierre-Julien would employ the rack without compunction, I felt sure. So it was that, while prophesying damnation for my enemies, I simultaneously applied my powers of reasoning to the possibilities of escape.

I reviewed those weapons still left to me, and asked myself how they could be employed.

'What is your name, woman?' Pierre-Julien was saying. And I heard Alcaya reply that her name was Alcaya de Rasiers.

'Alcaya de Rasiers, you are charged with the crime of contumacious heresy. Do you swear on the Holy Gospels to tell the truth, the whole truth, and nothing but the truth in regard to the crime of heresy?'

'Alcaya,' I interrupted, 'you must request time for consideration. You must demand proof of infamy.'

'Quiet!' The Seneschal pushed me with an abrupt, threatening movement. 'Father Pierre-Julien is finished with you.'

'Proof of infamy?' Alcaya said, clearly puzzled. But I was not able to clarify this concept for her, because Pierre-Julien thrust the Scriptures under her nose, and ordered her to swear.

'Swear!' he said. 'Or are you a heretic, and afraid to swear?'

'No. I will gladly swear, though I would never lie.'

'Then swear.'

She did so, smiling at the sacred text, and I was afraid. For I knew that, of all the women, it was Alcaya who had strayed most from the path of orthodoxy during her life. And I knew that she would not strive to conceal this fact from her tormentors.

'Alcaya de Rasiers,' Pierre-Julien continued, 'have you ever heard anyone teaching and affirming that Christ and His apostles possessed nothing, either personally or in common?'

'Alcaya,' I said quickly, before she could answer and condemn herself with her own tongue, 'you must request time for consideration. You must demand proof of infamy.'

'Be quiet!' This time the Seneschal struck me on the head with his hand, and I rounded on him, knocking his arm back.

'Touch me again,' I warned, 'and you will suffer for it.'

Roger's eyes glinted. 'Is that so?' he said, smiling a terrible smile. Then Pierre-Julien requested that I be removed from the chamber, and Roger professed himself delighted to be the agent of my removal. Naturally, I was keen to discover my destination; naturally, I appealed to the Prior for help. But the Seneschal forcibly prevented me from doing this, seizing my arms in an attempt to expel me from the room.

What would you have done? Do you condemn me for stamping on his foot, or, as his grip slackened, driving my elbow into his ribcage? Please recall that I had been most cruelly betrayed by this man, whom I had regarded for so long as a friend. Please recall that we were both of us locked in mortal combat, which was bound to manifest itself in acts of physical violence.

Be that as it may, I attacked him, and was attacked in return. Of course I could not hope to triumph. Though taller than the Seneschal, I was feebler, and untrained in the art of war. Furthermore, I had no sergeants at my back to support me. As Roger staggered away, holding his chest, the two soldiers at the door advanced in a single movement, and showered me with blows. Shielding my head with my arms, I fell to my knees, vaguely conscious of Johanna's horrified protests, before being propelled onto my face by a kick between the shoulders.

I recollect that I lay prone, flinching in preparation for the next punch. Only gradually did it become apparent that this punch had been withheld. Slowly, the ringing in my ears faded; I began to hear other sounds – cries, screams, calls for assistance. I sat up. Through tears of pain I saw an altercation taking place. I saw the Seneschal fending off Babilonia, who was clawing and biting like a wild animal, as the sergeants rushed to his rescue. One of them brought his staff down across her back, so that she buckled. Then Alcaya flung herself between the girl and the weapon, and Johanna flung herself on the soldier, and Pierre-Julien dived behind a chair. What followed is unclear to me, now, for I believe that the knock which I subsequently received to my temple drove the memory out of my mind. All I know is that, still crippled by injury, I attempted to pull Johanna out of the fray.

Whereupon I saw stars, and nothing else for a brief period.

I am told that I was felled by the same staff already used against Babilonia. I am also told that Johanna, thinking me dead at least for an instant, was so piercingly heartfelt in her lamentations that she brought the entire room to a standstill. Everyone faltered. The sergeants lowered their weapons. Nervously, the Seneschal felt for a pulse, while Alcaya began to pray. Then I groggily regained consciousness, and in a muted fashion it was decided that the assembly should perhaps disperse, for the present.

So it was that I found myself in the prison guardroom, without in the least knowing how it had come to pass.

Deliverance to the captives

I slept and woke, slept and woke. The first time I woke, with an aching head, I stumbled to the door and demanded an explanation: why was I immured in such inhospitable surroundings? For awhile no one responded. Then I heard Pons' voice from the corridor; he told me that I was an obdurate heretic, and a danger to others. He might have said more, but I have no memory of it. Overcome with dizziness, I returned to bed.

When I woke again, my mind was clearer. I knew where I was, and why; from the tolling of bells, I deduced that it was Sext, and wondered what might have occurred during the time that had elapsed since my injury. I was very, very anxious about Johanna. I was also thirsty, and stiff, and sore. My back hurt when I breathed.

Rising with some difficulty, I pounded on the door until Pons came.

'What is it?' he growled.

'I need wine. I am in pain. Fetch Brother Amiel, from the priory.'

There was a pause. Then he said: 'I must ask Father Pierre-Julien.'

'You will do as I bid you!'

'Not any more, Father. I must ask Father Pierre-Julien.'

Whereupon he left me, and it was thenceforth apparent that my prospects were dim. How was I to appeal to the Pope, if my appeal for the assistance of an infirmarian was so grudgingly received? Doubtless my fate would be scorn, isolation, neglect. As for my few friends, friendship must be strong indeed if it is to withstand the disapproval of the Holy Office.

Sitting on the bed, which formerly had been occupied by Vitalia, I considered my alternatives. They were few and unpalatable, for it was quite clear to me that if I were not to remain in prison, persecuted by Pierre-Julien and tormented by my fears for Johanna, I would have to escape. The very thought of such an action appalled me: how was it to be effected? The walls were thick; there were guards at the gate; the door of the guardroom was locked, and only Pons possessed a key. Then it occurred to me that I would have to rescue the women also, and my heart quailed. Truly, it seemed an impossible task. If they were incarcerated downstairs, it would be easy enough to release them, because the doors of the *murus largus* cells were barred from the outside. But my own door, as I said, was locked – and beyond the prison walls, the city offered no haven for a fleeing heretic.

Still, it behoved me to do what I could. It behoved me, at least, to ascertain Johanna's whereabouts.

'Pons!' I shouted. 'Pons!'

No one answered. But I persevered until the gaoler's wife, puffing and snorting, told me that her husband had gone to find Father Pierre-Julien.

'What do you want *now*?' she said.

'Those women. If they are not in here with me, where are they?'

'Downstairs, of course.'

'In the *murus largus*?'

'They are sharing a cell.'

'And does the cell have a window?'

'No it does *not*!' She seemed to derive some satisfaction from telling me this. 'It is at the southern end, near the staircase. No windows. Very damp. And your friends are eating like the rest of the prisoners.'

Clearly, my demand that the women be fed from her table had caused her great offence. Perhaps, on reflection, I had been unwise to ask it of her. Perhaps, if she was now my foe, I had only myself to blame.

Listening to the sound of her shuffling footsteps as she withdrew, I constructed in my mind a plan of the prison, and realised that Johanna was practically underneath me. The floor, however, was thick and well sealed; it offered no chink, no crack, through which I might have passed a note, or whispered a message. Not that I possessed the means of writing a note. I had no pen – no parchment. If I was to appeal to my influential friends, I would require the appropriate equipment. And who would dare bring it to me?

Durand, I thought. Durand would bring it to me.

I was reflecting upon this when Brother Amiel arrived, courtesy of Pierre-Julien.

'Here is your bonesetter,' Pons declared, jingling his keys. Then he opened the door, pushed Brother Amiel into the room, closed the door again, and locked it. 'If you need me, call me,' he said. 'I will be in the kitchen, just down the corridor.'

Brother Amiel made a wry face as the fading rattle of keys signalled Pons' departure. He surveyed the entire room, with evident disapprobation, before his gaze finally settled on me. Whereupon his luxuriant eyebrows rose almost to the line of his scalp.

'So,' he said, 'I see that someone has used you very ill, Brother Bernard.'

'Very ill.'

'Where is the pain?'

I told him, and he examined me for broken bones. Finding none, he seemed to lose interest; he said that the bruises would fade, and the swelling subside. He gave me a poultice of linen and paste, which he produced from a leather bag. 'Hyssop, wormwood, comfrey,' he declared. 'Some marjoram. And a draught for the pain, but it should be heated. Will the gaoler warm it for you?'

'I should think not.'

'Hold it under your clothes then. The heat of your body may suffice.' Placing in my hand a corked earthenware bottle, he said that he would wait until I had consumed the draught. 'They say that you are a heretic,' he added. 'Is it true?'

'No.'

'It seems unlikely. I said as much to Brother Pierre-Julien.'

'When?'

'Yesterday morning. He spoke to all the brethren, one by one. Asking about you.' Amiel's tone was somewhat detached; he had always impressed me as a man more interested in the dead than the living. 'He inquired about my hare.'

'Your hare?'

'My embalmed hare.'

'Oh.' I could imagine. 'You should be cautious,' I advised. 'He has odd ideas about dead animals.'

'What?'

'He sees sorcery everywhere. Be on your guard. He is not a rational person.'

Brother Amiel, however, was too wise, or perhaps too indifferent, to pursue this subject. I could not blame him; denigrating an inquisitor on Holy Office premises is probably best avoided. He inquired as to the colour of my urine, and observed that the guardroom was rather cold. I asked him if his draught would make me sleepy. He replied that it would.

'Then I had rather not drink it,' was my response. 'I need my wits about me, Brother. I have letters to write.'

'So be it.' With a gesture indicating that he relinquished all responsibility for my wellbeing, Amiel restored the draught to his leather bag. 'You should rest now. If there is bleeding, or fever, I should be summoned. But I can do nothing more for you at present – '

'Wait. There is *one* thing you can do. You can find Durand Fogasset, and tell him that I need to write some letters.'

'Durand Fogasset?'

'He is a notary. He works next door, where I used to work. A young man, untidy looking, with lots of black hair falling into his eyes. Usually covered with ink-stains. He should be in the scriptorium ... or he might be with Father Pierre-Julien. If he is, leave a message with one of the familiars.'

'Very well. And you say that you want him to write some letters for you?'

'I want him to deliver some letters for me. I want him to bring me a pen and parchment. Ink.'

Brother Amiel seemed to regard this as a logical request. He assured me that he would find Durand Fogasset. Then, having bade me farewell, he summoned Pons, who unlocked the door for him; without exchanging a single word, the two men retired, leaving me alone once again.

But this time, at least, I had the poultice to comfort me. It was cool and damp, and I pressed it gratefully to my throbbing temples. The smell of herbs seemed to clear my clouded mind.

Suddenly I remembered Lothaire Carbonel, whose father had been an unrepentant heretic.

He was a rich man, Lothaire, with a secret shared only by me, now that Raymond Donatus was dead. I wondered how much a rich man would sacrifice to keep so shameful a secret to himself. As far as I could recollect, Lothaire proudly maintained a stable of horses. Doubtless his kitchens would be well supplied. And surely he would not miss one or two items of clothing: a cloak, perhaps ... boots ... a short tunic ...

With a good horse, and the advantage of surprise, it might be possible to outpace any pursuer. But that still left unsolved the problem of keys, and guards. The morning shift was by no means overmanned, thanks to the strictures of the inquisitorial budget; aside from the two guards stationed inside the prison entrance, there were two who patrolled the interior of the building as a pair, and one whose task was to prohibit entry into headquarters through the outer door. The familiars so far assigned to this last duty had demonstrated a certain laxity, at least with regard to the exclusion of female trespassers ... and in any case, I thought, with growing excitement, the guard will not be there. Brother Lucius always arrives at dawn, and he will be in the scriptorium. He will not see us, because the door from the prison is on the ground floor of headquarters.

I considered this door. It was always locked at night, but was unlocked in the morning, with the arrival of Brother Lucius. Undoubtedly, a dawn departure would eliminate all manner of difficulties. Nevertheless, my heart sank as I realised that there remained the problem of the guardroom. Pons had the keys to the guardroom. He never surrendered them. If I were to escape, I would have to secure those keys, and what chance had I of accomplishing such a manoeuvre? It could only be done by attacking him. Once overpowered, he could perhaps be restrained, gagged, even locked up. His wife and children would be in bed, and I could easily avoid passing their quarters because the staircase practically abutted the guardroom door. Only one flight down lay Johanna's cell, and from there it was another flight down before one reached the entrance to headquarters. If I could avoid the patrol, lead my companions out through the stables, and escape on horses donated by Lothaire Carbonel – was this an impossible plan?

Not impossible, perhaps, but impracticable. Though somewhat stout, Pons was nimble enough, and no weakling. Furthermore, he often carried a knife. If called from his bed he might not be armed, but even so we were well matched; it was quite probable that *I* would be the one overpowered. And the scuffle would, in any case, surely rouse his family. One does not wrestle a man to the ground without occasioning some noise.

I fretted over this fact, and over the movements of the patrol, until Durand arrived. I heard him talking to Pons some time before I saw him; the gaoler made some brusque inquiries, but appeared to be convinced by Durand's murmured response.

(I could distinguish the tone of these remarks, if not their content, because both men were conversing in the kitchen.) In any event, the keys were produced, and the guardroom door was unlocked. When Durand crossed the threshold, I was surprised by the grateful warmth, by the relief and the joy, that his appearance aroused in me.

He was carrying several books as well as a sheaf of parchment. He looked pale.

'I brought some registers,' he remarked, glancing sideways as Pons, with noisy manifestions of discontent, closed and locked the door behind him. 'There are one or two things I want to clarify.'

'Indeed?' I could not imagine what, and was puzzled by his stilted delivery. But I soon understood, for when he thrust a register into my hands, and let it fall open, I saw a long, thin, wickedly sharp knife tucked between its pages. I recognised it as the knife that I normally employed for sharpening quills.

'Here, you see?' He was still looking at the door. 'I thought that you might know what to do.'

I was almost too shocked to speak. But at last I found my voice again.

'Durand, you . . . this does not concern you,' I said, choosing my words with care. 'Leave it be. Do not trouble yourself.'

'But it does concern me. It should be fixed.'

'Not by you, my friend. Now leave it.'

'Very well. I *shall* leave it.' Removing the knife from its hiding place, he moved towards the bed from which I had risen to greet him, and thrust the weapon under a blanket.

Seizing his arm, I drew him towards me.

'Take it back,' I breathed, with my lips to his ear. 'You will be implicated.'

He shook his head. 'If they ask me,' he responded, in the faintest of whispers, 'I shall say: yes, I gave him a knife to sharpen his quills. Why not?' Then, as if conscious of an unseen audience, he raised his voice again. 'Father Amiel was lucky to find me,' he announced, gazing intently into my face. 'I was at work all morning with Father Pierre-Julien, who was interrogating one of your lady friends. The older one. Alcaya.' I gasped, and he hastily assured me that the interview had not taken place in the lower dunjon. 'There was no need. She was very frank. She talked about Montpellier, and the book by Pierre Olieu, and ... and other things. Father, she was ... Father Pierre-Julien was very happy.'

This, I knew, was a warning. If Pierre-Julien was happy, then Alcaya must have condemned herself, in his eyes, as a heretic. And if Alcaya was condemned as a heretic, then I could be condemned as a hider and concealer of heretics.

'I must write some letters,' I declared, conscious of passing time. 'Will you wait, and deliver them for me? I shall not detain you for long.'

Durand assented; he showed me what he had brought in the way of writing materials. It seemed to me prudent that my letter to Lothaire should be concealed among others, so that the blame for my escape, if it occurred, would not fall upon one person, but upon many. Therefore I addressed appeals to the Dean of St Polycarpe, and to the Royal Steward of Confiscations, and to the inquisitors of Carcassonne and Toulouse. I asked if they would act for me as compurgators, in the knowledge that I was a man of unassailable piety, and orthodox belief. I stressed the need for cooperation, lest Pierre-Julien be encouraged to attack an ever-widening circle of Christ's good and faithful servants. I mentioned, and quoted from, the Scriptures.

Fortunately, I was not obliged to write every plea myself. Durand – who had brought with him several quills, and enough ink to drown a garrison – copied my first letter for me, amending only names and places (for each letter was identical in its phrasing). We sat head to head at the guards' table, scribbling away furiously, not daring to sharpen our quills. Twice we were interrupted by Pons, who evidently regarded the prolonged silence in my room as highly suspicious; our monkish industry, however, seemed to reassure him. On both occasions, he withdrew without comment.

Apart from a raised eyebrow, Durand also made no remark. He simply glanced at me, and smiled, and resumed his copying.

I wish to observe here that Durand, while slower than Raymond, could boast a truly exquisite script when circumstances allowed him to employ it. Odd that such an ungainly, dishevelled youth was able to produce such clean, graceful, harmonious calligraphy. But perhaps his writing was a reflection of his soul. For I have reason to believe that, beneath his somewhat dissolute habits and shambling appearance, lay a solid core of incorruptible virtue.

He was, in his very essence, a charitable man.

Of course, I say this now after long days of reflection; it was far from my thoughts at the time. At the time, I was preoccupied with my letter to Lothaire Carbonel. I knew that he could read, but only the vulgar tongue: he was not truly literate. Therefore I was obliged to compose my missive in Occitan, using simple words, as if addressing a child. Succinctly I informed Lothaire that I had found his father's name in the records of the Holy Office; that if he wished to retain his position, his property, and his children's good name, he must supply me with four saddled horses, a tunic, cloak, boots, bread, wine and cheese, to be transferred into my care outside the entrance to the Holy Office stables at dawn the following day. I added that, as proof of my good faith (for I was anxious to secure his unquestioning obedience), I would present him with the aforesaid records implicating his father, to dispose of as he pleased.

For it had occurred to me that Brother Lucius would present no problems. Through some oversight – or perhaps because no one could envisage my having the opportunity to use them – I still carried my keys to the record chests. If I was to deviate slightly from my course, and visit the scriptorium on my way out of the Holy Office, Brother Lucius could not prevent me from taking a register. He was so small and meek, and so obedient; if I told him that I had been released from prison, he would never suspect that I was lying. Why should he, if I had in my possession the requisite keys? Perhaps (and here my conscience smote me, somewhat) he would be subject to rigorous inquiry if the register's absence was ever noticed. But I doubted very much that he would fall under even the mildest suspicion of concealing a heretic. And if he kept his mouth shut – silence being his habit, after all – there was little chance that his lapse would be discovered.

Consequently, I made my aforementioned promise regarding the register, and underlined it for emphasis. Then I folded the letter carefully, until it was small enough to fit into the palm of my hand. Finally, I wrote Lothaire's name on it.

'Take this first,' I said, pointing to the name, and waiting until Durand nodded. Having received his confirmation, I tucked the document into the neck of his tunic, so that it fell down between his breast and the dull green wool that covered him. 'Do you know where to go?'

'Yes, Father.'

'You must go to him directly, and wait for a reply. Ask him: is it yes or no? Then find a way of telling me.'

'Yes, Father.'

'Perhaps you will find a seal on my desk. If these letters are sealed, it would make me happier.'

Again Durand nodded. There was nothing else to say – not, at least, within the gaoler's hearing. We rose together, as if in response to a silent bell, and the notary placed most of my correspondence (excepting that all-important letter to Lothaire Carbonel) between the pages of a register. For an instant he seemed to study me, looking up from beneath his straggling hair. Then he said: 'Go well' – in Latin.

I replied in the same tongue, as if intoning a prayer, 'May God bless you, my dear friend – and be careful'. We embraced each other quickly, but with fervour. I noticed that he smelled rather strongly of wine.

When I released him, he gathered up his books and quills

369

and parchment, and called for Pons. We said nothing as we listened to the approaching jingle of keys; perhaps our hearts were too full. But before he left the room, I said to him: 'Is your gut still troubling you, my son? I hope it does not prove a permanent impediment to your work here'. And he grinned at me over his shoulder.

That was the last I ever saw of him.

St Augustin spoke of friendship as one who has known such a blessing in its purest form. 'We taught each other and learned from each other,' he wrote of his friends. 'When some of us were absent we longed for them almost painfully, and welcomed them joyfully on their return. With these and similar signs the love of friends can pass from heart to heart, through facial expression, words and glances and a thousand friendly gestures. They were like sparks that set our souls on fire, and fused the many into one.'

What gesture could be more friendly than saving a friend's life? I know now, too late, that Durand was my true friend. I believe that we might have been friends as Tully defined the term and as Cicero celebrated it. But the notary's loyal affection was so restrained and retiring, such a modest and delicate flower, that I had all but trodden it underfoot. Dazzled by the flaming passion that I shared with Johanna de Caussade, I had not, at first, recognised Durand's quieter, cooler, calmer goodwill.

A gift like that is one of God's greatest blessings: greater, as Cicero says, than fire and water. I treasure the memory of Durand's friendship. I hold it close to my heart.

The grace of the Lord Jesus Christ, and the love of God, and the communion of the Holy Ghost be with him.

The rest of the day passed very slowly. I spent it sleeping and fretting, subject to an agitation of spirits that was almost too great to bear. Assuredly I prayed, but without finding peace. At Vespers, or thereabouts, a note was slipped under my door;

it was inscribed with the word 'yes', and I recognised the script as Durand's. Even this, however, failed to soothe my troubled soul. It simply committed me to a course which I could not help but regard as frightening, desperate and, in all probability, doomed to failure.

I saw nothing of Pierre-Julien. His absence told me that he was still busy with Alcaya and her friends; once he had obtained sufficient evidence against them, he would use it to implicate me. As you may expect, my concern for Johanna was overwhelming. What if I should unbar her cell door, only to find that ... God of mercy, that she was unable to walk? I remember how, when this possibility first entered my mind, I sprang from the bed wringing my hands, and paced the room like a caged wolf. I remember how I beat at my own temples with the heels of my palms, in a frantic attempt to drive the terrible picture away.

I could not allow myself to entertain such thoughts. They distracted me, and clouded my judgement. Despair would only result in defeat; if I were to succeed, I would require hope. *It is good that a man should both hope and quietly wait for the salvation of the Lord.* I would also require some means of binding the gaoler, and found it when I considered my garments. With my belt I would tie his hands, with my stockings his feet. The poultice I would put in his mouth as a gag. But how would I effect such a complicated procedure, while holding a knife to his throat?

If I were to kill him, of course, there would be no difficulties. For an instant I pondered this alternative, before dismissing it as barbarous. Besides, it occurred to me that I need not tie him up at all: I could take him with me. I could lock him in Pierre-Julien's book-chest, or ask Johanna to bind his hands.

He could serve as a shield if we happened to encounter the patrol at any time.

With such thoughts I occupied the long, lonely evening. When the bells rang for Compline, I recited the office as best I could. Then I retired to bed, knowing that the signal for

371

Matins, though faint, would rouse me – as it had for so many years. Between Matins and Lauds I would prepare myself, for the gates of Lazet were opened at dawn, and Lauds usually finished at the same time. Therefore, as soon as the Lauds bell sounded, I would put my plan into effect.

These were my intentions. But I found myself unable to sleep even between Compline and Matins; I lay sweating as if I had run from Lazet to Carcassonne. (Here indeed was a case of 'work out your own salvation with fear and trembling'!) I soon realised that there would be no rest for me while Johanna was in prison, so I immersed myself in prayer until the words of the Gospels began to calm my tormented spirit. *The Lord is my light and my salvation; whom shall I fear? The Lord is the strength of my life; of whom shall I be afraid?* Many faces passed before me that night; many regretful and wistful memories occupied my thoughts. I saw that my life, in one sense, was over. I could only hope that a new life awaited me.

From St Dominic, I sought forgiveness. From Our Lord God, I sought forgiveness. My vows lay shattered. I was cast adrift. Yet it seemed as if I had had no choice; love propelled me like the winds of heaven. How, I wondered, had I ever come to this? I had always regarded myself as urbane, moderate, sensible: a man given to pride and anger, certainly, but not governed by extreme passions. How had I come to forsake the path of reason – to abandon my own nature?

Through love, it seemed. For love is as strong as death, and if a man would give all the substance of his house for love, it would utterly be condemned.

Reflections of this sort did little to illumine the darkness around me. But as the night progressed I lost my fear, becoming resigned, and even impatient. I wanted to act. I wanted to cast my dice and see how they fell. Upon hearing the bell for Matins, I once again recited my office (in a whisper), omitting only those actions which accompanied the words. Then, with blindly fumbling hands, I ate the bread that had been given to me earlier.

What can I tell you of that final, blackest, longest period of waiting? I heard rats, and the distant cries of an infant. I felt the knife under my hand. I saw the faintest strings of light, seeping under the door and through the keyhole, shed by a lamp in the passage outside.

I felt wholly abandoned.

Sometimes I wondered if the night would ever end. I would think to myself: is the light changing? Has the dawn come? I must have dozed, at one point, for it seemed as if Johanna had entered the room, and had joined me in bed, and was caressing my tonsure. Naturally I thought, 'This cannot be', and woke with a start, terrified lest I had missed the bell for Lauds. But God, in His mercy, saved me from such a miserable fate. Even as I sat up, with a pounding heart, I heard a muted chiming, and knew what it meant.

The time had come. O Lord my God, I prayed, in Thee do I put my trust: save me from all them that persecute me, and deliver me in Thy righteousness.

Thrusting a finger down my throat, I vomited onto the floor. Then I lay down again, with the knife clasped to my bosom, and drew the blanket up to my chin. At first, when I called, my voice was a mere croak; I squeaked like the rats that scurried from corner to corner of my room. After clearing my throat, however, I was able to force more breath out of my lungs, so that my summons was louder. More urgent. Imperative.

'Pons!' I called. 'Pons, help me!'

Nothing stirred, though my cry seemed to echo like thunder in the silence.

'Pons! I am ill! Pons, please!'

What if the patrol heard me before Pons did? Such a possibility had not, until now, even crossed my mind.

'Pons! *Pons!*'

What if he refused to come? What if I was doomed to lie here, in the stench of my own vomit, until sunrise or beyond?

'Help me, Pons, I am *ill*!'

At last a grumbling, shuffling noise heralded the gaoler's approach. Ominously, however, it was accompanied by the plaintive whine of a female voice.

His wife was coming with him.

'What is it?' he growled, as his key rattled in the lock. 'What ails you?'

I said nothing. The door creaked open, revealing two figures, dark against the lamplit passage. One of them – the gaoler – waved his hand in front of his face.

'Faugh!' he said. 'What a stink!'

'Has he made a mess?'

'Father, what happened?'

Tensing, I muttered something inaudible, and groaned. The gaoler approached me.

'He can clean it up himself!' the woman snapped, where-upon her husband ordered her to shut her mouth. He advanced gingerly, careful to avoid the vomit, which was not easily discernible in the poor light. When he reached my bed he stooped and peered into my face.

'Are you sick?' he inquired.

I reached out for him with a feeble, trembling hand. I whispered a plea, and plucked at his shoulder. Frowning, he bent his ear to my lips.

And suddenly found a knife at his throat.

'Tell her to bring a lamp,' I breathed.

I could see his teeth glinting. I could see the gleam of his eyes. 'Bring a lamp!' he said hoarsely.

'What?'

'Bring a lamp, woman! Now!'

Mumbling imprecations, she waddled off to do his bidding. While she was gone, I told her husband, very quietly, that he must bid her to shut the door when she returned. Oddly enough, I felt no shame or repugnance as I lay there, though his pulse was racing under my hand, and his breath was warm on my cheek. Instead, I was conscious only of cold anger, and an iron excitement which was not, I fear, the kind of courage that God bestows, but something baser, and less virtuous.

'If you say anything foolish,' I hissed, 'you will die. You will die, Pons. Is that clear?'

He nodded, almost imperceptibly. As soon as his wife reappeared he said, 'Close the door' – and during the brief instant in which her back was turned I sat up, swinging my legs over the side of the bed.

She gasped when she saw what I was doing.

'If you scream, he dies,' I warned. 'Just put the lamp down.'

Her response was a whimper.

'*Put the lamp down,*' I repeated.

'In God's name, will you put the lamp down?' my captive expostulated. 'Do it! Hurry!'

She obeyed.

'Now – do you see that belt? And that stocking? Down by the foot of the bed?' I was careful not to look away from Pons. 'Take that stocking, and tie up his feet. Do it tightly, or I will cut off his ear.'

Of course I would have done no such thing. But my tone must have been convincing because the woman began to cry. I heard her groping around; I heard the clink of a buckle; all at once she was before me, clutching my leather belt.

I made the gaoler sit on the floor with his hands in his lap where I could see them. I watched his wife bind his feet, instructing her as to how it should be done. When this was accomplished, his hands were tied to the bed behind him, and I tested both ligatures, my knife always at the gaoler's throat. Finally, I stuffed the poultice in his mouth.

'Now, remove his belt,' I ordered. For Pons, though sketchily clad, nevertheless had taken the trouble to don his belt, perhaps because his keys were attached to it. 'Give me the keys. No, not the belt. I want you to tie your own feet with that belt. And I shall tie your hands.'

'Spare my children,' the foolish woman sobbed, as she

fumbled with her husband's woven girdle. I assured her that I had no intention of harming her children, unless she made a noise. And having secured her hands to the bed with another stocking, I gagged her with one of her own socks.

'Forgive me,' I said, rising at last, that I might survey my handiwork by the light of the lamp (which was an unexpected blessing). 'Forgive the smell. It was unavoidable.'

If Pons could have killed me then, he would have done so. But he had to content himself with a blistering glare, imbued with all the hatred natural to a man who has been humiliated in front of his wife. For my part, I went to the door, cautiously opened it, and peered out. I could see no one. I could hear nothing. Offering up a silent prayer, I slipped into the passage, and locked the guardroom door behind me. *I waited patiently for the Lord; and He inclined unto me, and heard my cry.* How miraculous my escape had been, thus far! How easily the first step had been accomplished!

But I was aware that I had no cause to rejoice, being ignorant of the prison watch bill. For all I knew, the morning watch was due to be changed; there might be guards in the gaoler's kitchen, or on their way to the gaoler's kitchen. Brother Lucius might not have arrived. Any number of circumstances might hinder me in my flight.

Furthermore, Pons and his wife were already making noises. Sooner or later they would succeed in expelling their gags, or freeing their limbs; sooner or later someone would hear them. I knew that I had very little time. Nevertheless, I was obliged to proceed with the most profound caution, step by step down the staircase, holding my breath as I listened for the sound of approaching familiars. Unfortunately, someone was ill in the *murus largus*. The resonance of his moans and curses, the abuse heaped on him by various prisoners whose sleep had been disturbed, made it difficult for me to distinguish the subdued rhythm of advancing footsteps. When I descended into the southern corridor, however, it was empty of movement – though filled with groans and snores and maledictions which might have come from spirits, so strangely disembodied did they seem (owing to the fact that the people responsible for them were shut up behind closed doors). And it occurred to me that this clamour would mask my own cautious progress.

Therefore, having identified the cell most likely to contain Johanna and her party, I approached it, and pronounced her name without fear of being overheard by a distant patrol.

'Johanna?' I said, nervously glancing down the stony corridor. 'Johanna!'

'Be-Bernard?' Her reply was faint, and full of disbelief. I was on the point of addressing her again when muffled laughter forestalled me; straining to listen, I recognised the chink of mail and the stamp of heavy boots. But from which direction?

From the stairs, I decided. A patrol was ascending from the floor beneath me.

It is fortunate indeed that the prison occupies one of Lazet's defensive towers, for all of the city's towers are equipped with circular staircases. Consequently, I was able to retrace my steps without being seen from a lower level, and without being heard, thanks to the groans of the sick prisoner. Hovering at the top of the staircase, conscious that the guardroom and its occupants lay just four paces from where I stood, I plotted the course of the two armed familiars and prayed that they would keep to their accustomed route.

Normally, they were not expected to patrol the top floor. Normally, it housed no prisoners. But if Pons had changed the watch, I was in grave peril.

'Lord, I cry unto Thee: make haste unto me; give ear unto my voice, when I cry unto Thee,' was my prayer. 'Let the wicked fall into their own nets, while that I withal escape.'

You can imagine my joy and gratitude when the sound of that heavy tread, the clink of armour, the loud exchange of remarks, began to die away. There was a sharp rapping, and an even sharper command – 'Stop that noise, or lose your tongue!' – followed by a deathly silence which seemed to suggest that this merciless injunction had been directed at the sick prisoner.

I waited until the guards were out of earshot, knowing that they would have to patrol the entire *murus largus* before returning to the *murus strictus* below. If I was quick, I would have time to usher my band of escapees down the stairs ahead of the patrol. But I would have to be very, very quick.

I would also have to be very, very quiet.

Upon reaching Johanna's cell again, I did not announce myself. I simply unbarred the door, wincing at every scrape and squeak, and pushed it open – to find that I was suddenly reunited with my beloved. She was standing before me (sound of limb, thanks be to God!) and I would have folded her in my arms, if our circumstances had been less hazardous. In the dim light, she looked drawn; her hair was untidy, and her beauty diminished. Yet I loved her more tenderly for her blotched complexion and furrowed brow.

'Come quickly,' I whispered, peering into the darkness behind her. Although the cell had been built for only one person, it was as overcrowded as the rest of the building. 'Babilonia? Come. Alcaya?' And then I saw a fourth shape. '*Vitalia?*'

'They brought her back from the hospital,' Johanna croaked. 'They burned Alcaya's feet.'

Her voice broke; her daughter began to sob noisily.

'Shh!' For an instant I was at a loss. Thoughts raced through my mind, and seemed to collide with each other. There would only be four horses – but Vitalia was on her deathbed. Alcaya was crippled, but she could ride, if she still had the use of her hands. Should I carry her? Should I give my lamp and knife to Johanna? And what about the guards? Already nearby prisoners were beginning to ask questions; soon they would be begging for release.

My wandering gaze found Alcaya. She looked very ill; her wet face glistened in the lamplight. But her eyes were still clear, and her suffering was tranquil.

'Alcaya,' I began, reaching out. Whereupon she shook her head.

'Go,' she said softly. 'I cannot leave my sister.'

'There is no time to argue – '

'I know. Come, my child. My rosebud.' And here I witnessed perhaps the greatest miracle of all. For when Alcaya embraced Babilonia, and whispered into her ear, the younger woman stopped crying. She seemed to listen intently, as Alcaya delivered some kind of prophetic utterance, inaudible to the rest of us, which infused Babilonia with an astonishing calm. I believe that it was God's hand, working through Alcaya at that moment, which soothed the demons in Babilonia's soul. All the stiffness left her frame; without protest, she allowed Alcaya to kiss and release her, rising heavily but submissively to stand beside her mother.

It occurred to me, all of a sudden, that I had not taken Babilonia into account. What if her demon should move her to an incomprehensible rage while we were still fleeing?

It was another reason to make haste.

'Come!' I urged Johanna. 'Now! Before the guards return!'

'Bless you,' said Alcaya, lovingly. And that was her farewell, because I would brook no more delay. I pushed Johanna and her daughter out of the tiny, noisome, tenebrous room, ordering them to go downstairs with all speed. While they hurried to obey my wishes, I barred the cell door again, hoping to delay the discovery of our flight. Soon I was treading on the hem of Babilonia's skirt, descending into the *murus strictus*.

At the foot of the stairs, however, I overtook my companions. Without a word, I led them towards the door that had become the subject of all my anxious cares. Would it be unlocked? Had Brother Lucius arrived? Would we encounter the guard from headquarters on his way to the kitchen upstairs?

If so, I thought, I shall kill him. And I raised my knife, in preparation for an attack.

But we were fortunate. The door was unlocked; there was no guard waiting in that familiar anteroom wherein I had spent so many long days, pursuing heretical morbidity. There was, however, a rather unexpected smell. It was the smell of smoke.

'Wait,' I said, alarmed at this development. Upon advancing towards the staircase, I was even more alarmed to realise that the smell was becoming stronger.

I turned and addressed my beloved. 'Wait here,' I whispered. 'If something happens, flee through that door. It opens onto the street. You might find some refuge.'

'Is there – are you – ?'

'I want to make sure that our way is clear,' I told her. 'If it is, I shall return directly. Watch and pray.'

I had to take the lamp; I had no alternative. Without it, I could not have found my way down to the door of the stables, or unbarred this door with any haste. Rest assured that I entered the stables with my knife at the ready, but having realised that the smell of smoke was far less pronounced at the bottom of the stairs, I was not anticipating any interference.

And I was correct in my assumption. No one attacked me as I burst into that malodorous cellar; by the feeble radiance of my lamp, I saw no fleeing shadows or glinting weapons, no torches or hot coals. Satisfied, I turned about. I climbed the stairs convinced that Brother Lucius must have lit a brazier in the scriptorium, for the smell of smoke grew more noticeable with each step.

And I was puzzled, because normally the brazier was only used after Christmas.

'Our way is clear,' I told Johanna. 'Take this lamp, and go down. You will find two big doors which open onto the street; our horses are on the other side of those doors.'

'What about you?' she inquired. 'Where are you going?'

'I must fetch a book. As payment for the horses.'

'Perhaps we should wait – '

'No. Hurry.'

She took the lamp. Without it I was at a disadvantage, for

the way to the scriptorium was not illumined; while my companions scurried downstairs, I had to grope my way up, until a faint glow informed me that I had almost gained the topmost step. Perhaps my preoccupation with this treacherous climb (for the stairs were very steep, and narrow) distracted me from the unusual nature of the sounds that were issuing from the scriptorium. At any rate, when I reached my destination, and looked up from the contemplation of my boots, I was, for an instant, paralysed with astonishment.

For there before me I saw Brother Lucius, setting fire to his place of work.

Now the events which subsequently unfolded did so with great speed. But before I recount them, I wish to describe to you the scene which confronted me as I stopped on the threshold, gaping. Both of the record chests stood open, and their contents were scattered across the floor. So too were many sheets of parchment and vellum. Flames were billowing from the chests, as if from twin pyres, and some of the dispersed documents were also alight: namely, those which lay the greatest distance from where I stood.

With his back to me, Brother Lucius was slopping lamp oil onto the littered floor. He held a torch in one hand. It was clear that he intended to drench the entire scriptorium in flammable oil before beating a retreat down the stairs. But he was never given the opportunity to complete his plan.

For when I gasped and exclaimed, he swung around in surprise. And suddenly he himself was a flaming brand, his habit on fire, burning furiously.

I have had many weeks to reconstruct in my head the cause of this mishap. The details seem to be incised (or perhaps scorched) into my memory: God knows, I shall never forget them. I recall that, as he turned, the lamp oil splashed all over him, spilling out of the receptacle in his right hand. At the same time, he dropped his torch – which, on falling, must have brushed against the oily fabric of his clothes.

His scream still echoes in my heart.

God forgive me, I was at a loss; I retreated as he advanced, for I was afraid to touch him. I found myself backing down the stairs, dropping my knife, fumbling to unfasten my mantle. When he lurched at me, his hair aflame, I stepped aside without thinking.

Of course he fell, and rolled, and came to rest some way down the stairs. I flung my mantle over him just as Johanna appeared; she was panting and wild-eyed.

'Stop!' I exclaimed, although she was in no danger of being burned. My mantle was a heavy one, and as effective as a candle-snuffer. I began to beat at the body beneath it with both hands.

'What is it? What happened?' Johanna exclaimed.

'Here.' I thrust at her the gaoler's keys. Let me explain the disposition of these keys: they hung from a leather loop, through which Pons' girdle had once been threaded. Since obtaining them, I had been wearing the loop around the middle fingers of one hand. Now I had cause to thank God that I had burdened myself with such a bothersome, noisy encumbrance. 'Lock the door to the prison!' I said, coughing and choking on the horrible stench.

'Which key?'

'I know not. Try them all. Hurry!' I suspected that Brother Lucius's scream might have been heard some distance away, and wished to secure headquarters against any kind of intrusion. But what was to be done with the injured man? Broken by the fall, burned by the fire, he would need help quickly. As Johanna fled, I turned back to him, and hesitated.

I hardly dared lift my mantle from his smoking head.

'God of mercy.' There are no words to describe his appearance, when it was unveiled. By why attempt a description? Doubtless you have seen heretics burned before.

Tears rose to my eyes.

'Ah, God of mercy,' I blasphemed. 'Lucius, what were you – what am I going to do? I cannot ... there is no ...'

'Father.' I swear to you, when he spoke I thought that I

382

must have misheard. I thought that someone else must have spoken. God alone knows where he found the strength. 'Father ... Father Bernard ...'

The smoke was almost suffocating. I wept with despair, for how could I leave him? And yet, conversely, how could I stay?

'I wish to confess,' he croaked. 'I am dying, Father, hear my confession.'

'Not now.' I tried to lift him, but dropped him again when he cried out in pain. 'We have to go ... the fire ...'

'I killed Raymond Donatus,' he whispered, in his raw and terrible voice. 'Absolve me, Father, for I repent.'

'What?' Once again, I was sure that I must have misheard. 'What did you say?'

'I killed Raymond Donatus. I set fire to the Holy Office records. I am dying in sin – '

'Bernard.' It was Johanna. 'I have locked the door. No one has come. But – '

'Shh!' If I had been threatened by a whole army of familiars at that moment, I would have stood my ground. Nothing mattered save the confession of Brother Lucius. (Such is the inquisitive nature of those customarily engaged in ferreting out the secrets of the soul.) 'Is this true, Brother? Lucius, talk to me!'

'My eyes ...' he moaned.

'How did you kill him? For what reason?'

'Bernard – '

'Shh! Wait! I must hear this!'

And so the confession was made. But because it was made clumsily, with many interjections, and repetitions, and calls for forgiveness – because certain gaps in the narrative have since been filled by my own suggestions and speculations – I shall not recount it word for word. Instead, I shall summarise it as best I can, sacrificing the dramatic excitement of reconstruction for the benefits of precision and clarity.

In effect, the sad tale was as follows.

Brother Lucius was the illegitimate son of a woman whose eyes had failed her. Poor and friendless, she would have been thrown onto the careless charity of an almonry or hospital, if not for the wages paid to her son by the Holy Office. These, with the approval of his superiors, he bestowed on a woman who accommodated and cared for his mother like a relative. The two women had lived together happily for many years.

But now Brother Lucius's own eyes were failing. He recognised the symptoms; he knew where they would lead. And while a blind canon may live out his life in the care of his brethren, what will a woman do whose only friend cannot feed her without pecuniary assistance?

Lucius could not bear the prospect of condemning his mother to the dirty, dreary life which so many crippled paupers are obliged to endure – if, indeed, they are lucky enough to live. Being of a proud and scornful nature, she was difficult to please; furthermore, she knew every step, every corner, every knot-hole of the house that she now occupied so happily. It was her home, and she moved around it with confidence. At her advanced age, she would never know any other home as well as she knew this one.

Brother Lucius therefore approached the Almoner of St Polycarpe for assistance. It was not forthcoming. The sum of alms offered – a customary sum, rarely transcended – was not sufficient. 'The chapter has many dependants,' Brother Lucius was told. 'They must accept what they are given.'

Confounded by earthly impediments, the scrivener therefore turned to prayer. He devoted himself to the contemplation of Christ's ineffable suffering. He immersed himself in the pursuit of God's love. He fasted, and eschewed sleep, and chastised his own flesh. But to no avail; still his vision continued to deteriorate.

And then, with the arrival of Pierre-Julien, he was presented with an alternative – a desperate one, to be sure, but by now he was a desperate man.

While copying depositions, he learned through the medium of Pierre-Julien's strange yet precise interrogatories, that one could conjure up demons to do one's bidding, if one performed certain specific rites. He learned that by dismembering a human being, and leaving the corpse at a crossroads, one might reasonably hope to attain a desired object. He learned that evil might perhaps result in some good.

It is my opinion that Brother Lucius was not of sound mind when he resorted to this extreme solution. Certainly, he babbled of 'numbness' and 'voices' and being 'tired – so tired'. It is when you are at your weakest that the devil's enticements seem most irresistible, and Brother Lucius was very weak from his self-inflicted penitential suffering. Nevertheless, he was still strong enough to sever Raymond's head with an axe.

He had done this in the stables, using an axe generally employed to chop wood for the Holy Office. There had been a great deal of blood, but most of it had fallen into the horse trough, because Brother Lucius had taken care to place Raymond's neck on the edge of the said trough. Raymond's blood had then been transferred to the brine barrels in a ladle borrowed from the gaoler's kitchen.

'I knew that ... no one would see,' the canon gasped. 'So dark. Wet. And the pigs ... all bloody ...'

'But was he *alive* when you cut off his head?'

'Had to be.'

'So you led him to the stables, and persuaded him to put his head in the horse trough – '

'No.'

It seemed that Brother Lucius's choice of victim had been dictated by one circumstance, and one only: the fact that he would often arrive at headquarters to find Raymond lying in a drunken stupor. Apparently, it was the notary's custom to spend the whole night on a heap of old cloaks in the scriptorium, after bidding farewell to his latest conquest. Brother Lucius would frequently have to rouse him with a shake, or a slap, or a pail of water.

I was given to believe that Raymond had died without regaining consciousness, one morning, when Lucius, on finding him in his usual state of oblivion, had dragged him all the way down to the stables and chopped off his head. The canon had accomplished this act unclothed, for fear of staining his habit. After the corpse had been dismembered, and deposited in the brine barrels, Lucius had washed himself and his tools very carefully before returning to work. His intention had been to transport Raymond's constituent parts to the grotto of Galamus, which lay at the centre of a crossroads.

'Three trips,' he faltered. 'Wrapped them in his cloaks ... used the register bags.'

'The register bags!' I knew them, of course. Whenever Lucius copied a deposition for the Bishop's library, or took a set of folios to be bound, or retrieved a bound register, he would carry these items in one or two specially designated leather bags. He was often to be seen setting out from headquarters with a bag under his arm. No one would have thought it remarkable if, burdened with two bulging leather bags, he had briefly disappeared from the Holy Office – not even on the day of Raymond's disappearance.

But the disposal of Raymond's body required three visits to the grotto, and three trips on the same day *would* have been remarked upon. Therefore Lucius was obliged to wait for a day so that he could complete one of his journeys before sunrise, when no one would witness it. (The other clandestine trip was accomplished in the evening, before the grotto was emptied.) Perhaps, he said, this lapse of a day had somehow spoiled the rites. Or perhaps Raymond should have been killed *at* a crossroads. Whatever the cause, no demon ever manifested itself to Brother Lucius.

He was at a loss now. Such acquaintances as he possessed were not in the habit of drinking themselves senseless – and thereby leaving themselves vulnerable to attack – in secluded places. But he did possess one last advantage. For he knew that a certain official, who shall remain nameless, had once offered Raymond a good deal of money to burn the Holy Office records. Raymond had made much of his own determined refusal to oblige this man and, without naming the culprit, had revealed to Brother Lucius that he would report the matter to Father Jacques.

But the matter was never reported – or, if it was, it had never been followed up. Indeed, when the notary complained of his expenses, he would often joke about 'burning the records'. It became such a common jest that he grew careless, and once, quite inadvertently, let slip the name of the official involved.

Armed with this name, Brother Lucius now went to offer his services.

'If I lost my sight,' he breathed, 'at least my mother . . . there would be some money . . .'

'I understand.'

'Bernard, *listen!*' Johanna was tugging at my sleeve, coughing furiously. 'Someone is at the door! Someone is knocking at the door! We have to *go*, Bernard!'

I knew that she was right. I also knew that, if we did not take Brother Lucius with us, he would perish in the smoke and flames before anyone else could break down a door and reach him.

But it will be quick, I thought. Quicker than what awaits him otherwise. For no one so horribly injured would survive long.

So I left him there, God forgive me. I left him because I had so little time; because it was already difficult to breathe; because, in my heart of hearts, I believed that he deserved such a punishment. I left him because I was frightened, and angry, and because I had had no opportunity to reflect.

A decision had to be made. Therefore, I made one. But I have lived to suffer the consequences. Every day since, I have endured such pangs of conscience, such arrows of remorse, that my face is foul with weeping, and on my eyelids is the shadow of death. I am filled with bitter sorrow, not so much because I left him, but because I left him without absolution. Absolution is what he sought – repentance is what he offered – but I withheld absolution, and left him to die alone. To face God alone. *Deliver me from bloodguiltiness, O God, Thou God of my salvation: and my tongue shall sing aloud of Thy righteousness.* I pray to the Lord that this cup will pass from me, for it is filled with gall and wormwood. I acknowledge my transgressions, and my sin is ever before me.

It was before me even then, as I staggered down the staircase and into the stables. I remember thinking 'Lord forgive my sin', while I unbarred the great doors that for so long had remained shut. Then I forgot about Lucius, because Lothaire Carbonel was confronting me, demanding his book, and I did not have it.

'The book!' he exclaimed, his features shadowy in the half light, his breath emerging in clouds of white vapour. 'Where is the book?'

'It is burned.'

'What?'

'It is burned. The books are all burned. See? Look up.'

We looked up, and behold! From the highest window of headquarters, clouds of smoke and showers of sparks were pouring. Soon the floor would catch alight, and collapse onto the rooms beneath.

'We only need three horses,' I gasped, mounting the first with some difficulty, for I was still coughing my lungs out. 'The fourth can stay.'

But Lothaire said nothing. He stood transfixed by this glimpse of a conflagration that he – and doubtless many more – had so often desired to witness. So I left him, much as I had left Brother Lucius. I set off, at a brisk but unhurried pace, towards the gates of the city. I fled, just as the first, faint cries of alarm were ringing in my ears.

It was the morning of the feast of All Souls. On that morning, I took Johanna de Caussade and her daughter, and I made my escape from Lazet before my absence was even remarked upon.

I can tell you no more. My story ends here. To proceed further would be to imperil many lives.

Conclusio

write this now from a secret place. I write in the bitter cold, and my fingers are numb and cramped, and my breath is like smoke before my eyes. I sit here like a leopard by the way, watching but unseen, a witness and a fugitive. I have sought refuge far – very far – from Lazet. Still, I am not ignorant of events as they have unfolded there since my departure. I have sharp ears, and the eyes of an eagle; I have friends who have friends who have friends. That is how my letter has come to reach you, Reverend Father. Like every other inquisitor of heretical depravity, I have an arm as long as the memory of the Holy Office.

Therefore I know certain things. I know that the fire lit by Brother Lucius devoured all of headquarters, though it mercifully spared the prison. I know that I am excommunicated, and summoned to appear before Pierre-Julien Fauré as a contumacious heretic. I know that Lothaire Carbonel was arrested as a fautor of heretics, having foolishly surrendered his own horses to my care. It is not easy to disguise the absence of three horses. He should have stolen them. Or purchased them from trustworthy relatives. God forgive me, for I was the agent of his downfall; it seems to me sometimes that destruction is ready at my side, and flowers wither beneath my passage.

Vitalia is dead. Alcaya is dead. By God's grace they died of bodily infirmities provoked by their incarceration, rather than on the pyre – or so I have heard – but my hands nonetheless are stained with their blood. Durand Fogasset is also dead, struck down by illness; if he were alive, I would not have mentioned his part in my escape. Undoubtedly he was a sinner, and perhaps his death served as punishment for his sins. But it is my true and earnest belief that he has found peace in eternal glory. For neither death, nor life, nor angels, nor principalities, nor powers, nor things present, nor things to come, nor height, nor depth, nor any other creature, shall be able to separate us from the love of God which is in Christ Jesus our Lord.

Reverend Father, I have told you all that there is to tell. I have told you a bloody tale of death and corruption, but these sins were not mine. Although I have sinned against my vows of chastity and obedience, I have not sinned against the Holy and Apostolic Church. Yet my enemies reproach me all the day; they are corrupt, and speak wickedly; violence covereth them as a garment. They seek after my soul, for wickedness is in their dwellings.

And I? I have eaten ashes like bread. Reproach hath broken my heart, and I am full of heaviness: I go mourning all the day long. Father, you must help me. Let them be ashamed and confounded together that seek after my soul to destroy it: let them be driven backward and put to shame that wish me evil. My enemies conspire, Reverend Father. They lie, and forsake righteousness. Their poison is like the poison of a serpent.

But you have inclined your heart to the testimonies of God. You have clean hands, and a pure heart, and you judge uprightly. Mine iniquity is before you, Reverend Father, and I ask you now: whose sin is the greater? Examine me, and prove me: try my reins and my heart. I have hated the congregation of evil doers, and will not sit with the wicked. Therefore turn thee unto me, and have mercy upon me, for my eyes are ever towards the Lord.

Reverend Father, I beg you – plead my cause. Plead my

cause with Pope John. Plead my cause with the Inquisitor of France. For it is the cause of a man condemned unjustly, who is persecuted among the righteous. My defence is here, in this epistle: consider it well. I am your loving son, Father. Do not cast me off, as so many have before. Look upon me with charity, and remember the words of St Paul: now abideth faith, hope, charity, these three; but the greatest of these is charity.

May you grow in grace, and in the knowledge of our Lord and Saviour Jesus Christ. To Him be glory and majesty, dominion and power, both now and forever. Amen.

Given at a place of sanctuary,
31 December 1318